BERNARDO
and the
VIRGIN

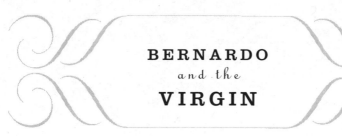

BERNARDO
and the
VIRGIN

SILVIO SIRIAS

LATINO
VOICES

NORTHWESTERN UNIVERSITY PRESS

EVANSTON, ILLINOIS

Northwestern University Press
Evanston, Illinois 60208-4170

Copyright © 2005 by Silvio Sirias.
Published 2005 by Northwestern University Press.
All rights reserved.

Printed in the United States of America

10 9 8 7 6 5 4 3 2 1

ISBN 0-8101-2240-5

Library of Congress Cataloging-in-Publication Data

Sirias, Silvio.
Bernardo and the Virgin / Silvio Sirias.
p. cm. — (Latino voices)
"Bernardo Martínez August 20, 1931, to October 30, 2000."
ISBN 0-8101-2240-5 (alk. paper)
1. Martínez, Bernardo, 1931—Fiction.
2. Mary, Blessed Virgin, Saint—Apparitions and miracles—Fiction.
3. Nicaragua—Fiction. I. Title. II. Series.
PS3619.I75B47 2005
813'.54-dc22
2004023372

♾ The paper used in this publication meets the minimum requirements of the
American National Standard for Information Sciences—Permanence of Paper
for Printed Library Materials, ANSI Z39.48-1992.

This work of fiction is based on actual events—
in the eyes of many. See "Posdata," page 441.

For the gang at Lario's

Bernardo Martínez
August 20, 1931, to October 30, 2000,
and
Joaquín Sirias, my father, who led me to this story
May 23, 1928, to January 30, 2004

With respect to private revelations, it is best to believe in them than not. This is because if you believe, and the revelations turn out to be true, your faith in our Holy Mother's apparition will earn you bliss. And if the revelations turn out to be false, you shall receive all the blessings as if they were true, simply because you believed them to be so.

POPE URBAN VIII

There are only two ways to live your life.
One is as though nothing is a miracle.
The other is as if everything is.

ALBERT EINSTEIN

contents

SEGUNDA PARTE: GUERRA

CHAPTER FOUR
Radix Sancta *(The Holy Root of Salvation)*
June and July 1979
Elías Bacon
107

BERNARDO
and the
VIRGIN

primera parte

INOCENCIA

ILLUMINATIO

(The Illumination)

April 1980

Bernardo

THE LIGHTS started coming on—all by themselves. That was the first sign. For a couple of weeks los cuapeños who live near the church saw them going on and off at strange hours of the night, but they thought the building was having problems with the electrical wiring. But, in my mind, my helpers had become careless. In nearly thirty years as sacristán, I always made sure that everything in la Casa del Señor was in order.

I had very little money for church expenses. Cuapeños, after all, are poor. On top of that, we are known throughout Chontales for being stingy: donations barely cover the cost of communion wafers. That's why, when I thought that the lights were being left on, I had no choice but to put a stop to the waste. I decided to visit doña Socorro and doña Auxiliadora, the women who help me at the church, to set them straight.

I was terribly upset when doña Tula told me that she had seen the lights on the night before; so the walk from my house to theirs, across the street from the church, was not enough to calm me down. "How many times do I have to tell these women," I mumbled on the way, "to turn off the lights before they leave?" I sometimes honestly believed that I'd be better off taking care of things by myself. By the time I arrived at doña Socorro's and doña Auxiliadora's house, I was still angry. But when they greeted me, I was struck by a glow of innocence that radiated from them. I can't explain how, but I knew they had nothing to do with the problem of the lights. Instead of lecturing them, I sat down, drank fresco de tamarindo, and caught up on the latest town gossip.

The day's biggest news was that doña Ermelinda's daughter was pregnant. The culprit was none other than Néstor Urbina, the son of don Casimiro the butcher. This was his third girl in three years. Doña Auxiliadora suggested that next castration season we lock Néstor in the corral with the bulls. It would be a service to the community to turn him into an ox as well.

The following day I called the electric company in Juigalpa. The office responded quickly, sending two technicians four days later. But as usually happens with government employees here, they were useless. La Revolución Sandinista, if anything, has managed to raise the levels of incompetence. These muchachos stood around with their hands on their hips, hemming and hawing, and in the end they only looked at a few wires. Then they said that they couldn't find anything wrong. So the problem with the lights remained a mystery. But after a couple of days had gone by, I placed the entire thing in the back of my mind. Maybe that's why I was completely unprepared for what happened next.

About two weeks later—the exact date was April 15, a Tuesday—I was running late to the meeting of la Comunidad Catecumenal. Our group met every Tuesday and Saturday to discuss what our role should be, as good Catholics, in la Revolución. We always ended our meetings by praying the rosary.

In those days, a lot was happening in Nicaragua. The Somozas, after controlling our lives for nearly fifty years, had fled the country just eight months before. The Sandinistas were still trying to figure out how to work in air-conditioned offices instead of running around in the jungles. Even our Catholic leaders were having trouble understanding the Church's role in la Revolución. People everywhere were arguing about everything. There were community discussions in every city, town, village, farming cooperative, neighborhood cantina, and home. And no one agreed on anything. I was not surprised, then, that like the rest of Nicaragua, Cuapa was becoming more divided each day. I was over an hour late for the meeting of los Catecumenales—of which I was the leader—because I had become involved in such a discussion.

Worried and out of breath, I arrived at the church. After fumbling for my keys, I opened the door. Once inside the building, I saw a soft, gentle light coming from inside la Virgencita's camarín: her rustic, wooden niche, painted blue and white. The light was just enough for me to walk between the pews without tripping. More than a light, I'd say it was a glow, like that of a moonbeam soaking through a hole in the roof.

That's what I first suspected. I checked the ceiling carefully, but I didn't find anything. I stepped outside and saw that the full moon was hidden behind a blanket of clouds. I walked around the building looking for a light post. Maybe the electric company had recently installed one without my noticing it. But no. Nothing from outside the building could explain the light.

Going back into the church, I walked toward el camarín. As I approached Nuestra Madre's niche, I was surprised that the glow seemed to come from her statue. The image of la Inmaculada Concepción gave off a soft, blue light. At the time I wasn't even thinking that it could be a miracle. I kept looking for a logical explanation. I searched inside el camarín. Maybe someone had hung several of those glow-in-the-dark rosaries around her. Or maybe some fireflies had chosen el camarín as their mating place. There had to be, I thought, a simple reason for the light.

After exploring el camarín, I checked la Virgencita's statue. I looked at her hands, her neck, her feet, and her dress. Everything about her glowed. The shine was real, but I couldn't explain where it was coming from. The statue was the one I had brought to Cuapa thirty-five years earlier. The same statue I had fallen in love with as a boy. The same rustic cedar statue I had known all of my life. But never, never, had I seen her so beautiful. La Virgencita's skin, from looking like that of an aged doll, was now perfect, almost lifelike. Her flesh reminded me of a rosy mango. Her face, the work of a masterful carver, but still a wooden face, had become enchanting. Her eyes, once flat, now seemed deep. She appeared to be alive. I was afraid and joyful at the same time.

I touched the statue to make sure that someone had not come into the church and painted her without my permission or that someone had not covered her in a shiny substance. But to my surprise, when I touched la Virgencita, something inside of her touched me back, producing a shock. Oh, but what wonderful pain! At that moment I began to believe that I was in the presence of something marvelous, holy. If I only had better light, I thought, perhaps I would understand what was happening.

I walked to the other side of the building and turned on the switch. But when the light came on, the glow from el camarín instantly vanished. I turned the switch off again. This time there was only darkness. I turned the lights on again and saw that the statue had returned to her former self. I was sad that the illumination had come to an end. Although I was still in shock, I remembered that los Catecumenales were waiting for me to call them to our meeting.

I went outside and rang the church bell. Suddenly, I felt the urge to tell everyone in Cuapa what had happened. I also felt the need to beg the townspeople's forgiveness for my sins. But only the usual group, about eighteen cuapeños, responded to the ringing of the bell. Since we already were more than an hour late, we decided to forget our discussion and just pray the rosary. As always, I led the prayers, but this night I did so distractedly. In fact, the more we prayed, the more anxious I became. Somehow, the illumination was compelling me to cleanse my soul.

As soon as we finished praying, I asked for everyone's attention. Although I knew that I'd be ridiculed, I told them everything that had happened to me earlier that evening. I didn't leave out a single detail. The older women repeatedly made the sign of the cross while invoking la Virgencita's name. But I could see the disbelief in the faces of the younger women and in the faces of the men. I began to feel like un idiota. But that's when my guilt got the best of me. I began to beg each person in the room for forgiveness, confessing every sin I had ever committed against them. As soon as I was done, I felt a profound sense of peace, of contentment. My work for that evening was complete, and my act of repentance moved everyone, even those who doubted my story.

"Please do not tell anyone what I told you tonight," I begged the members of the group before they left. But I have to admit that after my confessions I knew that I was about to become the town joke.

Of course, no one listened to my request. The town of Cuapa, although in the middle of the dry, dusty season, is like a raging river when it comes to gossip. A rumor flows quickly in all directions: uphill, to the east, past el barrio de los cabros, where you can't

escape the smell of the goats, and, beyond that, all the way to el Río
Murra. The gossip also travels west, toward the main highway that
runs north and south through Chontales. The news of the illumination spread rapidly throughout the town, running over the
unpaved streets like rainwater during a tropical storm. Each
person who had been at the meeting shared the experience with
another. And that person with another. And that person with
another, until by the end of the next day even the dumbest cow in
Cuapa knew about the illumination.

Doña Tula, our town's most notorious gossiper, jumped on the
bus to Juigalpa as soon as she heard what had happened to tell Padre
Domingo everything I had said. Cuapa at the time didn't have its
own parish priest. Padre Domingo showed up as often as he could—
traveling an hour and a half on a rocky road—to minister to us.
These days, however, we were seeing him more often because he was
helping us raise funds for the construction of a new church building.

The following Sunday, as soon as Padre Domingo saw me, he
said, acting innocent, "Bernardo, you have something to tell me."
But I can play dumb too. I talked instead about how most cuapeños
opposed the Sandinista's plan to send Cuban teachers here for the
literacy campaign. Haciéndome el loco is something I've always
been very good at. Padre Domingo listened patiently to my ram-
blings. He finally looked at his watch, saw that he was late, and
exited la sacristía to celebrate mass. I, as usual, assisted him.
Throughout the ceremony, he kept glancing at me out of the
corner of his eye. I pretended not to notice. In my nervousness, I
sang the day's hymns with extra enthusiasm—loud and out of
tune. After mass, back in la sacristía, as Padre Domingo removed
his sacramental garments, he said, once again, "Bernardo, you have
something to tell me."

Again, I played dumb. "The tailoring business isn't going well, Padre. I'm spending too much time on my responsibilities as sacristán. I may need to cut down on that. After all, I need to make money to pay off my debts." I could tell that Padre Domingo was becoming annoyed because I wasn't saying what he wanted to hear. He folded his chasuble roughly, showing his frustration, and began to leave the sacristy in a hurry. In his rush, Padre Domingo knocked over a container full of unconsecrated wafers. They rolled across the floor, and after they stopped we wordlessly picked them up. Then the priest, still angry, left the room. But he had not taken more than three steps out of la sacristía before he returned, his face the color of a ripe coffee bean.

"Bernardo, doña Tula told me everything about the illumination."

"Well, Padre, if you already know the story, why do you want to hear it again?"

"Because I want to hear it from your own lips, Bernardo. The entire truth, and in detail."

I had no choice. I did as he wanted. I told him everything. Padre Domingo listened carefully and didn't interrupt once. Sometimes he nodded, but barely. When I had finished, he remained silent, thinking, his head bowed. I was afraid that my story had angered him, and I was prepared for Padre Domingo to accuse me of making up the entire thing. At last, he lifted his head. He gazed at me with affection, so much so that I began to worry even more. Maybe, I thought, he's going to send me to the lunatic asylum. Then, reaching out, he placed a hand on my shoulder in a fatherly way, like a real father, not a priest.

"Bernardo," he said, his voice barely above a whisper, "if something like this happens again, ask la Santísima Virgen to state clearly what it is that she wants." I was surprised that Padre Domingo would even consider that la Virgencita was trying to talk to me. I said nothing and simply nodded.

"Vamos, let's go have lunch," he said, slapping me on the back. Padre Domingo didn't say anything else about the illumination for the rest of his visit.

I, on the other hand, already had plenty of things to worry about. The people of Cuapa were divided over politics, over the construction of the church, over the cooperatives the Sandinistas were creating in the region. I felt caught in the middle of it all.

The day after the Sandinistas triumphantly marched into Cuapa, don Caralampio asked me to vouch for his son before Elías Bacon, Blanca's kid, who was now el responsable of the garrison. Doña Filomena had accused don Caralampio's boy of being un oreja: a somocista informant. I told Elías that the entire accusation was really about a dispute over a finca, a quarrel between families that went back several generations. After my involvement in that case, Elías asked me to help him settle other conflicts where people, out of petty desire for revenge, accused their enemies of collaborating with the Somoza regime. Before long, I was assisting el responsable with all kinds of cases, such as who owned a particular pig. I soon grew tired of all the arguing, and like el rey Salomón, I wanted to tell them to cut the pig in half, take their portion home, and roast it. Elías still called on me to assist him. But whatever the outcome was, whatever my recommendation had been, no matter how fair I tried to be, my advice always made someone angry.

I had enough problems, and to all those I could now add this one—Nuestra Señora was apparently trying to speak to me. I had agreed that if she appeared I would ask Padre Domingo's question. But the question I really wanted to ask her, the question burning inside of me was: *Virgencita, why me?*

chapter one

HYPERDULIA
(The Veneration of Our Lady)

1931–1945

Padre Orlando García Sánchez

PADRE ORLANDO sat in el Parque Central, under the shade of el guanacaste tree, drinking his habitual midmorning glass of tiste. On this day, he greeted the passersby with a friendly smile, an eager wave, and, depending on how close they were, a chuckle. Instead of responding in kind, the people looked at him with suspicion, then simply said "Adiós, Padre" as they quickened their pace. The parishioners were not accustomed to seeing the cantankerous priest behaving so cheerfully. He was such an ill-tempered young man that they shuddered upon imagining what he would be like when he reached old age. What they didn't know was that on this day Padre Orlando felt like a man released from prison after serving a long sentence. Adiós, naive children, he thought. As far as the priest was concerned, he would never set foot in Chontales again.

Before Padre Orlando could begin to pack his belongings, one last item of business remained, having to do with Bernardo Martínez. That's whom the priest was waiting for in el parque. The deal they had struck turned out to be profitable for Juigalpa's parish. The people of Cuapa were getting something nice in return as well. They paid dearly for it, sure enough, but isn't Christianity all about making sacrifices? Three hundred córdobas—forty dollars or so. That represented a small fortune in the coffers of Juigalpa's parish. Los cuapeños had to reach deep into their pockets. That's why, when the priest thought about what Bernardo had done, the young man's deed seemed like a small miracle.

From the sale, all Padre Orlando planned to keep for himself was his boat fare to Granada. From Juigalpa, the first part of the journey would take nearly three hours by truck to get to Puerto Darío. From there, after another six hours on a boat, he and his belongings—mostly books—would be setting foot on the pier of what he called the most beautiful city in the world.

"Sí, sí, sí," he chuckled as a family rushed by, thinking that the parish priest had gone mad. "Adiós para siempre, Juigalpa."

Just two months before, Padre Orlando had received the letter he had been anxiously expecting for more than fifteen years. Fifteen long years stuck in these godforsaken backwoods: a rugged, mountainous region populated with sweaty hillbillies. Yes, here, in Chontales, he felt so far from God—thank you, Porfirio Díaz. His new assignment: parish priest of La Merced, in Granada. ¡Gracias, Dios, gracias! Regaining his freedom had taken more than fifteen years of ardent prayers and a lifetime of penance, or so it seemed. But Padre Orlando always had faith that the day would come when he could return to civilization. Throughout the years, he had struggled to let go of any bitterness over his forced exile. It was actually a good thing that his return to his hometown had taken this long, he reasoned with himself. The endless days of atonement would help him appreciate being back in Granada all the more. Yes, once he became the parish priest of La Merced he would never do anything to jeopardize the assignment.

"They're going to have to bury me in that church," Padre Orlando said aloud, but only to himself, as yet another passerby eyed his lively greeting with wariness.

Gran Poder de Dios. He seldom invoked the Great Power of God, but today the priest felt so holy, so blessed. For fifteen years he had been withering away in the hills of Chontales, among the earthy aromas of cattle and pigs. Here, there was nothing that stimulated Padre Orlando's razor-sharp intelligence—no literature, no theater, no concerts, no art exhibits . . . nothing. He, one of the best students in the history of Nicaragua's seminary, had spent a decade and a half surrounded by gullible, illiterate campesinos. He couldn't discuss his beloved readings with anyone. He couldn't even find someone to fix his phonograph. His classical music collection of 78s lay in a corner gathering dust.

In the entire region there was only one man he considered his intellectual equal, almost. He was a former classmate who left the seminary to get married and now earned his living as a schoolteacher and an organist. But Padre Orlando's friend lived in Santo Tomás, a long and bumpy bus ride away. Whenever they did meet they spent hours playing chess, discussing poetry, and drinking wines imported from France, which neither of them could really afford. Sadly, their meetings were far too infrequent.

Instead, Padre Orlando lived every day among monta-toros. Los chontaleños were gifted horsemen. More than that they were like the children of Ixion: centaurs. Unlike them, however, los chontaleños would never have been expelled from Thessaly because they were the only human beings nature would allow to live on this harsh land . . . and the only ones who would want to. Thus, Padre Orlando was condemned to live surrounded by men who could lasso a young bull, ride it, castrate it, and eat the testicles raw—all in five minutes flat. Los chontaleños were men of action, brave to the point of foolishness, but empty of thought. At least empty of any thoughts of substance, or so the priest believed. And the women, well, they were wholly devoted to their families and to their religion. But they were so bovine. They seldom talked, smiled, or expressed any emotions. They behaved like cows in a herd, patiently suffering the yearnings of bulls. Hardly anything interesting surfaced from their minds either.

Simpleminded people, really. "Take, for instance, their attitudes with regard to the rituals of the Catholic Church," Padre Orlando would often tell his former classmate. "These rites are designed to remind us of man's struggle to embrace what is good and pure," the priest would recite almost verbatim from the class on liturgy he and his friend had taken together. "These chontaleños," he continued, "although well intentioned, have turned the ceremonies of the Church into pitiful productions of ignorance and superstition. Their beliefs as indios have seeped into their Catholicism so deeply that no one, not even Su Santidad, el Papa, could straighten this mess out. Just look at how they walk on their knees, on pebble-covered roads, until their joints are a bloody pulp; how they dress like cows to fulfill a pledge to Nuestra Señora; how they spread the blood of a goat across a field in el Santo Nombre de Cristo when the planting season begins; and how they dance with the statue of a town's patron saint to a cantina and offer el santo a drink to start las fiestas patronales. The only thing that gives me hope is that their beliefs are not as perverse as santería, vudú, or candombe.

"But chontaleños still hold some of the most absurd notions to be true," the priest would go on as he moved his queen across the chessboard. "Just last month, for instance, everyone in the region was fearful because they believed a curandera's owl—her familiar—had scratched out don Tenorio's left eye because his daughters were witches. The lines at the confessional were so long the Friday after that it took me six hours to give everyone absolution. Absurd."

No wonder Padre Orlando had developed a severe case of gout—an old man's illness—while he was only in his thirties. Yes, the priest did eat a big, thick steak, with the blood still dripping, every day. But after all, he was in Chontales. And this *was* cattle country. Even so, he was sure that the agony of living among jinchos, among boorish campesinos, was the main contributor to his affliction. Now, every time he moved, his joints ached. No wonder he was such a crank.

Today was different. ¡O día glorioso! Padre Orlando could begin to celebrate the end of his exile and his return to Granada. At last, his destino had docked at his port. He would have been back in Granada a long time ago if the fates hadn't conspired to trap him in that sometimes-lethal mixture of national and Church politics. As a recently ordained priest, he had been outspoken about the Marines' presence in Nicaragua, boldly attacking U.S. foreign policy from the pulpit. He supported Sandino's struggle to force the Yanqui invaders out of the country (although he thought that el general de hombres libres overemphasized the role that ignorant campesinos should play in Nicaragua's future). But it wasn't only

Padre Orlando's political views that got him into trouble with Granada's bishop. The bishop's assistant and Padre Orlando had been classmates in the seminary. And they hated each other. Everyone knew that hell hath no fury like granadinos holding a grudge. They graduated the same year and were ordained within a month of each other.

But to add to Padre Orlando's bitterness, his pompous classmate received a choice appointment to serve as the assistant to the bishop in Granada only because he was also his Grace's sobrino: the son of the bishop's sister. And it so happened that the bishop's relative was a sobrino of Anastasio Somoza García as well: a no-good murdering, lying, and stealing hijueputa. Since way back when, long before Somoza became dictator, Padre Orlando had intensely disliked the head of la Guardia Nacional. The priest cursed the insignificant town of San Marcos, Carazo, for producing such a bastardo. He disliked el general almost as much as he disliked the bishop's toadying, dull-witted, and arrogant sobrino.

The young and impetuous priest insulted Somoza one time too many from the pulpit. The double-sobrino had the bishop's ear, and less than a year after being ordained, Padre Orlando found himself doing hard time in Chontales. Fifteen long years! His sentence, Bendito sea el Señor, had finally come to an end. The road back to civilization beckoned.

Padre Orlando was aware that he tended to exaggerate. Not everything in Chontales was all that bad. He had come to love the landscape. The stark lines of la Sierra de Amerrisque, its ragged edges looking like a row of crocodile's teeth, sometimes radiated a comforting blue light, a serene glow that seemed sacred. Other times, the sights of the peaks and valleys of Chontales touched something inside of him the way only those rare mystical moments of prayer could, when he felt himself in communion with Nuestro Señor. That's why, when a wealthy cattle rancher offered him a great deal on la finca named El Triunfo, half way up el cerro Tumbé, on the outskirts of Cuapa—a desolate little comarca of a few adobe houses that was under his jurisdiction—Padre Orlando went straight to the bank, withdrew his modest life savings, and purchased the property as an investment to help support him in old age.

More important, when the priest was totally honest with himself, he would admit that he had come to feel a lot of affection for los chontaleños. Although the barrenness of their minds and the simplicity of their thoughts would at times make him feel like buying a ticket on the next boat to Granada—and giving up the priesthood—he knew that they were good people. Salt of the earth. In spite of their poverty, their superstitions, and their ignorance, they possessed remarkable faith.

In a way, he envied their childlike belief in Dios; they seemed closer to the kingdom of heaven than the people he had grown up around. The peasants fully accepted the redemption promised in El Nuevo Testamento. And what perhaps impressed Padre Orlando the most about these campesinos was their faith in la Virgen's intercession. On their knees, they prayed before her statue for hours, asking her to help remedy wrongs and to bestow graces of every kind. And Nuestra Señora, perhaps out of pity and compassion, like in the Miracle of Cana, seemed to act on their behalf. Over the years he had witnessed a few things that he could only describe as near miracles. So, yes, being far away from civilization had hardened Padre Orlando's corazón—and his heart was already hard to begin with—but the simple ways of los chontaleños had left an imprint in him that would last forever.

A case in point: Bernardo Martínez. This was a young man

from Cuapa whom Padre Orlando respected. Not only that, the priest was genuinely fond of him. El cuapeño had been born on the feast day of his namesake: San Bernardo. And like the saint—who in life was nicknamed Dr. Mellifluus—Bernardo had the gift of persuasion. The priest met el cuapeño shortly after being assigned to Chontales. It was Padre Orlando himself who baptized him. From the moment Bernardo learned to talk, he showed a remarkable gift for piety, reciting long prayers with the ease of a prodigy. Of course, the boy's abuelita was responsible for such devoutness.

Doña Eloísa was as tough as the cast-iron bells of la Catedral de León. Even Padre Orlando, who inspired fear, feared her. And not only could the woman be stubborn, she could be prideful as well. Doña Eloísa made up this cuento loco about how she stole the infant Bernardo from her own daughter, Simeona, because she was angry with her for marrying un negro. No one in Cuapa believed the story. No one, that is, with the exception of the unfortunate Bernardo. The truth was that the couple gave the infant to doña Eloísa because they were so poor they couldn't afford to raise the child themselves. But the priest soon learned not to even suggest to Bernardo that his parents had given him up. Although he was usually a placid boy, he had a short fuse when snide remarks were made about why he lived with his grandmother rather than with his parents. The priest had broken up several fistfights behind the church building over this very issue.

One thing doña Eloísa did well, or so Padre Orlando thought, was to teach Bernardo to fear Dios, as well as to fear her. When the young priest taught el catecismo to children he was an unyielding taskmaster, forcefully drilling the Church doctrines into their trembling souls and demanding pinpoint memorization. Whoever missed a question that he thought easy would receive a sharp rap on the knuckles with the edge of a ruler. Nothing like a little pain, the priest believed, to motivate little ones to perform well. But Padre Orlando never had to punish Bernardo, for the boy always knew the answer. That is, until the day of the final examination.

That morning, doña Eloísa accompanied Bernardo to the church. She wanted, and deserved, to witness his stellar performance. Padre Orlando didn't mind her presence in the least. What's more, he approved of la abuelita's keen interest in the boy's religious life. The priest had been pleased, as well as impressed, when he learned that Bernardo was the only seven-year-old in Chontales who prayed the rosary every day. He had observed the boy kneeling alongside doña Eloísa on the dirt floor of their choza—about a kilometer west of Cuapa—before a plaster image of la Virgencita.

Yes, la abuelita was doing a wonderful job with the boy. And on this day the priest expected her to behold with due pride this important milestone in Bernardo's life. The children stepped forth, one by one, as Padre Orlando called their names. They all did remarkably well, better than the priest had expected. Finally, Bernardo's turn came.

"Bernardo, quiero que recités los Diez Mandamientos," Padre Orlando ordered. He leaned back in his chair, his eyes closed, ready to hear the boy enumerate, to perfection, the Ten Commandments. The priest waited. And waited. Surprised by Bernardo's silence, he opened his eyes. The child looked horror-struck. Bernardo's lungs appeared to have stopped working, the coloring on his face a reddish blue. The boy's eyes strained at the corners trying to catch a glimpse of la abuelita, who sat on a pew to the far right to better observe the proceedings.

"Well, then, maybe we should start with an easier question,"

Padre Orlando said, trying to give the impression of being a gentle man. "What's the difference between a mortal sin and a venial sin?" Again Bernardo remained silent. His entire body began to shiver, as if he had been locked in an icebox. The priest saw doña Eloísa's face begin to twist in anger, transforming itself into a corkscrew, the frustration visible in the corners of her clenched lips.

Padre Orlando quickly decided to ask a question he absolutely knew the boy could answer: "Bernardo, what are the five glorious mysteries of the rosary?" This time, not only did the boy seem to panic, but also la abuelita looked anxious, as if she too were being tested.

The priest had reached the limits of his scant patience. He stood, and wagging a stern finger before Bernardo's nose, warned, "If you don't pass the examination next week I will not allow you to take your primera comunión."

The child flinched in pain, as if he had been slapped. And la abuelita added to Bernardo's suffering. As soon as they stepped out of the church, she whipped the boy on the seat of his pants with a branch torn off a nearby tamarindo tree. Bernardo let out a loud wail, bawling as if it were the end of the world.

Padre Orlando approved of doña Eloísa's harsh discipline. Bernardo was toying with them. The priest was absolutely certain that Bernardo knew all the answers. The boy didn't tend to tease adults, but based on his experience, Padre Orlando believed that sooner or later every chontaleño rebels against authority. But Bernardo had surely chosen a poor moment to defy the Church.

What was the boy trying to prove? His primera comunión was too solemn an occasion for games. However, when the priest saw that doña Eloísa forced the boy to walk home in his bare feet, carrying his shoes as he stepped gingerly through thorny trails, his heart ached just slightly because he now thought that the lesson had gone too far.

The following week Padre Orlando tested the boy again. Virtually the same scene repeated itself. This time the priest became so angry at Bernardo's senseless stubbornness that he said, "Don't return for el catecismo until next year. Maybe then you will have outgrown your rebelliousness."

What Bernardo did next infuriated Padre Orlando. The boy traveled on horseback, on his own, all the way to Comalapa in search of Padre Ignacio. Bernardo told the other priest that Padre Orlando's temper frightened him so much that he forgot the answers to all the questions. He then asked Padre Ignacio to test him. Bernardo's persuasive, mellifluous tongue charmed the priest, and he agreed. He tested the boy, and Bernardo answered every question perfectly, concluding the examination by reciting the long, long prayer "Todo fiel Cristiano."

The following Sunday, Bernardo and doña Eloísa left before daybreak on the long trip to Comalapa—she on horseback and the boy on foot—for his primera comunión. And the Sunday after that Bernardo and his abuelita returned to Comalapa for confession and mass. But then word of what had happened reached Padre Orlando through Cuapa's overgrown grapevine.

When the priest reproached doña Eloísa, telling her that he didn't appreciate Bernardo's deception, nor her complicity, she simply replied, "Look, Padrecito, I had already had a suit made for his primera comunión. If we waited another year the pants wouldn't fit him any longer. His legs are stretching very fast these days. You know I can't afford that." Padre Orlando couldn't argue with her reasoning, but weeks went by before he forgot the incident. To his credit, he never let on that Bernardo's going around his back had slighted his honor. After all, the priest still needed doña Eloísa, and Bernardo, for that matter, to take care of the church.

Four slow, painfully uneventful years passed by in Padre Orlando's life. During this time, Bernardo's religious fervor continued to impress the priest. All the boy's peers had outgrown whatever childhood piety they may have once had. But not Bernardo. The boy now devoted more time than ever to the church. He and doña Eloísa made sure that the building was always spotless. She dusted and decorated the altar and los camarines while Bernardo swept and mopped the floors with the concentration of a monk. Padre Orlando was proud of Cuapa's church. The temple was the cleanest in all of Chontales. Because of this, the priest believed that Bernardo's destiny was to become the best sacristán in the region's history.

And the boy's devoutness was genuine. Every day he visited the church, praying the rosary before el Santísimo while kneeling on the hard, bare floor. Also, Bernardo never missed a mass and every week he religiously went to confession.

About once every three months, doña Eloísa and her nieto would make the long journey to Juigalpa. As soon as they arrived, they stopped by the church to pray and to greet Padre Orlando. After paying her respects to all the images, la abuelita would leave the church to visit relatives and friends. Bernardo preferred to remain there, sitting in the cool, dimly lit church, waiting until she had finished her rounds. Discreetly, of course, the priest would often observe the boy's routine. Bernardo would stop before each statue and say a brief prayer. But when he finally came before la Inmaculada Concepción, he would stand before her for the longest time, gazing upward. The boy always seemed lost in a trance, able to shut out all distractions, even the most annoying ones—like the people loudly selling cuajadas, chicharrones, pan dulce, and cajetas in the street. Once Bernardo awakened, he would pull a rosary out of its small leather case—which he always carried in his pants pocket—get on his knees, and pray. The priest wondered how the boy could remain in that position for so long. Padre Orlando's neck muscles would have cramped far beyond hope, becoming permanently locked into looking at the image of la Virgen, high in her camarín.

On one such visit to Juigalpa, after praying his customary rosary before la Purísima, Bernardo asked to speak to Padre Orlando. Rather than talking within the formal confines of his office, where the priest preferred to conduct business with adults, he took the boy to a pew far away from the handful of juigalpeños who were in church praying. Once they were seated, he let Bernardo speak.

"Padre Orlando, I want to become a priest." The boy's face radiated with eagerness, enough to illuminate the church if it had been night. Bernardo's desire to become a priest did not surprise Padre Orlando; he had been expecting the request for some time now. In his mind, the priest had rehearsed his response many times.

"Bernardo, why in Heaven's name would you want to become a priest?"

"I don't know, Padre. I mean, everything priests say and do seems so beautiful to me. I have prayed to Nuestro Señor that he consider me worthy. I want to serve him. And I have also placed myself under the protection of Nuestra Madre Santísima."

Padre Orlando was in no mood to encourage anyone to follow in his footsteps. "Bernardo, ¿vos un sacerdote? Dejate de disparates—

what you are wishing for is sheer foolishness. Don't you know that the roads in hell are paved with the heads of priests?"

Bernardo did not react as strongly to this response as Padre Orlando had envisioned in his head. Instead, the boy remained pensive for some time before finally replying, "Pues, Padre, if that's true, then I too want to be damned."

Padre Orlando rose to his feet with such a quick and violent motion that it startled Bernardo. The boy jerked back, banging his neck against the backrest, which would leave it stiff for days. The priest seemed ready to fly into a rage, his jaw and fists clenched so tight Bernardo feared that he would soon hear the sound of jaw-bones and teeth cracking. In mere seconds, though, a glint replaced Padre Orlando's burning stare. The priest then turned abruptly, giving his back to Bernardo. The boy saw his shoulders begin to quake. Whatever had possessed Padre Orlando seemed out of his control. At last, the priest broke out into loud, raucous laughter, smacking his open palm on the railing of the pew. He reached under his cassock, pulled a checkered handkerchief from his pants pocket, and wiped the tears from his eyes. The faithful stopped praying, looking at the priest in alarm. But he didn't care; he just waved them away. Slowly, they turned back to their devotionals.

Once Padre Orlando recovered, his tone became warm, hushed. "Bernardo, becoming a priest involves a lot of work, sacrifice, and time."

"I'm willing to do everything I'm asked to do, Padre. You know I'm a hard worker."

"Sí, sí, lo sé. But the work involves a lot of studying and, Bernardo, to begin with, you don't even know how to read. Catching up to the rest of the seminarians would take you years.

They've all had excellent schooling. Your sin, my son, is having been born poor and in Cuapa."

Although Padre Orlando had played this scene out in his mind beforehand, he never anticipated his own feelings of hurt upon witnessing the boy's dejection. Bernardo's lips trembled, and now his shoulders began to heave, but not in laughter. The priest sat down again next to the boy. He placed an arm around his shoulder and waited patiently for Bernardo to regain his composure. The priest knew that Bernardo would not persist with his petition, and he appreciated that the boy knew when to stop. Nothing is worse, he believed, than a spoiled child who begs relentlessly. Padre Orlando just hoped that Bernardo would someday understand that his frostiness toward supporting the vocation of others was based on his own tortuous experience.

"Oíme vos, Bernardo. What you should do is get married, have children, raise your family in the faith, and live and work on a finca. If you want to serve Nuestro Señor, you can do so as Cuapa's sacristán. I'll share a secret with you: finding good, responsible men like yourself is difficult around here. What's more, I'd like it very much if you'd work for me at El Triunfo." Padre Orlando meant the last comment. He knew that Bernardo would someday be the perfect caretaker for his finca.

The boy raised his face to meet the priest's sympathetic gaze. The spilling of tears had already passed, and his eyes now barely glistened, although the edges were spidery red. "Padre," the priest detected an uncharacteristic edge in Bernardo's voice, a scarcely traceable edge, but there nonetheless, "if I wanted to work in farming I could do so on the plot of land next to mi abuelita's house. And if I were going to become a common sirviente, then I would serve mi tío Félix, who owns a lot of property. At least he might leave me a good inheritance." The boy rose from the pew, thanked the priest, shook his hand, and left for el parque to wait for doña Eloísa.

And then Bernardo, true to his bullheadedness, did precisely what Padre Orlando had expected. The boy went to Comalapa to ask Padre Ignacio to help him become a priest. Padre Ignacio, being far more considerate, and much less blunt than his colega, did his best to let the boy down easily. He used the excuse—which was absolutely true—that he was paying for his nephew to attend the seminary. Because of this, he told Bernardo, he couldn't support another seminarian. He offered to pray for Bernardo so that Nuestro Señor would help him persevere in his quest to fulfill his calling. But not once did Padre Ignacio mention anything about Bernardo being illiterate. The boy already had a difficult road ahead as things stood, he believed.

In spite of both priests discouraging Bernardo in his quest for the priesthood, his piety remained as strong as ever. Bernardo's devotion to the Church continued to impress Padre Orlando. The young man—the priest began to refer to him as such when Bernardo turned fourteen—kept up his commitment to Cuapa's church, taking on greater responsibility for the building's upkeep, visiting el Santísimo, and praying the rosary before him every day. He always assisted in the celebration of mass. Only occasionally would he let another boy do so, as the experience allowed Bernardo to have some sense of what it must feel like to be a priest.

Whenever Bernardo and doña Eloísa visited Juigalpa, the young man would stop by the church to greet Padre Orlando (whom he still feared), los santos, and la Inmaculada Concepción. On one of these trips, the priest asked Bernardo if he was coming to the procession.

"What procession?"

"Las Hijas de María have bought a new statue of la Inmaculada Concepción, made by the best religious artist in Barcelona. She'll be very modern now. Imagine that, Bernardo, a statue of Nuestra Señora is coming to Juigalpa all the way from the land of Cervantes. She'll be here in a couple of months, before December 8. We'll be able to hold the best Fiesta de la Gritería in the history of this town. Once the date and time of the procession are set, I'll let you know so you can tell the people in Cuapa. But you, Bernardo, must come. Absolutely."

"Thank you, Padre." The priest, however, noticed that Bernardo seemed preoccupied.

"¿Qué pasa, Bernardo?"

"Bueno, Padre, what's going to happen to the old statue of la Purísima?"

At once, Padre Orlando remembered Bernardo's obsession since childhood with the rustic wooden image. Years before, doña Eloísa had told the priest a story about how Bernardo, when he was about five, informed her that when he grew up he was going to marry the pretty lady on the altar.

"¡Disparates!" la abuelita had scolded the child. "You're always thinking of nothing but nonsense." But throughout the years Bernardo kept visiting la Inmaculada Concepción faithfully, praying the rosary before her image every time he traveled to Juigalpa.

Seeing a business opportunity, Padre Orlando replied, "I'm not sure, Bernardo. Unless we find a buyer, and I doubt that we will, we'll have to burn the statue." Bernardo grimaced as the priest said this. In response, Padre Orlando quickly added, "It's customary in the Church to do so, Bernardo. You know, we aren't allowed to have two statues of la Inmaculada in the same building."

Bernardo found the idea of burning the image he had loved since time immemorial too appalling. "Padre, for how much would you sell her?"

Padre Orlando glanced down, thinking of the highest price a fanatic of la Virgen might pay. All the while he stroked his chin, trying to forget the throbbing pain in his joints that had been tormenting him for days. Surprisingly, in spite of the discomfort, the priest felt wonderful. What he had not shared with anyone, not even with his friend in Santo Tomás, was that December 31, 1945, would be his last day in Chontales. The letter he had been expecting for so long had finally arrived, just two months ago. Granada. La Merced. Civilization. Fifteen years of exile, an eternity, were almost over. Now he needed a little traveling money to get himself and his things to the other side of the lake.

"Trescientos córdobas," he stated flatly. He expected the fourteen-year-old to haggle, el regateo being a part of daily life in the region.

Instead, Bernardo, with singular determination in his voice, responded, "Está bien. Until when do I have to raise the money?"

"By December 8, Bernardito. She has to be out of here by December 8."

"Have Nuestra Señora ready, Padre. She's going to Cuapa."

"Well, if you manage to raise the money, don't bring me any coins. I'll only accept bills, Bernardo." Padre Orlando knew that if any person in Chontales could pull off the minor miracle of purchasing la Virgencita, Bernardo was the one. Still, the priest was skeptical. Cuapeños were as poor as the mice that lived under the altar floorboards. On top of this, they were miserly with what little they had. Nuestro Señor knew how Padre Orlando constantly struggled to get them to contribute something for the maintenance of their church, not to mention of their priest.

"Buena suerte, hijo," he muttered to himself as Bernardo hurried out of the building.

Initially, Bernardo went about Cuapa trying to persuade the adults to help him raise the funds to purchase the statue. "Please don't allow her to be burned," he would say, appealing to their sense of mercy. But less than a handful of adults supported the idea. Then Bernardo—a model of perseverance, as Padre Orlando would later describe him to the bishop—turned to cuapeños his age. Surprisingly, every one of them agreed to help. They formed a committee to direct the project. Pretty sophisticated, thought the priest, for a group of mostly illiterate kids. A local girl, Blanca Arias, whose father, the owner of a large hacienda, could afford to send her to school in Juigalpa, was appointed the record keeper.

The following Sunday, the entire group, armed with a pencil and a notebook, went from house to house, asking for contributions. When the campaign started off everyone gave—five, ten, fifteen centavos. A few households applauded their efforts; others contributed, but grudgingly. However, by the time the procession reached el barrio de la Sapera, word had gotten out that los rufianes of Cuapa were out raising money for illicit purposes.

"You say you want money to buy the statue of la Virgencita?" one wary woman yelled at them from her doorway. "Well, I say that you're going around tricking us out of what little we have so that you can buy kuzusa. What else do you vagos want to do but drink all the time? A bunch of vagrants, that's what you all are. I've known every one of you from the time you ran around naked, without diapers, your noses dripping with mocos. That's why I don't trust any of you. You're not getting a centavo from me. Not even half a centavo."

The woman's words ignited a wildfire. The rest of the day, hecklers greeted the group in every street of every barrio. By midafternoon, most of the volunteers had dropped out. "I'm not going to be treated like un pendejo," Casimiro Urbina said. And the other young men—and a few of the young women—left with him. Bernardo was the only male who remained.

Still, he was not discouraged. Sixteen girls vowed to continue until they had raised the three hundred córdobas. But by Monday, eleven informed Bernardo that their parents didn't want them to be part of any scam he had dreamed up. This obstacle, nevertheless, only strengthened his resolve.

"This is now the true test of our devotion to Nuestra Señora," he told the five that remained. Blanca, the record keeper, scribbled the following words down in the margins of the notebook: *We cannot let Nuestra Señora down. Have faith. She will reward it.*

And Padre Orlando firmly believed that from this moment on, the group came under la protección de la Virgencita. How else could you explain that a handful of adolescents were able to raise three hundred córdobas well before the deadline? Doña Tula told the priest that their collection efforts were something marvelous to behold. Bernardo and his five assistants moved stealthily about Cuapa, as if gliding upon an ocean-blue cloud, like sacred thieves whose victims cooperate because a mysterious force compels them to do so. What Padre Orlando found most difficult to believe was that the people of la Sapera, according to the notebook, in spite of being the poorest—and the fiercest in their harassment of the first group—were the ones who in the end gave most generously.

The committee arrived in Juigalpa on December 2, proud of their accomplishment. No one was more thrilled, though, than Padre Orlando. His exceedingly good humor—bordering on giddiness—perplexed the faithful youths. The priest was so elated that he didn't bother to count the money. Folding the bills in half, he lifted his sotana and placed the cash in his pants pocket. Then he thanked the committee members, praising them more than necessary and vigorously shaking each one's hand.

"So, Bernardo, when are you coming to pick up Nuestra Señora?"

"Within the next few days, Padre."

"Excelente, excelente," the priest said, rubbing his hands together. "You should be proud of yourselves. A job well done. Sí, sí, bien hecho." The priest smiled and nodded at the group. He then turned, intending to return to the church. Although he had his back to them, he sensed that no one was going to move. Padre Orlando turned again to face them.

"Well, is there anything else I can do for you?" he asked, lifting his shoulders and holding out his hands as if he were leading his congregation in saying el Padre Nuestro.

"We'd like a receipt, Padre Orlando," Bernardo answered. The young man tried to appear casual, but every person there could tell that he was bracing for one of the priest's feared tantrums.

Padre Orlando stared Bernardo down, making everyone else uncomfortable as well. He then looked intently into the faces of each one of the committee members. The color of his cheeks turned the shade of a ripening jocote.

"Why do you need a receipt?" he asked in a low, rumbling growl.

"This is an important moment in our parish's history, Padre. We want the people of Cuapa always to remember what they can do if they place themselves in the hands of Nuestra Madre."

Bernardo's response disarmed the priest. Padre Orlando's shoulders drooped, and he let out a heavy sigh. "I understand," he said. The priest left to go inside the church, to his office. The committee waited for him, sitting on the steps. When he returned, he handed Bernardo a sheet of paper. Bernardo passed the note to Blanca. She read it, nodded, and returned the paper to him.

Moving up one step, Bernardo turned to face the committee. "This receipt will remain forever in the archives of Cuapa's church. Consider this document a tribute to your faith in la Virgencita."

Unimpressed by the speech, Padre Orlando began to descend the church steps, waddling because of the ache that ran through every joint in his body. "Just make sure you get the statue out of here by the seventh."

"I'll be here at ten the morning of that day, Padre."

The priest, not bothering to look back, waved in the general direction of the group as he walked toward el kiosko in el parque.

Nearly a week later, Padre Orlando sat in el Parque Central, under the shade of el guanacaste tree, drinking his habitual mid-morning glass of tiste. Glancing at his watch, he saw that it was almost ten o'clock. He raised his glass in greeting to a passing group of schoolgirls. They giggled apprehensively, uncertain whether that was the correct response to the priest's friendly gesture. They were accustomed to his reprimands about the shortness of their skirts, the makeup they wore, or their interest in boys. They wondered whether he was drunk and continued walking, whispering nervously among themselves.

Padre Orlando checked his watch again. He then looked in the direction of the road to Cuapa. As if summoned by the exact time, Bernardo appeared on the horizon, riding alongside his tío Félix. Each of them led a riderless mule by a rope. When they spotted the priest, they rode to the edge of el parque, dismounted, and made their way to the shade of el guanacaste.

"Buenos días, Padre," don Félix said solemnly while he took off his sombrero, held it to his chest, and bowed before the priest.

The agility with which Padre Orlando rose from his seat surprised Bernardo. In all the years he had known the priest—really, all of the young man's life—he had never seen him grinning so brightly. "Bienvenidos, bienvenidos," Padre Orlando said with open arms. "You're right on time. And I'm ready to deliver Nuestra Señora to you."

Bernardo and his tío Félix followed Padre Orlando across the street. As they approached the church steps, the priest snapped his fingers at four unsuspecting young men who sat there, chatting. They glanced up in response to his call and he commanded them to help carry the statue out of the church. Once the group stood before la Inmaculada Concepción, Padre Orlando said, "There she is, Bernardo. And to reward your devotion to Nuestra Señora, I will let you have el camarín and el altar for nothing. How you will get those two things to Cuapa is beyond me. But if you can figure it out, they're yours." All Bernardo could do in response was to look at the gifts and nod thoughtfully. Padre Orlando clapped his hands loudly and rubbed them together. "Well, we're burning daylight. Come on, come on, gentlemen. Lift Nuestra Señora. Be careful. Don't be so clumsy! She's got a long, long way to go."

Once the young men placed la Inmaculada Concepción next to the horses, Bernardo and his tío Félix wrapped the statue carefully in layers of blankets and pillows. Tying the bundle to a board, they lifted the platform and tied it onto the flank of one of the mules. The two would take turns carrying her along the rocky twenty-five-kilometer path.

"Gracias, Padre. Por todo," Bernardo said.

"No, hijo, gracias a ti," the priest responded. For an instant, Bernardo thought that he had heard Padre Orlando's voice crack. Suddenly, the priest reached out and gave Bernardo a long abrazo. The young man wasn't quite sure how to respond, but eventually he returned the hug, awkwardly. "Andate ya, vos, you haven't got all day."

Bernardo nodded. He mounted his horse, spurred the animal gently, and turned it back in the direction of the road to Cuapa. Padre Orlando hobbled to el kiosko, sat down, and ordered another tiste as he watched Bernardo and his tío Félix disappear over the hill leading out of Juigalpa.

Bernardo's misfortune was that he had been born in Chontales, Padre Orlando believed. The young man certainly had potential. The priest shook his head, for the moment feeling somewhat disheartened. As Padre Orlando took the first sip of his drink, el Evangelio de San Juan came to mind. How appropriate, he thought. The priest nodded, and then asked himself, "Can any good thing come out of Cuapa?"

chapter two

DULIA
(The Veneration of Saints)

1949–1950

Teresa de Jesús Medina: From Her Journal

1949

January 23, Feast of San Ildefonso, early afternoon

Today I'm starting a new diary. Last July I lost the one I had been keeping for over three years. (I suspect that Justiniana, one of my classmates who has no friends, stole it. Suddenly she knew too much about me and she was trying to become close.) Losing my diary broke my heart, and even though Sor Conchita gave me a new one as soon as she found out about the tragedy, I was so depressed that for all these months it has stayed locked up in my nightstand drawer.

But today something happened that has made me want to start keeping a diary again. A special person knocked on our school door. His visit has left me confused, with an anxious, jumpy feeling—like when the stringy fibers of a mango get stuck between my teeth and I can't pick them out with my fingernails.

Visitors don't usually knock because the doorbell is clearly visible. Plus, there's a *huge* sign in the lobby that says POR FAVOR TOQUE EL TIMBRE. But today, as we were eating lunch, we heard someone desperately pounding out front, as if cornered by a jaguar. Sor Patricia, the eldest and most decrepit of las monjas, got up to answer. I followed her in case she needed someone to return to the dining hall with a message. El Señor knows that getting back would take her *forever.*

I was tempted to disobey the rule and open the door myself, but Sor Patricia had already read my mind. As I moved ahead of her, she reminded me that only a nun could answer the door. Sor Ada, the mother superior, whose specialty is to place obstacles in everyone's lives, made up the rule a few years ago, when I was only in el sexto grado, after two brothers had come to the door. They were from Cuba. One was very attractive, manly. The perspiration that soaked through his shirt gave off an aroma that left my older schoolmates trembling. At least that's what they said. The other brother, although also handsome, looked unbearably sad, and the scent of white lilies seemed to come out of every pore of his body. The first one—the really sexy one—spoke so seductively that the girls who answered the door later claimed that their entire beings shivered with desire the moment he started talking.

By the time las monjas discovered what was going on, the older students had formed a pressing circle around the men. The Cubanos explained to the nuns that they were looking for work, and Sor Ada, alarmed by the effect the men were having on the girls, instead ordered the brothers to leave, claiming that Satanás had sent them to tempt the young women. The students loudly protested the nun's decision. But la madre superiora remained firm. Knowing that their cause was lost, the handsome brother leaned daringly close to Sor Ada, and in a husky voice said, "It's too bad, Hermanita, because you look delicious. But it doesn't matter anyway. You see, we're músicos on our way to los Estados Unidos to become rich and famous." Ever since that incident only monjas have been allowed to answer the door.

Well, I could tell that Sor Patricia had already made up her mind that the person banging on the door was going to be trouble, just like the brothers. Because of this, I looked forward to seeing la madre superiora deal with the problem. But when the nun opened the door, standing before us was the most angelic man. It's not that he was handsome or beautiful, although he looked pleasant enough. What dazzled me was the startling aura that surrounded him, a soft blue luster. He was slightly older than me—about seventeen, I'd say—still gangly, and dressed like a jincho trying to pretend that he's from the city. But I found him very attractive. . . . And I still can't figure out why.

Will he be the first man I kiss?

I will continue with this entry after I finish my evening chores.

At night, shortly before bedtime

Continuing . . . the young man, named Bernardo Martínez, told Sor Patricia that he had come to Granada from Cuapa—a pueblito somewhere in Chontales—to attend school. Since he had no money, he offered to work in return for schooling. It seems that Bernardo doesn't know how to read or write. In that way he's just the opposite of the saint of the day, San Ildefonso, a true scholar and a doctor of the Church to whom la Virgen once appeared. Bernardo's illiteracy explained why he hadn't rung the doorbell. (In fact, I don't think he had ever seen or heard a doorbell before.) Sor Patricia then turned and asked me to call la madre superiora. I obeyed, dashing through the corridors as fast as I could until another monja stopped me, saying that proper señoritas don't run through buildings. After I returned with Sor Ada, she listened to Bernardo's story, impatiently interrupting him several times. Then she told the poor boy that there was nothing for him in Granada and that he should return home. (That monja—Dios me perdone—can be so coldhearted.)

Fortunately for this angel of a man, Sor Conchita, my favorite monja—de Italia—happened to be working in the office next to the lobby and overheard the conversation. Now *she* is a compassionate woman. She insisted to la madre superiora that there must be something they could do for a young man that wants to become educated. "After all, isn't that what don Bosco would have wanted?" she asked innocently but well aware of the impact of her words.

"Well, then," Sor Ada replied, being her usual bad-tempered self, "you handle it. I'm too busy."

Right away Sor Conchita started cranking the telephone, calling el Colegio Salesiano, one of the local boys' schools, to see if they had something to offer Bernardo. Watching him closely, I guessed by his puzzled expression that he had never seen a telephone before. He stared at Sor Conchita, his mouth slightly opened, as she spoke into the box. He probably thought she was talking to herself. That's when I decided to help out.

"Es un teléfono," I told him. "Through the wires you can speak to people far away." I saw his eyes follow the phone lines up the wall and out of the building.

"Gracias," was all he said. Then he offered me the most enchanting smile—inocencia e inteligencia wrapped into one.

As Sor Conchita hung up, she turned to Bernardo and said, "Go to el Colegio Salesiano. Ask for Padre Benito. He doesn't guarantee anything, but he will try to find work for you." She walked to where Bernardo stood and in a motherly gesture placed a hand on his shoulder. "Go with Juanito, our driver. He'll take you there."

I thought Bernardo was going to fall on his knees and kiss Sor Conchita's hand. She seemed to sense his intention and, grabbing both of his hands, steered him to the door while saying, "Don't disappoint me. Just work hard, and behave yourself."

"Sí, sí, Hermana. Muchas gracias." He looked in my direction and nodded. His angelic allure left me breathless. I stood at the doorway and watched as he climbed into the carriage and sat next to Juanito, who seemed surprised that Bernardo didn't prefer to sit in the back, like most passengers.

Sor Conchita stood behind me and placed both hands on my shoulders. "Come inside, Teresa. Whatever you saw, I saw it too. Come now, and keep a rational head. Don't let his spirit disorient you."

But it's too late. He's stuck between my teeth.

February 10, Feast of Santa Escolástica

As usual, our history class was interesting. Although none of the other girls really like Sor Julieta—because she is so tall, stern looking, and scary—she's my favorite teacher, and history is my favorite subject. Today she talked about Harry Truman's reelection as president of los Estados Unidos de América. "We can learn something from los gringos," la monja said. As a class, we had been following the elections closely, and we really expected el Señor Truman to lose. But after the votes were counted, he ended up the winner. If only elections were as honest here, I could hear us all thinking.

I'm trying hard to concentrate on my schoolwork. I'm only starting el segundo año de secundaria. I have four more long years to go, but I'm determined to graduate. With a high school diploma I won't end up working as a maid. Plus, I'm more likely to find a husband who's well off, and then I'll have maids of my own. But schoolwork is demanding, and graduating seems so far off in the future. As Sor Conchita keeps reminding me, though, I have to pick one guayaba at a time.

Also, I have a lot of responsibilities that keep me pretty busy—not like the rest of my classmates who have it easy. In addition to studying here, I help out in the kitchen and the dining room in order to pay for my tuition. Since the time my mother was a teenager she has been working at El Guapinol. (That's what the granadinos call the school because of the big tree that used to be on this corner before it was built. But the nuns hate the nickname. They always say to us: "Tell everyone that you study at la Escuela Profesional María Auxiliadora, and not at El Guapinol.") My mother is one of the cooks. That makes it kind of rough for me because my classmates make fun of my situation. But my mother will probably stay here forever because she is grateful that las monjitas didn't fire her when she became pregnant with me. And she still refuses to tell anyone, including me, the identity of my father.

So I have grown up in this place; it's the only home I know. Las monjitas are like my family, and they've given me the opportunity to study. "A good education cures poverty," Sor Conchita says. That's why I have to stop thinking about Bernardo. I have to stop wondering whether he will be my first kiss. But during today's reading of *Las vidas de los santos* I thought about how, at least once a year, Santa Escolástica got to see the person she loved most in the world: her brother, San Benedicto.

I want so much to see Bernardo again.

February 24, Feast of San Matías

Like the apostle San Matías, I've responded to the calling of love. But Dios me perdone, it's the love I feel for a man that's influencing my decisions these days, not my love for God. After the traitor Judas Iscariot hung himself, San Matías was chosen to replace him by drawing the longest straw. Like el Santo Apóstol, I feel that I've been chosen to fall in love with Bernardo through chance. How else can one explain Bernardo's appearance at our door and the immediate hold of those big, sad, brown eyes?

Today I went with Juanito to the house of the Delgadillo family to pick up food supplies for la Escuela. Sor María and Sor Julieta are sisters, and their family owns a huge hacienda in Chontales. But the family lives here in Granada and they always send us lots of food. I really like the cheeses they make. Anyhow, after we had loaded the cart, I asked Juanito if he would take me by el Colegio Salesiano.

"¿Y para qué, Teresita?" Juanito has known me since birth, and sometimes I think that he can read my mind. But what worries him now is that he's under strict orders not to take any detours. So I was as honest with him as I could be.

"I want to see how it's going for the young man you dropped off there." And I spoke the truth, in part. Juanito just smiled and drove the cart down la Calle Real all the way to el Colegio. Instead of ringing the front doorbell, which would have raised many questions, Juanito drove to the side entrance, the one nearest to La Polvora—the old Spanish fort and now headquarters for la Guardia in Granada. At the gate he asked for el Colegio's driver, whom he knows well, and then asked him to call Bernardo.

My hands released fat beads of sweat as I waited. I felt hot, as if I had accidentally swallowed a chile congo. As I waited for

Bernardo, the sides of my skirt became damp from wiping my sweaty palms on them. When he finally showed up, I was sad not to see his aura, probably because of the intensity of the morning sun.

At first Bernardo didn't recognize me, so I reminded him of his visit to my school.

"Ah, sí. Ahora recuerdo," he said, smiling. He seemed so happy then to see me that I almost melted into a puddle of sweat. "Sudor seré, mas sudor enamorado," I thought, paraphrasing Quevedo, the Spanish poet, whom we had recently studied in our literature class.

"I came by to see how you were doing. Sor Conchita wants to know as well," I lied. But why should my interest in him be obvious?

"Estoy bien," he answered. "I'm working hard: gardening, sweeping, mopping, painting walls." Suddenly, a sad thought crossed his mind. I could see it dim his cheerfulness. He looked so much like a lost schoolboy that I said a quick prayer on his behalf to San Juan Bosco. "The problem is that I want to go to school, and Padre Benito says that it's not possible here. He also says that I should be prepared to return to Cuapa. He doesn't expect any jobs to open by the end of the month."

I felt so terrible I almost began to cry right then and there. Honestly. Then an idea occurred to me. I told Bernardo that he should talk to Sor Conchita. She always seems to be able to think of something.

"¡Claro!" he said excitedly, almost shouting. "Nuestra Señora must have sent you. I was beginning to think there was no way out of this." He was so grateful I thought he was going to kiss me. Sadly, he didn't. "I'll stop by your school sometime next week. Gracias, and thank Sor Conchita for her kindness."

I couldn't, obviously, tell him that Sor Conchita didn't have a clue that I was there.

March 1, Feast of San Rudecindo

Bernardo came to El Guapinol today, looking just as valiant as San Rudecindo when el santo fought off the Muslim infidels (why they're "infidels" I don't know, but that's what Sor Ada called them this morning) at Santiago de Compostela. Sor Conchita received the "boy with the glow," as she has taken to calling him, and immediately telephoned the Jesuits at el Colegio Centro América. (Frankly, I believe that's a better school than el Colegio Salesiano—the boys are handsomer and come from better families. In fairness to los Salesianos, Padre Benito gave Bernardo eighty córdobas in payment for his work.) Padre Mauricio, the director of el Colegio Centro América, promised Sor Conchita that he'd speak to Bernardo. He also told her that if he liked the boy he would find work for him *and* allow him to attend classes.

After thanking Sor Conchita over and over, and smiling sweetly in my direction, Bernardo left for el Colegio Centro América. Once again, he sat on the driver's seat next to Juanito.

When Juanito returned, the grin on his face immediately let me know that things had gone well for Bernardo. But still, Juanito wouldn't tell me anything in spite of my pestering. Instead, he waited—I think to kill me from the suspense—until we found Sor Conchita. He then announced that Padre Mauricio had accepted Bernardo. ¡Gracias, Padre Mauricio!

"I like that young man," said Juanito, winking at me while Sor Conchita wasn't looking. I just smiled at him, saying nothing.

But I agree. I agree. I agree.

March 25, Feast of San Juan Capistrano (and La Anunciación)

I couldn't wait any longer. For nearly a month I have neither seen nor heard from Bernardo. My grades are going down fast. I can't concentrate. His virtuous face and tender voice drift like clouds of cotton, clogging my mind when I try to do my homework. I desperately need to see him. So I went to talk to Sor Conchita. I knew she would understand.

And she did. She gave me permission to visit Bernardo once every two weeks on the condition that I pull my grades back up again. "But keep the relationship chaste," she said. "Place yourself under the protection of San Juan de Capistrano. Remember what you heard at today's reading of *Las vidas de los santos*? He was married before he joined the Franciscans. That means he understands relationships between men and women. But although San Juan de Capistrano took that unfortunate misstep, he remained forever chaste after taking his religious vows. Do you understand what I'm saying?"

I told her that I did, of course. But I also remember hearing in this morning's reading that after San Juan de Capistrano helped defeat the Turks in battle, he died from a horrible disease he contracted because of the rotting corpses that were left lying in the streets of Belgrado. The flesh, then, got him after all. What a waste! He died without having one last kiss.

April 2, Feast of San Francisco de Paula

I could hardly concentrate during today's mass because I was so excited about seeing Bernardo. But afterward I did pay attention as Sor María read from *Las vidas de los santos*. That was because today's santo, San Francisco de Paula, reminded me so much of Bernardo—kind, gentle, and thoughtful. And now that Bernardo lives at el Colegio Centro América, he overlooks the lake, the same way that el santo overlooked the waters of the ocean during the years he lived as a hermit.

Bernardo was surprised to see me at el Colegio. I went there with Juanito, who agreed to act as my chaperone, even though I don't really need one. As Bernardo and I sat down on a bench close to those hideous stone idols from la isla de Zapatera, I lied again, telling him that Sor Conchita was interested in learning how he was doing.

He seemed much happier with los Jesuitas than with los Salesianos. He attended classes every day after his work was done. So far Bernardo's work has been to sweep and mop el Colegio's endless corridors and to tend the garden, the usual things someone without an education does.

I was hoping that today he'd want to learn a little about me. You know, maybe show some interest in who I am. But he didn't ask a single question. (The nuns say that all men are like that: interested only in themselves and their *needs*.) Since Bernardo is so quiet, it didn't take long before I had run out of things to talk about. I sat there thinking about what excuse I was going to use to visit him next time. I was sure that before long the Sor Conchita pretext was going to wear thin. I didn't say a word, hoping that the awkward silence would force Bernardo to declare his love for me, ask me to be his novia, and give me my first kiss. No such luck. We sat there for ten minutes without saying anything. That was all I could handle.

As I rose to leave, I noticed that Bernardo became anxious so I asked him if there was something I could do for him. "Yes," he answered. I hoped that he would ask me for a kiss. I quickly moistened my lips with the tip of my tongue. Instead, Bernardo told me that he had dictated a letter for his abuelita to Padre Mauricio. He had just received her answer, so now he needed to write another one. "I'm afraid I'm just now learning how to read. Could you help me write it? I don't want to impose on Padre Mauricio again." The sweetness of his petition made me feel lightheaded. Plus, I was touched that Bernardo really seemed embarrassed to ask for my help. And although my lips had been tingling in anticipation of my first kiss, I rejoiced because I now had an excuse to see Bernardo more often.

I tried not to show my elation and calmly agreed to act as his amanuensis. Bernardo looked at me blankly. His expression reminded me of the puzzled look on Sor Ada's face the time I asked her if she liked Glenn Miller's music. I realized, then, that Bernardo didn't know what the word *amanuensis* meant. (I had just learned it myself in Sor María's language class.) So I told him I would gladly write down whatever he had to say during our next meeting.

"Gracias, gracias, Teresita," he said. "I'll be waiting for you." After waving good-bye, he turned and hurried back into el Colegio. I stood there thinking that a kiss on the cheek—to show his gratitude, of course—would have been a nice gesture.

April 16, Feast of Santa Bernardina (one of Bernardo's favorite saints!)
I arrived as early as I could at Bernardo's colegio. Since I've been starting to do well in my studies again, Sor Conchita gave me permission to leave before breakfast. She also liked the thought of me helping Bernardo write letters to his grandmother.

For once, Bernardo seemed happy to see me. That made me happy as well. After briefly catching up on what we had done the past two weeks, we sat down on a bench, with a pad of paper and my trusty pen, to answer his abuelita's letter. But first he asked me to read aloud what she had written. "I don't feel that I can ask this of anyone here, except for Padre Mauricio. But I trust you,

Teresita." My heart raced when I heard that; and then it beat faster when our hands touched as he passed the letter to me. His abuelita's reply went something like this:

> *Querido Bernardito:*
>
> *Thank you for your letter. It made me very happy to know that you are safe. It has also made me happy to know that you're with good, moral men like Padre Mauricio. But I'm still somewhat upset because you went away without telling me. You left me alone with a lot of work: Who's going to feed the pigs, the cows, clean and plow the fields, help me clean the church? Promise me that you'll learn to read as quickly as possible and come right back.*
>
> *Blanca is writing this letter for me. She comes to visit me almost every night and we talk about you for hours. She wants you to return to Cuapa as well. She's a fine girl and will make some fortunate man a fine wife someday.*
>
> *Please come back soon. I have a long list of things for you to do. Don't forget to pray the rosary every day, go to confession every Friday, and to mass on Sundays.*
>
> *Dios te bendiga,*
> *Tu abuela*

I told Bernardo that the letter was very nice, and that his abuelita sounded like a wonderful woman who genuinely loved him. I then asked the question that was weighing heavily on the tip of my tongue. Who's Blanca? He told me that Blanca is the smartest girl in Cuapa. She was going to school in Juigalpa and she helped him with the record keeping when the townspeople bought the statue of la Inmaculada Concepción: the very same Inmaculada

Concepción that appeared last century to today's saint, Santa Bernardina, in Lourdes, Francia.

He then told me the entire story, including how he received a hero's welcome when he brought her from Juigalpa. The entire town had waited for him—and Nuestra Señora, of course—at la Piedra de Cuapa (sort of like la Piedra de Gibraltar, I guess). Los cuapeños had organized a grand procession with plenty of music and fireworks. I have to admit that after hearing this my admiration for Bernardo grew. Imagine having such a hero for a husband. That's why I'm so jealous of Blanca. Dios me perdone.

We then went on to answer his abuelita's letter. Bernardo's reply went something like this:

> *Querida Abuelita:*
>
> *I pray that la Virgencita is keeping you in good health. I have received your letter. Thank you. And thank Blanquita for being so kind to us.*
>
> *I've begun classes and I'm now working on the alphabet. I'm also learning my numbers and a little arithmetic. Pretty soon, si Dios quiere, I'll be able to write to you myself. I now have Teresita de Jesús Medina writing this letter for me. She's very intelligent, just like Blanquita.* [I didn't appreciate the comparison, but I kept my feelings to myself.]
>
> *I'll be back to help soon. Padre Mauricio says that he does pastoral work in Chontales. He has noticed that I go to mass not only on Sundays, but every day. He likes that. He has asked me to accompany him on his next trip, which should be within a couple of months. I'll be his assistant. He says that we'll be stopping by Cuapa. So you'll see us*

soon. Please ask don Isidoro if Padre Mauricio can stay at
his house.

    I apologize for leaving home without saying a word.
But you know that I believe that I'm not destined to be a
campesino. I want to do much more than plow fields, fight
weeds, and take care of animals. I don't want to live by the
blade of my machete. I can do better than that. The life of a
campesino is not the life I want, abuelita. Please try to
understand. I need an education so I can become someone
you'll be proud of.

    Don't worry, abuelita, I pray the rosary every day. I
have not forgotten Nuestra Señora. I know that she
watches over us, her devoted children.

    Give my best to Blanquita, and thank her again for me.

Con respeto, su nieto que mucho la quiere,
Bernardo Martínez

After I wrote the letter, it was almost time for lunch. As I got
ready to leave, Bernardo thanked me and held out his hand for me
to shake. What is he waiting for? Where's my first kiss?

August 20, Feast of San Bernardo (and Bernardo's birthday too!!!)
Although several months have gone by, and Bernardo and I have
spent a lot of time together, I still have no idea where our relationship is going. We've become good friends, but that seems to be the
extent of it. What am I doing wrong? Why hasn't he kissed me
yet? I'm drinking plenty of pitahaya juice because my mother says
that it will make my lips redder. Every time I see Bernardo I wear
my hair differently and I put on my prettiest dresses, but he doesn't

seem to notice. Where's my kiss? Today's his birthday; maybe it'll be my lucky day as well.

I've not told Bernardo how I feel because I don't want to frighten him. But I'd like to become more than just friends. I'd like for us to become novios!

I told Juanito how I feel. He's very wise for a carriage driver. But this time he had no advice. He suggested that I be patient. "Time will tell if something more is to become of your friendship." And he's right, I guess. I'll just have to wait. "A patient heart earns great glories," says Sor Conchita. She's italiana, so she knows a lot about love. Although lately we haven't discussed Bernardo much, she knows that our relationship has been progressing very slowly.

I continue to help Bernardo answer his abuelita's letters. But these have become less and less frequent. She says she gets tired of writing, even though she really dictates them to that girl, Blanca. (Incidentally, I wrote Blanca a polite letter informing her that Bernardo and I are *very* close.) It's just as well that his abuelita doesn't write much anymore. That way Bernardo doesn't hear as much about Blanca, and that way I get to spend more time talking to him.

I confess that I became dreadfully jealous when he went to Cuapa for a vacation. He was there for only a week, but I couldn't sleep thinking that he was spending all that time with Blanca. When Bernardo returned he told me that although she spent a lot of time at his house, he was out plowing his abuelita's field, cutting the weeds, feeding the animals, visiting friends, and visiting el Santísimo and the image of la Inmaculada Concepción. I can't believe how much he loves Nuestra Señora. That's why I gave him a statue of her for his birthday. It's carved from cedar wood, just like the one in Cuapa. A beautiful piece, if I may say so myself. He wouldn't open the package while I was there, though. But I know he will love her.

In his love for la Virgencita, Bernardo reminds me a lot of the saint for whom he is named. Today's reading of *Las vidas de los santos* said that San Bernardo was one of the wisest men in the history of the Church. It also mentioned that he was devoted—in body, mind, and soul—to Nuestra Señora. Through the order he founded, the Cistercians, he spread the devotion of la Santísima Virgen throughout Spain, Portugal, Hungary, Poland, and other countries (I think I heard England too, but I'm not entirely sure).

The reading also stated that San Bernardo could be a difficult, stubborn man. I wish my Bernardo would be easier to deal with as well.

October 15, Feast of Santa Teresa de Jesús (and my birthday too!!!)
I woke up excited today thinking that perhaps, on *my* birthday, Bernardo might finally ask me to become his novia. No such luck.

Sor Conchita gave me permission to use the carriage all day. After putting on my prettiest dress—the new mamón-colored one with the white collar—Juanito and I picked up Bernardo and took him for a ride throughout Granada. I think that he had a lot of fun. He's acting more like someone who belongs in the city rather than on the cattle ranches of Chontales. He seems more at ease and no longer stares at everything with his mouth open. He was in a particularly good mood today. Because of his dedication to work and to his classes, the Jesuits have allowed him to begin serving various apprenticeships. Last week he worked under the master tailor, and he likes this trade a whole lot more than plumbing or electrical work.

We were enjoying our carriage ride when, suddenly, in front of the church of La Merced, Bernardo began to act strangely. He crouched low in the passenger seat and slowly slumped down onto the floorboard, where passengers rest their feet. That bothered me because it's filthy down there. He said that he suddenly got a bad cramp in his leg, but I swear he was trying to hide from someone. Still, the only person I saw in the street was the parish priest, Padre Orlando, who's one of the nicest, most cultured men I've ever met. After we had driven past La Merced, Bernardo started to relax again, although he was as pale as a mono cara blanca for quite some time (and after he got up from the floorboard he smelled like a white-faced monkey too).

When we reached el Parque Colón, I asked Juanito to stop the carriage. Bernardo and I walked to el kiosko where we each ate a vigorón and drank a glass of chicha. And he insisted on paying for it! Then Juanito drove us down la Calzada all the way to the pier where we stopped, got out, and sat on a bench. We watched the waves crashing against the dock as workers unloaded a banana boat that had come from Ometepe. Afterward, they began loading the fruit onto freight cars headed for Corinto. Eventually those bananas will end up in the United States of America—maybe on Harry Truman's table. Bernardo and I just sat there watching the men work while we enjoyed the cool breeze coming off the lake's surface. Then Bernardo surprised me. He said that we should take a boat to Chontales sometime so I could see how beautiful Cuapa is for myself. That's the closest he has ever come to saying that he loves me.

At that moment I felt like Santa Teresa during one of her episodes of rapture. My spirit was lifted and I envisioned myself in holy matrimony with Bernardo. I pray that someday this vision will become reality.

After I returned to la Escuela, Sor Conchita somehow sensed that I had experienced a blissful moment. I don't know how she does it but she always seems to know what I'm thinking and feeling. "Do you have anything you would like to tell me, Teresita?" she asked. "No," I answered, and then I paused for dramatic effect, "only that Bernardo said that someday he would like to take me to Cuapa," I added, happily suffering the oncoming blush. Sor Conchita smiled and said, "Well, the young man is becoming bolder."

Bolder . . . I wish he would become as bold as Santa Teresa was when as a young girl she ran away from home and headed for the south of Spain to fight the Muslim infidels.

I'm waiting for Bernardo to storm my castle and take me prisoner.

November 10, Feast of San León Magno

Today during mass, Padre Eustacio read aloud Pío XII's proclamation in which he states that María, Madre de Jesús, ascended in body and soul to heaven. I found it appropriate that this proclamation was read during the feast day of the brave pope who confronted Attila the Hun when the barbarian and his hordes of infidels were about to sack Rome.

When I told Bernardo about la Asunción de la Virgen, he simply said, "I've always known that. She is, after all, la Madre de Dios. How can one even think that her body would be allowed to rot on earth?"

Sometimes it really bothers me when Bernardo acts like he knows everything. I mean, he's still learning how to read.

December 8, Feast of la Inmaculada Concepción

For tonight I invited Bernardo to the last procession of the nine-day feast in honor of La Purísima. Each year the final one is held on la Calle Atravesada, the street where the most illustrious citizens of Granada live. This neighborhood always does a magnificent job with her altar, as well as with the float that takes her back to la Catedral. Knowing how much Bernardo loves Nuestra Señora, I thought he would enjoy seeing how granadinos rejoice over la Inmaculada Concepción.

The throngs of people who had come to see la Virgen astounded Bernardo from the moment we approached la Calle Atravesada. Although we were far from the train station—near where her altar is set up—the multitude was so dense it was difficult for us to move forward. Bernardo seemed uncomfortable in such a huge crowd, so I asked him if he would prefer to go elsewhere instead, perhaps to a movie.

"No," he said, "I want to see her. I'll be fine."

As we advanced slowly along la Calle Atravesada, up the slight hill heading north toward la estación, I could see that Bernardo was still nervous. "¿Estás bien?" I asked. I was becoming concerned because he looked as if he were about to faint.

"Sí, sí," he answered impatiently. "It's just that I'm eager to see her."

"Within another block we should have a good view of the altar," I said.

As we continued inching our way forward, I told him how Nuestra Señora's statue had appeared mysteriously, floating on the lake. Her image was in a box, and the box wouldn't let anyone near until the people had finally called a priest. When the priest at last arrived, the box came to him, gliding on the waves like a lazy turtle, and after he ordered the people to open it they found the statue we still venerate today. I had just finished the story when

Bernardo came to a complete stop. He remained frozen, himself as still as a statue. I stopped as well, prepared to ask him, once again, what was wrong. Then I saw that he was looking, mouth wide open, in the direction of the altar.

Nuestra Señora was, indeed, a beautiful sight. Lights shone upon her from all directions, transforming her into a resplendent being, glowing alone on this starless night against the persistent drone of the electrical generators.

Bernardo was speechless, and after a few moments, I saw tears rolling down his cheeks. "She's the most magnificent being I've ever seen," he said at last. Looking at me—for the first time ever in a passionate way—he added, "Teresita, thank you for bringing me here."

He hardly said a word the rest of the evening. When we arrived at the foot of the altar, he brought out his rosary, got on his knees, and began to pray. He remained like that for two hours. I must confess that I soon became so bored that I considered leaving him there and going to the movies instead, by myself. But I was patient, and at last I was relieved when the band struck up the music to mark the beginning of the procession. Bernardo rose and along with the rest of Granada accompanied Nuestra Señora back to la Catedral. During the entire route, Bernardo didn't say a word.

Once they had taken la Virgen inside the church the crowd began to disperse, everyone heading home. But Bernardo remained inside la Catedral for a while, praying what must have been his twentieth rosary that night. When he finished, he came to me and said, "Gracias, Teresita, muchas gracias. If you don't mind, I think I'd like to walk back to el Colegio Centro América. I need to be alone."

And forgetting that I existed, he left, looking dazed; lost on some luminous inner journey—just like the portraits I've seen of Santa Teresa while she's having a mystical experience.

1950
February 27, Feast of San Leandro

Today Sor Julieta told us about how the American Congress amended their constitution to limit the terms a president can serve to two. That means that a man can only be president for eight years. No more. "There's a lot we can learn from los gringos," she said again. I looked around and saw all my classmates nodding in agreement.

When I mentioned this to Bernardo, he said that neither priests nor nuns should be allowed political opinions. After all, he said, Dios gives us the governors he deems best suited to rule over us. I tried to argue with him, telling him that Dios is not fond of dictators. But I couldn't convince him.

Sometimes Bernardo can be incredibly stubborn. Like San Leandro, bishop of Sevilla, who argued adamantly with the visigodos and with the arians (I looked the term up in the encyclopedia: these heretics did not believe in the Holy Trinity) until he finally convinced them that the doctrine of the Holy Roman Catholic Church was the only correct one.

Bernardo's also stubborn when it comes to our relationship. Why doesn't he ask me to be his novia? Where's my first kiss? I'm beginning to lose my patience.

March 24, Feast of San Patricio

Today Bernardo had the nerve to ask for my help with a letter he wanted to write to Blanquita of Cuapa. Of course, I refused. I was angry. I do have my pride. How long does he expect me to wait for him to ask me to become his novia? How long does he expect me to wait for my first kiss? Instead, he has the insensitivity to ask me to write a letter to "the most intelligent girl in Cuapa."

Bernardo took my refusal calmly, saying that he understood perfectly. He, of course, thinks that I'm tired of writing letters for him. He told me that he thinks that he's now ready to write the letters himself. (He *doesn't understand* at all.) (And how can I be tired? We haven't written a letter to his abuelita for almost a year: ever since the old woman got "tired" of answering his letters.)

In some ways Bernardo reminds me of San Patricio. When el santo was a boy, in Scotland, he was captured, sold as a slave, and held captive in Irlanda for many years. After an angel appeared to him in a prophetic dream, he escaped and made it all the way back home. He later returned to Irlanda to convert the pagans. But, like Bernardo, San Patricio learned to read and write late in life. Still, I think San Patricio would have been much more sensitive toward any novias he may have had. I think I'll stay away from Bernardo for a while to see if he even notices that I'm missing.

August 20, Feast of San Bernardo

Nearly five months have passed, and not once has Bernardo tried to contact me. The first few weeks were horrible, I missed him so much. I thought I was going to die. But as time passed it hurt less and less—sort of like when a deep wound on your finger begins to heal after you cut it while chopping onions with a sharp knife. I now wonder what I really feel for him. I'm beginning to think that maybe he's not worth the aggravation.

Yet Bernardo has called Sor Conchita several times. She says that he always asks how I'm doing. She also said that I should have gone to see him, that I was being prideful. Doesn't she understand how much it hurt that he didn't seem to have any feelings for me? I'm a woman now but no one seems to notice. Where's my first kiss? I'm already in el tercer año and after I graduate my mother says that I should start thinking about getting married. But I'm not sure now about becoming anyone's wife. Maybe I'll become a monja like Sor Conchita. I mean, if all men are like Bernardo, then what's the point?

And now I'm discovering things about men and women that I find troublesome. That includes the holiest, most sacred of beings: los santos. For instance, while reading about the life of San Bernardo in the school library, I discovered a legend that has left me confused. The book says that la Virgen visited San Bernardo and rewarded his devotion by giving him three drops of milk from her breast. The book also had a print of a painting by a Spanish artist named Murillo where San Bernardo lies back in ecstasy as he suckles on Nuestra Señora's bosom.

I went to Padre Eustacio with my questions about what I had learned. "It is better not to think of la Santísima Virgen in this way," he said, his face turning the color of a pitahaya. "Go along, young woman, put this out of your mind, pray the rosary, and get ready for your classes."

I then turned to Sor Conchita. "What a wonderful legend!" she said. "Nuestra Madre in this way becomes real to San Bernardo and she nourishes him the same way she nourished the Redeemer. What a blessing for el santo."

I do try to think of the entire thing the way Sor Conchita sees it, but I can't.

October 15, Feast of Santa Teresa (and mi cumpleaños as well!!!)
I had two big surprises today. The first was an early morning visit from Bernardo. He brought me a gift: a beautiful light blue blazer that he had cut and sewn himself. He said that it would bring me

good luck in my relationships. (What's *that* supposed to mean?) He also said he was able to guess my measurements by comparing me to Blanquita, since we are about the same size. You know what surprised me the most about this? I wasn't upset in the least. I was even happy for Bernardo. He has truly become an artist at the sewing machine, and he seems happy. Looks like his destino after all is to become a tailor.

The past few months hiding from Bernardo have been good for me. I'm no longer drawn to his angelic aura. I don't even see it anymore. The feeling of being crushed by rose petals whenever I'm around him has disappeared (it's the same feeling Santa Teresa reported having whenever she saw Jesús). I look back now on how I used to feel, and I feel so foolish. I was just an immature little girl back then.

Bernardo and I spoke for a while in the lobby. He couldn't stay long because he was leaving for Cuapa with Padre Mauricio. As Bernardo said good-bye, he leaned forward and gave me a kiss on the cheek. A year ago I would have died and awoken in heaven. Today, it was nothing more than a kiss between friends. It was so nice to see how I've outgrown him.

The second and best surprise happened later during the day when I went out with some classmates from El Guapinol to celebrate—my birthday, that is. I wore Bernardo's blue blazer for the occasion and my friends said it made me look striking, like Rita Hayworth. At el kiosko in el Parque Colón we all ordered chicharrón con yuca and chicha. We were having a wonderful time imitating the most obnoxious nuns, and laughing scandalously. (At least that's what Juanito said as he scolded me on the way back home. But I don't care; I've not felt this happy in ages.)

Then, as Sor Conchita once told me, when you're least

expecting it, when you're not really looking, love comes your way. Seated a couple of tables away from us was a group of boys from el Colegio Salesiano. Among them were two brothers (at least it was obvious to me that they were brothers). Several times I caught the younger one staring at me. He had a sweet, innocent expression, as if the world had never hurt him in the least. Although I wouldn't call him handsome, there was a shy, gentle, yet manly way about him. When he stood up, I noticed that he was tall—the tallest in the group—and athletic looking, as if he swam, played a lot of baseball, or something like that.

Whenever he looked my way I would quickly glance in another direction, trying to appear as nonchalant as possible, in spite of my galloping heart. Before long, all the boys were staring at me. I could see them coaxing the young man with their elbows, encouraging him to come talk to me. Of course, my friends soon caught on to what was happening as well. They began to tease me, making the whole thing so very awkward.

At last, after much goading—or perhaps to stop the goading—he walked toward me. I was surprised that although he seemed athletic his stride was lumbering. He moved like an ox. I heard my friends giggle when they saw this. "Stop it!" I ordered. "I think the way he moves is cute. He reminds me of a tall, thin troll." We all burst out laughing.

"Buenas tardes," he said once he was standing next to me, "Me llamo Nicolás." I was overwhelmed; what he lacked in gracefulness he made up with the most beautiful voice. He sounded like un ángel.

Our friends, unfortunately, didn't let us talk much. They tried to eavesdrop on every word. But after he found out my name and where I lived, he promised to drop by to visit.

Will Nicolás be my first kiss?

I think I'm in love.

December 6, Feast of San Nicolás (and Nicolás's cumpleaños too!!!), morning
Today I placed myself under the protection of San Nicolás, santo patrón of unwed women. During his last visit, Nicolás told me that on his birthday he'd come by to ask my mother's permission to become mi novio. When Sor Conchita found out about his plan, she called Padre Benito at el Colegio to learn more about mi enamorado. The priest told her that Nicolás was a fine young man with great potential, and that he had no objection to our becoming novios.

Nicolás's mother is also a cook, just like mine. We have so much in common. He's an excellent student as well. After he graduates this year he plans on studying medicine.

I'm so in love. And I'm also so nervous. I'll continue this entry after his visit.

At night, right before bedtime
I have a novio!!! (Is it because I wore the light blue blazer?) My mother gave Nicolás permission to visit me twice a week. She said that his intentions seem honorable. Does that sound old-fashioned, or what? After Nicolás received my mother's consent to court me, she stepped aside so we could have a moment of privacy (¡Gracias a Dios!), and he then asked me if I would accept him as mi novio. Of course, I said sí.

Sor Conchita, who stood alongside my mother, witnessing the whole thing, escorted her out of the room. As they were leaving, she whispered to me, "You have exactly thirty seconds." I knew what she meant. But Nicolás, that sweet young boy, was slow in catching on. So I put my hand behind his neck, pulled him toward me, and we shared our first kiss. (My first kiss!!!) The coming together of our mouths was so breathtaking I almost fainted.

¡Gracias, San Nicolás! Maybe thanks to el santo I'll become a doctor's wife. And to think that only a few months ago I would've been delighted to be the wife of a simple tailor.

PRIMA VISIO
(The First Apparition)
May 8, 1980

Bernardo

I COULDN'T sleep at all the night before her first apparition. The humidity made things unbearably hot and not the slightest breeze entered through my bedroom windows. The air was so dense I had trouble breathing. Everything was absolutely still. I could clearly hear the buzzing of mosquitoes and the lonely croaking of frogs. To make matters worse, I couldn't stop thinking about my problems.

To be honest, what people were saying about me was what worried me most. Many said that I was crazy because of what I had said about the illumination. About la Revolución, a few believed that I was in league with Elías Bacon, the Sandinista officer responsible for Cuapa; others said that I was a contrarevolucionario. But everyone agreed that I was a dreamer who wasted his time on disparates, always thinking of nothing but nonsense, like mi abuelita used to say.

I was also worried about money. I was flat broke—palmado, sin un centavo. I still worked as the town's sacristán, but taking care of the church was volunteer work; I didn't get a single córdoba. And the comments my relatives were making about my devotion to the

Church were beginning to really irritate me. They said that I was un gran baboso, unquestionably dim-witted.

"El Vaticano is loaded with money, Bernardo. If Padre Domingo wanted to, he could easily pay you," my cousin Toribio said, and the rest of my clan nodded in agreement. Cash was so scarce that I was forced to ask my friends and relatives to collect their kitchen waste in buckets for machigüe, to feed my pigs. I couldn't remember ever being that poor.

To make things worse, the day before the apparition my cousin Pedro stopped by the church while I was leading a prayer service. He demanded that I repay the money he had loaned me. It's true that I was overdue, but he didn't need to be disrespectful. He yelled at me, in front of everyone, when I asked him to be patient, to give me a little more time.

I was very depressed. That's for certain. The only thing I found comforting was that people were no longer talking about the illumination. That was a big relief because I was tired of being the town's favorite topic of conversation.

That entire night, then, as I tossed and turned in bed, drenched in sweat, all I could think about was how much I hated my life. I lay there, staring at the ceiling while asking myself whether life was worth living. Not even the two Rosaries I prayed freed me from feeling miserable, tired, unwanted, and unloved.

At dawn I climbed out of bed to feed the pigs. While watching them dig their snouts deep into el machigüe I decided to spend the day down by the river, near one of my pastures, el potrero farthest from town. My plan for the day was to sit by the stream in the shade of the trees, catch some fish, pick some fruit, and relax. As I left my house all I took along was an old white nylon sack and my machete.

When I reached the river, I waded across easily. It was toward the end of the dry season, so the water barely rose to my ankles. I kept on walking, slightly beyond the curve, until I reached the entrance to mi potrero. Once inside the pasture, I took the path that descends to the river. I decided to rest under the shade of a genízaro. I dropped my sack and my machete on a sandy knoll and sat down on a large, smooth rock.

After I had cooled down a little, I got up to start fishing, which I do with my bare hands. Within an hour I had caught three sábalos, four guapotes, and three barbudos. "This is a miracle," I said to myself. I had never caught that many fish in such a short time, and big ones at that. I strung them together on a tigüilote branch.

Feeling much more relaxed, I stopped at a guapinol tree. I saw that its branches were loaded with ripened pods. I climbed onto a large boulder from where I picked two from a low-hanging branch, then sat down, cracked the pods in half, and poured the sweet yellow powder into my mouth. From the top of the boulder, I looked out upon my entire pasture. "I'm truly blessed," I said aloud, looking over mi potrero with pride.

Looking up at the sun, I saw that it was almost noon. This made me sad because I didn't want to return to Cuapa. I was sure that nothing but unhappiness awaited me there.

But I still had a few hours left, so I picked up the tigüilote branch that was now heavy with fish, and dropped it into the nylon sack. Feeling a little hungry, I walked to the mango tree on the opposite side of el potrero. I picked two large, low-hanging fruits, and ate them. They were perfect: the meatiest, juiciest, sweetest mangos ever. Not a single fiber got caught between my teeth. I then found a nice spot under the tree and sat down to rest. Feeling drowsy, I lay down and soon fell asleep.

When I awoke, I glanced at the sun to check the time: three o'clock. I needed to get back home to feed the animals. If I don't give the pigs their supper they follow me to church, and today I didn't want to be embarrassed by their loud snorts during the evening's prayer service. But the thought of returning to Cuapa still made me sad.

I checked the sun again. It was then that I realized that something about it was different. Instead of the harsh light that always makes me squint, the sun had become a clear, friendly circle, easy to stare at without hurting my eyes.

When I was halfway to the gate of mi potrero, a sudden flash of light startled me. It was so intense that I braced myself for the deafening crack that always follows. I waited, but the sound of thunder, which always makes me jump, never came. Relieved, I made the sign of the cross. I glanced up at the sky looking for rain clouds, but it was spotless and clear. Although I still can't explain why, I knew something incredible was about to happen.

When I was only a few steps away from a pile of volcanic rocks set between two trees, a morisco and a cedro, there was a second flash. Out of the corner of my eye, to my right, I saw a cloud descending, and I could feel a powerful presence within it. I became so frightened that I threw myself flat on the ground, covering my head as it came closer. I began to shake, as if the weather was bitter cold, and I shut my eyes, like a child at bedtime who's afraid of seeing ghosts. Then, without explanation, my terror disappeared. It was replaced by a sudden urge—an urge I found impossible to resist—to get on my knees and greet whatever was before me.

I opened my eyes. My entire body froze as the cloud stopped moving. The mist shot off colorful beams of light in all directions. The cloud came to rest on top of el morisco, entirely covering the small tree. Standing above it, magnificent to behold, was a beautiful señora. (And although I respectfully thought of her as a señora, she looked only about eighteen, much younger than me.)

On my knees, and no longer frightened, I stared in wonder. I first noticed her bare feet. All I could really see were her toes, but they were perfect—slender and straight. The señora wore a long white dress, long sleeved and modest, with a wide, light blue ribbon tied around the waist. A cream-colored shawl covered her head. The cloth was wrapped loosely around her neck. It hung over her left shoulder and reached all the way down to her knee. The ends of the shawl were embroidered in a splendid gold thread.

La señora's skin was white, radiant, and it shone like glass. Framing her head, like a halo, was a crown made up of twelve sparkling stars. Her hands were clasped in front of her chest, which made her look very peaceful.

I rubbed my eyes. For a moment I thought that I was still asleep under the mango tree. Perhaps I was dreaming about the illuminated statue of a couple of weeks ago. But when I removed my hands from my eyes, she was still before me, floating on the cloud. And now something had changed. Her skin had lost its shine; she had become human. I looked into her eyes . . . and I gasped when she blinked.

She's alive, I thought, amazed at the transformation. I began to tremble. I tried to speak, but my tongue had become heavy.

La señora then spread both arms apart, moving them away from her sides. She stopped when her hands reached the level of her waist. Her open palms were facing me. Suddenly, they released strong beams of light, more intense than the light of the sun. The rays struck me squarely in the chest. At once, I could move my tongue again.

"What is your name?" I asked. She smiled at me, and for a moment I couldn't breathe because I found her beauty so stunning. I knew at last what a man feels when he first sets eyes on the woman he's going to marry.

María.

My knees weakened when I heard the sweetness of her voice.

She's alive, and now she has answered me, I thought. So I asked the question that had been haunting me ever since the illumination: "Are you la Virgen? Do you really want to speak to *me?*"

Yes.

Although I was now sure that I was talking to la Madre de Nuestro Señor, I asked the next question naturally, as if I were speaking to a friend. "What do you want?"

I want everyone to pray the rosary, every day.

She spoke slowly, carefully pronouncing each word. This let me interrupt her, by saying, "But we *are* praying the rosary, Señora. Padre Domingo has asked us to do so every day during the entire month of May."

I don't want you to pray the rosary only in May. I want everyone to pray it every day, with their family. Teach your children to pray the rosary as soon as they are old enough to understand. Pray the rosary at the same time of the day, once the chores of the home have been completed. El Señor does not like prayers that are said in a hasty, distracted, or mechanical manner. Make sure that when you pray you take time to reflect upon the appropriate passages of the Bible. Renew the first Saturdays. You received many favors from el Señor when you last did this. And above all, I want everyone to live la Palabra de Dios.

"What are the biblical passages you are talking about, Señora?" I asked, not knowing what she meant.

Search for them in the Bible. They are there.

She smiled at me, as if amused by what I had asked, and then she continued, *Love one another. Fulfill your duties and obligations to each other. Forgive one another. Work for peace. Do not ask el Señor for peace. You need to work to make peace among yourselves; otherwise it will never happen. Do not choose the path of violence. Never choose the path of violence. Since the earthquake, your country has suffered much, and now dark, menacing clouds cover it again. Your suffering, as well as the suffering of all humanity, shall continue if people don't mend their ways.*

She paused. The brightness of her clear, honey-colored eyes made me sigh. For a long time we just stared at each other. At last, she continued speaking.

Pray, mi hijo. Pray the rosary for the entire planet. Tell believers and nonbelievers alike that grave dangers threaten the world. I am begging el Señor to delay his judgment. However, if you don't mend your ways, your dependence on violence as a way to settle differences will bring forth Armageddon.

"Señora, do I have to tell this to everyone?" Although I was honored that Nuestra Señora had come to me, I really didn't want the responsibility of being her messenger.

Sí, Bernardo.

This was the first time she had mentioned my name. Hearing it from her made me feel brave enough to protest.

"Señora, I already have enough problems. I have money problems, problems with the people of Cuapa, and even problems with the Church. Couldn't you choose someone else?"

No, Bernardo. El Señor has chosen you for this task.

Her answer was firm. I knew that nothing I could say would change her mind. But in spite of her sternness my feelings were not hurt. I became very sad when I saw the cloud beginning to rise, taking her away.

"Just a moment, Señora. Don't leave. Let me run into town to bring back a few people who want to meet you. Doña Tula, for one, has many questions she wants to ask."

No, Bernardo. Only you are able to see and talk to me. Those who believe that I am here will see me later, in heaven. Now go. Do as I've asked and tell everyone what you have seen and heard this afternoon.

After she said this, she raised her arms and the cloud began ascending, becoming brighter the higher it rose.

I will return on June 8, she said, now looking straight down at me. The vision slowly faded and then vanished completely when the cloud cleared the top of el cedro.

I remained on my knees, unable to move. From early on, my fear had been replaced by a sense of wonder. The entire time I felt as if I had been speaking to someone I had known all of my life. But now, I felt like cussing. And who could blame me? The whole thing had been incredible. La Virgen María doesn't just appear to anybody. But mi abuelita Eloísa always said I should never use profane language, *especially* regarding things that are holy.

A couple of minutes after la Virgencita had left, I gathered my sack and my machete. But before starting for home, I decided to pick some coyol berries for the pigs' supper.

At first I had every intention of obeying her, of sharing her message with everyone. But on the walk back to Cuapa, every worry that had kept me awake the night before came back to haunt me: how cuapeños believe I'm crazy, that I'm a fool, a pathetic dreamer. Then I remembered how the community was also bitterly divided over politics, and something like this could divide them even further.

When I started to imagine how people would react, I knew that I would become el hazmerreir of Cuapa, the laughingstock, the center of ridicule. To avoid more problems, I thought it best to keep my mouth shut about what I had seen and heard that afternoon. Maybe, if I didn't do as she had asked, she would look for another messenger.

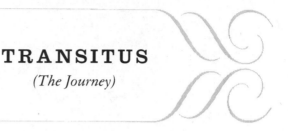

chapter three

TRANSITUS
(The Journey)

1954–1978

Blanca Arias

IF A MURALIST were to lay out Blanca Arias's life along the smooth surface of a building's wall, Bernardo Martínez's face would appear throughout—from her childhood to the present. He had helped hold Blanca steady during her most difficult moments, and he had been by her side to share many of the happy ones as well. El Señor knows that their relationship was never a romantic one, even if doña Eloísa, his abuelita, had hoped it would be. That girl from Granada—Teresa something or other—surely thought it was. What's more, when Bernardo was away, studying in Granada, she had sent Blanca a frightening letter. *Stay away from him or else,* it read. Back then, Blanca had become angry, but now, many years later, the incident was a mere sapling in her thick forest of memories; and with the passage of time, when she looked at it through the tinted lenses of nostalgia, what had once been a threat was now merely another amusing episode in her life.

Blanca had always been very fond of Bernardo. She would never deny that. From the time they were children she had admired his religiosity, his enterprising spirit, and how he always tried to make his abuelita proud. She also enjoyed his gift for storytelling, laughing at the way he could take the simplest experience and turn it into an adventure. But what she liked the most about Bernardo was his sincerity and his compassion. He was the one man in the world with whom she always felt safe.

That's why Blanca missed him terribly when he left for Granada. Only Bernardo, of everyone in Cuapa, fully understood her desire to continue going to school, to continue learning. Had it not been for Bernardo she would never have attended la escuela secundaria, let alone graduate.

After Blanca completed the sixth grade, her father, don Isidoro, asked, "Why do you want to go on studying if all you're going to do is get married, have children, and take care of a family?" And then he added, "What's more, with the land and cattle I own, and with that pretty face of yours, you're bound to marry into a wealthy family from Chontales or Boaco. You'll never have to work, Blanquita. Just forget about the whole thing. You don't need more schooling."

But Bernardo asked Padre Mauricio, during one of the Jesuit's pastoral visits to Cuapa, to convince don Isidoro to support Blanca's ambitions. In his presentation, the priest appealed to el hacendado's pride.

"Think of it this way, don Isidoro, you could be the first man in Cuapa to have a daughter who has graduated from secundaria. And you'll be setting an important example for other fathers."

Blanca's father didn't buy the argument at all, but he deferred out of his deep respect for the priesthood. Still, Blanca•thought, if it hadn't been for Bernardo, Padre Mauricio would never have intervened.

When Bernardo returned from Granada, Blanca was about to enter the fourth year of secundaria—only one more year to go after that. Since there wasn't a single school in Cuapa, she had to continue living in Juigalpa with her aunt Dorotea, a florist. In spite of the years Blanca spent in a bedroom next to the shop, she never became accustomed to the smell of azucenas. The pungent, rich, sickly sweet scent of the white lilies of the tropics, which were present at every wake and funeral, would remind her of death for the rest of her life.

Still, Blanca loved the years she had spent in the city. In particular, she enjoyed her last two years of secundaria because Bernardo, after returning from Granada, had also moved to Juigalpa to continue studying. They met every afternoon in el Parque Central, under the guanacaste tree, to drink tiste and chat. In those intimate moments, Blanca shared her dreams, her loves, and her hopes for the future. Back then, she could never have imagined the twisted and sometimes tortuous paths that lay ahead for each of them.

"Bernardo, you know what I would love someday? To have educated people all around me, and to marry a man who loves to read and owns lots of books. And to have children who love to read as well."

Blanca would then look toward Bernardo only to see that his mind was somewhere far away, lost in the heavens. Bernardo seldom seemed to listen, which frustrated her. As a small measure of revenge, she'd secretly laugh when Bernardo's preteen classmates would tease him as they passed through el parque.

"Oye, viejo. Come help us cut down some cocos. And while you're at it, buy us some cigarettes and a few beers," they'd shout, mocking his height and age.

"This is the part I hate the most about going to school, Blanquita: being twenty-two and still in primaria. It's so humiliating!" But in spite of that unpleasantness Bernardo persisted, completing the fifth and sixth grade.

After graduation, Blanca returned to Cuapa. For days, she summoned all of her courage to ask for her father's permission to go to college. To help soften don Isidoro's heart she sat at his feet, embracing his legs. "Papi, can I attend the university in León? Lots of girls are studying there now."

"¡Allí ya no!" he replied resolutely, rising from his favorite rocking chair and storming out of the living room.

The only plan possible then in Blanca's future was to wait patiently to see what life held in store for her. And, really, when she thought about it, that meant marriage and filling don Isidoro's house with grandchildren. Blanca would have no problem finding suitors. She had become an attractive young woman who had the good fortune of inheriting her mother's long and shapely legs. But the man of her dreams—the one who loved to read and owned plenty of books—was nowhere to be found in Chontales. Don Isidoro's only child, then, had no alternative but to wait.

During this time of Blanca's life, her days were limited to staying at home to keep her mother company and help her supervise the maids; or to taking long horseback rides on her father's vast hacienda. Bored beyond redemption, she prayed that her destino would soon reveal itself.

Bernardo returned to Cuapa the same year as she. "I want to go on studying, Blanquita, but my uncle Emilio moved to

Comalapa and mi abuelita now lives alone. I need to be here for her." Blanca felt sorry for her friend because, more than anything, he wanted to finish school. Since Bernardo refused to work in the fields, he opened a tailor shop next to his bedroom.

His business, from the beginning, went well. Bernardo's tailoring was highly regarded. Wealthy hacendados from Juigalpa made the trip to Cuapa to have him custom make their pants and white linen suits. And, cautiously, since Bernardo was conservative with money, with don Isidoro's advice he bought land and cattle. Over the years, he purchased three potreros, totaling close to eighteen acres of fertile green pastures that spread throughout the gentle slopes running along el Río Cuapa.

"Look at me, Blanquita, I've become quite a capitalist," Bernardo would say jokingly, but with a trace of pride as well. "What do you think?" Bernardo didn't own much, really, but for a cuapeño who had started off with nothing, Blanca thought that what he had accumulated was rather impressive.

All of these events took place, of course, before el escándalo. At least, that's how cuapeños referred to the events that changed Blanca's life forever. Yet the scandal filled Blanca's soul with some of the most beautiful memories of her life, as well as the saddest.

El escándalo began when two Franciscan priests, both Americanos, came to Cuapa for a few months to perform missionary work. Shortly after they arrived, they found that although they had studied Spanish in preparation, the formal language of the classroom proved useless when they spoke to campesinos chontaleños.

"Padrecitos, aquí tienen unos bollitos," said don Fabio after his grandson's baptism, the day following the priests' arrival. "Y de ipegüe, un chanchito. Y no vayan a olvidarse de darle su machigüe, porque si no, tendremos velorio." The priests looked at each other bewildered, one of them holding a córdoba in coins and the other a piglet while don Fabio walked away chuckling to himself. Neither Franciscan had the slightest idea what the campesino had said. The communication gap worried them so much that they immediately began to search for someone who could act as their bridge. Bernardo recommended Blanca.

She was delighted at the prospect of having something to occupy her time, and she was especially excited with the idea of working for two Americanos. Blanca, since childhood, had dreamed of someday visiting the United States, ever since her favorite aunt from Managua, her tía Carmen, had moved to San Francisco. Also, secretly, never having told anyone, not even her confidant, Bernardo, Blanca had fallen in love with several rugged American movie stars in the dim, smoke-filled safety of Juigalpa's theater. Watching films with Tyrone Power, more than any other actor, made her release involuntary sighs of repressed yearnings.

When presented with the opportunity of working with the Franciscans, Blanca didn't hesitate. She had never met a gringo in person, but without knowing why, she fully expected the experience to inspire her. Blanca came to think of their arrival as a gift from heaven. She had been praying to la Virgencita to help her escape the distressing loneliness of being an educated person cast adrift in a sea of ignorance.

Called upon by Padre Francisco, Juigalpa's parish priest (as well as Cuapa's, whenever he could spare the time), Blanca hurried to the church to meet los Americanos. The priest introduced her to Padre Antonio Calvino and Padre Róger Bacon. Padre Antonio was tall and thin. His silver hair made him look strikingly distinguished. He wore glasses with thick black plastic frames that were far too big for his face, but that didn't detract from his warm Italian smile. Padre Róger, on the other hand, was short, barrel chested, and balding. But he had beautiful green eyes that reminded Blanca of an emerald ring her mother owned. She stared at them intently because they were the first green eyes she had ever seen. Still, she thought that they were too small and set a little too close together. But Padre Róger wore small, wire-rimmed glasses that in Blanca's opinion suited his face perfectly. Padre Antonio was older and, as she would later discover, much wiser than Padre Róger. Observing the way they behaved toward each other, Blanca guessed that Padre Antonio was the younger one's adviser. She placed Padre Antonio around forty-eight, and Padre Róger around thirty-three.

The Franciscans spoke haltingly in Spanish when they first met Blanca, pronouncing each syllable a little too carefully and pausing for long stretches in midsentence as they searched for the perfect word, and the perfect grammatical construction.

"Yo espero que en este trabajo, usted. . . . Róger, what's the subjunctive of *tener—usted* form?"

"Let me think . . . usted . . . tuviera, . . . no . . . tuviese, . . . no . . . I got it . . . *tenga!*"

"Yo espero que en este trabajo usted tenga mucha . . . no . . . muchas, res-pon-sa-bi-li-da-des." But soon the priests felt comfortable enough around Blanca to allow themselves to make mistakes, which she corrected with masterful subtlety. At the end of the meeting, they implored her to help them with their work in Cuapa, and she happily accepted.

At first, Blanca served strictly as their interpreter. But within a few weeks, the singsong accent of the chontaleños ceased to disorient the priests, who for a while had believed that people were talking to them in an indigenous language rather than in Spanish. By this time Blanca had made herself indispensable. She had become a superbly organized assistant who kept the Franciscans' business in perfect order. With her help, during their short stay in Cuapa, the priests performed more marriages, baptisms, confirmations, and first communions than the combined efforts over the past ten years of Cuapa's part-time parish priests. And with the help of the Franciscans based in Managua, the missionaries persuaded the government's Ministerio de Educación to open the town's first escuela primaria.

Bernardo dropped by to help whenever he could. He sewed an outfit, at no charge, for every boy receiving first communion. He also devoted more time than usual as sacristán. The Franciscans were impressed with how everything in the church was always well arranged and immaculate. And every evening Bernardo joined them in praying the rosary, staying afterward to chat until far beyond his usual bedtime.

After the first couple of weeks, although Blanca liked both priests, she found herself preferring Padre Róger's company. Perhaps it was his youth that made her feel that they had more in common. This, in spite of Padre Antonio being the more outgoing of the two. During the afternoons Blanca took long walks with Padre Róger. Their favorite destinations were the swimming hole of La Paslama and, when they had more time, la Piedra de Cuapa. Blanca told the Franciscan about the legend of el Duende de la Piedra: the mischievous gnome who lived atop the monolith and came down to attempt to seduce young, virginal girls. Blanca also warned the priest that if an outsider swam in La Paslama, he was condemned to marry a local girl and never leave.

During one of their hikes to the rock, he ran ahead of her and climbed to the top. The ascent took him close to an hour. At the summit, once he spotted her, he pounded his chest and shouted down, "Yo soy, de la Piedra de Cuapa, el Duende. Muy, muy pronto, vengo a usted, a buscarle." Because of his heavily accented Spanish and twisted syntax, Padre Róger's joke about being el Duende and coming after her seemed harmless, even charming.

Whenever Blanca needed to attend confession, she preferred Padre Antonio. His counsel was wise and full of empathy. By this she didn't mean that Padre Róger was neither wise nor sympathetic; it was just that Blanca, for reasons unknown to her, did not want him becoming aware of her shortcomings. One Friday, the week before the beginning of Lent, about three months after the Franciscans had arrived, Padre Antonio was out of Cuapa, having been called to a meeting in Managua. Blanca, then, turned to Padre Róger.

When she asked him if he would hear her confession, he surprised her by replying, "Only if you hear mine first."

When she raised her bowed head, he reached out and lovingly held her face in both hands. "Niña, estoy enamorado de ti," he said.

His declaration of love baffled her. Blanca bolted out of the church, shocking Padre Róger. She didn't stop running until she reached her house—the elegant one with seven caoba pillars out front—on la Calle de los Laureles. She entered, crying and out of breath, and went straight to her room, refusing to answer the questions of her alarmed parents. The following two days Blanca only came out at mealtimes. She'd join her family at the table only to push her food with a fork from one side of the plate to the other.

"Señorita, you either stop that or go back to your room!" don Isidoro would say, irritated at his daughter's sudden and unexplained sullenness. Relieved, Blanca would rise from the table and lock herself in her room again.

On the third day, Bernardo came looking for her. Without hesitation, she left the safety of her room to see him. He was the only person in the world for whom she would do so. Alone, in la sala, with no one to overhear their conversation, they talked.

"Padre Róger told me what happened. He asked me to speak to you," Bernardo said, his voice gentle, understanding.

"He told you? He told you everything? How could he?" Blanca felt betrayed, and guilty, although she knew she was not responsible for the feelings of the priest.

"He feels terrible. And he apologizes for frightening you."

"But he says that he has fallen in love with me, Bernardo. Priests aren't supposed to fall in love."

"I know, Blanquita. I know." Bernardo leaned forward, placing his hand on her shoulder. Blanca struggled to keep from crying. Bernardo gave her his handkerchief and waited in silence until she had regained her composure. Then he continued, "Priests aren't supposed to fall in love, Blanquita. But they're human, just like the rest of us."

"I know, Bernardo. I know. But how can I continue working with him? How can I face him? I'm so embarrassed. I feel guilty and I haven't done anything."

"You need to speak to him, Blanquita. He wants to talk to you."

What disturbed Blanca the most about the entire incident— especially after her reflections of the past two days—was the realization that her feelings were the same as Padre Róger's. His declaration awakened a passion inside of her; sentiments that crossed the lines of what she had believed was nothing more than an innocent attraction toward an unattainable man. His confession had forced Blanca to face her own emotions.

She suddenly became aware that her arms tingled whenever she saw his stout figure walking along Cuapa's main street; that she loved to make him laugh just to hear his loud cackle, which her parrot had quickly learned to mimic; that her face flushed whenever he complimented her perfume; and that she lingered before the closet, like never before in her life, to pick out a dress she was sure he would like. Troubling Blanca more than anything was the thought of her being the cause of Padre Róger's abandoning the priesthood. Still, she agreed to meet with him.

The next day, as the early morning mist hovered above the valley of Cuapa, Blanca and Padre Róger took a walk along the road to Juigalpa. At first they spoke of nothing important, trying to return to the haven of trust from which they had drifted. But as soon as they waded across the river, Padre Róger began to confide that for more than a year he had been questioning his commitment to the priesthood. He told Blanca, as he wiped away his tears with the sleeve of his cassock, how he loved being part of the Franciscan community and how he found great joy in the brotherhood in which they lived, worked, and prayed together as seminarians. But once he was assigned to a small Texas parish, doubts began to plague him. Before long he felt drained, empty.

"Are celebrating the Eucharist every day and listening to the repetitious drone of bland confessions what God really intended for me, Blanca? Coming to Nicaragua gave me a chance to think about my future. It is somewhere apart, far enough from the unhappy man I've become. Here, I had hoped to put things back into perspective."

Padre Róger stopped for a moment, fixed his eyes on Blanca's, and continued. "What I hadn't counted on was meeting you." Blanca winced, and the priest rushed to clarify. "But don't worry, Blanca, I promise not to speak of my feelings for you again for as long as I remain in Cuapa." Certain that Padre Róger was a man of his word, Blanca returned to work.

Their last month together went by peacefully, time flowing in a way that reminded Blanca of the soothing rush of her favorite mountain stream, in el Cerro de Chavarría. She continued working closely with both Franciscans. The group once again became at ease with one another, even playful, getting into a silly fruit war once by throwing ripe nancites at each other. And Padre Róger kept his promise, behaving as if he had never said anything.

The problem now was that Blanca looked at him differently. In her mind she now stood at the top of the monolith—a female duende calling down to this virginal man with silent urgency. In spite of her efforts to censor her thoughts, Blanca would discover herself fantasizing about Padre Róger as her husband, and as the father of her children. She tried to put these distractions out of her mind by praying at least two Rosaries every night. But afterward, when she lay in the shadowy solitude of her bed, trying in vain to sleep, an intense warmth took possession of the sanctuary between her thighs, a desire for the stroke of an amorous hand tormented her, filling her soul with anguish.

On the last day of the Franciscans' mission in Cuapa, Blanca and Padre Róger took one last walk to La Paslama. Golden and light blue sparkles bounced off the quivering surface of the swimming hole as the sun entered the waning moments of its descent. The trees and vegetation that lined the water's edge had turned an ardent jungle green after the first two downpours of the rainy season. Suddenly, while they were seated on a boulder, engaged in quiet conversation, to Blanca's surprise and horror, Padre Róger stood and took off his cassock, then his shoes, and then his socks.

"What are you doing, Padre?" she asked, glancing around in fear that someone might discover them.

"I'm going in for a swim." Blanca turned her back as Padre

Róger began to unbuckle his belt. She turned around again after hearing the splash. Blanca became alarmed when the priest remained underwater for what she thought was too long a time, and just as she was about to shout for help, his head broke the surface. The Franciscan, paddling across the swimming hole, looked delighted, just like a child.

"Padre, you know what people say happens to an outsider if he swims here," Blanca said mischievously, whispering just loud enough to be heard on the other side.

"Blanquita, that is precisely why I jumped in here."

The implication hung suspended above the water, tempting and disturbing at once. This time, Blanca did not feel threatened. After all, Padre Róger had not really broken his promise. Later that evening, as they said farewell, Blanca knew with all certainty that their relationship was only beginning.

About a month after the Franciscans returned to the States, Blanca received a letter from Padre Róger. In it, he told her that he had requested permission from his superiors to leave the priesthood. His request had been forwarded to his bishop, who in turn sent it to Rome. *I'm at peace with my choice. I have made it after calm, serene contemplation,* he wrote in handwriting so delicate that Blanca found the script feminine. *I'm certain that God has blessed my decision.*

In his next letter, he asked Blanca to call him simply Róger, and he promised to teach her, whenever they met again, how to pronounce his name in English. From that point on their correspondence became a steady flow of missives that traveled up and down the narrow strip of land joining the continents. Although their letters were chaste, Blanca suspected that even the most casual reader would have detected the passionate undercurrents stirring the sediments of their friendship.

For a year and a half, Blanca and Róger exchanged letters, the pace increasing feverishly until they wrote every day, and sometimes twice a day. The only person with whom Blanca shared what was happening was Bernardo, and he clearly understood where things were headed.

"I pray every night to la Virgencita for the both of you," he would often say.

At last, nearly two years after Róger's declaration, Blanca received the letter she had eagerly been awaiting. Written on green stationery that reminded her of the spirited vegetation surrounding La Paslama, the message was succinct and to the point:

> *Querida Blanquita:*
> *The Vatican has granted me permission to leave the priesthood.*
> *Would you now grant me permission to court you? If your answer is yes, I will be there as quickly as possible.*
>
> *All my love,*
> *Róger*

Blanca answered yes, of course. But now came the task she had been dreading for the past two years: telling her father, don Isidoro. Blanca knew exactly what he would say: "The entire family will be cursed now that you've stolen un hombre de Dios."

Many a rum-filled Saturday night, when the seventh bottle of Flor de Caña was nearly empty, don Isidoro would entertain his card-playing buddies—who always lost at desmoche to stay in his good graces—with a tragic story about the son of a talented goldsmith from nearby Acoyapa. The son had left the priesthood to get married, and God punished him. The former priest became a worthless alcoholic, left his first family and his second family, and was now working on his third. Like a sorrowful soul cast into the deepest recesses of purgatory, he would never be able to find peace.

Worse yet, "The goldsmith also became cursed because of his son's folly," don Isidoro would proclaim loudly, pointing his right index finger toward the heavens. The goldsmith's prospects had once shone brightly. President José Santos Zelaya had become fond of the goldsmith because the artist had created a wondrous, intricately adorned golden egg that he presented to the dictator during one of the strongman's expeditions to the east coast. As a reward, the president granted the goldsmith the rank of general in the Nicaraguan army, even though the artist had never shot a weapon in his life. Years later, not long after the goldsmith's son had committed the unforgivable sin of forsaking his duty to God—and the U.S. Marines had forced Zelaya from power—those who had become envious of the goldsmith's fortunes ostracized the entire family. And as if that hadn't been enough, their membership in el Club Social de Acoyapa was revoked.

"¿Por qué?" don Isidoro would always ask, pausing dramatically. Although his friends knew the answer perfectly, they pretended to be spellbound, awaiting the conclusion with their mouths slightly open. "Because the son had left the priesthood."

Blanca's prediction turned out to be correct. When she informed her parents of her relationship with Róger, on the eve of his arrival, don Isidoro exploded with the fury of a volcano that had been amassing its fiery rage for centuries.

"I'm going to have my men shoot that godforsaken priest as soon as he steps into Cuapa!"

"Papi, Róger's no longer a priest."

For a moment, don Isidoro didn't know what to reply. Through clenched teeth, he answered, "Once a man wears a cassock, he will always want to wear a dress."

"What's that supposed to mean, Papi?!"

"This is what comes of educating daughters: lack of respect."

Surrendering to the inevitable, don Isidoro sat in el patio, under el almendro tree, cradling his head in both hands, and crying disconsolately. His wife's heart almost broke when she heard him repeat, over and over, "Now we and all of our descendants are doomed."

The following day, when Róger arrived—hot, sweaty, and dusty from the long bus ride over bumpy dirt roads—Blanca embraced him shamelessly in the middle of Cuapa's main street. Fortunately for them, Bernardo was the only witness to their reunion. Róger was staying at the sacristán's house because don Isidoro had forbidden a man who had betrayed el Señor from setting foot in his. Doña Eloísa, Bernardo's abuelita, also believed that some of the curse would rub off on her for harboring a fallen priest, but Bernardo had Padre Francisco make a special trip from Juigalpa to tell her that no such curse existed. Even so, as Bernardo later told Blanca, doña Eloísa resisted until the priest finally ordered her, in the name of the Catholic Church, to provide Róger with lodging.

"But don't expect me to be nice to him," she warned both Padre Francisco and her nieto.

Regrettably for Blanca, los cuapeños didn't take long to figure out what was going on. The scandalous relationship soon became the talk not only of Cuapa but also of all of Chontales. Doña Tula assumed the responsibility of monitoring the couple's every move.

And it was she who informed don Isidoro, as well as the rest of the townspeople, that she had seen Blanca and Róger swimming together in La Paslama, en pelotas—buck naked.

Blanca didn't mind the hastily arranged wedding one bit. In fact, she was relieved as don Isidoro's rush to salvage what little was left of her honor bypassed a formal courtship that could have delayed their coming together for months, or perhaps even years. Blanca felt that a lot of time had already been lost, and she wanted, without delay, to devote herself to making Róger happy. She even insisted that Padre Francisco perform an abbreviated wedding ceremony. At the reception, the bride and groom danced until they collapsed from exhaustion. And don Isidoro buried his public shame by slaughtering two young bulls, seven turkeys, and four pigs for the occasion.

"Maybe if I throw the biggest wedding party in the history of Cuapa everyone will forget that my daughter has stolen un hombre de Cristo," he confided to his wife.

The day Blanca and Róger announced that they were moving to los Estados Unidos, her family, instead of crying, breathed a collective sigh of relief. To their way of thinking, the distance would free them of the curse. And if Blanca left, then maybe los cuapeños would forget how she had tarnished the family's reputation. What Blanca's relatives couldn't understand was why the couple was moving to Los Angeles. Wasn't San Francisco where all Nicaraguans in los Estados Unidos lived?

The farewells were unexpectedly tearful. After all the resistance, after detonating the full charge of his macho bravado in threats and curses, don Isidoro had grown to appreciate Róger. He liked the gringo's kind, gentle manner. At the moment of the final despedida, don Isidoro clung to Róger, crying uncontrollably. Everyone present became convinced that don Isidoro would miss his yerno more than his daughter.

When Blanca climbed on board the Pan American Airlines four-engine plane she was terrified. During takeoff, she dug her nails into Róger's arm, leaving quarter-moon marks that were visible on his skin for weeks. She wouldn't stop asking, until he finally begged her to please stop, how that chunche, that contraption, stayed in the air. To make matters worse, the flight made stops in Tegucigalpa, San Salvador, and Guatemala City; and Blanca physically tortured Róger during each takeoff and landing. But by the time they reached the capital of México, la cuapeña behaved as if she were a veteran of years of travel. On the long flight between México City and Los Angeles she was Róger's nurse, as he filled three airsickness bags. She also felt confident enough to laugh out loud when, during a severe bout of turbulence, a woman's bag overturned, spilling hundreds of mamones, the fruit rolling up and down the aisle like green marbles.

Róger's parents, brothers, and sisters were at the airport to greet them. They accepted Blanca as family from the moment they met her; and she, in turn, was relieved that they didn't seem the least bit concerned about the curse she was bringing down upon them. Of course, she couldn't really be sure of that since she didn't speak a word of English, and they didn't speak Spanish. But Róger worked tirelessly as her interpreter, and although Blanca at times experienced the sensation of being submerged under clear waters that nevertheless distorted all of her senses, her husband's doting made her feel safe in his world.

A week after their arrival, Róger rented a house, south of downtown, not far from the Coliseum. It was small, two bedrooms, but had a large backyard with fruit trees: oranges, figs, and avocados. Blanca liked to sit out there when she felt homesick, imagining herself back in Cuapa. Among other reasons, Róger liked the house because it was within walking distance of his parents' and only a few blocks from his new job with Catholic Social Services.

Los Angeles left Blanca breathless. The city was so alive, vibrant, sprawling, the streets lined with palm trees, freeways that seemed endless, businesses that at night glowed fervently with the reflection of neon signs, and staggering vistas of oceans and mountains. Róger enjoyed how his hometown displayed itself for Blanca's benefit. He took her to the observatory, the zoo, the museums, and her favorite place of all, Grauman's Chinese Theatre. There, she slipped her hands into Tyrone Power's sidewalk imprints, their smallness surprising her.

"That's Hollywood," Róger said, with an amused smile. "Nothing but illusions."

To the couple's joy, shortly after their visit to the Chinese Theatre, and after only three months of marriage, they discovered that Blanca was pregnant. About the same time, their own illusions of a long, happy life together began to fade, and reality intruded like an unwelcome guest, one they couldn't get to leave. At first, Róger became unexplainably ill: weak and feverish. He was also losing weight rapidly. When his condition didn't improve, in spite of Blanca's and his mother's care, they visited a clinic. The expression on Róger's face when he came out of the doctor's office would be etched in Blanca's memory for as long as she lived. The dread in his eyes frightened her as much as his pallor.

Leaving the clinic, Róger clung to her tightly as they walked to MacArthur Park. They found a bench far from everyone, although few people were there on that chilly, overcast day. Sitting closely together, he held her hands tenderly. Although Róger tried to appear confident, Blanca could see that he was terrified.

"Mi amor, tengo cáncer." Before the words had their full impact, he added, his smile hopeful, "But, please, try not to worry too much, we'll get through this."

With the hope of God granting Róger a miracle, they began an interminable chain of visits to doctors' offices and clinics. At the same time they were delighted by the miracle growing within her. But as Blanca grew larger with each passing day, Róger's size diminished. From a once stout man, he became thin, bony, with sunken cheeks. His new wife at times found it difficult to recognize the person she had married. But Blanca remained hopeful, keeping a dozen lit candles before the small cedar image of la Inmaculada Concepción she had brought along with her from Cuapa—a wedding gift from Bernardo.

She and Róger attended mass as often as they could. On the days Róger felt well, he insisted on going twice. "I'm saving up in case the time comes when I can't go any longer," he'd say, attempting to shield his fear behind the joke.

Blanca's pregnancy progressed well, in spite of the paralyzing anxiety that began to crush her. As Róger's illness got worse, what buoyed his spirit was the thought of holding his child in his arms for as long as God would allow him that grace. But by the seventh month of Blanca's pregnancy, the pain made his nights almost unbearable. Their worst fears began to consume them, depriving them of any rest. They'd cry together in bed, each of them resting a loving hand on Blanca's swollenness.

The night Blanca's labor pains began, Róger called his parents asking for a ride to the hospital. While Blanca suffered as quietly as she could through long hours of labor, Róger also had to be admitted.

His parents, Blanca later found out, kept him updated on her progress, but sometimes they found that the painkillers had plunged him deep into a stupor from which they had difficulty bringing him out. Finally, at five in the morning, thirty hours after Blanca's labor pains had started, Róger's father shook him, startling him awake. Róger tried to sit up, but could only do so with his father's help.

"It's a boy, Son. He's healthy. And Blanca's doing fine as well. She's exhausted, but fine."

"Thank God. That's wonderful news," Róger said, bravely smiling through his discomfort. He reached out and held his father's hand. "Dad, we're going to name him Elías, honoring the man who took over the order from Saint Francis."

Later in the day, in a wheelchair, Róger sat before the nursery window, wistfully contemplating his son. He thought that Elías looked exactly like Blanca, with the exception of inheriting his light complexion and green eyes. Róger then went to visit his wife, and as soon as they saw each other they cried because at that precise moment they realized that precious little time remained for them to be together. Their future was an album of family photographs that would always be incomplete. And fate, as if to prove them right, never allowed Róger to return home.

Blanca, upon seeing the end of her husband's life approaching, called Padre Antonio, who caught the first plane he could to Los Angeles. The Franciscan and Róger talked often and for as long as the doctors, nurses, and medication allowed. They shared a good laugh when Padre Antonio commented that at least they had lived long enough to see a Catholic in the White House, Kennedy having been inaugurated just the week before. And Padre Antonio baptized Elías while Róger, sitting up in bed, held the infant. The priest stayed until his friend's death, almost a week later. In a tearful ceremony, attended by hundreds of mourners, with Blanca sobbing the entire time in the arms of her father-in-law, Padre Antonio laid Róger to rest.

Before his death, Róger made Blanca promise that she would not surrender to grief, that she would make a valiant effort to go forth and enjoy the rest of her life. He also made her promise to stay in Los Angeles, where Elías would have more opportunities to pursue whatever path in life would most fulfill him, and where he could hear—from his grandparents, aunts, and uncles—stories about his father. Although Róger insisted that Blanca move in with his parents, she never promised this. She loved her in-laws, they were the kindest people she had ever met; but she felt a strong attachment to the house where she and Róger had lived, if only for a few months, in bliss. Blanca believed that she would feel his spirit there, in the home they had decorated so lovingly, and that his presence would help her fight off despair. Besides, as Blanca had reminded him, his parents lived only three blocks away. So what she promised instead was that she would visit them every day.

Without Róger, however, Blanca's new world suddenly became meaningless and intimidating. She had lost her interpreter—and in ways that went far beyond language. Blanca, feeling devastated and utterly alone, tried to remain strong, hiding behind a veneer of fortitude, for Elías's sake. Mother and son spent hours at a time rocking on a swing Róger had installed on the front porch, watching the automobiles pass by. Each time Blanca saw a red one she cheered and clapped Elías's little hands together, a silly game she had invented to distract herself.

One sunny afternoon, about a month after Róger's funeral, Blanca met her next-door neighbor: Esperanza, a young woman, in her early twenties, from Chicago. Although Esperanza appeared to be from Latin America, in a Spanish that Blanca found convoluted, her neighbor explained that her father was from México but that, sadly, she had never visited that country. She was una Americana, born and raised in the United States, but with a lot of México in her heart, or so she claimed. Blanca glanced down at Elías, who slept in her arms, and grew troubled when she realized that he would have more in common with Esperanza than with his own mother if they remained in los Estados Unidos.

The neighbor was a petite, artistic person who wrote poetry, in English, which Blanca, to her regret, couldn't understand. Unlike any woman Blanca had met before, Esperanza freely pursued her dreams. The biggest one of all, it appeared, was to own her own home. At the moment, Esperanza shared the house with a broad-shouldered gringa named Catherine. Their relationship puzzled Blanca. Back in Cuapa the thought of two single women living together who were not related to one another would have never occurred to her. All Blanca knew about Catherine was that she worked during the day and that she was extremely reserved, limiting her exchanges with Blanca to a terse wave of greeting, sometimes without even offering a smile. On the other hand, Esperanza, who reported to work in the late afternoons, was outgoing, constantly joking and laughing—except for an occasional melancholic mood when Blanca imagined her missing her family in Chicago.

The gringa-mexicana, as Blanca thought of her, spent much of her free time helping to cheer the widow. She took Blanca to the markets, showed her how to get around in the bus, and cautioned her about the dangers of living in Los Angeles. In particular, Esperanza urged Blanca to keep her doors and windows locked at night.

"Be careful, Blanca," she said. "I don't want to scare you, but during the last few months several women living in the area have been raped and murdered. A woman who survived the attack said that the killer had watched her house from across the street, standing in the shadows for hours, while bouncing a rubber ball."

"Remember," Esperanza continued, sternly pointing a finger at Blanca, "lock yourself inside, and after dark never, ever open the door for anyone you don't know."

Blanca, without question, heeded Esperanza's warnings. At least three times each evening she checked every door and window. And before going to bed—which now, without Róger, had become a lonely, painful undertaking—she checked one last time.

One evening, three weeks after Esperanza's warning, Blanca, while taking the trash out, thought she spotted someone lurking in her neighbor's backyard. She ran to her back porch from where she had a better view. Blanca stayed there until she became convinced that she had lost control over her fears and imagination. Still, the feeling of danger clung to her, like the dull gray haze she saw draping the San Gabriel Mountains on certain mornings. As soon as Blanca stepped into the house, she triple-checked every window and door.

By then the golden hues of dusk were encroaching from the west. It was a time when, in Blanca's mind, Los Angeles began its daily metamorphosis into endless rows of dim streetlights and whirling automobiles that carried within them the anonymous profiles of desperate, lonely people trying to find their way home. She settled down in bed to feed Elías, and fell asleep. Somewhere, far off in her dreams, she heard the springy recoils of a ball pounding the sidewalk—one, two, three, four, five times until the sound faded away, in the distance.

Shortly before midnight the blare of sirens startled Blanca

awake. What happened that night forever remained an entangled, confusing burst of images that bounced around randomly in Blanca's mind: the patrol cars pulling in front of the house next door, their wheels screeching; the flashing lights; the police jumping over fences, searching the neighborhood; the questioning; the stretcher loading a sheet-covered body onto an ambulance; the incomprehensible human voices layered over the blast of static on the police car radios; and Esperanza crying hysterically.

Blanca found the policemen remarkably compassionate, genuinely trying to console her surviving neighbor. But their sympathy didn't help diminish Esperanza's wails, which pierced Blanca's heart, her neighbor's grief mirroring her own.

When Róger's parents arrived, they took both Esperanza and Blanca to spend the night with them. Later, with Esperanza sedated and in bed, Blanca understood perfectly, in spite of not knowing the words, what her in-laws were saying to her: "Don't worry, everything's going to be fine."

But everything is not going to be fine, Blanca thought, feeling terrified and forsaken. She couldn't remain in Los Angeles any longer. Absolutely not. She had to return home. Róger was the reason she had come to the United States, and he had helped her understand life here. How could she even consider raising their son alone in a country so treacherous?

Róger's family begged her to stay. With the help of a Costa Rican woman from their parish, they explained that the odds were against Blanca ever witnessing something like that again. But she was already convinced that her decision was for Elías's own good. Yes, Blanca would break her promise to Róger. But after what had happened that night, she was certain that he would have understood.

Blanca did vow, though, that she and Elías would spend every Christmas, Róger's favorite holiday, with the Bacons.

When Blanca's flight landed in Managua, Bernardo was among those who had traveled all the way from Cuapa to greet her. Both of her parents cried as they embraced their daughter. All the while Bernardo cradled Elías in his arms. Although don Isidoro didn't once mention the curse, Blanca was sure it was on his mind. The following day, back in Cuapa, everyone came by the seven-pillar house on la Calle de los Laureles to pay their respects. Los cuapeños had many wonderful things to say about Róger, and they were sincere. After all, in a short time the Franciscans had done much for the town. But more important for Blanca, Elías Bacon, the fair-skinned, green-eyed son of a gringo former priest, was received like a prince. From this time forward, she lived her life for the boy.

On the child's first birthday Bernardo arrived early for la piñata, dressed in a light blue suit—of his own making, of course. Strangely, his face was turning the blood-red shade of a ripe zapote, his eyes bulging because his tie was knotted too tightly. But Bernardo also had the woeful look of a man whose thoughts were strangling him.

"Bernardo, is something wrong?" Blanca asked. "And why are you all dressed up?"

"Blanca, Elías needs a father," Bernardo replied. "I know that I can never replace Róger, but I want to do what's best for the boy." Bernardo then got down on one knee and proposed marriage.

At first Blanca remained silent, too shocked to react. Then, in spite of her bravest efforts to contain herself, she crumbled into a thousand tremulous bits, laughing so hard that she showered Bernardo with spittle. Once Blanca could speak again, she said, "Bernardo, you wonderful, wonderful man. Do you really want to get married?"

Although at first stung by the realization that he was being rejected, Bernardo soon let out a long-contained sigh of relief. "Blanca, . . . honestly, . . . no."

"What I need, Bernardo, is for you to continue being my friend: my best friend in the whole world. That'll be more than enough for me and for Elías. Besides, there will never be another man in my life: Róger lives on in here," she said, tapping her heart with two fingers. "But I do appreciate your proposal, and I love you now even more for it." Reaching out, Blanca held his face in both hands and gave him a long kiss on the lips. "That, Bernardo, seals our friendship forever."

From that moment on Bernardo became the man Blanca and Elías most needed in their lives. He doted on the boy as if he were his own. He sewed outfits for him, taught him the catechism, taught him how to pray the rosary, and other useful things: how to rope a calf, wield a machete, catch fish in the river with one's bare hands, and carve wooden animals with a pocket knife. Like everyone else in Cuapa, Bernardo affectionately called Elías "Chele," because of the boy's light skin. And every December, when Blanca and Elías traveled to Los Angeles to visit Róger's relatives, Bernardo felt desperately alone, as if his wife and son had taken off on a long vacation, leaving him behind. But when doña Eloísa, his beloved abuelita, died early one December, el sacristán didn't allow Blanca to cancel her trip, even though that became the loneliest Christmas he ever spent.

Life went by uneventfully, as it usually did in Cuapa, in the stately seven-mahogany-pillar house on la Calle de los Laureles. Blanca devoted herself to Elías and to learning to run la hacienda, anticipating the day she would take it over from her father.

When el Chele began the sixth grade, Bernardo started a

campaign to bring una escuela secundaria to Cuapa so the boy would not have to live in Juigalpa, like his mother before him, to attend high school. The government at first replied that there weren't enough students in Cuapa to warrant opening one. Bernardo refused to accept this answer. Instead, he signed up every eligible person in town, including don Gumersindo Zamora, who was ninety-nine and blind, and he took the applications personally to el Ministerio de Educación, in Managua. By the beginning of the next school year, Cuapa had a high school, and Elías and Bernardo were the first two students to enroll. They completed the first three years of secundaria together, seated every day at desks next to each other. But before the fourth school year began, as a sixth decade of Somoza family rule loomed on the horizon, the clouds of war were darkening the skies.

After much reflection and prayer, Blanca decided to send Elías to live with his aunt Georgia, Róger's older sister who now lived in Albuquerque, so that he could finish high school there, in safety. In spite of the still terrifying memory of Catherine's murder, Blanca had come to believe that Nicaragua was becoming as violent as, if not more so than, los Estados Unidos. It was especially dangerous for boys Elías's age because la Guardia suspected every young person of being a Sandinista.

But the boy resisted. He told his mother that under no circumstances would he leave. He protested as loudly as don Isidoro or Bernardo would allow. Yet in the end, seeing that he was unable to bend his mother's resolve, Elías had no choice but to accept her decision. Don Isidoro invited all of el Chele's friends to a farewell party that was held on the eve of Elías's departure. In his nieto's honor the old man slaughtered a young bull and a pig. The gathering was bittersweet; the young men laughed as they nostalgically recalled past pranks, and they cried over the uncertainty of the future. Because it was such an important occasion, Blanca, for one time only, allowed the hired bartenders to serve Flor de Caña to Elías and his friends; and although they did get drunk, it was only slightly so.

The guests left shortly after midnight, their arms draped over each other's shoulders, singing mournful rancheras through the streets of Cuapa. Only Felipe and Carlos, Elías's two best friends, stayed behind. Their farewells became an unending affair. They embraced and cried, cried and embraced, told a joke and laughed, cried and embraced. Finally, Blanca, reaching the limits of her maternal patience, ordered the boys to go home because her son had to get up before dawn for the long trip to Managua.

Standing somewhat unsteadily, thanks to the rum, Elías, with a slight slur, told Bernardo how much he would miss him. He then gave el sacristán a long hug, followed by a slobbery kiss on the cheek. He did the same with his mother and each of his grandparents. He bowed solemnly, bade goodnight to everyone in the living room, and left, staggering slightly, for his room.

The sun had yet to rise when Blanca knocked on her son's door to wake him. There was no answer. Warning Elías that she was about to enter, Blanca opened the door. On his bed, still neat from not having been slept in, she found a note:

> *Adorada Madrecita:*
>
> *I'm sorry to have to break your heart this way, but I cannot leave when la patria needs me the most. While many people my age are dying for freedom, you want me to flee to the United States, the nation responsible for our*

suffering. Just ask yourself, Mamá, who placed the
Somozas in power? In good conscience, then, I cannot go.
Neither can I avoid my duty to mis compatriotas any
longer. We have all been called to make sacrifices, and my
turn has arrived.

Te besa, tu hijo,
Elías

PATRIA LIBRE O MORIR

s e g u n d a   p a r t e
GUERRA

chapter four

RADIX SANCTA

(The Holy Root of Salvation)

June and July 1979

Elías Bacon

I DON'T REMEMBER my father at all; I was less than a month old when he died. He's an absence, a blind spot that only my imagination can fill. People tell me that he was a good man, with a big, kind heart. They also say that I look a lot like him: my fair skin, green eyes, and all. I know for sure that my mom misses him. She's faithful to his memory, and she has turned down several suitors— who for all I know may have been after mi abuelito's hacienda—to devote herself to raising me. I would appreciate it more, though, if she didn't remind me every time I get into a little trouble of all the sacrifices she has made. I know it's been difficult for her, but sometimes she just needs to back off a bit and not try so hard to fill the void my father left behind, if you know what I mean.

Mi abuelito has tried to be a father figure. But grandfathers can't do that because they are, well, just that: *abuelitos.* They're too old to be fathers. As far back as I can remember, my mom's father has been ancient. He's always been too cranky to have anything to do with me. When I was a little kid he wanted me to be dressed up in neat vaquero clothes, looking like a miniature version of Chontales aristocracy while I sat upright in a chair all day without making a sound. "Niños callados, como venados," he would say. Yes, he wanted me to be as quiet as deer. Doesn't leave much room for becoming close, does it?

To be honest, Bernardo Martínez has been the closest thing I have known to a father. He always insisted that I call him Papá Bernardo. So I did, and eventually I dropped the Bernardo part and began calling him just plain Papá.

He and my mother have an interesting relationship, one I haven't quite been able to figure out. She doesn't have many close friends. I would even say that Papá is her only friend; in the sense of having someone you can trust completely, like the way I trust Carlos, and the way I trusted Felipe. My mom and my papá can talk for hours, and about the dumbest things: the price of milk, the latest fashions, the things they used to do for fun as kids (which seem *so* boring to me), religion (Papá's favorite topic), and what everyone else here has been talking about for the last couple of years: politics.

All in all, Papá is what my gringo cousins in New Mexico would call a nerd. I learned the word last year when I visited my aunt Georgia and her family in Albuquerque. I would hate for anyone to call me that. But it fits Papá. What can I say? For starters, he lives for the Church. He's the town's sacristán—cleaning, washing, and helping Padre Domingo—but he gets nothing but grief for it. The past couple of years Papá has been trying to raise money to build a new church. Now you tell me, why does Cuapa need a new church? The old one only fills up during Easter, Christmas, and las fiestas of San Juan Bautista, our santo patrón.

Then there's his obsession with the rosary. Papá beats the beads all the time. I've seen him pray it three times in one sitting! But that's not enough for him; he wants everyone else to pray it as well. When I was little he made me pray the rosary with him every day, saying that his abuelita made him do it and that's why he turned out to be so religious. Does he really think that's how I want to turn out? Now, though, he won't even try to get me to pray with him. He knows I won't.

A few months ago Papá began an observance he called First Saturdays. This meant that on the first Saturday of each month people in Cuapa came together to pray the rosary to ask for peace in Nicaragua. At first most cuapeños did participate. I have to give Papá credit for that. But in the end many just stopped going, saying that they didn't believe it was working. A few did argue that because of the First Saturdays Cuapa was spared the violence and death that devastated the rest of the country. But don't even suggest that to Felipe's mother.

Another thing Papá did, several years back, was to get everyone organized for that escuela secundaria thing. I, for one, am grateful to him for bringing a high school to Cuapa, but did he really have to enroll and become my classmate? *That* was embarrassing. For three long years everyone teased me. Did Papá do your homework for you? Do you study with Papá? Did Papá pack your snack for you? Did Papá prepare your cheat sheet? The guy was approaching fifty, and there he was trying to hang out with my friends and me. Definitely embarrassing. At the same time, he acted as if he were my father, getting on my case when he thought I had done something wrong, and in front of the guys! Man, he really did cramp my style. Bernardo, the nerd.

But you know what? He's able to pull off things like no one else I know. I've seen it with my own eyes. I mean his faith, his belief in his Virgencita, seems to work miracles. Papá must have saved at least twenty lives over the last couple of months. I'm not kidding. Sure, they were not the Clint Eastwood–shooting-off-powerful-guns type of rescues, but in his quiet, geeky way he was able to get people to change their hearts, and thus avoid a lot of bloodshed. Honestly, he *did* save lives. For starters, he saved mine.

When I left to join the Sandinistas it broke my mother's heart. But I just couldn't take off for the States and leave behind everything I loved and believed in. We were in the middle of la Insurrección, and I wanted to help. Half a century of one family running things was enough. Don't you agree?

Plus, there was Magdalena. No one knows about this, but we had a pretty good thing going. Since her father was a strict, mean, conservative old zopilote—hovering around her like a buzzard wherever she went—we had to keep our relationship secret. He would never let her have a novio. So I found the ideal place for us to meet: the church. Her parents thought that their daughter was becoming very pious. It made them proud. Can you believe that? I'd borrow the keys from Papá, telling him that I was going to clean up the place a bit, and Magdalena and I would have the building all to ourselves. Dios nos perdone for the things we did in there, but we were talking about maybe getting married, so we figured it was all right.

Our secret nearly got out one day when we were skinny-dipping in La Paslama, and doña Tula, who's always on the prowl for something to gossip about, came by and almost caught us. We hid behind some bushes and were forced to stifle our screams when we discovered that we were squatting right on a hill of fire ants, and they were swarming all over us. After the woman left, I kissed the bites on Magdalena's tender canela skin until they were all healed, and that was cool because the bites made her coloring even more like cinnamon. And while I was taking care of her, we said, what the heck, and went on from there.

So you see, I had plenty of reasons to stay in Nicaragua. Besides, a couple of acquaintances who had joined the Sandinistas told my buddies and me that more and more women were signing up, and that they were, well, pretty liberated, if you get my drift. Whoever said that la Revolución wasn't sexy?

Carlos and Felipe volunteered for el Frente before I did. Not only did they despise Somoza, his family, and la Guardia Nacional, but more than anything they wanted to be part of la aventura. That is precisely how we thought of it: an adventure. Running through the jungles, climbing mountains, fording rivers, shooting the bad guys—just like those old Hollywood movies my mother likes so much—and all the while we'd be delivering our country from the evil clutches of a wicked dictator hated throughout the world. I mean, what more could young macho studs like us want?

So my buddies put me in touch with a Sandinista recruiter: Oscar, his name in the "underground." We met for the first time in el parque of Juigalpa, in the shade of the guanacaste tree.

"El dictador tiene hemorroides." He whispered la contraseña to me.

"Y Dinora también." I answered the password with the correct reference to Somoza's mistress.

As we talked, Oscar acted very nervous, constantly glancing around as if he were afraid someone was following him. He was so stressed that he never drank el tiste I had ordered for him. My first impression was that he was a character out of a poorly written spy novel. He distractedly asked a few questions about why I wanted to join, and I guess I passed the test because we agreed to meet again, within a few days, along the old road to Juigalpa, by the river, behind one of Bernardo's potreros.

On the next occasion Oscar was far more relaxed. We talked, fished, drank a few cervezas Victoria, and dreamed up the idea of my vanishing the night before I was scheduled to leave for the States. Felipe would join me in the mountains three weeks later, and then Carlos in another three weeks. That way, Oscar said, our disappearances wouldn't draw much attention. There was one condition about joining that I didn't like, though: I couldn't tell anyone. Still, although I cheated and left a note for my mother, I didn't tell Magdalena. But that was all right because she had agreed to wait for me until I "returned from los Estados Unidos."

The night I fled, Oscar and I met in Juigalpa. That was the beginning of my life as a Sandinista. I was sent to a secret camp along the Honduran border for military training and political education. But the truth is, I soon became disappointed with the whole thing. There were not enough weapons to go around for a proper military training; living conditions were terrible; the political indoctrination boring; and, worst of all, la Revolución wasn't sexy at all. The women who had joined closed ranks around a ballbuster of a woman with the code name Sandra (her real name was Tatiana). Let me tell you, no guy in his right mind would ever mess with her. If he did, she'd put a gun to his head. Because of Sandra's influence,

the compañeras grew dead serious about becoming expert guer-
rilleras, and they began to talk about how la Revolución would
bring about equality between the sexes. ¡Mierda! The loose chicks
everyone talked about didn't let their sex-starved compañeros into
their circle. What a bunch of shit! Yes, it was looking like I had
made a big mistake.

But it's interesting, you know, a person can get used to anything. And I did. I began to grow up. It reminded me of when I
turned thirteen and my voice started to crack, slowly becoming
deeper and in the end making me sound serious. After a few
weeks of training I was ready, even eager, to go fight la Guardia. By
the time Felipe showed up in camp I felt like a seasoned veteran.
The first thing I did when I saw him was to give him a big hug.

"How's Magdalena?" I asked when we finished greeting each
other. After all the time in the mountains without a woman I was
missing our secret meetings.

Felipe looked embarrassed as he stared in silence at his shoes.

"Come on, Felipe," I insisted, "tell me." Refusing to look me
in the eyes, he began to kick the dirt.

"Elías, I hate to be the one to tell you this because I know that
you're kind of hung up on her, but right after you left she hooked
up with Gerardo. Several of our friends saw them behaving like
crazed animals out in the countryside. They were even scaring the
cows and stuff. Then doña Tula discovered them swimming in La
Paslama without a stitch of clothing on—en pelotas. Her father, to
save face, rushed them to the altar."

I was dumbfounded. How could Magdalena do that to me?
She was out there humping that wimp while I was in the jungle
sacrificing myself for la patria, and surrounded by a bunch of

amazons who eat men's testicles for breakfast. But, you know, I soon got over it. As I said, a person can get used to anything.

A few weeks later, after Carlos had arrived, I was called in to see Comandante Wilmer. I was about to receive my marching orders and I was ready: prepared to fight anyone, anywhere. Where was I headed? To the columns that were going to attack Estelí? To León? To Monimbó?! I was ready.

I stepped into Comandante Wilmer's tent and performed my most enthusiastic salute. He wore a scraggly beard and smoked a cigar. In my short time as a Sandinista, I had noticed that a lot of the guys had Che/Fidel complexes, especially los comandantes. The rustic table before him was covered with maps.

"Felicitaciones, compañero," he said, without looking up from the maps. "You have your first assignment. You're going back to Cuapa to coordinate our activities there."

I was stunned. My jaw must have hung open for a long time because he finally looked up and asked, "Is something wrong, compañero?"

"¿Cuapa, Comandante?" was all I finally managed to say.

"Yes. Our informants say that everyone there, including la Guardia, thinks that you're in the United States. You've got a perfect cover."

"But, Comandante, what's there to do in Cuapa? I'm ready for some serious fighting."

"When the final offensive begins, compañero, and that will be very soon, we'll need small diversions to stretch la Guardia's resources. You'll organize one."

"But . . . , Comandante . . . ," I began to protest, but he waved me away as if I were a fly, with the back of his hand. At that moment I cursed the pledge of obedience I had taken when I joined.

Before I knew it, I was on a bus back to Cuapa, wearing brand-new American clothes, new American sneakers, and carrying a new American suitcase so that it looked like I had just returned from los Estados.

I arrived in Cuapa during the early afternoon, siesta time. The streets were deserted. The deathly stillness reminded me of a scene out of a western, right before the big showdown. Only the tumbleweeds were missing. I walked down la Calle de los Laureles until I stood before mi abuelito's house, the one with the seven caoba pillars. Taking a deep breath, I knocked on the door. My mother answered. When she saw me she started screaming. Mothers can be so escandalosas sometimes. She began hugging and kissing me, over and over and over. Then she began to cry and call out for mis abuelitos. Before I knew it everyone in the house, even the maids, were pressed against me in the living room, greeting me as if I had returned from the dead. Once I was alone with my mother, I asked how it was that no one in Cuapa knew that I had left to join the Sandinistas.

"That was Bernardo's idea," she replied. "That way, he argued, if you decided that it all had been a mistake, you could return home safely. The day you left he even made us drive to the airport so everyone would think that you had gone to the States."

Well, what could I say to that? I followed the thread by telling my family that I had indeed made a *big* mistake, and that I was home for good, out of politics forever. That made my mother and mi abuelito Isidoro very happy. Plus, as I had been instructed, nothing beats a solid cover, and under no circumstances was I to blow mine. My orders were to coordinate the operation and let others do the fighting. If things went wrong, Comandante Wilmer told me, I was to remain in Cuapa and await further instructions.

Man, was I disappointed, all that training for nothing. But . . . I had sworn obedience.

The day after returning, I began to plan the attack on Cuapa. The objective: to capture the garrison and declare Cuapa part of Nicaragua Libre. We expected la Guardia to send reinforcements from Juigalpa. The compañeros would resist as long as they could before fleeing into the mountains. If everything went well it would be an effective diversion, without casualties on our part. A neat plan, or so I thought.

Before I could do anything, though, I needed room to operate. Mi abuelito Isidoro hated the Sandinistas so passionately that I really couldn't work out of his house. "Those godless communists, enemies of democracy and free enterprise," he would often say, for anyone's benefit. He had become totally paranoid. He convinced himself that his hacienda and his precious seven-pillar house would be confiscated. He probably checked under his bed for Sandinistas every night before going to sleep. Now that mi abuelito Isidoro thought that I had quit, I told him and my mother that I needed some time away to reflect on my future. I then asked them if I could move in with Papá. Well, they were thrilled with the idea. I mean, how much trouble could I get into hanging out with a nerd in his late forties?

The night of June 11, my plan went into motion. The rain poured incessantly without showing signs of letting up. Along the main road the water ran as strong as a river. But that wouldn't be a problem. If anything, the rain would provide a good cover for los compañeros. Shortly before midnight, I heard the knocks at Papá's front door. He already had been sleeping for a couple of hours. I, of course, had been waiting anxiously for los compas to arrive. I rushed out of bed and opened the door. Four compañeros, soaking wet, stepped into the house, Carlos and Felipe among them. I embraced both of my friends, getting soaked myself. Papá stepped out of his bedroom. He had a sleepy yet puzzled look as he checked out the gathering. When Papá saw that Carlos and Felipe were there, notorious now in Cuapa because the word had leaked that they had joined the Sandinistas, he instantly knew something was wrong. Without even greeting los compañeros, he motioned for me to join him in his room.

"¿Qué está pasando, Elías?" By the tone of his voice and his stern expression, I knew that he would only accept the truth. So I came clean. I told Papá *everything*. I have never seen him that angry in my life, I swear. I honestly thought that he was going to give me a whipping.

"They're just spending one night here, Papá. They'll leave before dawn."

"Make sure they do, Elías. If la Guardia discovers that we're hiding them we'll all be in a lot of trouble. More than you can imagine."

As soon as we came out of Papá's room, a compañero I had never met before had the bright idea of announcing that he was hungry. Well, that did it. I could see by the way Papá clenched his jaw that he was about to lose his temper. I quickly jumped between them and offered to go get some food, while asking myself where in the hell I was going to find food in Cuapa at that hour of the night. But I wanted to keep Papá from yelling at los compas. Instead, surprising me, he heaved a loud sigh of resignation and said that he would get everyone something to eat.

"Besides," he added, "the walk will do me good."

When the door closed behind Papá, one of los compañeros I didn't know asked, "Do you think he'll turn us in?"

Carlos, Felipe, and I looked at each other for a long moment. Finally, Felipe answered, "Impossible, compañero. Don Bernardo would die before he let something happen to el Chele."

After that, I asked the guys to show me their weapons. They pulled out four small-caliber handguns. "These were all el Frente could spare," answered Felipe. "But don't worry, Elías, they'll do."

Papá returned with half-a-dozen nacatamales. How he managed to get them at that hour beats me. But like I said earlier, he has a way of making things happen.

Los compañeros at the kitchen table ate like they had not seen food for days. After they finished, Papá told them to lay down wherever they could. Shortly before dawn, they left for the hideout I had selected in the foothills of el Cerro Tumbé—a secluded spot where Carlos, Felipe, and I used to play as kids. At noon, Oscar and a group under his command would meet them there, bringing food. Later, after nightfall, the combined units would take Cuapa's lightly guarded garrison.

Well, sometimes plans have a way of not working out the way you want them to. Oscar, the super-Sandinista recruiter, didn't show up. Neither did any of his compañeros. ¡Qué hijueputas! By midafternoon, mis compas were starving. On their own, then, they decided to come out of hiding, go to doña Sinforosa's pulpería on the outskirts of town, buy some food, and return to the hideout to wait for nightfall.

But there's a Judas Iscariot in every community. Some cuapeño saw Carlos and Felipe and ran straight to the garrison to inform la Guardia. I'm sure the bastard who told on them picked up a few silver dinars—just like Judas—for selling out my comrades. The four guardias stationed in town followed los compañeros' trail straight to the hideout. Papá and I were feeding the pigs their afternoon machigüe when we heard the shots. Dropping the bucket, Papá ran inside the house, grabbed his rosary, got on his knees before the statue of la Inmaculada Concepción, and began to pray. I, on the other hand, felt like going out there to see what was happening, but I remembered the strict orders not to blow my cover . . . under any circumstances. At that moment I loathed this obedience thing.

All I could do was pace up and down in Papá's small living room while biting my fingernails. After the initial shots, though I listened intently, I heard nothing more. I assumed that los compas had escaped. When Papá finished praying, he came to me, his eyes filled with gloom.

"Chele, I have something to confess," he said. "I have sinned. I was so frightened that I ended up praying that there be no wounded, that anyone shot would be dead so they wouldn't talk. If la Guardia gets ahold of one of your compañeros, that'll be our end as well."

You know, I couldn't get angry at Papá because the exact same thought had run through my mind, although not as a prayer.

I had no other choice but to wait. I wanted to help los compañeros, but what could I do? It would have been foolish of me to even try. Instead, I sulked around, feeling useless and afraid. Papá was in the living room with me, praying the rosary—over and over and over.

A couple of hours after the shots, a truckload of Guardias coming in from Juigalpa roared past the house. The soldiers were on their way into town to help search for los comunistas. I sat next to Papá and began to pray to la Inmaculada Concepción for los compañeros' escape.

That evening, as we sat at the kitchen table listening to the

radio to see if the news mentioned anything about the failed operation, there was a knock at the door. Cautiously, I opened it.
Carlos and one of the other compañeros burst in. Their clothes
were ripped to shreds and they had scratches all over their legs,
arms, and faces from running and hiding in the bramble. They
were dripping wet and looked utterly exhausted.

"The whole thing was a disaster," Carlos said after Papá served
them bread and coffee. "Before we knew it we were being attacked.
We became separated as we fled, and because we were afraid of
being captured we ditched our guns. By sheer luck, the two of us ran
into each other. But we have no idea what happened to the others."
After a long pause, Carlos looked at Papá with pleading eyes and
asked, "Don Bernardo, could we spend the night here?"

"¡No! ¡Absolutamente no! Por favor, find another place,"
Papá replied. In all the years I've known him I've never seen him so
fearful.

"We can't," Carlos said bleakly. "We don't have anywhere
else to go."

"Of course you can stay here," I said. At that moment I didn't
care what Papá was thinking; I was not turning my back on mis
compas.

Papá accepted my decision without protest. As punishment,
though—or so I thought at the time—he told los compañeros to
sleep in my bedroom. "You," he said, pointing sternly at me, "get to
sleep on the kitchen table." To be honest, at the moment I had no
problem with that.

Around midnight, a forceful knock on the door startled all of
us awake. The first thing I noticed was la oscurana. It was pitch
black because the streetlamp was out. Cuapa, once again, had lost
electricity.

Papá came out of his room. Moving swiftly, he went into my room and whispered something to los compañeros before going to the front door.

"¿Quién es?" Papá asked. I wondered how he had managed to sound so calm because, honestly, I was about to pee my pants.

"La Guardia," came the reply, polite, but firm. "Por favor, let us in. We need to get out of the rain."

"Un momentito, por favor. I have to find some candles. I can't see a thing in here," Papá answered. And it was almost true. Still, in spite of the dimness, I saw Papá motion for me to sweep the dirt floor. I got off the table, grabbed the broom, and swept as quietly as possible while Papá searched for candles.

"Vamos, what's taking you so long, cabrón?" said another guardia. Papá and I recognized the rough, raspy voice belonging to el Muerto, a guardia stationed in Juigalpa. He was absolutely feared throughout Chontales. People claimed he was responsible for so many deaths that he now lived among the dead. When I finished sweeping the floor, Papá lit a candle and opened the door.

"Buenas noches, Señores. What can I do for you?" El Muerto pushed Papá aside, and five other guardias followed him in. Two of them had been stationed in Cuapa for years, and they knew perfectly well who Bernardo and I were. A young lieutenant whom we had never seen before—probably a recent graduate of la Academia Militar—was in charge of the squad.

"Buenas noches," he greeted us as he stepped into the house. "Earlier today unos criminales tried to rob a store in el pueblo. Have you seen anyone suspicious around here?"

"Not at all, teniente. We've been asleep for at least a couple of hours. Everything has been quiet," Papá replied.

"Would it be all right, then, if my men and I spend the rest of the night here? It's no use continuing the search in this weather," the well-mannered lieutenant asked.

"I would be honored if you stayed with me," Papá answered. My pulse was racing, and I believed that if one of them looked closely at my throbbing jugular we'd be found out. Fortunately, los guardias barely took notice of me. Evidently the ones stationed in Cuapa had informed the others that Bernardo's nerdy kid lived with him, and for once I thanked Nuestro Señor for that identity.

El Muerto, rude as ever, demanded a drink of water. Papá quietly obeyed, pouring a glass for each of them. "Make yourselves comfortable wherever you can. I'm afraid my house is small."

"Sí. Muchas gracias," replied the lieutenant. Although for years I had hated guardias, this man seemed sincere and compassionate.

Papá and I bid los guardias good night and headed for our rooms, but as we opened the doors, el Muerto snarled: "Mi teniente, I think we should search the house. Los comunistas may be hiding here."

The lieutenant picked a candle off the table and held it up while he inspected the floor. Satisfied, he gently placed the candle back.

"Sargento, I see no evidence that anyone else has been here. Besides, from what I've heard about el Señor Martínez, es un hombre de honor." Tilting his head in our direction, he concluded, "Buenas noches, y gracias."

I went into my room. Los compas were hiding under my cot. I lay in bed the entire night, fingering the beads. I knew that Bernardo would be doing the same in his room. This is surely a miracle, I thought. It was as if Papá's Virgencita had placed a veil over the lieutenant's eyes. At five in the morning, we heard the front door slamming shut. Papá and I waited another half hour before we allowed los compañeros to come out.

"¡Váyanse ahora mismo!" Papá ordered. "Carlos, take the old road to Juigalpa. It'll get you out of here safely. You know it's not used much anymore. Take as many of the trails that run alongside it as you can."

Carlos embraced us, and without saying another word, he and the other compa left.

For thirty minutes Papá and I didn't move from the kitchen table, listening to every sound. At last, certain that los compañeros had escaped, and still shaken over the close call of the previous night, I let out a sigh of relief.

"Vamos. Let's make some coffee," Papá said smiling. Obviously, he also believed that the danger had passed. We were putting heaping teaspoons of sugar into our cups when we heard a loud noise in the living room. We rushed over to check. On the floor, with a gunshot wound to his leg, was Felipe. He looked awful: his color a dull yellow, as if he were sick with malaria.

"¡Ayudame, Hermano!" he said, reaching out to me.

Without a word, Papá and I helped Felipe get up off the ground and climb onto the kitchen table. Using a pair of scissors from the tailor shop, Papá cut Felipe's pants to get to the wound. It looked serious. The lower part of his leg was entirely caked with dry blood around a gaping bullet hole. Papá went into his room, returning with alcohol and bandages. Just as he began to clean the wound, a military boot kicked the front door open. Before us stood el Muerto.

"¡Quietos!" he ordered in a deep growl. Both Papá and I raised our hands. "So you *were* hiding one of los comunistas. I knew it!" He began to threaten us, using cusswords I had never heard before.

"¡Oíme, vos, no seás estúpido!" Felipe shouted, interrupting el guardia's tirade. "I just got here. And I threatened to kill them both if they didn't help me." Felipe's bravery surprised me. I had known him since we were little kids, and I never would've imagined that he possessed such courage.

"Bueno, pues, where's your weapon, pendejo?" el Muerto asked, glancing around the room while still keeping one eye on us.

"I don't have one. But they didn't know that."

El Muerto didn't say a word. Instead, he jerked Felipe off the table, threw him to the ground, and began kicking him. Angered, I stepped forward, ready to fight el hijo de la gran puta. But Papá reacted quickly, standing in front of me and holding me back. He said nothing, only shook his head. I obeyed. But I swear, if a gun had been within reach, I would've shot el comemierda right on the spot.

El Muerto was about to beat Felipe with the butt of his rifle when Bernardo stepped between them. "No," he said firmly. "En mi casa, no."

"¡Maricón insolente!" el guardia yelled, his face just inches from Papá's. "I should beat you too for helping him. But I'll deal with you later." As he shouted, I imagined his sour, pestilent breath. Papá calmly met el Muerto's glare, not blinking once. El guardia then turned toward me and ordered, "Bring me a rope. You're going to tie this subversivo up. I'm taking him to headquarters."

With a nod, Papá ordered me to obey. El guardia supervised every knot I made. Without consulting with el Muerto, I tied Felipe's hands in front so that he could still use them. Once I had finished, el Muerto made Felipe rise. My friend cried out in pain as he placed some weight on the wounded leg. El Muerto then pushed him out the door, beginning a forced march of more than a kilometer to the garrison.

The news spread fast of Felipe's capture, and as we entered el pueblo, a crowd awaited us. The gathering parted as Felipe, followed by el Muerto, began his trek down the main street toward the garrison. Papá and I walked behind Felipe. The other cuapeños began to fall in silently behind us.

We had advanced nearly a block when doña Filomena stepped forward to offer Felipe a jícara full of water. Felipe stopped and, with her help, took the gourd to his mouth. He began to drink greedily, but after only a couple of gulps, el Muerto knocked the jícara out of doña Filomena's hand, spilling the water onto the ground.

"Keep moving, comunista de mierda!" he ordered.

Two blocks later, don Armando offered the prisoner all he had at that moment—a banana. Felipe reached out and accepted the fruit.

"Don't give the prisoner anything!" el Muerto shouted as he turned in a circle, waving the barrel of his Galil rifle at the crowd. But Felipe defiantly peeled the banana and took a bite. Outraged by the challenge to his authority, el Muerto, in one swift, powerful move, smashed the butt of his weapon against the side of my friend's face. The sound of Felipe's jaw fragmenting into countless pieces was followed by a collective gasp. Felipe fell to the ground, almost losing consciousness. El guardia quickly grabbed the prisoner's arm and forced him back up. I was enraged when I saw my friend's jaw hanging loose.

But I was not the only one pissed. The crowd's fury started first as a low murmur, building in intensity, until a woman shouted, "¡Maldito guardia, rejodido, hijo de la gran puta!" Others began to shout insults. I saw el Muerto's own fear as his eyes darted about wildly. He smelled the beginnings of a lynching, and instinctively pointed his Galil at anyone who moved. The commotion by now had drawn the attention of los guardias at the garrison, a block and a half away. Three soldiers, readying their rifles, ran toward us.

Felipe now could barely stand. His legs wobbled like a rag doll's. Blood oozed in a gooey stream from his mouth. Leticia, a girl we've known since primaria, stepped forward to wipe Felipe's face with a towel soaked in water. El Muerto pushed her away so violently that she fell on her back, crashing down at the feet of Cuapa's two oldest sisters. These began to cry, begging el guardia to stop, to spare Felipe's life. A woman behind me began to wail loudly, and I could now hear the men uttering threats under their breath.

The other guardias arrived just in time to save el Muerto. The situation had gotten out of his control. Together, the soldiers retreated to the garrison as quickly as Felipe could move. We followed closely, a few of us crying, while others boldly shouted threats. The soldiers stepped into their building and slammed the doors shut. We then heard the clicking of bolts.

We stood there for a few moments, all of us wondering what to do next, when, suddenly, someone shouted, "¡Patria Libre!" And the crowd, in a single cry that I swear made the earth shake under my feet, responded, "¡O Morir!" I felt Papá clinging to my forearm, and it was not until then that I realized that he had been holding on to me the entire time. I looked to him for advice, and he shook his head slightly. I understood perfectly: *Don't get involved.* And then Javier Gutiérrez—who I always thought was nothing but a useless punk—suggested that we burn down the garrison. Everyone agreed. A couple of men started to run home to get containers of kerosene.

Abruptly, startling every one of us, the garage doors of the garrison burst open. Several guardias emerged, their rifles pointed directly at the crowd. Soldiers from Juigalpa had obviously been left behind. We instantly became silent. A jeep stormed out: one guardia drove, another was seated next to him, his weapon ready, and el Muerto sat in the rear, guarding Felipe. The vehicle took off hurriedly down the dirt road leading to el Cerro de Chavarría, to the south, where la Guardia had a small station guarding the radio tower.

While we stared at the jeep, the windows to the garrison opened with a loud slap that made us all jump. Rifles pointed out at us.

"¡Váyanse a sus casas!" a corporal shouted. "We don't want to have to shoot anyone. But we will if necessary. Go home! Now!"

Papá, holding both hands up, turned to face the crowd. "Amigos, let's do as el cabo says. Let's remain calm and see how we can work our way through this."

Papá then turned to the corporal and said, "Please tell the lieutenant that we've known Felipe all of his life. This Sandinista talk has just confused the boy, that's all. Besides, he's pretty badly hurt, so he's not a threat anymore. Please assure el teniente of that."

The corporal nodded.

Just as we began to disperse, Felipe's mother, who lived high on the northern slopes of Cuapa, along the dirt road to Comalapa, came running down the street. As she approached I could hear her crying, begging the soldiers to release her son. Papá calmly intercepted her. He explained the situation, giving her hope that Felipe would be released. He then asked several of her friends to stay by her side until the ordeal was over.

Everyone did just as Papá asked. He and I went straight home, neither of us saying a word along the way. After entering the house, Papá went straight to his room and returned, rosary in hand. "Sit down, Elías. You're praying with me." I didn't protest at all. As we prayed, I implored la Virgencita to save Felipe, pledging to quit the Sandinistas if she spared his life.

We had barely finished reciting the rosary when two shots echoed throughout the valley. I jumped out of my seat and headed for the door. Papá, moving more quickly than me, blocked my way. "There's nothing you can do now, hijo. There's nothing anyone can do. Felipe está en las manos de Dios." He reached out and embraced me, and I began to cry like a child.

That night I couldn't sleep. The shame I felt for not having the courage to save Felipe haunted me in the darkness. At dawn, Papá came into my room. As if guessing my thoughts, he repeated, "There was nothing you could do, hijo. It's no use having the both of you dead. Besides, Felipe had obviously accepted the consequences of being captured. He didn't tell them anything, Chele. If he had, we'd be with him right now, among the dead. He sacrificed himself because he wanted you to go on living."

That day, jeeps loaded with guardias patrolled Cuapa and the outskirts. I doubt that they were looking for more revolucionarios. They were just trying to intimidate us. Their menacing presence said it all: *Submit to our authority or else.* And los cuapeños obeyed, including myself: everyone remained behind their doors that entire day.

That night I was so tired that I finally fell asleep. I don't know if it was the exhaustion or what, but as I slept I drifted to a place in my mind I had never visited. I floated on a cloud. The color of the sky was the most stunning light blue. In the middle of the night, I awoke, startled by the incredibly vivid dream I just had. I called out to Papá. He came into my room, sat at the edge of my cot, and paid close attention while I spoke.

"Papá, I was walking down the hollow where los compañeros

were hiding when I ran into Felipe. We embraced and I told him how happy I was that he was still alive.

"Felipe smiled and then, very softly, said, 'I'm no longer with you, Chele.' I felt so sad that I began to sob. Placing an arm around me, Felipe continued, 'You really should be delighted for me. I'm now free from pain, from bitterness, from want. This is a wonderful place, Chele.'

"Felipe smiled again, and it was clear to me that he was truly happy. Suddenly, he grew serious, and said, 'I've come to ask for a favor, Chele. It's a big one—one that I'll appreciate for eternity. I want you to find my body. I want it to be buried in the cemetery, next to my father.'

"Of course, I agreed to help. We embraced once more, and then Felipe said, 'Chele, I'll be waiting for you when your hour comes.' He smiled, turned, and headed up a mountain path. Before I could ask him when that would be, he had vanished."

Papá listened intently. He considered what I had told him for a long time, and at length he said, "We must do as Felipe has asked."

We got up at dawn and after a quick breakfast we saddled three bestias. Papá filled an alforja with food, water, and two large plastic trash bags, and then we left. On the way out of el pueblo, we stopped by to see don Edmundo, the carpenter. Papá asked him to prepare a coffin for a man of average size. Don Edmundo didn't even ask whom it was for. He already knew.

We then stopped by the telephone station and Papá called Padre Domingo in Juigalpa. "Could you come to Cuapa to celebrate a funeral mass?"

"I can't," the priest answered. "No one can leave the city. Martial law. Besides," he added quietly, as if someone were eavesdropping on the conversation, "I have plenty of funeral masses to conduct here." He asked Papá to lead the community in praying the rosary during the wake, and then to have everyone say the Lord's Prayer at el cementerio. "I will conduct a proper mass for Felipe whenever I can make it to Cuapa."

Papá and I then headed for the garrison. This time, the young lieutenant was there. "Teniente, I need your permission to retrieve Felipe's body to give him a Christian burial," Papá said. Instead of pretending that he didn't know what we were talking about, the lieutenant simply nodded. He looked exhausted and his eyes were weary, full of sorrow. El teniente filled out a safe conduct for us to enter the radio tower area and stamped it with his seal. "Buena suerte," was all he said.

The trip to the tower took a good portion of our morning. When los guardias at the station spotted us, they shouted, "¡Váyanse! You can't be here! ¡Es determinantemente prohibido estar aquí!" They aimed their rifles at us, and I was absolutely sure they were going to fire. But Papá calmly waved the order above his head, and shouted back that he had the lieutenant's permission to search for Felipe's body.

"Dismount and come forward. Con las manos en alto," one of them ordered.

When Papá gave them the lieutenant's signed order they seemed surprised. Although neither of them seemed to know how to read, they recognized their commanding officer's seal.

"Well, then," the older of the two said at last, "I guess you do have permission to be here. Go ahead and search."

"Would you please show us where the body is?" Papá asked. But both guards shook their heads, refusing to say another word.

From the summit of el Cerro de Chavarría, Papá and I looked out over the countryside. The plots of tilled farmland and the forested areas stretched out like a beautiful green quilt that lovingly covered a lumpy bed of hills, mountains, and valleys. It made me sad to think that a country so beautiful should suffer so much. The thought of ever finding Felipe in the immensity sprawled before our feet dismayed me even more. His body could be anywhere. Papá insisted on descending and heading south. After a kilometer or so, he stopped and dismounted. He then sat on a rock under the shade of a cedro, pulled his rosary from his pocket, and began to pray. This time I lost my patience.

"Papá, now's not the time to pray! We have to find Felipe!"

"Where do you suggest we look, Chele?" I remained silent. He was right. Felipe could be anywhere. "Chele, I'm praying to la Virgencita. Maybe she'll give us a sign. Maybe she'll help."

Well, we have nothing else to lose but time, I thought. Besides, I was getting a bit hungry. So while Papá prayed, I ate lunch.

Papá also ate, once he had finished. Afterward, he rose and began to scan the sky. I did the same, shading my eyes from the noonday sun. About half a kilometer south, high above our heads, we spotted a few black specks gliding on the wind currents in effortless circles. I stared at los zopilotes with both hope and dread. "The body must be there," was all Papá said. We mounted our horses and headed in the direction of the circling vultures.

We followed those dreadful beacons in silence. The horses seemed honed in to their signal, and holding loosely to the reins, we just let them take us there. We advanced until los zopilotes were flying directly overhead. But still we saw no sign of Felipe's body.

"Let's begin moving in a circle, making it slightly larger each time," Papá suggested. "That way, Chele, we are sure to stumble upon whatever is attracting los zopilotes." We did so, and within fifteen minutes the stench of decomposition began to repulse me.

Now using our noses as guides, we followed the gruesome scent. Still, we could see nothing.

Soon, an insistent buzz, the high-pitched murmur of insects, drew our attention. The sound made my stomach queasy. Our ears guided us. I took out my bandana and tied it around my face, covering my nose and mouth—like a bandit from a cowboy movie, or like an urban Sandinista, for that matter. The drone led us to a dense bush. As we approached, we saw a dark cloud wavering from side to side behind the bramble. I quickly dismounted and parted the growth to look on the other side. There, blackened by what must have been a million flies, was Felipe's body. The sight forced me to turn away. I gagged and puked up everything.

Papá, on the other hand, calmly got the plastic trash bags out of his alforja. After my sickness had passed, he motioned for me to help him place the body inside. When we turned Felipe over—the flies scattered just for a moment before returning to torment us—I saw two gunshot wounds in his face. I have no memory of what happened next, but somehow I managed to help Papá. It wasn't until after we were done that I realized that I had been crying all the while. We carried the body out of the brush and laid it across the riderless horse. Then we started back for Cuapa.

As we entered el pueblo from the south, across the river and onto la Calle de los Laureles, the townspeople came out of their homes to stare at the black plastic bulk containing Felipe's body. The horse carrying his remains had a look of resignation, patiently bearing the burden of our country's political sins. The people's anger, although muted, was visible in their faces. News of our arrival spread quickly. By the time we rode up to the church, almost all of Cuapa was there waiting. The cries of Felipe's mother painfully pierced my heart, like a long, cold needle.

"What a horrible way for la aventura to end," I muttered to myself. Papá, after dismounting, walked straight to Felipe's mother. In a soft, gentle voice he advised her that it would be wisest to leave the body wrapped. He then turned to face the gathering.

"The funeral service will be this afternoon at four." Without a word, los cuapeños dispersed. Many accompanied Felipe's mother to her house, where the coffin awaited. The crowd followed the horse, which seemed to know the way. Papá and I went straight home to clean up. When we returned, the church was overflowing; nearly every person in Cuapa was there. As I entered the building I could feel waves of sadness and anger spreading from the gathering like swells during a storm. The impact was so overwhelming that I had to hold on to a pew to steady myself.

Bernardo walked to the front, and as Padre Domingo had instructed, he led us in praying the rosary. The entire time we prayed, my being yearned for una teología de justicia, and of vengeance. After we finished, all of Cuapa headed for el cementerio. In mourning, the townspeople were like a spring pushed back to its limit, ready to recoil in fury. At Felipe's tomb, next to his father's, Bernardo led us in praying El Padre Nuestro.

Our Father, who art in heaven . . .

Everyone remained afterward until don Gilberto, the town albañil, had finished sealing the crypt. We then walked home in silence, our rage under control—for the time being. That entire day los guardias had locked themselves in the garrison, fearful that if they showed themselves los cuapeños would riot.

A week had passed since Felipe's funeral, and I grew impatient, awaiting my next orders. I was ready to finish what my friend had started, especially since I took his death as a sign that la Virgen wanted me to remain with the Sandinistas. By this time I began to think that mis compañeros in el Frente had forgotten that I was here, stuck in Cuapa, while the war against Somoza and his Guardia Nacional raged on throughout the rest of the country. Just when I was about to give up hope of being called into action, a compañero I had never met before stopped by the house while Papá was at church.

"El dictador tiene hemorroides," he whispered when I opened the door. He used the same contraseña I had used with Oscar. His name in the underground was Mambo, and he explained that the reason Oscar and the others didn't show up was because la Guardia discovered their safehouse and killed every single one of them, including Oscar.

"So," I said to myself, "it was a day of mourning for all of us."

. . . hallowed be thy name . . .

Mambo gave me my new orders. I was to join a guerrilla unit assembling on the outskirts of Juigalpa. Within a day or two we would take the city. From there our columns would advance—south, east, and then north—until all of Chontales had been liberated.

"The bigger cities are falling like dominoes, compañero," Mambo said with a huge grin. "Before long the dreams of Augusto César Sandino and Carlos Fonseca Amador will become reality." Although just a little over a week ago the Sandinista rhetoric would have moved me to tears, after Felipe's death el compañero's words sounded empty. Still, by the time Papá returned from church, I had already left. Mambo, like Oscar before him, didn't allow me to leave him a note.

The final offensive was more successful than any of us could've anticipated. La Guardia crumbled as we gained momentum. My unit took Juigalpa after firing just a few shots. Somoza's soldiers couldn't raise the white flag soon enough. From there we went to La Libertad, then Santo Tomás, Acoyapa, and Comalapa. Each time the opposition dissolved into nothing within minutes of our arrival. Five decades of living under the threatening thumb of a selfish dynasty were coming to an end with a whimper.

At last, the day before Somoza fled on a plane bound for Miami, I was ordered to lead a unit to capture Cuapa. I returned to my hometown in full combat uniform, with the rank of Responsable and in command of a ragged but enthusiastic group of young rebeldes. Los cuapeños were astounded when they recognized me, draped in the seductive aura of power and giving orders with an intimidating Uzi hanging from my shoulder.

. . . Thy Kingdom come, thy will be done . . .

Cautiously, los compañeros and I surrounded the garrison. We ordered los guardias to surrender. There was no response. The silence didn't surprise me. Guardias had been fleeing in droves, ditching their uniforms and running for their lives as their reign of terror collapsed. Before I sent mis compañeros to search the building, don Juan Espinoza hurried out of his house, which was next door to the garrison. This man, known in town for the goofy-looking animals he carved out of wood, crossed the street with difficulty, moving with as much speed as his aging bones allowed.

When los compañeros brought don Juan before me he couldn't speak: first because he was winded, and second because of his surprise at seeing me in charge of the operation. Once recovered, he said, "Chele, I overheard los guardias talking about going to la Piedra. You're going to have a hard time getting them down from there."

The old man was right. Los guardias could hold out at the top of the monolith for as long as they had food and water. We wouldn't even be able to approach the rock. We'd make easy targets. The situation had the markings of a long standoff.

Mis compañeros and I left for la Piedra, a kilometer beyond Papá's potrero, along the old road to Juigalpa. As soon as los guardias saw us, they fired a warning shot that hummed above our heads. We quickly took cover. Surrounding the rock was out of the question: I simply didn't have enough men. As los compañeros and I discussed our options, Papá appeared. He didn't even say hello to me. He acted as if I had said good-bye to him just five minutes earlier.

"Chele, let me go up there and talk to them. But before I do, I want your word that if they surrender none of them will be harmed. If you can promise me that, I think I can get them to come down peacefully."

... *On earth, as it is in heaven* ...

Because it was Papá, I didn't hesitate for a moment. I gave him my word. He smiled, patted me on the shoulder, and left for la Piedra. As news of the standoff spread, cuapeños left their homes and gathered near our base camp. Soon, the siege took on the feeling of a fiesta. Vendors appeared out of nowhere, selling raspados, rosquillas, cajetas, fruits, and drinks.

... *Give us this day, our daily bread* ...

A couple of musicians brought their guitars and started singing revolutionary songs. Everyone, including los rebeldes, joined in when they played "El Cristo de Palacagüina." We did have a reason to celebrate: the end of the war was within sight.

About three hours after Papá had left, el compañero I had assigned as lookout reported that los guardias were coming down from la Piedra. Before long we could see them headed our way, walking along the road with their weapons held high above their heads. Papá, unarmed, walked in the lead. As los compañeros and I went to meet them, I said a brief prayer, asking for their peaceful surrender.

When we found ourselves within shouting distance, they stopped. The corporal came forth to meet me. He asked for my personal assurance that they would not be harmed. I gave him my word, and we shook hands. He then motioned for his men to lay their weapons on the ground. The crowd broke into cheers and applause, as if it all had been a circus performance.

I could see the fear on the faces of los guardias as they approached. And once they began to pass by, I spotted el Muerto. Instantly, I barked an order for los guardias to halt. I walked up to el Muerto, staring at him while saying nothing. I let the hatred that surely burned in my eyes speak for me. El guardia then revealed himself for what he truly was: a coward. He fell to his knees and clasped his hands together at his chest.

"Por favor, no me mate. Tengo una familia. Por favor," he wept, begging for his worthless life.

. . . *and forgive us our trespasses* . . .

The crowd, angry at what he had done to Felipe—and to countless others—began to press in around us. Felipe's mother was the first to cuss at him. Then Leticia, angry still because of how el Muerto had treated her when she tried to wipe the blood off Felipe's face, stepped forward and spit on his.

"Shoot him!" a man yelled.

That did it. Everyone's desire for revenge boiled over that very instant. Even mine. The surge of hatred was so forceful that it began to cloud my judgment. Without thinking, I grabbed a pistol from one of my men. I held out my arm, straight and firm, pointing the weapon directly at el Muerto's face.

"I'll only shoot you twice," I said, "just like you did to Felipe." My finger felt a pleasurable decisiveness as it curled itself around the cool waist of the trigger. The other guardias, seeing that I was going back on my word, began to squirm. Suddenly, Bernardo climbed onto a rock where everyone could see him, and he spoke—not just to me, but also to all present.

"If we are going to build a new, just nation, we must begin by forgiving those who have hurt us the most. Now's the time for us to be compassionate. Now's the time to practice forgiveness. That's what el Señor expects of us."

. . . as we forgive those who trespass against us . . .

"Don't listen to el sacristán, Chele! He's a wimp!" a nameless voice shouted, lost in the anonymity of the crowd. "Remember what that bastard did to Felipe!"

The tension of my finger indeed increased as I recalled what el Muerto had done. I was not about to fail Felipe this time. Then I remembered the dream.

. . . and lead us not into temptation . . .

With tears of rage welling up in my eyes, I lowered the gun.

I turned to mis compañeros, my voice becoming a low, rumbling growl that frightened even me, and I ordered, between clenched teeth, "Take this hijo de la gran puta and lock him up in the filthiest cell you can find."

. . . but deliver us from evil . . .

Amén.

VISIO OPPROBII
(The Apparition of the Reproach)
May 8–18, 1980

Bernardo

AFTER LA VIRGENCITA first appeared to me, I went home, cleaned up, and rushed to the church to pray the rosary. On my way back home, I ran into several friends, but I didn't tell a single person what I had seen or heard. I was terrified of being ridiculed.

That evening, sitting at home, alone, I once again began to feel depressed. A deep sadness flowed straight through me, as if my heart had been pierced with a stake. I had trouble breathing; my chest fluttered, my lungs felt like they were full of moths. So I went to my room, grabbed my rosary, and began to pray. I asked Nuestro Señor to free me from temptation, for I was starting to believe that it had been the devil himself who had appeared to me. If Satanás had the nerve to tempt Jesús in the desert, then who am I to believe myself safe from his wiles?

Even though I was feeling terribly sad, shortly after it got dark I managed to fall asleep. I don't know for how long I had been out when the Voice startled me awake.

Tell.

I climbed out of bed, grabbed my rosary, and went into the

living room, where I got on my knees before the crucifix that hangs on the wall. But no matter how much I prayed, I still felt miserable. Therefore, I tried to pray straight through the night so I could forget my sorrow, but I couldn't concentrate. In time, feeling exhausted, I went back to bed.

"I can't possibly tell," I said aloud to myself. "If I do tell people about the apparition, I'll be el hazmerreir of Cuapa as sure as parrots prefer to roost in guanacaste trees." And I am too proud to ever want to be the laughingstock of el pueblo. I spent the rest of the night staring at the ceiling. The thought of seeing her again tormented me, so I decided never to return to el potrero.

After the first apparition, time almost stood still; the days went by with agonizing slowness. Still, I stubbornly kept what I had seen and heard to myself. But the weight of my secret grew far too heavy. Her message was beginning to crush me.

To distract myself, I spent time with anyone who was willing to spend time with me. I didn't want to be alone. I even joined los muchachos at the pool hall every evening for a few beers. That, I'm sure, quickly became part of Cuapa's grapevine. But I was ready to do anything to keep from thinking about the apparition, to keep from thinking about her.

The nights were the worst part. By far. Shortly after I'd go to bed the heat would become unbearable. It felt as if I were trying to sleep inside an oven . . . or in hell. And I'd sleep in fits, if I got any sleep at all. But when I did manage to doze off, the Voice would wake me up.

Bernardo, why haven't you told everyone, like I asked you to?

I'd then get up and pray the rosary until daybreak. Eight days and nights went by like this; my secret was tearing me apart. Nothing I did helped keep my mind off the apparition. I couldn't eat, I couldn't sleep, I couldn't concentrate on my tailoring. I started to feel so depressed that I even stopped taking care of the church. In just a week's time I lost nearly twenty pounds, and I was turning pale.

"Are you feeling all right, Bernardo?" people would ask.

"I'm fine. Estoy bien," I assured them. But I insisted on remaining quiet, although I became convinced that my silence would soon kill me.

On May 16, eight days after the first apparition, I woke up feeling a bit happier. Late in the morning, I decided to tend to my calf, Rondita, whom I had left in the smallest of the three potreros I own. The day was so hot that I felt guilty for having left her out in the sun all day. Although la ternera has plenty of grass to graze on in the pasture, and the river is nearby, with lots of trees, she sometimes is too plain dumb to look for shade. Before lunch, I thought it would be a good idea to take her to the river, and while there I would take a quick dip myself.

When I arrived I scanned the hillsides and I didn't see la ternera anywhere. Perhaps, I thought, Rondita had gone on her own down into the gully where the river runs. I was proud of her because the sun that day showed no mercy.

I was halfway across el potrero, headed for the gully, when a flash of light made me jump. No sound followed. I checked the sun. Noon. Not a cloud was in the sky. Before I could begin to worry about the meaning of that flash, there was another one so powerful that its brilliance outshone the day's harsh light.

And there she was. La Señora. Floating before me on a glowing cloud. A sparkling light blue aura surrounded her. She looked exactly the same as the first time I saw her. I fell to my knees.

"Now I'm really in trouble because I was disobedient," I

whispered to myself. Feeling ashamed, I tried not to look at her, but I couldn't help myself. Her presence attracted me the same way an iguana is attracted to sunlight.

Like the first time, la Virgencita held her hands together, as if she were in prayer. Slowly, she spread her arms apart and lowered her hands, the open palms facing me. Two powerful beams of light came out and met at the center of my chest. And then she spoke.

Bernardo, why haven't you told? Why haven't you done as I've asked? Her voice was melancholic. A deep sadness flooded my soul because I knew I had let her down.

"Señora," I answered, "it's because I'm afraid. I'm afraid of becoming el hazmerreír of Cuapa. I'm afraid of everyone making fun of me. Most of all, I'm afraid that people won't believe me. And whoever doesn't believe me will think that I'm un loco de remate or, worse yet, a liar." I didn't even try to fool la Virgencita because I was certain that she knew every thought hidden in my heart.

She smiled, and I rejoiced. She had forgiven me. She, the most merciful being in heaven.

Bernardo, do not be afraid. I will help you. Also, go tell the priest. He will help you as well.

With that there was another flash. I was blinded for an instant, and by the time I could see again, she had vanished.

I shook my head, dazed. After I had recovered, I continued to look for Rondita. I found her on the other side of the hill, grazing in the shade of a madroño tree. I greeted her, took her to the river, and while she drank, I bathed. When I was done, I returned home.

There, I changed clothes and went straight to the church, where I prayed the rosary. After I had finished, because my friend Blanca was out of town, I rushed to doña Socorro's and doña Auxiliadora's. I told them everything I had seen and heard. They listened attentively, not interrupting me once. When I had finished, they began to scold me for having disobeyed la Virgencita. And then they began working on the remedy.

"We'll tell everyone to drop by the church tomorrow because you have something important to say. And you will tell them everything, Bernardo. Just like you told us," said doña Auxiliadora.

"We'll ask doña Tula to spread the news about the meeting. Tomorrow morning, ten o'clock," said doña Socorro, her face beaming with pride over their plan.

"But la Virgencita told me to tell Padre Domingo. I think I should tell him first," I answered, worried that I might again be disobeying her.

"¡Disparates!" charged doña Auxiliadora. "Stop talking nonsense, Bernardo! Didn't she tell you to tell *everyone* the first time you saw her? Well, that's what you're supposed to do. Tell *everyone.*"

What doña Auxiliadora said seemed reasonable, so I promised to share my story with whoever showed up the next morning. We said good night and I returned home, stopping first by don Casimiro's to pick up some chicharrones. They were delicious, with fresh tortillas and, to drink, cacao. My appetite had finally returned. That night I slept deeply. I woke up refreshed, the misery of the week before completely forgotten. Miraculously, all of my problems, all of my worries, had also disappeared.

The following morning I felt so good that I stayed home, sitting in the cool shade of the mamey tree in my backyard, listening to the birds sing. I had completely forgotten about the meeting. When I finally remembered, I checked my watch and was shocked to see that I was running late. I got up and made my way as fast as I could into el pueblo. Along the way I noticed crowds of people walking in the streets. More people than I realized lived in Cuapa. Until that day, I hadn't been aware how much el pueblo had grown. Interestingly, everyone was going in the same direction as me. At first I thought that maybe the circus had come to town, but then I understood that doña Tula had done her job. Every single person in Cuapa, it seemed, was going to the church.

When I appeared at the door, the friendly chatter between neighbors died down. Normally the silence following my entrance would have scared me, but today nothing could change the feeling of peace that I had. The church was more crowded that morning than during Semana Santa. And the people, when they saw that I had arrived, parted to let me walk through, just like the Red Sea did for Moses.

I walked to the front, turned to face the crowd, and amid gasps, tears, signs of the cross, and snickers, told my story.

When I had finished, I offered to answer any questions. That part of the meeting went for a couple of hours. I saw belief, admiration, and wonder in the faces of some. Others thoughtfully analyzed everything I said. A few sat there in stunned silence, their expressions giving away nothing. And others, of course, made fun of me, saying out loud that I was completamente loco.

But la Virgencita had given me the strength to overcome my fear of being ridiculed. I really didn't care if people made jokes about me. I was at peace and I was experiencing great joy after having revealed my secret. That was all that mattered.

And Nuestra Señora had given me another gift; a gift that I still carry with me: I somehow know who believes in the apparition, and who doesn't. It's a sort of sixth sense.

After my talk I returned home to rest. But that became impossible. Not because I was anxious—if anything I had never felt so much at peace—but because of all the visitors. People came by my house all afternoon to ask more questions, and a few also came to continue making fun of me. But I took it all in stride, with far greater patience than I ever knew I had. I figured that talking to people, even the incredulous, was part of being la Virgencita's messenger.

The visitors asked mostly questions about their personal lives. They thought that she had given me a crystal ball. For instance, doña Regina wanted to know if her husband was fooling around, doña María Marta wanted to find out who was the father of her second child, and don Gumersindo wanted to know how many calves his cows would bear next season. I kept on telling everyone that I couldn't answer those questions, that I knew nothing about their futures or their pasts, nor did I think la Virgencita would tell me. But they persisted in asking these impossible questions until Camilita, Leticia's little girl, said, "Don Bernardo, am I going to heaven?"

"Yes, my dear, you most definitely are." The naturalness of my reply surprised me. I hadn't given the answer a moment's thought, but I knew that I was right, and I figured that in Camilita's case la Virgencita had interceded.

Well, that opened the floodgates. Everyone started shouting at once. They all wanted to know if they were going to heaven. People began pushing each other, begging for me to tell them. But I didn't know. Really. Only in Camilita's case had the answer been as clear as the waters of a stream in la Sierra de Amerrisque. But my ignorance made me happy. After all, how do you tell someone, "No, you're not going to heaven"?

Finally, as I grew tired, doña Auxiliadora and doña Socorro forced everyone to go home. Doña Tula tried to stay behind to ask questions about other cuapeños. "To help them find the road to salvation," she said. But I told her that I was exhausted and sent her home as well.

The next morning I caught the first bus to Juigalpa to see Padre Domingo. I found him in the church. We walked to la Casa Cural and made ourselves some coffee, and I then told him everything about the apparitions. After some thought, he said, "Bernardo, maybe someone is playing a joke on you? You know, taking her statue from the church to the pasture, hiding behind it, and making you think that you were talking to her?"

"No, Padre. That's impossible. I was right in the middle of el potrero. There's nowhere to hide there. No, Padre, impossible. I would have easily seen anyone trying to carry her statue through the fields."

"Well, Bernardo, perhaps then the devil is tempting you?"

"No, Padre," I answered. But then I considered his suggestion for a moment. "Well, to tell you the truth, I wouldn't be able to say whether it's the devil tempting me or not. I don't know about these things. All I know, Padre, is what I saw and what I heard. And I know that now, after telling everyone about the apparition, I'm at peace."

"Well, that brings up another point, Bernardo. I'm somewhat upset because you disobeyed Nuestra Señora. Didn't she ask you to tell me first? Instead, you went and told the entire town."

For an instant I became angry at doña Socorro and doña Auxiliadora for their bad advice. But rather than blaming them, I decided to accept full responsibility. "Lo siento, Padre," I said, my head bowed in shame.

"What's done is done, Bernardo. You have my permission to continue telling people what you have already experienced. But if she appears to you again, you are only to tell me, and no one else. Understood? Can you promise me that?".

I nodded.

"Good. Now, I want you to say the Act of Contrition and then pray the rosary. And when you return to Cuapa, go to the apparition site and recite the rosary once more. If she appears to you again, make the sign of the cross. Do not be afraid. Even if it's the devil that is tempting you, nothing bad will happen if you place your faith in Nuestra Señora. Remember, she has defeated Satanás before."

The priest smiled and embraced me. Although I felt at peace, joyful even, I left Juigalpa with a great burden on my shoulders. The gift I received from la Virgencita, my sixth sense, made it painfully clear to me that Padre Domingo, the person I most wanted on my side, was not a believer.

chapter five

PARTUS
(The Birth)

December 1980

Sofía Velázquez

THE THREE-AND-A-HALF-HOUR drive from Managua to Cuapa gives one plenty of time to think. Word has reached the newspaper that la Virgen appeared there to a campesino named Bernardo Martínez. People from all over the country are making the journey to Chontales to hear him tell the story, as well as to visit the site where she appeared. Don Ernesto, my boss, asked me to go find out what's going on.

"Probably some nut case," he said. "But people still have a right to know."

As far back as I can remember I've wanted to be a reporter. There's something about investigating a story, writing it, and sharing it with readers that satisfies me immensely. I still get chills up and down my spine when my byline appears in bold letters on the front page. Maybe that's why I haven't needed a man in my life.

One of the earliest memories I have of my father—and I don't know what else to call that maricón—is of him lying in a hammock on the porch of his hacienda, reading the newspaper. La Fidelidad, his farm, was located just outside of Niquinohomo, the birthplace of our greatest national hero, General Augusto César Sandino. From a distance I'd watch him read and listen to the rustle of the paper as he turned the pages. Whatever existed on those pages mesmerized him day after day. After he finished, he'd fold the paper neatly, place it on the coffee table, climb into his jeep, and drive off to supervise the campesinos at work. Sometimes, after his wife, my half-brothers, and my half-sisters (all older than me) had finished reading the newspaper, I was allowed to take it to my room. I would spend hours gazing at the photographs and dream that someday I would meet the people in them.

Shortly before I turned seven, my mother and I moved to Managua. Although she never said a word to me about why we left La Fidelidad, I guessed that she had finally had enough. You see, my father was her patrón. She had been working on la hacienda since she turned thirteen. That's when she began washing and ironing his family's laundry. One night, while drunk, when my mother was just sixteen, he crawled into her bed and had his way with her. But there was nobody a poor illiterate india could turn to for justice, or for another job. In those days there was not a single policeman or a single court in Nicaragua that would investigate a rape charge brought by someone of her class against a wealthy hacendado with a respectable last name. To make matters worse, he never admitted to being my father.

"I know your kind, india," he said to her. "Any man on the hacienda could be the father." Thus, el bastardo never recognized me. That's why I carry her surname—Velázquez—and proudly, I might add.

Once in Managua, my mother found a job working in the household of a colonel in la Guardia Nacional. But he wasn't the hardcore military type, the kind everyone in Nicaragua feared back then. Those men rose high in the ranks because of their ruthlessness. No. This was a kind, gentle, calm, and patient old man. His name was Roberto López, a physician who had joined la Guardia when it first started. The U.S. Marines, back in the late 1920s, had recruited him when he graduated from medical school and trained him as a medical officer. They paid him well, too. Dr. López would often tell me long, detailed stories about how he served in the war against Sandino, chasing guerrilleros throughout the mountains of Nueva Segovia and Jinotega. He seemed to recall the experience with fondness; but he once shared with me that if he had to do it over again he would decline. He had been young, rash, and foolish then. The war against Sandino had been far too dangerous and, in the end, "What was it all for?" he said. Afterward, Dr. López would remain silent, staring off somewhere safe and distant where I couldn't follow his thoughts.

Dr. López was a serene person, who moved about slowly. At times he reminded me of a tortoise. On the other hand, his wife, doña Natalia, was high-strung, nervous, always in motion, and constantly checking to see if the maids had performed their chores according to her very precise directions.

The couple had only one child, a daughter, who eloped with her boyfriend a couple of years before my mother and I arrived.

The young girl had run off because doña Natalia didn't approve of her boyfriend's pedigree; he didn't have the right last name or sufficient education to become part of the López family.

Still, in spite of this display of snobbery, she—and Dr. López, of course—were good to my mother and to me. I guess because of the many years doña Natalia had been married to Dr. López, much of his kindness had rubbed off on her. Since we lived in their house, they insisted that I receive an education. They paid for me to attend a private Catholic school. One for poor girls, of course, but a good school nonetheless. For that, I will always be grateful.

My mother says that I was lucky because Dr. López was fond of children. The couple treated me nearly as a daughter. Every afternoon, over my mother's objections, Dr. López would allow my two best friends from school to come play. Sometimes he'd call us together, have us sit on the floor around him, and read us stories.

On those occasions I'd receive a double treat because late in the evening, right before bedtime, Dr. López would set me on his lap and read the newspaper out loud just for me. He'd let me choose the articles. I treasured those evenings with him. I did notice, however, that the older I got, the longer Dr. López's hand would linger on my upper thighs whenever I sat with him. And sometimes, when I sat a certain way, I could feel his once dormant bulge hardening. But I didn't mind. Even thinking about it today doesn't offend me. Beyond those hapless indiscretions, the colonel never did anything improper to me or to my mother.

I was happy. I really was. I enjoyed living in Managua far more than on la hacienda. The capital was full of life. Everywhere I went I would see and hear interesting stories, the kind one reads in the newspapers. And, yes, the Lópezes made it a happy home for me, and for my mother as well. Then it all came tumbling down. Literally.

I remember the excitement of Navidad approaching. Ever since we had been living with the colonel and his wife, they made sure that el Niño Dios brought plenty of gifts for me. That Christmas, I couldn't wait to see my new wardrobe, courtesy of Dr. López and doña Natalia.

December 23, 1972. No one who came out alive from that horrible experience will ever forget that date. I know I never will. My mother and I had been asleep for three hours when a low rumbling sound awoke us. While still lying in bed, with my head on the pillow, I imagined that I had put my ear on the intestinal tract of the earth. The rumbling suddenly turned into a booming sound, and everything began to sink, shake, and sway. I was so terrified that I couldn't even climb out of bed. All I could do was sit up and scream. The earth's fury was so intense that I couldn't hear myself shout above the groans of the building. The electricity went out. At once, the night turned pitch black. I couldn't even see my mother, whose bed was just a couple of yards away from mine. Above the noise, I faintly heard her calling my name. The terremoto kept going on and on, the quaking not wanting to end. After what seemed like a lifetime of the earth's churning, I heard the crunch of the walls of the house as they began to crack. By then I had panicked beyond reason; I had become part of my bed, feeling as if I had been welded to the frame. What terrified me further was that I knew that if the shaking continued for a few seconds more, the house would cave in on us.

Unexpectedly, the beam of a flashlight stung my eyes. Beyond the source I recognized the tortoiselike silhouette of Dr. López. Moving as quickly as he could, he helped my mother stand on her feet and led her through the door. Then, with surprising strength, he scooped me up and carried me out of the room. As soon as we were past the doorway, the bedroom wall collapsed, crushing my bed. We waited in the small courtyard, clinging to each other until the shaking stopped.

Then Dr. López said, "Sofía, let's get out of the house before the aftershock comes." We rushed out of the building. Once outside, I cried in relief when I recognized my mother and doña Natalia, safe and anxiously waiting for us. And then we felt the aftershock. After a couple of seconds, the entire section of the house where everyone slept buckled in and crumbled with the sound of a million bones being ground to dust.

When los temblores at last ended, we sat on the sidewalk and waited for daybreak. It was the most dreadful night of my life. From where our house once stood, near Tiscapa and the presidential palace, on a hill overlooking Managua, we wept at the sight of entire neighborhoods of the capital going up in flames, the smoke rising toward the heavens like funeral pyres. Throughout the night we heard the cries and moans of people trapped in the rubble, as well as the wails of those who had lost loved ones. Ten thousand Managuans never witnessed the sunrise. At dawn, I said a prayer of thanks to el Señor and to la Inmaculada Concepción for sparing us that night—a night that marked several generations forever.

The next morning, somehow, amid all the death, destruction, and chaos, Dr. López found a truck to hire. We rescued the few possessions we could pull from the house and left for Granada. We moved in with doña Natalia's sisters: two spinsters and a widow. Once Dr. López got us there safely, he rushed back to Managua to report for duty. When at last he returned, three days later, his gaunt, shattered appearance shocked me. Witnessing a suffering that nearly surpassed human capacity had come close to breaking this caring man.

"I've never seen so much death, so much misery, so much devastation," he said as he let out one long, exhausted sigh. He went into his new room without pausing to inspect it, fell on the bed, and slept for twenty-four hours straight.

My mother and I remained in Granada for six months. Although doña Natalia's sisters lived in a huge colonial home—where they claimed the ghosts of their Spanish ancestors roamed during the night—so many relatives had also moved in, refugees from el terremoto, that we were all living far too closely together. Doña Natalia and Dr. López, as always, were kind to us, but other members of the family were unbearably bossy. They ordered my mother and me around as if we were their slaves. Doña Teresita was the worst of the lot. She was married to this nice man, don Nicolás, a distant nephew of doña Natalia, who had a roving eye for women. Doña Teresita relished treating us as if we had been created to fulfill her every whim. The irony was, as my mother and I learned, that doña Teresita's mother had been a cook and her father a carriage driver at a local school. Because of this, no one could understand from whom doña Teresita had inherited such pretentiousness. You'd think that she, of all people, would have been more sympathetic toward us.

My mother and I, then, fed up with all that rudeness crammed into one house, returned to Managua. With the money Dr. López gave my mother as a farewell present—"For all your years of loyal service," he said—we bought a small lot in one of the many barrios that were springing up on the outskirts of what once was Managua. With Colonel López's help—his military rank always got things done quickly—the shell of a prefabricated house, part of the foreign assistance pouring into the country after the earthquake, was up and ready to be our new home within a week. It wasn't much of a house, granted, but at least it was ours.

My mother had decided never again to work as a maid. Instead, she began to take in laundry, washing and ironing six days a week, from sunup till sundown. I offered to help, but she insisted that I continue attending school and getting good grades. "It's the only way you'll escape being poor, Sofía," she said, while her prematurely wrinkled hands wrung a bed sheet. I did my best to please her, putting in long hours of study because I wanted to excel in every subject.

When I was seventeen, my mother agreed, as a favor to a neighbor who had gone to Bluefields to attend her father's funeral, to do the laundry, for two weeks only, in the home of Dr. Pedro Joaquín Chamorro. This was a gift from Providence. Here was my mother working in the home of el Gran Hombre of Nicaraguan journalism. I asked her to speak to him on my behalf, to tell him about my dream of becoming a reporter.

"¡No!" she replied.

"Por favor, Mamá. Por favorcito," I begged.

"¡No!" she said again, this time more firmly.

"Then let me go there with you so I can speak to Dr. Chamorro myself."

"You are not to disturb Dr. Chamorro. Ever. Do you understand, Señorita? He already has enough on his mind, and we're in no position to ask him for anything."

I answered yes. Very meekly. But I had already decided to disobey her and deal with the consequences later.

Early the next morning, I flagged down a taxi and followed

my mother's bus all the way across town to Dr. Chamorro's house.
I waited across the street for him to leave for work. When I saw
Dr. Chamorro come out of his house and get into his car, I rushed
to meet him. The driver's side window was down, and he was
about to turn the key in the ignition. He stopped when he saw that
I wanted to talk to him.

"¿Sí?"

I had to struggle to control my nervousness. It was the first
time that I was face to face with someone known to every single
Nicaraguan. "Dr. Chamorro, I've always dreamed of being a jour-
nalist," I started. I know I stammered through the rest because I
caught him smiling a couple of times at my blunders. "I really
admire *La Prensa*. I work hard in school and I always receive the
award for being the best student in my class. The problem is that I
live alone with my mother, and we're very poor. Would you please
help me?"

He looked at me thoughtfully and then turned his head,
facing forward and staring off to who knows where, a faraway
expression on his face. Then he looked at me again, smiled, and
said, "Bring me your next report card. If it's true that you're the
best student, I will pay for you to study journalism." He smiled
again, rolled up the window, turned the ignition key, pulled out of
the driveway, and drove off.

I did as Dr. Chamorro asked. And he kept his word. He took
an interest in my education and before long I was working at *La
Prensa,* earning little but learning as much as I could about the
trade. Yes, I made the most of my apprenticeship. After Dr.
Chamorro saw my dedication, he began assigning small, unimpor-
tant stories to me such as the vampire invasion that plagued
Granada, or the story of the boy from Ticuantepe who was going to

try to get into the *Book of Records* by shoving twenty peanuts, out of their shells, of course, up his right nostril, or the story of the girl from Nagarote who memorized seventeen of Rubén Darío's poems—backwards. Although these assignments were beneath the dignity of a serious reporter, I was on top of the world. Within a couple of years, Dr. Chamorro began to give me more challenging, complex stories.

And then, on January 10, 1978, just as we were getting to know each other well, my mentor, Dr. Pedro Joaquín Chamorro, was assassinated.

His murder shook the entire nation, almost as badly as the earthquake. My boss had been a symbol of resistance after a lifetime of bravely confronting dictators. His death made him a martyr and a saint, in spite of his shortcomings. Everyone blamed Somoza for Dr. Chamorro's death, and while covering the funeral, as part of a team from *La Prensa,* I could see that Nicaragua was on the verge of erupting.

Sí—las cosas se pusieron calientes. Dr. Chamorro's death lit the powder keg we had been sitting on after nearly half a century of one family ruling over us with an iron hand. During the Sandinistas' final offensive, I reported on the battles taking place in the eastern barrios of Managua. After that experience I understood how Dr. López felt seeing all that death and destruction during the earthquake. But this was worse: a civil war where brother killed brother—and sister. Although I missed Dr. López terribly, I thought it was fortunate that he had died from a heart attack three years earlier. God had spared him from yet another round of our people's suffering.

During la Insurrección, being a reporter became a dangerous occupation. I was young and naive; I didn't know any better, like

Dr. López when he had fought in the war against Sandino. If offered the same assignment today, I'd refuse. Flat out. Back then I came close to being killed—several times. For instance, I was only a block and a half away when la Guardia captured and executed that American television reporter, Bill Stewart. The poor man didn't speak Spanish; he couldn't even try to talk his way out of it. He was innocent, a member of the profession just doing his job. If something good came out of that tragedy it was that his crew filmed the entire thing and people in los Estados Unidos got to see our suffering on television, incarnated in the martyrdom of one of their own. The war in Nicaragua, overnight, became real over there, and Somoza swiftly lost Washington's backing.

On another occasion, I was trapped in el barrio El Dorado while it was being bombed. I barely escaped alive from that one. Planes from Somoza's air force indiscriminately dropped barrels loaded with five hundred pounds of dynamite on the people below. Seeing the mangled corpses of innocent civilians, entire families blown to bits beyond recognition, was what made me a fervent Sandinista.

All of Nicaragua got together on July 19, 1979, in la Plaza de la Revolución—renamed thus on the crest of the rebels' victory—to celebrate the fall of nearly fifty years of Somoza rule. Although journalistic standards dictated that I take no sides, I proudly wore a red and black bandanna around my neck. The early days of la Revolución were heady, our prospects for the future exhilarating. Even though, in comparison to the terremoto, we had five times the number of dead to bury, we were a new nation, brimming with hope and optimism. Out of the rubble we would create a utopia. And the entire world was behind us. Or so we thought.

Before long the cracks in the wall began to appear, and that's talking only about what was happening within our borders. Even our journalistic family began to come apart. Half of Dr. Chamorro's children were critical of the Sandinistas, and they controlled *La Prensa*. The others were staunch supporters of la Revolución, and they left to work for the new government's newspaper, *La Barricada*. When asked if I planned to stay or join the new venture, I didn't hesitate one instant. I thought the Sandinistas had all the answers to our nation's problems, and I wanted to be a part of the solution. I wanted to help lead our people to la Tierra Prometida, the Promised Land.

The early days of *La Barricada* were the most exciting of my life. Starting a newspaper from scratch was quite a learning experience. Not only did we represent the voice of the people, but we educated them as well.

"The press can inform, but it can also form," don Ernesto, my new boss, would tell me. "We are under a moral obligation to teach Nicaraguans to think differently, to break the paradigms imposed on us by a colonial system, to work toward an egalitarian society: that's our sacred mission," he would conclude. And those of us who left *La Prensa* and joined his staff began working with unbridled passion to transform Nicaraguan society.

But even then I could see storm clouds blowing in from the north. Rumors abounded that former members of la Guardia Nacional were in Honduras, and that with the help of the CIA they intended to put a stop to la Revolución. Shortly afterward, we were informed that because of this threat, members of el Ministerio del Interior would be checking our articles before they went to print. El Ministro argued that now, more than ever, it was the duty of the press to teach Nicaraguans what to think, to put the right ideas into their heads.

In the beginning, I had no problem with el Ministerio's input. I did, after all, want what was in the nation's best interest. But as of late, I've seen a few things that concern me. For one, the government is becoming rather heavy-handed with dissenters. People labeled as contrarevolucionarios are terrorized by state-sponsored mobs, turbas: bullies that wield clubs, throw rocks, and shout insults. Or worse, rumors are circulating that our prison cells are filling up. And the surprising thing is that in spite of this, Nicaraguans are becoming more outspoken against the Sandinistas. Take my mother, for instance.

"If I wanted to live in a communist country, I'd move to Cuba," she says to anyone who will listen. "I'm a faithful Catholic. I've raised my daughter to be a Catholic as well. And I refuse to live among atheists."

There are also the shortages, which my mother sees as a sign that la Revolución is failing. "I can't buy soap for my laundry business," she complains, "and soon the people who hire me will be going into exile. I can feel it. Who am I going to work for then?"

Also, during the earliest days of la Revolución, I had something more important to worry about. For weeks my mother had not seemed well. She had lost weight and looked ashen. At first I thought it had to do with the trauma of the civil war. Once an energetic woman, my mother began to tire easily. After a lot of pestering on my part, she finally agreed to visit a doctor. He found a lump on her left breast, and a biopsy showed that it was cancerous.

You know what those Sandinistas my mother hated so much did? They put her on a plane to Cuba. She came back delighted with the island's hospitals, its doctors, and the treatment. She now loves the Cuban people. Yet to this day she remains adamant about not wanting to live in a communist country.

I was thrilled to have her back. But although she seemed

healthy, she didn't return whole: her breast had been removed. What's worse, the Cuban doctors couldn't guarantee that the cancer wouldn't return. That is why I was secretly thankful when don Ernesto asked me to investigate the apparition of la Virgen, in Cuapa. Although I still support la Revolución, I could never renounce my faith. My mother's right about that. I could never become one of those militant, atheistic Marxists. Because of my mother, I grew up devoted to Nuestra Madre. La Virgen loves me, she protects me, and she helps me when I'm in trouble. I know I'm not supposed to say this, because the nuns in grade school told me that my belief was heretical, but María, la Madre de Jesús, is, in my eyes, a goddess. She is much more accessible than her Son; or her husband, for that matter, whoever that may be. And while I'm being honest, I think that she's just as powerful as either one of them. So while I was on this assignment, I intended to petition her to intercede for my mother's health. I need this miracle.

By the time I arrived in Cuapa it was midmorning. I stopped at the first pulpería I saw as I drove into el pueblo, got out of the car, stretched my legs a bit, and went inside. "Do you know where I can find Bernardo Martínez, the man to whom la Virgen has appeared?" I asked the storeowner.

A customer, an old woman, short in stature, with wild white hair and inquisitive eyes, replied, "Bernardo goes to the site every morning at eleven o'clock to talk about the apparitions. If you want to see him you should go there." The old woman stared at me intently, making me a little uncomfortable, until she finally asked, "Are you a believer?"

I didn't quite understand the question, so I answered, "I'm a reporter from *La Barricada*. I'm here to write a story about the apparition."

"Oh, good," she replied, her interest in me growing. "Yesterday un muchacho from *La Prensa* was here asking questions as well." That was terrible news. I hate being a day behind our biggest rivals on any story.

"Where's the apparition site?" I asked.

"I'll take you there myself," the old woman volunteered.

I invited her into the car. Once we were on our way she introduced herself as doña Tula. We returned along the road I had taken into Cuapa until we came to a turnoff that she called el camino viejo a Juigalpa. Precisely at the turnoff, she pointed to a humble adobe house that stood all alone, without any neighbors in sight.

"That's where Bernardo lives," she said.

I stopped there for a few moments, took a couple pictures, and then we went on. Along the way, doña Tula told stories about Bernardo. "You know," she said, "when the statue of Nuestra Señora illuminated, the people from Juigalpa came here trying to get her back. Fortunately, Bernardo had saved the receipt from when we bought the image. They returned empty-handed. La Inmaculada Concepción is ours."

The old woman told other stories, but there really wasn't much to them. The most interesting thing I learned was that he had more preparation than your average campesino, since he was a tailor. But as far as I could tell, up to the time of la Virgen's apparition his life had been rather uninteresting. Then doña Tula shared with me what other people in town were saying about Bernardo, but that information sounded like malicious gossip. As a result, I tuned her out.

Shortly after we crossed a little stream that doña Tula insisted was a river, I spotted a gathering of people—about forty persons—on a pasture to the left of the road. Several cars were parked to the right, next to the barbed wire fence.

"Is this the place?" I asked.

"Yes," doña Tula answered. "I don't see Bernardo out there, but he should be here soon."

"Are most of these people from Cuapa?"

"Santos cielos, no. Everyone who lives around here knows the story. And, really, we can talk to Bernardo anytime we want. No, now people are coming from all over the country to hear about the apparition. On Sundays, there are usually hundreds."

I parked the car and we got out. I was taking a few photographs when, through my telephoto lens, I recognized the Japanese ambassador. There were a few other Japanese with him. I walked over to where they were gathered, approached the ambassador, identified myself, and requested permission to ask a few questions. Graciously, he acceded, and we conversed about the apparition for several minutes.

As the interview was winding down, the ambassador, with a serene smile, said, "Go sit somewhere, by yourself. Experience the peace. This is, I believe, a sacred place." He nodded, glanced around the green hills, and took a deep breath.

I thanked him and followed his suggestion. I found a shady spot under a tree, sat down, and began to empty my mind of worries. Before long, I knew exactly what the ambassador meant: a sense of contentment, of peace, came over me. And then, without thinking, I began to pray for my mother, for myself, and for my country. Somehow, I had the certainty that my prayers were being heard. As I was finishing, the gathering stirred excitedly. Bernardo Martínez had arrived.

He didn't look at all the way I had imagined him: a short, stooped, toothless old campesino. If Bernardo was of peasant stock, it really didn't show. For one, he was taller than most Nicaraguan men. Although I could partly see his indio ancestry, the European side of his mestizaje stood out, like with me. His hair was unruly and beginning to turn white, which gave him an air of distinction. No, Bernardo wasn't your common campesino. He had a charisma you normally don't find in people from tierra adentro.

The pilgrims quickly gathered around him. He greeted and shook each person's hand. As he did this, doña Tula came to stand next to me. "Bernardo has lost a lot of weight. We're very worried about his health," she whispered in my ear.

I tried to imagine, then, what he would look like with a few added pounds. I concluded that, if anything, with a fuller face he would be handsomer. When I thought about it, he did look rather undernourished, depleted, tired, as if for quite some time he had been carrying a big weight on his shoulders. His appearance reminded me of my mother's when she was ill.

After the seer had welcomed everyone, we gathered around him, and he began to speak. As he narrated la Virgen's first appearance a few of the women gasped. At one point, when Bernardo mentioned that Nuestra Señora looked to be about eighteen, an old woman fainted. He stopped talking until she had been revived and we were sure that she would fully recover.

When Bernardo finished his story, he asked everyone to join him in praying the rosary. The Japanese, although they didn't pray with us, respectfully remained with their heads bowed throughout. As for myself, I prayed with greater intensity than ever before in my life.

After we finished praying, people began to say farewell to Bernardo. It was then that the spectacle started. I'll always be at a loss for words to describe what took place that day. It all began when a woman shouted, "Look up at the sun!" I did. The usually ardent globe appeared to be wrapped in a transparent, gauzy veil that I could stare at easily. The orb then began to spin on itself, clockwise, first slowly and gradually increasing its pace until the motion became a continuous mad whirl. A single clamor rose from the crowd. Stunned, we witnessed a second sun detach itself from the original, as if the star had given birth. The replica moved playfully above our heads: an enormous dull silver ball bouncing, dancing in slow motion. The second sun then began whirling and, abruptly, broke free from the heavens, plunging toward the earth, on course to crush us with its huge fiery weight. We gasped as the sphere dove in on us, coming closer and closer, and just as we were about to crouch, fearing the worst, the second sun began to rise, slowly ascending until it returned to its normal position, becoming again a single sun. Immediately after the stars came together, I had to shield my eyes from the light—the protective veil had disappeared.

I glanced around and saw that most people were on their knees. Some were making the sign of the cross and beginning to pray the rosary again. I walked up the slight hill to where the Japanese ambassador stood, looking over the crowd with folded arms, as if he had been presiding over the event.

"Señor Embajador, ¿vio usted eso?" I asked.

"Yes, I did see it. Definitely. Magnífico, ¿no?" he said, smiling beatifically.

I then went to talk to Bernardo. After introducing myself, I requested an interview. He smiled and said, "Yes, of course. I can see that you're a believer."

Although perplexed by his comment, and perhaps because I was still stunned by what I'd seen, I didn't ask him to explain. I assumed this was the way cuapeños greeted other Catholics. I pulled a notebook out of my bag and began asking questions. I didn't find

Bernardo to be un loco. On the contrary, he seemed quite normal: balanced and sincere. And I didn't find that he was a simpleminded campesino either. He was, if anything, quite a storyteller, vividly narrating what had happened to him. To be honest, I found him a little self-centered. He seemed to enjoy having an audience. I could see how those qualities may lead others to doubt him, but after what I had experienced that day, I didn't.

Before returning to Managua, I ate lunch at doña Queta's and then bought a large bag of rosquillas from doña Octavia, both on the recommendation of doña Tula. When I reached the capital I was hot and exhausted, but I wanted to write the story while the details were still fresh in my mind. Instead of going back to the office I drove straight home, showered, changed clothes, and sat down in front of my typewriter.

LA VIRGEN APPEARS IN CUAPA

By Sofía Velázquez

Bernardo Martínez, a tailor, says: "I still find myself asking, 'Why me?'"

CUAPA, CHONTALES. On May 8 of this year, in a pasture beyond the nearly dried-up Río de Cuapa, along the old road to Juigalpa, la Virgen María allegedly appeared to Bernardo Martínez, a forty-eight-year-old tailor who lives a kilometer west of town. Since childhood, Bernardo has been devoted to la Virgen. In addition to being a tailor, he's been Cuapa's sacristán for many years.

During the afternoon of May 8, after Bernardo had finished taking a peaceful nap in the shade of a mango tree, la Virgen appeared to him and asked that he share her message with the world. According to Bernardo, she asks us to pray the rosary every day in family, to work for peace, to avoid the path of violence, and to forgive one another.

Already many people have begun making pilgrimages to the apparition site. An average of forty people travel each day to Cuapa to listen to Bernardo's story, which he tells at eleven o'clock every morning in the pasture where la Virgen appeared.

Among those who have visited the site is el Señor Kohei Tomokiyo, Japan's ambassador to Nicaragua. "Although I am a Shintoist Buddhist, and not a Christian, I believe this place is sacred, holy. During this visit I experienced something that I can only describe as being in communion with the divine. I also heard a voice tell me to work for peace in Nicaragua. That is what I intend to do," said Ambassador Tomokiyo.

Since the first apparition, la Virgen has appeared to Bernardo another four times. Her message is constant, unwavering: prayer, peace, and forgiveness. She has also stated that if her message is not heeded, Nicaragua will enter a period of suffering unlike any the country has experienced in its history. Bernardo implores us all to listen and to act as la Virgen asks.

The Office of the Archbishop has initiated an investigation into the apparition. So far, a spokesman for the Bishop of Chontales confirms that investigators have found the message from Cuapa to be profoundly biblical, and that it agrees perfectly with the teachings of the Catholic Church.

After I had finished composing the article, I read it to my mother. She listened attentively. Afterward, she asked many questions about my trip to Cuapa, about Bernardo, about what he had said, and about what I had seen. She wanted to hear every single detail about la Virgen's appearance and about my visit. Once she had finished, she remained silent, as if meditating. After a long pause, she said, "Sofía, do you believe Nuestra Señora appeared there?"

Although I was caught off guard by my mother wanting to know what I thought, without hesitation I answered, "Yes, I do."

She got up from her rocking chair, went directly to the statue of la Virgen that's in our living room, and lit a second candle before her. My mother then went into her bedroom and returned with her rosary. She placed a chair before la Virgen, sat down, and began to pray.

"May I join you?" I asked. The question surprised her. We had not prayed the rosary together since we had lived with Dr. López and doña Natalia. My mother nodded, smiling gratefully. I placed a chair next to hers, and together we made the sign of the cross.

The next morning I was the first reporter at work. As soon as don Ernesto arrived, I went to his office and gave him the article. He read it, smiled, and said, "Good." Taking off his reading glasses, he looked directly at me and asked, "Do you think this Bernardo fellow is crazy?"

"He seems quite normal, actually." While answering don Ernesto's question, I tried not to show my real feelings. "He sincerely believes that la Virgen appeared and spoke to him." The editor nodded, swirled his chair around, put his feet on his desk, and then placed his hands behind his head. Without saying another word, he sat there, staring out of the window. I went back to my desk to begin working on my next story.

Around midmorning, don Ernesto called me into his office. With him was the press officer from el Ministerio del Interior. He was a short man with slumped shoulders, dressed in an olive-green uniform. To me he looked like a wicked gnome. The editor motioned for me to close the door.

"Compañera Velázquez," said el duende, "we think that your article is too sympathetic to the alleged apparition. What you wrote could be—how shall I say it?—counterproductive to the goals and objectives of la Revolución."

His comment stunned me. "I don't understand," was all I could stammer. "I'm just reporting the truth. I don't make an assertion one way or another about whether she appeared there, or not. Excuse me, but I don't see anything in that article that endangers la Revolución."

The man from el Ministerio del Interior stared at me without saying a word. What bothered me most was that he never blinked and his beady eyes were fixed on my breasts. When he finally spoke, he did so calmly, paternalistically, as if he were speaking to a young child. "What you don't seem to understand, compañera Velázquez, is that our government is beginning to enter—how shall we call it?— a very delicate phase in its relationship with the Catholic Church. The Church is in a position to make things—shall we say?—complicated. If people begin to make pilgrimages to Cuapa because they believe la Virgen has appeared there, well, that will just get everyone riled up about nothing. The National Directorate doesn't want that. What's more, los comandantes have reason to believe that the Church, working with the CIA, has contrived this . . . hmm . . . fairytale. We are asking that you write an article discrediting Bernardo Martínez's story. Do you understand me now?"

I swear that as the gnome was speaking his ears grew bigger and bigger. I looked at my boss, expecting him to defend my right to report the truth. But he just stared out the window—a sad, distracted expression on his face.

"Yes, I understand," I said, resigned to having no other choice.

El duende nodded and left. But I still didn't understand why my article would create a problem. I didn't understand it at all. What I did know was that for the first time el Ministerio's interference had infuriated me. I felt that my integrity, my obligation to tell the truth, was being compromised, far beyond what I was prepared to accept. But Nicaragua had become a battleground in the cold war. Because of this anything I would say or do contrary to el Ministerio's "suggestion" would make my loyalty to la Revolución and to the Sandinistas suspect.

"Do you have any ideas about how I should rewrite the

article?" I asked don Ernesto. He leaned forward, picked the last prized Marlboro from the pack that lay on his desk (American cigarettes having become a revered commodity), lit it, and blew out the match. He took a long, deep drag that channeled the nicotine to every nook and cranny in his lungs, and exhaled slowly, as if he were trying to expel demons the olive-green gnome had left behind.

"You must have heard something while you were in Cuapa that would help you write a story along the lines of an 'alternate truth.' Am I right?"

I thought about it for a moment. Some of the things doña Tula had said started to come to mind, but everything had been so gossipy, so bizarre, that at the time I had largely ignored her. Still, I recalled bits and pieces of the conversation—anecdotes and incidents that in my memory were now shrouded in a misty light blue haze—that I might be able to turn into a story. I thought, already anticipating my repentance, if I wrote these things, I would be betraying Nuestra Señora. What would be my penance to earn her forgiveness?

"Yes, I think so," I answered.

"Good," don Ernesto said. "Have your article on my desk before the end of the day. *La Prensa* already beat us to the punch. You have to counter what they've printed." He handed me a folded copy of our rival's paper.

I went to my desk and read the article. The reporter for *La Prensa* had treated the news of the apparition with great reverence, far more than I had. I even thought his report was somewhat extreme, suggesting that Nuestra Señora had come to save Nicaragua from socialism. I saw straight through that reporter's tactics. Really, there has to be some objectivity in our profession.

I scribbled down a few notes, and, after recalling some of the things doña Tula had mentioned, I produced the following article:

LA VIRGEN APPEARS IN A CUAPA LIGHTBULB

By Sofía Velázquez

Bernardo Martínez, a campesino who neighbors say smokes marijuana, asks: "Why is this happening to me?"

CUAPA, CHONTALES. On the afternoon of May 8 of this year, Bernardo Martínez, a forty-eight-year-old campesino from Cuapa, saw la Virgen María appear inside a lightbulb. At least one other person, who has requested anonymity, also admits to having seen the image of la Virgen inside the bulb, while lit.

"I haven't been the only one. Don Casimiro the butcher, his son Néstor, doña Octavia, don Joaquín, and others saw her as well. I saw la Virgen's image as clearly as I'm seeing you right now," the unnamed source stated.

Bernardo Martínez, in addition to farming, cleans the church. Cuapeños describe him as being obsessed, ever since childhood, with la Virgen. They also affirm that Bernardo's grandmother used to say that he was always saying nothing but disparates. Several of Cuapa's youth believe that Bernardo smokes marijuana, and that's why he still hasn't stopped saying nonsense.

"His lifelong obsession with la Virgen has now led others to believe that they are seeing her as well," explains the anonymous source. "Why, when he was a little boy he used to tell everyone that he was going to marry her. Can you believe that?"

Bernardo also claims that la Virgen has spoken to him. Her message is clear, he says: pray the rosary every day, be kind to one another, be forgiving, and devote yourselves without questions to making Nicaragua a socialist country the world can look to with pride.

In its investigation, the Catholic Church found nothing objectionable in the message that la Virgen relayed to the nearly illiterate campesino. Nevertheless, since the Vatican hasn't officially approved the apparition, pilgrimages to the site are discouraged.

As soon as I finished writing the article I rushed it to don Ernesto. He thanked me for my promptness. Within thirty minutes he called to inform me that the gnome from el Ministerio del Interior was very pleased with my work. El duende had also commended my solidarity with la Revolución.

I asked don Ernesto for the rest of the day off.

"Go ahead, Sofía. You've earned it."

I drove straight home, jumped in the shower, put on fresh clothes, and began rummaging through some papers we had stacked in the living room. I was still doing this when my mother returned from el Mercado Oriental.

"What are you looking for, hijita?" she asked.

"Doña Natalia's latest letter."

"I put that away in my room. Let me get it for you."

Doña Natalia had been among the first Nicaraguans to leave the country after the Sandinistas came to power. She had moved to Houston, Texas, to live with her daughter and son-in-law. They've had a happy reconciliation. Doña Natalia's son-in-law had opened an electronics repair shop in the late 1970s and, according to her letter, was doing well. But she was now old and frail, and her letter invited my mother to move to Houston because our former patrona could use her company, as well as her help.

My mother and I, of course, had declined, telling her that, come what may, we planned on staying in Nicaragua. And that seemed easy because I had a position of privilege with *La Barricada*. But after what happened today, I wonder if I really want to stay here. Can I remain somewhere where I'm forced to live a life contrary to my beliefs? Can I continue working as a reporter when I'm forced to distort the truth?

Is exile a form of penance?

chapter six

ECCLESIAE
(The Church)

March 1981

Father Damian MacManus

IN THE EYES of Father Damian Innocent MacManus, if life wasn't lived as a crusade, it wasn't worth living at all. That his campaigns were more political than religious didn't matter. As long as Father MacManus was engaged in battling the enemies of the One True Church, the Church that Christ himself had bequeathed to Saint Peter, he was fulfilled. Nothing made him happier than defending the Holy Apostolic Cause of Rome and the pope. Nothing. The problem for Father Damian Innocent MacManus was that he had been born four centuries too late, for he would have made an excellent inquisitor.

His readiness to obey orders unquestioningly made him the Company's most valuable special envoy in Latin America. The priest carried out his assignments with fanatical single-mindedness and sometimes with ruthless abandon, but Father MacManus's superiors could always count on his getting the job done. And now that the Church was facing its gravest threat ever in the region, he was executing his orders with added diligence, as well as with divine pleasure.

Damian Innocent MacManus was born in Boston, the year before the United States entered the Second World War. His father was a policeman, and his mother—a saint, in his eyes—was a mystic housewife who embraced angels, fought off demons, and had daily conversations with the Virgin Mary. Damian's father believed in raising children with sternness. He'd make the boy sit on the window ledge of their fifth-floor apartment for one hour, regardless of the weather, whenever he broke one of a thousand house rules. That's why Damian, to this day, was terrified of heights. But he had become a believer in harsh discipline as well, for it made a God-fearing man out of him.

Damian Innocent MacManus was an only child. He had survived his twin brother, who died at age one. The death so anguished his parents that it left his father embittered and his mother barren. The tragedy, however, opened her eyes to her numinous gifts.

While growing up, Damian felt trapped between his father's unforgiving nature and his mother's mystical voyages. From his father he learned obedience and respect for authority. The police officer always demanded immediate and silent compliance with his commands. From his mother he learned piety. Every day the boy accompanied her to St. Cosmas for mass, and later they'd pray the rosary. The child's early devoutness pleased her immensely.

But once, when Damian was six years old, his mother emerged howling from a mystical rapture because the Virgin had said, *I am sorry to tell you this, but your son will always be an outcast.* That's when Damian's mother decided that if he was to be scorned on this earth, it might as well be as one of Jesus's most valiant soldiers. She vowed to make it the boy's mission in life to see that Catholics comply faithfully with the teachings of the Vatican and to lead those who stray away from the Church's doctrines back to the bosom of Our Lord.

Although Damian was well behaved in school, his performance was quite unremarkable. He dreaded taking home his report card because his father would fly into a rage over his grades, which were average, and then send him out on the ledge for two hours. His mother also disciplined the boy by making him sit in a steaming bubble bath with her and forcing him to remove the calluses from her feet with a pumice stone, then he would have to massage them until his fleshy little arms cramped. This punishment usually went on for weeks at a time, until she felt that he had done enough penance. When Damian entered the third grade, his father visited St. Cosmas School to ask why his son's performance was so mediocre.

"Damian is a good boy," the nun who taught third grade said, smiling as she tried to sound encouraging. "He doesn't give us any trouble and he's very, very obedient. We know that Damian tries his hardest, but he seems to have . . . well . . . a warped imagination. For instance, he believes that God has put him on earth for a holy purpose, but says that he can't reveal it to us. Plus, he has difficulty making the connections between different subjects. He sees everything in black and white. The best way I can put it is that I've never seen a mind so turned in on itself. He can be very inflexible. But, Officer MacManus, Damian's very well behaved. He's a wonderful lad."

The father didn't give a damn whether the boy was a good lad or not. He wanted to know why Damian brought home such lackluster grades when at home they made him study three hours every day. He now believed that the boy only pretended to study. As punishment, he would add another hour to the regimen.

"Well, Sister," the father said, glancing coldly at the boy, "with grades like these he'll never amount to much. Am I right? He'll probably end up being an elevator operator in some department store, taking shoppers to the bargain basement."

What Damian's father never suspected was how determined, stubborn, and cunning his son could be in the pursuit of personal goals that, according to his mother, were in harmony with God's plan for him. What he lacked in flexibility, he made up in persistence. His main objective: to fulfill his mother's greatest wish. Damian Innocent MacManus would, at any cost, become a priest.

Although Damian's grades were average when he graduated from St. Cosmas, his dogged, yet polite, lobbying for admission convinced the director of the Theological Institute in Brighton to accept him. The recommendation of the nuns helped. On the form, the mother superior wrote: *Although Damian's scholastic work is less than impressive, he is the best-behaved student in the history of our school. He is exceedingly obedient and pious—key ingredients for the priesthood. Besides, since childhood, there has been nothing else that he has ever wanted to be. To become a priest, it appears, is his destiny.*

At the same time Damian attended the Theological Institute, he enrolled in the college across the street where he studied Spanish, the language of Spain, the nation he admired for being the most devoutly Roman Catholic on earth. Even though Damian's performance in the seminary was satisfactory, he bewildered his Spanish professors. They admired how he gobbled up grammar, memorizing every single rule. Still, he never did master the subjunctive. ("How can a tense be determined by emotions and perceptions? That's absurd," he'd say.) But they gave up on Damian ever becoming a successful student of literature because his interpretations of the readings were always the same.

He had been so moved by a poem by the Spanish mystic poet San Juan de la Cruz—about a profound religious experience described as a clandestine meeting between lovers—that he interpreted everything he read as if it were that poem. Everything. Other poems, essays, short stories, plays, and novels were all about the human soul rejoicing upon meeting Jesus. To arrive at his standard elucidation, Damian turned the simplest of metaphors into highly complex literary devices. His skewed imagination stretched the meanings of the works he read beyond his professors' belief and patience. Still, defying his father's dire prediction, Damian graduated from both college and the seminary.

Once ordained, Damian was assigned to a parish in an impoverished black neighborhood of Boston. At first, as would always be the case with Father Damian, he charmed everyone around him, for he could appear to be most likable. But after a couple of meetings the crusader would kick into gear, and he'd begin to shame his parishioners into behaving like "faithful" Catholics.

It didn't help matters that Father Damian was physically intimidating as well. He was very tall and broad-shouldered—a scaled-down giant, in fact. Since he had never exercised in his life, his rather grotesque flabbiness saddened him when he stood before the full-length mirror prior to his daily steaming bubble bath. But his ever-present black cassock, as well as the biretta he always wore on his head, concealed his amorphousness.

Young children, especially, after the charm faded, became terrified of his presence. As a result, the parish's catechism classes
dwindled from about three dozen to only a handful. And it did not
take long before Father Damian's highly judgmental nature began to
offend his adult parishioners. His need to intimidate others into following his highly conservative brand of Catholicism, coupled with
some of his other pastoral practices, alarmed them. But the recur-
rent yet unsubstantiated accusations of racism were what ultimately
forced the archbishop to transfer Father Damian to another parish.
And the same thing happened all over again. And then again.

The problem of Father Damian MacManus greatly distressed
His Grace. But just as the archbishop had begun to run out of hope,
Providence intervened. On a freezing January morning, His Grace
received a secretive telephone call from Washington. The person
on the other end of the line introduced himself as Victor Phillips,
chief of special operations for the Central Intelligence Agency,
Latin American Division.

"Your Grace, a retired agent, who's a member of Father
MacManus's parish, informed me that his unique outlook on life
would fit in perfectly with the joint efforts of the Catholic Church
and the Company in Latin America.

"Your Grace," agent Phillips continued, "you'll be receiving a
request from the archbishop of Santiago, Chile, asking that Father
Damian be assigned there. The Company would consider it a
great service to your country if you agreed to the transfer." The
archbishop found Victor's harsh, gravelly voice mesmerizing. Of·
course, he consented to the request, and gratefully so, since he had
run out of options about what to do with the priest.

A year after Padre Damián arrived in Chile, the socialist

government of Salvador Allende crumbled under a hail of bullets and cannon fire. Many of those imprisoned during the massive sweep of Allende sympathizers, once released, spoke of a tall, broad-shouldered gringo priest, dressed in a black cassock and wearing a biretta, who'd stroll up and down the hallways, between packed jail cells, brandishing his aspergillum like a medieval mace as he sprinkled holy water on the captives.

"Renounce the demons of communism and accept the teachings of the Holy Roman Catholic Church, Christ's One True Church, as your road to salvation," the priest would extol in a booming voice during his ministerial visits. Because his appearances always coincided with the start of another round of tortures—from which many prisoners never returned—they took to calling him el Sacerdote de la Muerte.

Once the Chilean military government had completely restored order, Padre Damián vanished. Soon after, reports began to surface of a tall, broad-shouldered gringo priest living in Argentina, a spiritual warrior in that country's Dirty War. There, the priest promenaded up and down the prison hallways, aspergillum in hand, spewing terrifying religious exhortations. In those cells, the prisoners nicknamed him Pater Mort.

Padre Damián was now in Nicaragua, assigned to the archdiocese, and placed in charge of strategic planning. He lamented that the Company had waited this long to send him here. Things are out of hand, he thought. They were far worse than they had been in Chile or Argentina. In a letter, Padre Damián had written: *The situation in Nicaragua has reached a critical stage, Mother dearest. The enemies of the Holy Roman Catholic Church are seemingly in control.* The tall, broad-shouldered American priest placed part of the blame on the Church itself for the predicament.

Months back, during a Sunday sermon in Buenos Aires, Padre Damián had preached: "The spiritual legacy that the Church inherited from St. Peter has been forsaken and replaced by a lenient, perverted, and misguided form of humanism. God, and only he, is at the center of the universe, not man. And it is to his will, and the will of the pope—his holy representative on earth—that we should kneel in blissful submission. The Church's first mistake was to permit the Second Vatican Council to take place. Yes. That gathering of apostates made drastic, harmful changes that will take decades, nay, centuries of spiritual coercion to remedy. And only a few years later, the bishops of Latin America met in Medellín, Colombia. This gathering of heretics opened the very gates of hell, and out of Satan's mouth a nauseating vomit called liberation theology oozed forth. Believe me, that will be a worse curse on us than the plagues Almighty God cast upon the infidels of Egypt. This heresy is the work of the devil, I tell you," Padre Damián concluded, raising his voice to a shout while pounding his fist on the pulpit.

The devil's work. That's the only thing, according to this American priest, that could explain the crumbling of the solid, simple, uncomplicated Catholic values he had grown up with. That was when the world was in perfect order, making sense, and he wanted more than anything to restore it to that state. Nothing would stop him. As his mother had written in a letter: *My cherished son, a soldier of Christ and of the Holy Roman Catholic Church cannot despair while he's engaged in spiritual warfare. He must boldly move forward, with faith and righteousness as his allies.*

As Padre Damián saw matters, his mission in life was straightforward: to help the Holy Roman Catholic Church and its followers find their way back to orthodoxy. Nothing more, nothing less. People are more comfortable, he believed, in a world that's black and white. *Priests must never negotiate with those who question the doctrines of Christ's One True Church. We must not surrender to those who see shades of gray in the Church's doctrine,* he wrote in a letter to his beloved mother.

Although Padre Damián would deny it, that's why he kept a framed portrait of his personal hero, Tomás de Torquemada, on his nightstand. The American priest thought that history had given this Great Man a bad rap. Padre Damián had read everything written by and about the grand inquisitor of Spain, and these readings made him yearn for those days when the authority of the Holy Roman Catholic Church and the absolute truth were as one. As far as he could tell, both he and Torquemada were exactly alike: sincere, incorruptible Roman Catholics who scorned luxury, worked feverishly for the One True Church, and rejoiced in the opportunity to serve Christ by hounding heresy. The American priest was sure that God had guided the inquisitor's hand.

I know that, like my role model, Tomás de Torquemada, I'll never be canonized, Padre Damián had written in a letter to his mother, *but at least I'll be remembered as one of the most loyal servants in the Holy Army of the Vatican. After all, Mother dearest, someone has to do the grunt work.*

Indeed, in Nicaragua, the priest was prepared to give his life in the war against liberation theology, that satanic aberration that had found fertile ground in la Revolución Sandinista. It revolted him to see renegade priests and apostate nuns fly in from all over the world to participate in this sacrilegious uprising against the authority of the Holy See. Not since that renowned heretic, the accursed former Catholic priest who had nailed his theses on a church door in Wittenberg—whose name Padre Damián refused ever to let pass through his lips—did the One True Church of Our Lord and Savior Jesus Christ face such grave danger.

In a preliminary report to Victor Phillips, the Roman Catholic crusader wrote: *These intellectuals in the guise of priests and nuns know nothing about the One True Christian Faith: Catholicism. They lie to the people, telling them that it's possible to build a Marxist-Christian paradise on this earth. But faith means the acceptance of things as they are; accepting what God has disposed for you with humility and gratitude. That's the most important lesson I've learned in life, and now I feel that it's my sacred duty to teach it to others, regardless of the means.*

Yes, Padre Damián was on a holy crusade against Catholics throughout Latin America who nonchalantly traded the word of God for the collected speeches of Fidel. *Infidels, infidels, that's what they are!* Padre Damián wrote to his mother. *While celebrating mass they glorify the example of Gaspar García Laviana: a Spanish priest who, during the uprising against Somoza, died in battle after sacrilegiously giving up the cassock for a guerrilla uniform. Worst yet, Mother dearest, after the Sandinistas' triumph, the communists rewarded heretical priests with government posts.*

Seeing how bad things were now in Nicaragua, Padre Damián regretted that Victor hadn't sent him earlier, before the Sandinistas gained power. The American priest was sure he could have helped Somoza restore order, and thus saved the One True Faith.

"The one sign of hope," Padre Damián had said to Victor, "the one thing that gives the Holy Roman Catholic Church a chance to win the war against the apostates and the communists in this country is the archbishop's popularity. I'm impressed with the large crowds His Grace draws wherever he goes. However, Victor, the archbishop has no clue about how to use this power. But that's no longer a problem—I'm here to advise him."

Padre Damián, now in charge of strategic planning for the archdiocese of Nicaragua, was working on a line of attack that would help the Holy Roman Catholic Church assert the full weight of its history against the Sandinista infidels, when the chief of special operations for the CIA, Latin American Division, came to see him.

"Father Damian, ask the archbishop to appoint you to head the commission investigating the appearance of the Virgin Mary in Cuapa." Victor's voice reminded the priest of the sound of gravel being crushed.

"Are you sure, Victor? I'm about finished with a plan that would eliminate all the radical, terrorist priests. They're the reason you're losing Central America, you know." Since the CIA agent had not contacted Padre Damián for several weeks, the priest had been acting on his own, and enjoying his independence.

"Save your plan for later, Father. I've got a hunch that this thing going on in Cuapa can be put to good use. Look into the matter and send me a report as soon as possible."

For a moment, Padre Damián became angry with the CIA chief of special operations in Latin America. "Who in Heaven's name does this guy think he is?" the priest muttered to himself as he was dialing to make an appointment with the archbishop. "At times he can be just like my father. He bosses me around without ever caring about what I think or feel. And Victor is so pathetic. Doesn't he see how ridiculous his secret agent persona appears to others? The man takes himself way too seriously. Victor Phillips: alias Victor Murphy; alias Victor Forsythe; alias Victor Sullivan;

alias Victor Hubbard; alias Victor Patzia—and where on earth did he come up with *that* last name? The fool spends too much time reading bad spy novels."

Once the priest remembered what his mother had always told him—"Son, God most loves those who are obedient"—he was able to bring his anger under control. Thus, following Victor's orders, Padre Damián visited His Grace to present his petition, but even though he explained that the request had come directly from the U.S. Embassy, it was denied because another priest was already working on the investigation.

"Good," Padre Damián muttered to himself. "Now I'll be able to continue working on my project." He called Victor to inform him of the archbishop's decision. The agent listened calmly without interrupting once.

"Hang up, Father. But stay close to the phone. I'll call you right back." Within five minutes, Victor was back on the line. "Pack your bags, Father, you're going to Cuapa. And be careful with las garrapatas," the agent said, chuckling. "Their bites will make you scratch yourself raw." And Victor was right, those horrid crablike insects burrowed themselves under Padre Damián's skin, and the itching lasted for weeks after he had returned from Chontales.

The month Padre Damián spent in Cuapa was the longest of his life, in large part because there were no bathtubs. At first, los cuapeños were curious about this tall, seemingly likable gringo priest, especially because he was the new man in charge of the investigation into the apparition of la Virgencita. They hoped that he would proclaim the miracle authentic so that the name of their pueblito would be spread throughout the world. But the more they talked to him, the more they shared their thoughts, the more judgmental he became, freely commenting on how each of them fell far short from the perfect lives Nuestro Señor and el papa wanted them to live. Before the first week was over, the cuapeños were keeping their distance from the priest.

Even the children soon realized that Padre Damián wasn't the kind man he first appeared to be. Inspired by one of their favorite movies of the time, *La guerra de las galaxias,* which Padre Domingo had taken them all to see in Juigalpa, they baptized the broad-shouldered priest in the black cassock and biretta after one of the film's characters: Darth Vader. None of the children, of course, ever had the nerve to call him that to his face.

What Padre Damián disliked most about his stay in Cuapa was the time he had to spend with the seer, Bernardo Martínez. The gringo priest lamented having to squander more than a week of his life on this uneducated Christian. He chased him around with a tape recorder to catch everything the man had to say. Finding that el campesino tended to ramble, the priest would forcefully interrupt him to keep the conversation on track. During the evenings, when Padre Damián played back the recordings, he frowned at the number of times he heard himself disrupt Bernardo's long-winded narrative. It was almost impossible to keep the visionary on track. The priest already knew that transcribing the man's account of the apparitions would be a nightmare. There were many unnecessary details he would have to weed out: all that talk about pigs, calves, mangos, iguanas, jocotes, machetes, fish, and so forth. The priest looked longingly at Torquemada's portrait and wondered if the grand inquisitor had also experienced trouble keeping the subjects of his investigations from rambling.

For two weeks, Padre Damián spent a lot of time talking to

anyone who claimed to have anything to do with the apparition. He spoke to doña Socorro, doña Auxiliadora, don Casimiro the butcher and his son Néstor, doña Filomena, Leticia. In essence, he interviewed almost everyone who lived in el miserable pueblito. And Padre Damián taped each of their statements as well. The priest just hoped that the archbishop and Victor wouldn't insist on a thorough report. He would hate to listen all over again to those meaningless conversations, to all that incessant babbling. Padre Damián had thought that Bernardo rattled on, but in comparison with the rest of los cuapeños, he was remarkably coherent and to the point.

The only person in el pueblo who made perfect sense to him was doña Tula. She told the priest, succinctly and conspiratorially, all the secrets in the lives of each cuapeño. He appreciated her disclosures. People with her talent were always helpful in his crusades; they instinctively knew how to uncover and concentrate on a person's weaknesses.

The Franciscan parish priest of Cuapa, Padre Domingo, was the person who made Padre Damián most uncomfortable. Merely a couple of minutes into their first meeting, the American had figured out that his so-called brother in Christ was one of *them,* one of those Marxist heretics. The American planned to mention this prominently in his report to the archbishop: *The town of Cuapa has fallen under the spiritual control of the enemy. Swift action is necessary to remedy the situation.* But in Padre Damián's estimation, Padre Domingo was a priest of little consequence, not worthy of the American's time, or of his unique talents. Thus, he thought it best to leave that problem in the hands of the archdiocese.

With regard to the Blessed Mother's apparition, Padre Damián was rather indifferent. "What's special about the Virgin appearing in Cuapa? She appears in my mother's Boston tenement every single day. And that saintly woman never made a big deal about it," he'd mumble to himself.

"Mystical experiences are a private matter," his mother assured him. Padre Damián agreed wholeheartedly. He only wished that Bernardo Martínez had been bright enough to recognize that he should have kept his mouth shut. Instead, the fool goes around shouting the news, getting the entire country riled up at a time when they should be concentrating on disrupting "la Iglesia Popular Sandinista" and worshipping Our Lord Jesus Christ in a proper, orthodox, Holy Roman Catholic manner.

That is why Padre Damián didn't understand what Victor could possibly see as useful in Mary's appearance to an unsophisticated campesino in this godforsaken pueblito. What here could help the Holy Roman Catholic Church combat the Marxist heretics? The priest believed that his investigation would lead nowhere. In Nicaragua, there were much bigger battles to fight. But as always, he sought comfort in the knowledge that God rewards obedience above all things.

At last, after a debilitating three weeks in Chontales without the possibility of relaxing in a steaming bubble bath, Padre Damián felt that he had enough information to begin composing his report. The archdiocese had provided him with the documentation submitted by a Spanish priest who had started to investigate the case. The American threw that report in the wastebasket, considering it the work of a rank amateur. Since Padre Damián might need to ask a few more questions, he fought the urge to return to Managua. On the positive side, he thought that his stay in Cuapa, stranded amid ignorant peasants, would be enough penance for any sins he may have inadvertently committed while conducting his work.

After a week of pounding furiously on his portable typewriter, he finished his report. He called the archdiocese and they sent a vehicle to rescue him. The next morning, Padre Damián personally submitted his report to the archbishop:

FINDINGS OF THE COMMISSION
INVESTIGATING THE APPARITION
IN CUAPA

AUTHORED BY: Padre Damián MacManus

SUBMITTED TO: His Grace,
the Archbishop of Nicaragua

MARCH 25, 1981

BE IT KNOWN:

I. To all appearances, Bernardo Martínez, the individual claiming to have experienced visions and locutions from the Holy Virgin Mary, possesses sound judgment and considerable common sense.

II. The subject, Bernardo Martínez, appears to be both psychologically and emotionally well balanced.

III. The individual at the center of this investigation appears to be sincere and humble rather than prone to exaggeration and mindless storytelling. (His narratives, though, tend to ramble and lack conciseness.)

IV. Bernardo Martínez contacted the appropriate religious authorities in order to seek guidance with regard to the apparitions. (Although there are some questions about whether or not he disobeyed a direct command from our Blessed Mother.)

V. The information that the Holy Virgin Mary provided to the visionary concurs with commonly accepted articles of religious faith and morals as determined by the Holy Roman Catholic Church.

VI. As a result of the apparitions, there are clear manifestations of healthy religious devotion and increased
spirituality in the community.

VII. The investigation indicates that Bernardo
Martínez has never accepted personal favors or money
in exchange for his allegedly prophetic insights.

VIII. The visionary did, in fact, consider the possibility
that his visions may have been a delusion. This
increases, as Your Grace well knows, the credibility of
the subject.

IX. The subject proved highly obedient when the local
parish priest ordered him to remain silent with regard
to his visions. (This act has significantly elevated his
credibility in the eyes of Your Humble Servant, the
Head Investigator.)

X. Bernardo has remained calm and at peace with himself despite the potentially disturbing nature of his
visions.

XI. The investigation substantiates that Bernardo
Martínez, to the best of the Head Investigator's knowledge, had led a moral and Christian life, well within
the margins of the orthodox tenets of the Holy Roman
Catholic Church.

XII. The visionary appears to enjoy the attention
focused both on himself and on his narration. (This
point is of great personal concern to the Head
Investigator. In Your Humble Servant's estimation,
Your Grace, the visionary relishes the limelight a little
more than is usual among bona fide visionaries.)

XIII. Also of concern: Bernardo Martínez was forty-
eight years old when the apparitions began. As Your
Grace well knows, most visionaries are children at the
time that these types of events begin to take place.

(However, young mothers who have suffered excruciating losses are exempt from this rule.)

XIV. Academically speaking, the subject is woefully deficient. Plus, the Head Investigator has serious concerns regarding the seer's intellectual capacity—or, to be more precise, lack thereof. Still, this point coincides with the profiles of most Marian visionaries.

XV. The apparition occurred in an isolated, quiet, restful site during a time when the beliefs of the One True Christian Faith are under attack in this part of the world.

XVI. Bernardo Martínez never anticipated the visions he received; they came to him as a complete surprise.

XVII. The Virgin Mother has warned the visionary that he will not be happy in this lifetime. (Blessed is he who suffers in the name of the Lord!)

XVIII. The subject has been consistent in his narratives with regard to the contents of his visions. During the investigation he has not contradicted himself on any major points of concern (with the exception of perhaps exaggerating about the number and size of the fish he caught just prior to the first apparition).

XIX. The messages provided during the apparitions call for increased prayer, repentance, and penance. These worthy practices promote the orthodox values and virtues of the Holy Roman Catholic Church.

XX. To date, several occurrences, impossible to explain, such as individuals being cured of serious illnesses, have been attributed to la Virgen de Cuapa.

WHEREAS:

I arrived in Cuapa, Chontales, Nicaragua, on February 25, 1981, at the behest of the nation's archbishop, to head the commission investigating the Blessed Mother's alleged apparition in a cow pasture located alongside the old road to Juigalpa. After reviewing the documents submitted by the original investigator, I began interviewing all those who claim to have been involved in the apparition, in particular the visionary Bernardo Martínez.

I spent a week interviewing the subject, taping the entire proceedings on cassettes. I have culled through hours of recordings and I have transcribed the highlights of these interrogations, presenting them in the voice of Bernardo Martínez to give the reader a greater sense of intimacy. (Besides, Bernardo's version of events was easier to transcribe this way.) Your Grace will find a condensed version of my interviews with Bernardo Martínez in the appendix, titled *Relación sobre los sagrados eventos de Cuapa*.

In addition, I have interviewed virtually every inhabitant of Cuapa (a highly time-consuming task), since they all claim to have been personally involved with the apparitions. Their comments invariably corroborate Bernardo Martínez's assertions, with the exception of those statements made by individuals known to be sympathetic to la Revolución Sandinista. (Your Grace, as you are well aware, the word of communists, as is also the case with the word of their Protestant brethren, can't be trusted.)

Throughout the investigation I found the information supplied by doña Tula to be the most helpful. With her assistance I was able to determine within a brief period whether an informant has led a moral life under the light of the One True Christian Faith, or not.

Finally, although I found Cuapa's parish priest, Padre Domingo, to be helpful and cooperative, I must warn Your Grace that I believe him to be one of *them*. (My belief doesn't reside in something he has said or done, but rather on a feeling, an intuition, that truly orthodox Catholics experience upon meeting one of our own.) I comment on Padre Domingo only as a precautionary measure, and I leave the matter of how to deal with him in Your Grace's wise hands.

THEREFORE:

I. This Commission finds nothing objectionable in the messages received in Cuapa. The statements Bernardo Martínez has made thus far are all in agreement with the doctrines espoused by the Holy Roman Catholic Church.

II. The Commission recommends that devotion to la Virgen de Cuapa be allowed to continue. As a result of these apparitions, many people have returned to the fold of the One True Church, as opposed to "la Iglesia Popular Sandinista"—a vicious cancer that is spreading throughout the country.

III. The Commission also recommends that the Church allow liturgical services to take place on a steady basis in Bernardo's cow pasture. (The subject of the apparition should also be urged to donate this parcel of land to the Holy Roman Catholic Church.)

IV. Although Marian apparitions have become commonplace in the twentieth century (I personally know of someone very close to me who has conversations with the Blessed Mother on a daily basis), the events in Cuapa merit a closer look. The investigations of this Commission indicate that the apparitions could very well be genuine.

RESPECTFULLY SUBMITTED BY
Padre Damián MacManus
Chairman, Commission Investigating
las Apariciones en Cuapa

Immediately after Padre Damián finished writing his report for the archbishop, he composed the following letter to Victor Phillips:

CLASSIFIED DOCUMENT

March 25, 1981

Mr. Victor Phillips (FYEO)
Consular Section
American Embassy
Managua, Nicaragua

Dearest Victor:

Per your request, I have investigated the apparition of Our Blessed Mother in the town of Cuapa, Chontales. I have submitted the results of this investigation to the archbishop. Included in the packet you'll find a copy of my report.

I must confess that I still don't understand what you expected me to find there. I differ with you, respectfully so, with regard to the area that should be of utmost concern to the Holy Roman Catholic Church. Our real enemies are the false priests and nuns who have embraced heretical theologies. In doing so they have become agents of Lucifer. Moreover, I believe, the parish priest of Cuapa is one of them. If I may suggest, meekly, of course, someone of my dedication, discipline, and talents should invest all of his time and efforts in combating this insidious evil.

Still, in remaining obedient to your noble office—and grateful, as always, for your generous patronage (my mother thanks you for the recent "contribution" sent to

her) — I have tried to fulfill your request to the best of my
abilities. I hope that you'll find that my hard work provided
fruits both satisfactory and helpful. Please feel free to call
me if there is anything else you wish to discuss with regard
to my investigation.

Yours faithfully in Christ,
Father Damian MacManus

Before the day had ended, as Padre Damián sat in a steaming bubble bath removing garrapatas from his right calf with a pair of rusty tweezers, he received a telephone call from Victor.

"Father, you did good! Congratulations! I think we can put this thing happening in Cuapa to use. Well done, my friend. Well done. The Company is going to print several thousand copies of the appendix you submitted to the archbishop. We will include it among the anti-Sandinista booklets we plan to distribute throughout Nicaragua." Victor coughed, and Father Damian distinctly heard the welled up phlegm coming loose from the walls of the agent's lungs.

"Victor, I'm sorry, but I don't understand. How is the apparition of Our Blessed Mother in a hick town like Cuapa going to help our cause? You're going to have to forgive me for saying so, but I just don't get it."

"Father, it's easy, really. Sometimes in the espionage game the simplest plans are the best because the enemy fails to see the inherent danger. Remember the Trojan Horse, Father? Look . . . it works like this: the Sandinistas consolidated their power this past year. They've crushed the business sector, the political parties opposed to them, the labor unions, and now the press. There's only one institution that remains intact: you guys, Father, the conservative wing of the Catholic Church. Los comandantes now consider you their most dangerous political rivals. I bet you're now asking your-self, how does the apparition of Mary tie in? Easy, Father. The archbishop needs a rallying point, something that can help him rouse the people: that's where she comes in. If the Church declares the apparition to be legitimate, thousands will come flocking to you, and in doing so they'll be turning their backs on the Sandinistas. Get it?"

"But Victor, that is *too passive*. It means that all I can do now is just sit and wait."

"Ah, Father, I know you're a man of action. But one lesson I've learned from our mistakes in Vietnam is that at times it's more important to win the hearts and minds of the people. It's easier, cleaner, and certainly less costly than military conquest. Don't you agree, Padre?"

"I pray that you're right, Victor. I pray that you're right."

"Yes, Father, do pray," Victor coughed again, and Padre Damián had to refrain from telling him to give up those stinking Cuban cigars. After the fit, the agent continued, "I do have a ques-tion for you, Father. What's Bernardo Martínez like?"

"A simple man, really. He has a good heart. Although, like I said in my report, I think that he enjoys being the center of attention a bit too much."

"You believe his story, then?"

"What's there not to believe, Victor? Apparitions of the Blessed Mother are more common than you think."

"Really? I thought you Catholics were picky about these things."

"We are, Victor, we are. But, for instance, I know someone to whom the Blessed Mother appears every day. Only this saintly woman doesn't advertise it, nor does she seek the Holy See's endorsement. She merely sees herself as having been profoundly blessed by God. That's all."

"Well, I think I understand, Father." Victor paused for a moment, before going on. "Tell me, then, what makes this Bernardo guy tick? Is there anything we can offer him that will guarantee that he'll stick to his story and continue to proclaim it out loud?"

"There's only one thing he asked from me, Victor, but it'll be impossible to grant."

"And what's that?"

"He wants to become a priest."

"I'd think the Church would welcome that, Father. What's the problem?"

"Victor, he didn't even graduate from high school. You have to be academically gifted to become a priest, you know. Besides, he's already fifty years old. That would make him, by far, the oldest as well as the most poorly prepared student in the seminary."

"Father, what does age have to do with religious vocation?"

"Funny, Victor. That's exactly what he asked. I told him that he would be in his sixties by the time he was ordained. And you know what he responded? 'How old will I be by then if I don't become ordained?'"

"There you go, Father. The man's clever. Personally, I think you should help him out. Think of what a great rallying point he would be for the Church if he became a priest. What did you end up telling him?"

"I told him to forget it, Victor. I told him that he doesn't have the intelligence necessary to make it through the coursework."

"Ouch! That's a bucket of ice water on his head, Father. But I guess you know the Church's business far better than me. Still, I think you're missing a golden opportunity here. Anyhow, it's time for you to move on. I've got your next assignment, and it's right up your alley. For the moment, your work in Nicaragua is done."

"Sure, Victor, what is it?"

"I want you to go to El Salvador. The Jesuits have a university there. They're giving our friends in the military a hard time. Those damned priests are actively calling for the Organization of American States to investigate human rights violations. I'd like you to handle the matter."

"That, Victor, would be my pleasure. Yes, definitely my pleasure."

SECUNDA VISIO
(The Second Apparition)
June 8–24, 1980

Bernardo

JUNE 8 ARRIVED at last: the day la Virgencita had promised to return. This time, a group of women and children joined me, including doña Auxiliadora, doña Socorro, and doña Tula. They all wanted to see Nuestra Señora for themselves. We arrived at el potrero shortly before noon and stopped before the morisco tree where she first appeared. We got on our knees, sang a few hymns, and then prayed the rosary.

By the time we finished, it was half past noon. The people who brought their lunch shared with those of us who hadn't. It's just like in the early Christian communities, I thought. An hour later, we prayed the rosary again. By the time we finished, a few in the group were becoming impatient.

"Bernardo, when is she coming?" doña Tula asked.

All I could do was shrug. Every single person in Cuapa knew that I had said that she would appear again today. I felt that I was letting everyone down. But I have to admit that those who were with me that day were very understanding. They waited quietly until midafternoon, then most of them returned home. Later, as the time to prepare dinner approached, the handful of women who had stayed behind gathered their things and left as well. Thankfully, no one said an unkind word. Only doña Tula said something that worried me.

"Maybe you committed an awful sin, Bernardo, and la Virgen is so offended that she decided not to come."

I didn't say anything. How could I? I began to think that maybe doña Tula was right, that somehow, without knowing, I had betrayed la Virgencita's trust.

In the end, only I remained in the pasture, hoping that she would decide to appear now that the others were gone. I waited until dusk. Nothing happened. Not wanting to stumble along the road in the dark, I also left. I was sad all the way home. Maybe she had decided that I was not worthy of being her messenger. La Virgencita had promised to come, but she hadn't. In my mind, that could only mean one thing: I had failed her.

That night, before going to bed, I got on my knees and prayed the rosary before my statue of la Inmaculada Concepción. As I prayed, I begged her forgiveness and asked for another chance to prove my love. Once I finished, I went to bed and, without being able to help myself, began to cry. Before long, I started to doze off. This night something about the way I fell asleep was different. I entered a beautiful tunnel, with transparent, light blue walls. It was like being inside a long glass tube surrounded completely by clear water.

Then I began to dream. But it wasn't a regular dream either. I don't know exactly how to explain it. I was dreaming, but I was aware that I was dreaming. I knew that I was in a dream within a dream. And, all the time, I could think exactly the same way as when I'm awake. Everything I saw, heard, said, and did in my dream was very real.

When at last I walked out of the tunnel, I found myself in the pasture, standing before the morisco tree. Everything looked and felt just exactly the way it had during la Virgencita's first appearance. I pulled my rosary out of my pocket and began to pray.

When I finished, I saw the flash of light. By now I knew what that meant. My heart swelled with joy. Then the second flash came and, as I expected, she descended slowly, standing on a bright cloud that stopped right on top of the morisco.

"What do you want, Madre mía?" I asked as soon as the rays of light from her hands struck my chest. I desperately wanted to fulfill her every wish. Nuestra Señora responded with the litany that I had already memorized. She repeated everything she had said the first time, word for word. She reminded us to pray the rosary every day, in family; to pray it during the calmest part of the day, without distractions; to love one another, and to fulfill our obligations to each other; to forgive one another, and to work for peace; to avoid the path of violence; to change our ways so we can avoid Armageddon. And she asked me once again to share her message with the world.

"Sí, Madre, I'm already telling everyone, just like you asked. But thank you very much for reminding me." I paused for a moment to gather my courage, and then I continued, "Señora, I have a favor to ask. The townspeople have a few petitions they've asked me to present to you." Although I was dreaming, I reached into my shirt pocket and pulled out the list I had been compiling since the last time I had seen her.

"Don Casimiro would like to make more money; doña Rosa

would like for you to heal her foot—she has a corn that has been killing her for weeks; doña Carla would like her daughter to marry a man who doesn't drink; doña Socorro would like to learn how to better please el Señor; doña Tula would like to become a better listener; doña Auxiliadora would like to be able to love those who have hurt her; don Benjamín wants to win over the girl of his dreams—he says that you know who that is; don Roberto, the teacher at the high school, wants his students to lose their fear of math; and don Humberto wants to know if he will ever get the respect he deserves. What should I tell them, Madre mía?"

Tell them that some of their wishes will come true, and that others will not.

I stood there, expecting to hear her say which ones would and which ones wouldn't. But she didn't add anything more. "What kind of answer is that, Señora?" I wanted to ask, but I decided that would be too disrespectful.

While I was thinking this, she smiled at me, almost playfully. Then, she lifted her right arm and pointed slightly above the hills, saying, *Look toward the sky.*

Her finger was aimed at the patch of light blue between the jícaro and the palm trees. This became a brilliant theater screen, and on it the clearest movie began to play. The first scene was of a group of people, all dressed in white, walking toward a rising sun. They moved joyfully, singing the entire way. I could hear them clearly, but I didn't understand a word they sang. Their celebration was heavenly. What most struck me was that these were beings of light; each person glowed with pure happiness, giving off a holy radiance. And then la Señora spoke.

Behold, Bernardo. These were the first Christians. They lived in communities shaped by love. Many of them were martyrs.

She paused, looked at me intently for a long time, and then asked, *Bernardo, would you like to become a martyr?*

I didn't hesitate for an instant. "Sí," I answered.

That is good, Bernardo. You will suffer much because of your beliefs. You will not be happy in this lifetime, but you shall have your reward when Nuestro Señor finally decides to call you.

Although I knew what she meant, and I was aware that I should have been disturbed, I was rapt in her presence and in the vision she was sharing with me. I looked again toward the screen, and a second group of people appeared. They were also dressed in white. In their hands they held rosaries that glowed brightly. The beads were as white as the meat of a coconut, and they radiated light of the most wonderful colors. The leader of the group carried a thick book. He opened it, and began to read. After he finished a section, they all stopped to meditate in silence. Upon the reader's signal, they recited the Lord's Prayer, followed by ten Hail Marys. I prayed along with them.

When we finished praying, Nuestra Señora said, *These are the first people to whom I gave the rosary. This is how I want everyone to pray.*

"I understand, Señora," I answered.

A third group then appeared on the screen. They were all dressed in brown and looked familiar. I think they were Franciscans. The prayer scene repeated itself, and I joined them as well.

When I finished praying with this group, la Señora said, *These received the rosary from the group you saw before.*

Then a fourth group appeared on the screen. This, by far, was the largest. There were so many I couldn't have counted them if I'd tried. An enormous crowd passed before my eyes in an endless procession. They looked like an army, only that they carried rosaries instead of weapons. They were dressed the way we dress today, with so many different colors, so many different styles. I rejoiced because I knew that I belonged in this group. I was an outsider with the first three, but the ones now before me were my people. Just when I believed that I found my place, I glanced down at my hands. The sight made me want to cry. In comparison to theirs, my hands were dark and filthy. Then I looked at the people again and saw that they were like the others, their bodies glimmered. I looked at la Virgencita and pleaded, "Señora, I want to go with them, I want to be a part of this group."

No, not yet, Bernardo. Your time has yet to come. You have far to travel before you can join them. You have to go back now and tell everyone what you have seen and heard. I have shown you the glory of Nuestro Señor. Whoever obeys him, whoever perseveres in reciting the rosary, whoever puts the word of Nuestro Señor into practice, will earn the right to be part of this group.

After saying this, she slowly raised both hands, palms up, and her cloud began ascending into the heavens. Soon, she faded from view.

I immediately woke up, turned on the lights, got out of bed, and prayed the rosary. When I finished, I climbed back into bed and went back to sleep, feeling very happy.

The next morning, I left on the first bus to Juigalpa to tell Padre Domingo about my dream. I found him sitting at the dining room table, eating breakfast. I told him everything that had happened at el potrero the day before, and then I told him about the dream.

"Have you told anyone else, Bernardo?"

"No, Padre, you asked me not to."

"Good," he said, and then he remained silent, thinking. I also didn't say a word, but I honestly expected him to tell me that it was fine to share my vision with everyone in Cuapa. Instead, he said nothing.

After several minutes, I couldn't bear the silence any longer, and I asked, "Padre, may I tell people about the dream?"

"No, no, Bernardo. I want you to keep it a secret." That was all he said. I would have preferred an explanation, but I kept quiet, trying to be obedient. At that very instant, my chest began to burn inside, and no matter what medication I took the rest of the week, it wouldn't go away.

When I returned to Cuapa, I fought against my need to talk. I kept on hearing her voice, saying, *Tell,* but I had to obey Padre Domingo. I kept my mouth shut, even though my silence tormented me all over again.

The next few days I lost a lot of weight again. When Padre Domingo returned to Cuapa, on June 24, for the feast of San Juan Bautista, santo patrón of el pueblo, the first thing he noticed was my appearance.

"Are you ill, Bernardo?" he asked as I helped him prepare for mass.

"Padre, remaining silent about the dream is killing me. I keep on hearing her voice. She's telling me to share everything."

The priest said nothing. But I couldn't bear the fire in my chest any longer.

"Padre," I pleaded, "please let me tell. If not, I'm afraid I'm going to die."

Padre Domingo looked worried. I could see his eyes filling with compassion. At last, he simply nodded and placed his hand on my shoulder. We stepped out of the sacristy and into the church. As usual, I assisted during the mass. Because that day was the feast of our santo patrón, the building was full. People were standing several rows deep in the rear. Everyone I knew was there, except doña Tula, who had come down with dengue.

Before beginning the mass, Padre Domingo announced, "Please listen with respect to Bernardo. He has something he wants to share with you concerning Nuestra Señora." He stepped aside and motioned for me to stand at the center.

That morning I talked about what I had seen and heard in my dream, and the more I spoke, the lighter the fire burning in my heart, until finally, toward the end, I felt nothing but joy.

When I had finished, the entire congregation remained silent. But I didn't care what they were thinking, really. Padre Domingo came forth and said, "Please keep this information to yourselves. It's important that I swear each of you to secrecy. This news must not leave the building until I've had the opportunity to consult with the bishop."

To the credit of every cuapeño, no one said a word about my dream. All those who attended mass on the feast day of San Juan Bautista proved their loyalty and their obedience to the parish priest.

As Padre Domingo said mass, I was transported. Our small community that day looked like the ones Nuestra Señora had shown me on the screen. Everyone gave off a faint light. And as they said the Lord's Prayer together, I realized that I had never witnessed such devotion to Nuestro Señor Jesús as I did that morning in Cuapa.

chapter seven

O FELIX CULPA
(O Happy Sin)

October 14, 1982

Flor de María Gómez

I WOKE UP early this morning. Quite a few stars were still out—glittering centurions of God's wonderful universe. The night was so humid that my bedsheets got cold. My bones were chilled, but I can't call on just anyone to bring me a blanket, since I'm confined to this silence and unable to move for myself. I rely only on Rocío. But last night I thought it best to let my daughter sleep.

I don't like living in Pedro's house, although I grew up in it, as did three generations of my family. I know that I'm a burden on my brother. In spite of everything, Susana, his wife, is kind to me. She doesn't seem to mind taking care of me. Pedro, though, barely tolerates my presence. I know he would be happier if I lived elsewhere. But I'm not complaining. After all, I asked to be like this. I only need to be close to my daughter and no one else. Rocío is very good to me, always nearby, giving me far more affection than I deserve. So I'm happy, really. I couldn't ask for more.

Rocío, my only child, has always been the perfect daughter. Her father left me for another woman during our first year of marriage, after he realized he would never get a hand on the fortune my family had made in the hardware business. Since then, he never showed an interest in having a relationship with Rocío. But that didn't bother either of us. Rocío is all I ever needed to fill my life, and for many years I seemed to be all she needed as well. A mother couldn't ask for more.

As a child, my daughter was pretty, sweet, loving, funny, talkative, and talented. Very talented. People would visit us just to hear her recite Rubén Darío's poetry: "La marcha triunfal," "Sonatina," "A Margarita Debayle," and "Lo fatal." Rocío's memory astonished everyone. She captivated our guests, who held their breath during her long recitations. And she never made a single mistake. From the moment Rocío was born, she has been the center of everyone's attention. She has the gift of making people around her feel happy.

Although it's still early in the morning—the sun's just now beginning to rise—the day is already muggy. Before long the cooler night air will dissipate, and we'll all be breathing in gulps, like fish. My brother's shadowy figure comes into my room, lifts me out of bed, and places me in the wheelchair. Pedro always speaks gruffly to me, but I choose not to listen. I only listen to Rocío, whom I now see coming down the hall. She reaches us and walks alongside me as Pedro pushes the wheelchair out into the living room.

"Buenos días, Mamá," she says as she leans over to kiss me on the cheek. "I slept wonderfully last night. How about you?"

My brother leaves me in my usual spot in the living room: in front of the window. From here I can see the blurs of cars and people passing by. My daughter gets on her knees and gives me a hug. She reminds me that yesterday was the second anniversary of la Virgen's final appearance in Cuapa.

"And you know what happened, Mamá?" she says excitedly. "Thirty-five thousand people showed up at the apparition site for mass. Can you imagine that? All of them were there to honor the Barefoot Madonna Who Rises into Heaven. The archbishop himself presided over the event. He did a beautiful job. You know, Mamá, doña Eloísa, Bernardo's grandmother, told me about how, when he was a little boy, he had a dream in which a great multitude traveled from all over to gather around him. Doña Eloísa told him to stop having those thoughts, that he was committing the sin of vanity believing that he would ever become that important and that he spent far too much time thinking only disparates. But you know what, Mamá? Bernardo's childhood dream was divinely inspired. No question, it was a prophecy. The multitudes were certainly there, gathered around him, yesterday."

I tell Rocío that she's privileged to know as much as she does about la Virgen de Cuapa. And I'm not joking. I'm proud of my daughter's intimate relationship with Nuestra Señora.

"But here's the best part, Mamá. Shortly after the archbishop left to go back to Managua—that poor man is always in such a rush!—the sun started to dance in the sky. At first it became a disk within a disk, and then it began to rotate clockwise. Along its edges you could see long, thin blond ponytails wildly rising up and then falling. Over and over again, the multitudes saw this. And then, from a celestial cone, the sun shot extraordinary colors at them: light blue, orange, soft green, red, violet, copper. Most of the people there witnessed the miracle. The majority fell to their knees and praised the Queen and Mother of the Heavens. Isn't it marvelous, Mamá?"

I answer that it's marvelous, indeed. Rocío told me before about the miracles the sun performed at the apparition site, but I don't remember such a big crowd ever being present.

"I'll be right back, Mamá. I'm going to see what's keeping your breakfast."

Shortly afterward, my sister-in-law Susana places a chair next to me. She then brings my usual breakfast: bread soaked in café con leche, with lots of sugar. It's the only thing I like to eat. Susana patiently spoon-feeds me the bread, so drenched in the coffee that it's falling apart. She speaks to me with genuine affection; I can tell by her tone of voice. But when I look at her, it's as if a thick fog separates us. That's just fine, though. I do, after all, have to stay within myself. When Susana finishes feeding me, she wipes my mouth and chin and returns to her housework.

I like it when my brother and his wife leave me alone because it's then that my daughter usually comes to keep me company. She can't stand to see me sitting here by myself. Even as a teenager she was attentive and loving. Rocío was never rebellious, like most girls are during that time in their lives; and she never, ever, got into trouble. I was the envy of all mothers. And although she was not the best student, her grades were respectable.

The reason Rocío didn't shine in school was because of her popularity. Her friends were always visiting, and my house was open to them. I preferred that they gather there rather than where they could get into trouble. The boys especially liked coming. They were all in love with Rocío, who was a big flirt. But she couldn't help herself; she was just absolutely adorable. Needless to say, spending time with her friends didn't leave Rocío much time to study.

When mornings are as hot and humid as this one, the house swarms with echoes. Sounds that have been hiding in the crevices for ages come out for air. And I hear conversations, but they sound ancient, as if things our ancestors had said centuries ago are just now being released from a long sleep. Rocío's return makes the ghosts flee.

"How was breakfast, Mamá?" she asks as she hugs me. This time she sits in the chair Susana brought in earlier. I tell Rocío that breakfast was fine, as usual, and that my sister-in-law, as always, treated me with love and concern.

"Yes, tía Susana is a wonderful person," Rocío says, kissing me on the cheek. "Would you like for me to tell you about another miracle from Cuapa, Mamá?"

I answer, yes, of course.

"Well, the Blessed Daughter of San Joaquín and Santa Ana is still appearing to Bernardo. Only this time, the messages are not for the rest of us, but only for the leaders of her Son's Church. She tells Bernardo to warn the archbishop that he must not waiver or compromise on Church principles, that the Church is in danger of becoming permanently divided, and that he and his bishops must present a united front until this menace passes. After Our Mother Who Fled into Egypt gives Bernardo a message, he immediately visits the archbishop to tell him what she had to say. Amazing, isn't it, Mamá?"

I say yes. I never want to dampen my daughter's enthusiasm for la Virgen de Cuapa. After all, it is through her intercession that we're still together.

"I'll be back, Mamá. I'm just going to check on Lourdes."

Lourdes is Rocío's daughter, my granddaughter. Because I'm in this state, I can't see the child, much less hold her. But Rocío keeps me updated, always letting me know how the baby's doing.

When Rocío graduated from high school, she enrolled in the Jesuit university. Luckily, she studied there before the Sandinistas came to power. Back then you could still get a good education here. My daughter surprised me, deciding to major in pharmacy. I always thought that she would choose something more artistic, like literature. Pharmacy didn't come easily to Rocío either. She had to work hard at it. During those years she became serious about her studies. Her aim, she said, was to help make the people of this country healthier. "A healthier people will build a better nation," Rocío used to say. Back then, you know, that's what every young person of her generation said. Nice sentiments. But you can't run una revolución on passion alone, as we're all learning.

One good thing that came out of Rocío's years at the university was her first serious boyfriend, Guillermo Villanueva. I really liked that young man. He was from a good family, with a last name that's highly respected in Nicaragua. What I liked the most about Guillermo was that he was a devout Catholic. I didn't raise Rocío to be particularly religious. We went to church most Sundays, and on occasion we prayed the rosary. But one would never have labeled us *devout* Catholics. Guillermo, on the other hand, was so committed that at times I thought he would have been happier as a priest. It was through him that Rocío first became interested in religion. They joined youth action groups that worked in the community to try to improve the lives of the poor. "As Christ would have done himself," Guillermo would say. Bless the boy; at least he had his heart in the right place.

The heat has become insufferable. The cooler air of the

morning has risen. It now feels like we're being steamed over a slow fire. The weather usually gets this way right before a downpour. I've always thought that this swampy inferno feels as if the world were waiting to be born again. Suddenly, Rocío returns from checking on the baby. I immediately forget that I was suffocating.

"The baby's sound asleep, Mamá," she says, smiling lovingly while she places an arm around my shoulders. I ask her how Lourdes is able to sleep in this weather. "They've put two fans directly on her. She's far more comfortable than we are right now." I smile at my daughter and nod. At times like these we really don't need to waste words.

"Mamá, let me tell you about the miracle of the boy and the fish." Sometimes Rocío doesn't remember what she has and hasn't already told me. I've heard the miracle of the boy and the fish many times now. But I can't disappoint her. To make my daughter happy I smile, nod my head, and pretend to listen closely.

"Well, Mamá, there was a six-year-old boy from Managua who had been sick for weeks. His parents took him to several doctors, including some of those who have come here from Cuba. All agreed that the child was terminally ill. I don't really know what disease the boy had, but the parents had been told that there was no hope. Well, then, armed only with their faith in the Woman Clothed in the Sun, the couple decided to make a pilgrimage to Cuapa to ask for her intercession. Because of their son's frail condition, they weren't going to take him. The boy begged to go, but his mother remained firm, insisting that he stay home.

"But that night the boy had a dream. Nuestra Madre appeared to him and said, 'Go to Cuapa. Go fishing at the river crossing. You will catch a fish, and your parents will cook it for you. After you eat it, you will be healed.'

"The next morning the child told his parents about the dream. The mother didn't believe him, saying that he had made it up just so they would take him along. But the boy's story moved his father. He argued with his wife, trying to convince her to let their son join them. After a lot of coaxing, the mother gave in. The father packed a line and a hook, and on their way to the apparition site they stopped at the river crossing. Almost immediately the boy caught a guapote. Then they went to the apparition site where they prayed the rosary. Once back in Managua, the mother cleaned and fried the fish, and the boy ate it, just as the Queen of Heaven Crowned by the Trinity had told him. And you know what, Mamá? The child was cured. The doctors were astounded and couldn't explain what had happened, but they announced that the disease had vanished. Marvelous, isn't it, Mamá?"

Rocío tells the story with such enthusiasm that I always smile and answer that it indeed is marvelous.

"Mamá," she says, "you're sliding down in the wheelchair. I'll go get tío Pedro. He'll help you sit up straight again."

Soon, Pedro's vague figure arrives to help me out. Just as quickly as he arrives, he disappears into a thick fog.

I remember how, upon graduation, Rocío got a job with el Ministerio de Salud. This was during the first weeks of la Revolución, and everyone's dream was to have free medical care. Rocío loved her job with the Ministry of Health. She believed that she was making a difference in people's lives. I had never seen her that happy. That's about when she and Guillermo began talking about marriage.

This was also around the time everyone started to say that la Virgen had appeared to a campesino in Cuapa. Excited by this news, Guillermo and Rocío helped our parish priest organize a pilgrimage to the apparition site. And I, through a friend, helped them rent the bus.

On the day of their trip, the worst person imaginable also went along: Agustín Dávila, el Demonio. From the moment el Demonio saw Rocío, he desired her. Agustín is the most useless man on God's earth—and I question if it was really God who put him here. His mother, Nora, another one of God's oversights, has never known what to do with her worthless son. On that day, she was taking him to Cuapa hoping that Nuestra Señora would take pity on the miserable creature.

After Agustín had graduated from escuela secundaria, Nora sent him to study in los Estados Unidos. He remained there for years, lying to her, telling her that he was attending college. Every month she sent him all the money she could spare. All along, Agustín said that he was on track to graduate with a degree in engineering. Finally, after six years, Nora woke up and sent her brother to check on him. The brother found out that Agustín was nothing more than a drunk and a drug addict and that he had not completed a single course. El pendejo had already been twice married and divorced, both times to women who shared his addictions. Once the mother found out that she had thrown away a fortune, she put a stop to it. With no other way to support his wicked habits, Agustín returned to Nicaragua.

On the way to Cuapa, el Demonio spoke to Rocío, trying to get close to her. Fortunately, Guillermo was there to guard her. But on the return trip, the bus lost its brakes and sped out of control, overturning on a sharp curve. I know I can't prove it, but I'm sure that el Demonio was responsible for the accident. There was only one death: Guillermo's. Without that angel to protect my daughter, I knew to expect yet another tragedy.

Suddenly, it's become dark. The rain clouds are so dense it looks like dusk. Strong winds, flashes of lightning, and thunder are laying siege on us. No rain yet, though. Paper and dust swirl in the streets. Through the shadows I see the ghosts of indios and conquistadores skipping excitedly among the people running for shelter. I like tropical storms. I almost want to come out of my confinement to go out and dance with the spirits. I can hear them laughing as they fling handfuls of sand and dirt through the windows. Soon, Pedro, who is dressed, ready to go to work, comes into the living room and begins to close the windows. I see his blurry outline turning the shutter handles in panic. At the same time he scolds me. His resentment doesn't bother me. I've never been tempted to listen to him.

Rocío rushes back into the living room, drawn by the fury of the storm. "Oh, that's good, Mamá. Tío Pedro has closed the windows. But look at yourself, you're covered with dirt." I tell her that it doesn't bother me, that I would rather have her sit down and tell me about another of la Virgen's marvels.

"Well, then, let me think. Ah, yes, this miracle happened to someone who lives right there in Cuapa. Her name is Dolores. It turns out that she discovered a lump on her breast. She was sure she had cancer. She visited a doctor in Juigalpa who had to perform a biopsy and send a sample to a laboratory before he could diagnose anything. He scheduled Dolores the following week for an appointment. In the meantime, he gave her a lotion to rub on the breast because it had become sore. After visiting the doctor, Dolores went straight to the apparition site to ask for the intercession of the Mother of Sapphires. As she prayed, a voice in her head said, 'Apply the lotion above the lump and then squeeze. And have faith. If you do this, you will be healed.'

"That evening, after praying the rosary with her husband, Dolores locked herself in the bathroom and did just as the voice had ordered. She applied the lotion and then squeezed. Within a couple of minutes, a mass came out that looked like a ball of corn-meal you feed a parrot. Dolores disinfected the small wound with kerosene—which is not really a disinfectant, but she's from Cuapa—and the following day took the lump to the doctor, who sent it straight to the laboratory. The report said that it was indeed cancerous, but since the mass had been squeezed out intact, Dolores was declared healed by the grace of the Dispatcher of Satanás. What do you think about that, Mamá?"

Rocío has told me this miracle a couple of times already, but I smile and say that Dolores is blessed, just like us, through Nuestra Señora's intervention. I don't share with Rocío how sad it makes me that la Virgen de Cuapa couldn't spare us the entire suffering el Demonio caused.

Guillermo's death devastated my lovely daughter. For weeks she walked around like a survivor of the earthquake: not knowing, not seeing, not hearing, not feeling anything. Throughout the months that followed, Agustín came by every day to visit. At first he behaved well, and I must admit that he even had me fooled for a while. He can be charming—as I'm sure all demons can be—when he wants to. By the time Rocío came out of her daze, she had become attached to el Demonio. But enough time had passed for me to see the true nature of this evil man. For one thing, I never saw him do anything productive. He was always looking for the perfect job because he wanted a position that fit someone of his high social standing. As Agustín kept reminding us, he was, after all, a *Dávila*.

After this, I knew that el Demonio was no good. I tried to

warn Rocío, but she refused to listen. What she did do was tell Agustín what I thought about him, and he ran straight to his mother. Nora—a woman with no neck and the body of a plug—stormed into my house.

"How dare you say those things about my son!" she shouted. "If anything, you should feel privileged that a *Dávila* would even consider marrying someone of your class."

Marriage? Marriage? They were talking about marriage? At that moment, I decided to put a stop to their plans.

But it was already too late.

El Demonio had run off with my daughter. On my bed, I found a note in which Rocío implored me not to worry, to trust that la Virgen de Cuapa would protect us all.

The storm clouds are directly overhead. They have opened their floodgates as punishment for all sinners. This is a tropical downpour of biblical proportions. All one can do is look out the window and watch as the waste of the world floats by upon sad, frothy waves. The water pounds like a thousand hammers on the rooftop. I distinguish the shapes of Pedro and Susana; they are shouting instructions to each other at the top of their lungs. But I close my ears to the storm, for Rocío is sitting next to me, and it's enough for her to whisper. I can clearly hear every single word she's saying. Putting the tempest out of my mind, I listen as my daughter tells me another story of the wonders performed by la Virgen de Cuapa.

"One evening, Mamá, in Cuapa, a group of friends met at doña Filomena's house to pray the rosary in honor of the Patroness of Marriages. They had just finished praying and were sitting around chatting when, without warning, they heard the ringing of bells: melodious, sweet, rich beyond words. The chimes played stirring melodies that seemed to come from everywhere: out of the air, the living room walls, the roof, out of the people themselves. They all ran to the corner to see if the music was coming from the church. It wasn't. The building was dark and empty. Doña Filomena then looked up, astonished. The sound was softly descending from the stars. The tolling went on for more than five minutes, and the group just stood out there, listening in wonder, without anyone saying a word. Finally, as the music faded away, everyone who had been in doña Filomena's house began to cry, missing that heavenly creation. They did, fortunately, recover, but the memory of that night will follow them around forever. Without a doubt, Mamá, the chimes were a gift from the Culmination of Womanhood. Miraculous, isn't it?"

She has told me this story before. Still, I assure Rocío that Nuestra Señora's generosity has no limits, that she even gives away the music of the spheres to those who honor her. My daughter smiles and nods. If only we had always agreed.

When Rocío and Agustín returned—tragically now a married couple—they had nowhere to live. Her salary wasn't enough for them to rent a house and, of course, he had yet to find the right kind of work for someone as princely as himself. Desperate, Rocío pleaded with me to let them live in my house until they could find a place of their own. Against my better judgment, I agreed. Before a month had gone by, Agustín had taken off the mask: he had become el Demonio. He began to disappear into Managua's slums on his quest for drugs. Poor Rocío. She repeatedly humiliated herself, searching for him in the worst bars, the worst neighborhoods of Managua (he had a preference for Jorge Dimitrov because there he could find the cheapest cocaína), and, once she found him, she'd spend hours begging him to come home. When he'd finally return, I'd lecture him, telling him to behave responsibly, like a real man.

"Who the hell do you think you are!" Agustín would yell at me. "Idiota, you're a nothing! I'm a *Dávila!* I'm better, I'm more intelligent, than anyone in your miserable family. Besides, I'm now the man of the house. From now on you're to obey me without question."

This went on for weeks until the day came when, during one of our arguments, el Demonio shoved me. That did it. I told him to leave and never set foot in my house again. Poor Rocío. My daughter was unhappy, caught between the two people she loved most in the world. As Agustín climbed into the taxi that would take him to his mother's house, Rocío ran into her bedroom, locked the door, and lit a candle before her statue of la Virgen de Cuapa. She remained in there for three days without coming out, even to eat. Finally, just when I was about to hire someone to take the door off its hinges, she reappeared.

"Rocío, you're much better off without Agustín. He's ruining your life," I told her.

My daughter just smiled and looked at me sadly. "It's too late, Mamá," she said. "I'm pregnant."

The house is flooding. The downpour is defeating us. Pedro postponed cleaning the drainage in the courtyard. Now, because of his carelessness, the edges are overflowing. Even though my brother is wrapped in clouds, I can tell that he has taken off his shoes, has rolled up his pants, and is frantically poking a broomstick into the hole, hoping to dislodge whatever is blocking the drain. Lightning strikes nearby. Susana's outline runs about the house, unplugging the stereo, the television, and the refrigerator.

She and Pedro are shouting instructions, but I don't think they can even hear themselves, let alone one another. But what do I care? Rocío is here, next to me, holding my hand.

"Mamá, have I told you about how the Sublime Model of Chastity restored the sight of a young man who had gone blind in one eye?" Although I have heard this miracle before, I shake my head. That way I know that she will repeat the story, and I'll continue having the pleasure of her company as well. "This miracle also happened in Cuapa. A young man, a welder, was working one day—foolishly, I might add—without a protective mask. Well, a splinter of scalding metal flew and lodged itself in the center of his eye. His screams could be heard throughout every street in el pueblo, all the way up el Cerro Tumbé. His coworkers carried him home, and his poor mother made them hold him over the sink, with his face directly under the faucet. Frantic, the poor woman poured water on her son's eye, but that didn't help. His screams grew louder. She then ran to light a candle before her statue of the Merciful Sweet Señora Overflowing with Goodness and said a quick prayer. Immediately after she had finished, without even hearing a voice, she knew exactly what to do. She ran to doña Auxiliadora's house and asked to borrow the dress that the statue of la Virgen had worn the night of the illumination. She ran back home and wrapped the dress around her son's head. By that time he was thrashing in pain. But within less than a minute he was resting in peace, soon falling into a deep sleep. He didn't wake for three days. When he finally sat up, she unwrapped la Virgen's garment from his head: his eye had been healed. Astonishing, isn't it, Mamá?"

That's one of my favorite miracles. I really don't have to pretend to be enthusiastic. It comes naturally. And Rocío is pleased to see my joy.

"I'll be right back, Mamá. I'm going to help mi tío Pedro unclog the drain." Already, the water is coming close to reaching the footrest of my wheelchair.

After my clash with el Demonio, both he and Rocío went to live with his mother. I knew that would be a disaster, since Nora is such an unpleasant person, almost as unbearable as her son. My daughter is far too sensitive to deal with people like her. I was absolutely right. Within a month, Nora slapped Rocío after my daughter suggested that Agustín enter a rehabilitation clinic. The one good thing that came out of that mess is that they separated. Rocío returned home to live, and el Demonio stayed with his mother. Life became a little more peaceful then, although he'd call my daughter about ten times a day. But Rocío and I continued to argue loudly over the money she still gave him and because she still humiliated herself by following el Demonio into seedy bars to try to persuade him to return to his mother's home. Plus, a couple of times, she borrowed money from her tío Pedro to bail Agustín out of jail. Her husband was hopeless.

Every day, Rocío prayed fervently before the statue of la Virgen de Cuapa, asking her to have pity on Agustín's wretched soul. All along, I'd tell her that she should be praying for her own soul instead. Sadly, we had all been caught up in this dreadful drama. The nine months of Rocío's pregnancy passed without the usual joy. At last, she gave birth to a beautiful baby girl she named Lourdes.

The storm is letting up, and the thunder and lightning are growing distant, heading west. El Señor has spared our lives yet again. His pity, his mercy, are what keep us afloat in this valley of misery. Pedro and Susana are sweeping water through the front door. It's as if they are trying to push our sins out of this house. During the flood they moved my wheelchair to the dining room.

I'm facing the wall where I can distinguish, through the haze, a painting of the Last Supper. For an instant I focus on Judas Iscariot; his right hand holds a bag full of silver dinars, already having betrayed the Redeemer. I believe Agustín would have been capable of doing the same thing.

Rocío has returned. "Mamá," she says, "mi tío Pedro didn't need my help after all. And you know what? Lourdes slept straight through the storm." She smiled and then continued, "Let me tell you about another miracle performed by the Most Holy Being. A little girl from Comalapa was born with a deformed foot. Back in the days of Somoza, the mother didn't have enough money to take the child to the doctor. But now that la Revolución has given us access to medical care, she brought her daughter to Managua where a Cuban doctor said that the only remedy for the little girl, now four years old, was to have an operation. The mother then returned home to raise money to pay for their lodging in Managua while her daughter recovered. While back in Comalapa she and the little girl made a pilgrimage to the apparition site. There, the mother saw people gathering dirt from the spot where la Virgen had appeared. She decided to do the same, placing the soil in the bag in which they had brought their lunch. When she returned home, she decided, all on her own, to mix the soil with water, and then she packed the mud around her daughter's foot. The little girl slept like that the entire night.

"The next morning, after the mud cast was removed, the girl's foot looked normal, but the mother couldn't really be sure. She thought that maybe it was her imagination. A week passed, and they returned to the capital. When the Cuban doctor examined the foot, he was startled. 'Señora, what did you do to your daughter's foot?' he asked. The woman, fearing that she would be scolded if she revealed her faith in the Most Perfect Human Woman to an atheist, said nothing. 'Bueno,' the doctor said, 'your daughter's foot is healed. She no longer needs the operation.'

"Then the little girl spoke up, 'Mami, the mudpack did it! It cured me! La Virgen did it!'

"'Please, Señora, tell me what you did,' the doctor pleaded. When the woman had finished telling the story, he said, 'Thank you very much for trusting me.' With tears in his eyes, the doctor continued, 'I will also make a trip to Cuapa to ask for la Virgen's intercession. My wife's very, very ill.'

"What do you think about that, Mamá?"

I've never heard this story before. Delighted, I thank Rocío for sharing the miracle with me. I only wish that I could move my arms. That way I could make the sign of the cross. But I do so mentally. My daughter smiles delightedly, seeing that the story has made me happy.

It's wonderful that things are going well between us again. Our relationship was strained after Lourdes's birth. My granddaughter was a beautiful baby, just as her mother had been. But I had trouble fully accepting her because part of el Demonio also lived inside. I know the child's not to blame, but I couldn't help myself. It didn't help that during the entire pregnancy Rocío and I argued constantly. I nagged and nagged her about Agustín, begging her to divorce him once and for all. But she was horrified that I would even suggest such a thing. "I'm a faithful Catholic, and divorce is out of the question, Mamá." I then urged her to get an annulment, but she refused to consider even that. I could tell that Rocío was growing tired of my pestering. The daughter who had never talked back now argued constantly with me. It seemed that fighting was the only thing we had in common, and our arguments were horrible. Between Agustín's addictions, Nora's hatefulness, and my scoldings, Rocío, my once vivacious daughter, became deeply depressed.

One day, after a particularly nasty disagreement, my daughter said, "Mother, I'm miserable. I hate my life. I'm going to kill myself." Well, I had never put up with a tantrum when she was a child, and I wasn't about to start now. I decided to call her bluff. I dared her to kill herself. I knew that Rocío didn't have it in her; I knew that she could never commit suicide.

The rain falls softly on the banana plants outside, silently sliding down their long leaves and pouring in tender streams onto the ground. The earth is soaked; the world looks like a pool of bubbling water. The clouds slowly move west, exhausted from their work. On the windows, fat drops scurry down in glittering cascades.

"Mamá, I'll tell you the last miracle of the day, and then I have to go. I have a lot to do," Rocío says. I nod in agreement. "A strange man arrived at the apparition site. No one really knows who he was, or who he is. But we do know that he's an apostate, having forsaken everything that is holy. Anyway, he was looking for a way to offend the Queen of the Holy Rosary. It so happened, then, that one night, when no one else was at the site, he showed up, went to the exact spot where la Virgen appeared, pulled down his pants, squatted, and prepared to defecate. But the Madonna of the Apocalypse would not allow him to desecrate her Holy Site. Early the next morning, devotees of Nuestra Señora found him still squatting, pants down to his ankles, unable to stand up straight. She had frozen him in that position. The people carried the man, still squatting and with his pants around his ankles, all the way to

Cuapa. There, they put him on a bus to Juigalpa with instructions for the driver to drop him off at the hospital. Isn't that interesting, Mamá?"

I hadn't heard this story either. But I don't like it. I've always told Rocío that I don't think that stories involving bodily functions are appropriate to tell in front of others, and I remind her of that. Besides, I don't think of that as a miracle. La Virgen de Cuapa would never punish anyone like that. That's not a miracle, I tell Rocío. Well, that upsets her. She looks at me and I can see the hurt in her eyes. Without saying a word, my daughter leaves the room.

This reminds me of the last time I saw her alive. After I told her to go ahead and kill herself, she stared at me for the longest time. Her gaze was lost somewhere between hurt and anger. Rocío went into her room and came out with a bottle of sleeping pills. "I'm going to take the entire bottle, lie down, and wait for my death," she announced out loud for the maid to hear as well.

"Go ahead!" I challenged her. "Don't just talk about it, do it!" She stared sadly at me, and then she looked toward our maid before going into her room and closing the door. I had dared her because I was certain Rocío would never do such a thing, but the maid thought otherwise.

"Señora, you have to stop her," she said.

"No," I answered. "And stay out of this. It's none of your business. Besides, Rocío won't kill herself. All she wants is my attention." The maid nodded and let an hour go by before she spoke again.

"Señora, please check on niña Rocío," she pleaded.

"No," I said. "Let her stay in her room. She'll come out soon enough, once she realizes that I will not tolerate her insolence."

Two hours passed. Let's see who can be more stubborn, I

thought. Sooner or later, Rocío will have to come out. The maid, though, was becoming frantic. Against my strict orders, she went into the room and tried to wake Rocío. She came out crying hysterically.

"She's pretending," I said.

"No, she's not, Señora!" The maid then ran to the phone, intending to call el Demonio.

"Put that phone down!" I ordered. "Rocío's fine. She's just pretending to be asleep. She's a devout Catholic. She would never kill herself, don't you see?" Tearfully, the maid disappeared into the kitchen, which I thought was just as well. Rocío always needed an audience, ever since she was a child and used to recite Darío's poetry to everyone's delight.

I did not know that the maid had left the house through the back and run next door. From there, she called el Demonio. Before I knew what was happening, Agustín and Nora were in my house. I tried to stop them, but Nora shoved me aside, her tubular body being much stronger than mine. They rushed into the bedroom and Agustín picked Rocío up and carried her to a waiting taxi, which rushed them to the hospital. The maid just stood there, staring at me and crying.

"You'll see," I said, "Rocío's only pretending."

Not two hours had passed when Agustín and his mother returned. "It's your fault Rocío's dead!" Nora yelled at me. "She made a big production of her suicide just so you could save her, and you let her die! What kind of mother are you?"

What kind of mother am I?

What kind of mother was I?

With those questions turning over and over in my head, I went into my daughter's room, locked the door, and lit five candles before the statue of la Virgen de Cuapa. I called upon her as Rocío had taught me: "María, you are my Mother, Mother of all of us, sinners," and I implored her to perform a miracle. I begged her never to let me be separated from my daughter. I prayed and cried so desperately that Nuestra Señora took pity on me. Everything in the room began to swirl. Sounds, thoughts, images, everything blurred together into a whirlpool that began to spin out of control. And soon I lost consciousness.

Or did I?

When I opened my eyes again, la Virgen stood before me. She was *so* beautiful. She is the most stunning creature imaginable. We didn't say a word, and we just smiled at each other. But in spite of the silence, I didn't need her to tell me that she would grant my wish.

I fell into a deep sleep. When I finally awoke, Rocío was on the bed, sitting next to me. I knew, right then, that I could no longer pay any attention to the living. If I did, I would slide back into that desolate, lonely world. I never want to return there. I'm happy here, existing only for Rocío. And she exists only for me.

After I was released from the psychiatric hospital, I went to live with Pedro. I had no other family. Sadly, Pedro didn't want to take care of both Lourdes and me. That meant that Agustín and Nora ended up keeping my granddaughter. There was nothing I could do about that; if I fought to keep Lourdes I would have lost Rocío. I had no choice. I cut myself off from the sorrowful thought of el Demonio keeping a piece of me. I simply had to let go of my granddaughter. There is some consolation: Rocío visits her several times a day and keeps me updated.

My brother, hoping for a miracle, pleaded with Bernardo de Cuapa to visit us. The seer came today. The instant he entered the house, I let myself slide out of seclusion, paying close attention to one of Nuestra Señora's favored sons.

"Please, don Bernardo, heal my sister. Please bring her back to us."

"I don't perform miracles," the visionary answered. "Everyone performs their own miracles, based on their faith. But I'll be happy to pray over her."

With that, Bernardo placed both hands on my head and began to pray, asking for la Virgen de Cuapa to have pity on me. After he finished, he turned to my brother, startled. The seer then got on his knees so that he could look straight into my eyes. I must admit that Bernardo is handsomer than your average campesino.

"I don't understand," he said.

"Understand what?" Pedro asked.

"La Virgencita has already performed a miracle. This is the blessing your sister desired."

And upon hearing that I retreat, going back into myself and firmly locking the exit. I see Rocío, standing next to me, delighted because la Virgen's messenger is here. And I know that Bernardo sees us both clearly, my daughter and me—shadows among the living.

chapter eight

PROTOSPATHARI
(The Royal Guard)

February 1983

Tatiana Altamirano

TATIANA ALTAMIRANO took great pleasure in the blast of hot air
that greeted her the moment she exited the offices of el Ministerio del
Interior. Leaving the air-conditioned coolness of the building for
the sweltering tropical heat reminded her of the exploding containers of gasoline that Somoza's air force dropped on the city of
León, during the last days of the dictatorship. The scorching tem-
peratures brought back memories of buildings engulfed in flames.
But they were also memories of victory: that stirring time when,
after decades of struggle, the triumph of la Insurrección became
inevitable. Thus, Tatiana loved this weather. Besides, she absolutely
hated air-conditioning.

Tatiana had just left a meeting with her boss, el sub-comandante
de seguridad nacional, Jorge Pineda. The assistant chief of national

security had called her to his office, stating over the phone that it was urgent. When Tatiana arrived, his unkempt appearance shocked her. Normally her jefe was immaculate, always wearing starched, sharply pressed olive-greens, as if he were about to attend a gala dinner where Fidel would be present. But today his uniform was crumpled and sweat-stained. Jorge also had big dark circles under his eyes, as if he had stayed up all night talking to the ghosts of former political prisoners. And they were beginning to haunt him, at least that's what his subordinates were whispering these days. When Tatiana entered her jefe's office, he was leaning back in his leather chair with both boots up on his desk. In his hand, he held a penlight, which he turned off and on, off and on. With a casual gesture, Jorge motioned for her to sit in the chair across from him.

"Sabes, compañera," he started without preamble, "I miss the early days of la Revolución. Back then it seemed that nothing could stop us. I believed that our hopes and dreams for Nicaragua would become reality merely because we wished them so. But those times seem far away now."

"I know exactly what you mean, jefe. But the setbacks we're having will disappear soon. Once we neutralize the opposition, we'll be able to create the just society that Sandino and el Che envisioned."

For the first time since Tatiana had walked into the office, Jorge stopped playing with the penlight. He looked directly at her. "Do you really believe that, compañera? The people have made many sacrifices already. And all I see are more sacrifices ahead. How much longer do you think they'll continue to trust us, to believe in us? At this point, I doubt that the radical changes we had dreamed of will be possible."

Tatiana was startled to hear her jefe express his pessimism so openly. He sounded, she feared, like a counterrevolutionary. Maybe Jorge no longer belonged in this job, she thought. Maybe she should report him to el Ministerio del Interior. These thoughts were going through Tatiana's mind when, as if reading them, her boss said, "Forgive me, compañera, I've not slept for three days. I'm just exhausted, that's all. I've been touring the northern part of the country, and the contrarevolucionarios are causing a lot of damage. The trip has left me depressed. I'm afraid they're hurting la Revolución, Tatiana. And they're getting stronger every day. They've penetrated as far south as Chontales. Just a few months ago I would've said that was impossible. But the help they're getting from the United States has made a big difference. Do we have the resources to match that? No. The people will be asked to make greater sacrifices, compañera. What I'm about to tell you is top secret: los comandantes are thinking about imposing a military draft. There seems to be no other choice. That's why I've called you here."

"Sí, jefe," Tatiana said. She sat upright in her chair, eager to serve la Revolución.

"The minister of the interior and the chief of national security expect the archbishop and his cadre of pingüinos to openly oppose the draft. Compañera, you've got your work cut out for you. The comandantes are highly complimentary of everything you've done so far: the naked priest caper, shutting down Radio Católica, organizing our writers to respond to the archbishop's political pronouncements, the protesters who have taken over churches throughout the country. All work well done, Tatiana."

"Gracias, compañero."

"I mean it. Good work. Now, tell me, what are you planning for the pope's visit next month?"

"Members of la Iglesia Popular will be sitting up front during the pope's mass in Managua. They'll interrupt his sermon, chanting slogans for peace. We hope that their cry for justice will force the pope to denounce the contras."

"I hope it works, compañera. If he condemns U.S. aggression it will certainly help our struggle." Jorge then remained silent, staring intently at Tatiana. She knew what this meant, the stare always preceded his concern about something she was working on. "What about this Cuapa thing, compañera? It refuses to go away. Los comandantes are beginning to find the growing devotion somewhat worrisome. People are going there by the thousands every week. We've almost silenced the Church, but now the faithful are showing their support by traveling to Cuapa. What are you doing about it, compañera?"

"Bernardo Martínez has been in custody for ten days now," Tatiana said as calmly as she could, trying not to appear on the defensive. "He's in El Chipote. We're trying to get him to recant, but he refuses. He's sticking to his story. When it comes to the apparition, he can be extremely uncooperative."

"Have you asked him if the CIA helped fabricate this children's tale?"

"Yes, compañero. We've asked him that many times. But I honestly believe that he has no idea what the CIA is. If it weren't so damn frustrating I'd find his answer funny: at first he thought we were talking about a chair—*la silla*. I think he's genuinely clueless when it comes to politics. For instance, the one thing that scares him most about la Revolución is his belief that all Sandinistas are atheists."

"Well, compañera, you need to silence him once and for all. And do it quickly. You have a lot of work ahead with the pope's visit. I know you've been completely devoted to all of your assignments. I commend you for that. But the game hasn't even begun to get rough yet. Soon we'll be playing hardball with the Church. You need to do whatever it takes to neutralize them. But first, let's get rid of this Cuapa problem. Keep me informed, compañera."

As Tatiana sat in the rear of el ministerio's Soviet-made Lada, on her way back to El Chipote, she thought about how she would neutralize the visionary. "We'll see now, Bernardo Martínez, which one of us is more hardheaded," she said to herself.

Since childhood, Tatiana had been tenacious. Plus, she'd always detested passive people. Tatiana especially hated her parents' meekness. Although her family wasn't rich, she wouldn't call them working class either. Her father earned a living by giving injections to mostly overweight, middle-aged, hypochondriac women. He bridged the gap between doctors who were too busy to make housecalls, and patients too lazy to walk to their offices. Her father charged seven córdobas per shot—one dollar. Because he wanted to save the money he'd spend on cab fare, every two months he wore out the soles of new shoes from walking endless kilometers up and down the streets of León. Tatiana's father had seen so many flabby bourgeois buttocks, swabbing them down with cotton balls soaked in alcohol, that he had become complacent, ignoring the insults these women hurled at him as he buried the needle deep into their shapeless, trembling mounds of flesh.

Tatiana's mother owned a pulpería. Every day she had to remind her regular customers that she didn't sell anything on credit. On blistering March afternoons, the poor woman sat behind the counter, dripping with sweat while she waved a hand-held fan before her face, hoping that the heat would move people to buy more soft drinks. Tatiana's parents worked like slaves because they wanted their six children—four girls and two boys—to go to León's best Catholic schools.

Tatiana and her sisters attended La Pureza de María, across the street from la Catedral. The wealthier girls teased her mercilessly, making fun of the worn uniforms she inherited from her older sisters. Tatiana hated the way these girls set themselves apart from their poorer classmates. She liked the nuns, though, believing them compassionate. It wasn't until many years later, after Tatiana had studied Karl Marx, that she realized that these seemingly kind monjitas, all along, had been filling her head with outdated, archaic ideas about social class, and about a woman's place in the world.

As far back as she could remember, class differences made her angry. Even at home, Tatiana couldn't understand why her beloved Tina, the maid who had served the family faithfully since before her birth, couldn't sit down at the same table to eat with them. If there was one thing she could change on this earth, it would be the way the rich treated the poor.

During Tatiana's senior year in high school, in the late 1960s, she joined a Catholic youth group. The priest who led it taught her to read the New Testament in light of Christ's commitment to the dispossessed. The group visited Subtiava once a week—the section of León where los indios lived—to distribute food and medicine, and to teach adults how to read. Tatiana loved this. She felt she was helping to change the world.

Tatiana continued working with the group when she entered la universidad. But halfway through her first semester, she met Edmundo Rojas, a handsome young student from a Managua family of means. He had an intense gaze, which his thick, dark eyebrows accentuated. The marked cleft on his chin and the slight gap between his front teeth reminded her of a young Omar Sharif, one of her favorite movie stars. It was Edmundo who first noticed Tatiana at a protest rally. She stepped up to the microphone and told the crowd that, in spite of the work they were doing on behalf of political prisoners, they should not forget the plight of the poor.

After Tatiana had finished speaking, Edmundo approached her and said, "I liked your speech. You're one of the handful of students who understands what this is really all about." They began to meet frequently over drinks of cacao to discuss ways of transforming the country. While they agreed that Nicaragua needed drastic changes, they completely disagreed on the means.

"The transformation must happen peacefully, gradually, in a Christian spirit," Tatiana would argue.

"You're joking, right? You think Somoza and la Guardia will allow meaningful changes to take place? I'm sorry, Tatiana, but you're fooling yourself. Only an armed revolution can bring the things we're talking about," he would counter.

By this time, Tatiana had noticed that Edmundo never attended classes. He just hung around campus, carrying books on Marxism under his arm.

"La universidad is full of political agitators, Tatiana," her mother had warned. "Stay away from them. If not, they'll get you into trouble." But each passing day the young woman grew closer to Edmundo.

What he had to say opened her eyes. She began to see la Guardia Nacional as a repressive, brutal army at the service of a tyrant. Before long, Tatiana announced that she agreed with Edmundo; the only way to combat Somoza's despotism was by force. As soon as she admitted this, he said, "I think you're ready for the next step: to join el Frente."

The invitation to join the Sandinistas startled her. Although

Tatiana knew that Edmundo was a political activist, she would have never guessed that he was a member of the revolutionary group. "Join el Frente?" she whispered in disbelief. "You may as well ask me to rob a bank with you! You guys are nothing but a handful of extremists who keep getting slaughtered. It'll be centuries before you overthrow Somoza. Right now it's hopeless! If I join el Frente, I'll be signing my own death sentence!"

"That's what Somoza would have you believe, Tatiana," Edmundo said, "I'm a Sandinista and I'm still alive. And there are dozens more just like me, young people ready to take up arms against the dictatorship. The thing is to be careful and not get caught, to be always on guard. That's why secrecy is essential. That's why we recruit only those we can absolutely trust." Tatiana didn't need much convincing since by now she was far too much in love. She would have joined Edmundo in any scheme, no matter how reckless.

Before joining a rebel cell, Tatiana had to read a large stack of books on Marxism. Edmundo also gave her mimeographed copies of essays written by Carlos Fonseca Amador, the movement's founder. Tatiana proved an excellent student. She read everything avidly and afterward had passionate discussions with Edmundo. Within a few weeks she had let go of her "Christian trappings." In Tatiana's life there would be no more masses, confessions, communions, or rosaries—nothing more to do with the Church.

"Catholicism is largely responsible for conditioning the masses to behave submissively before the dehumanizing demands of imperialistic powers," she excitedly told Edmundo one evening as they discussed her readings.

Once satisfied with Tatiana's progress, Edmundo introduced her to the other members of his cell. They immediately assigned her a few tasks: buying clothes, food, and supplies for those who had gone underground; acting as a courier; listening to Guardia activity over a radio scanner and keeping detailed records; securing medicines and, if possible, weapons. Tatiana performed her responsibilities with supreme dedication. She went as far as to steal two small-caliber pistols while visiting her father's best friend, which her fellow cell members wildly celebrated.

Before the year was over, the cell had grown to six men and three women (who joined after Tatiana). But by now the sexism within the Sandinista movement was infuriating her. Although the rebels claimed to lead a struggle to ensure equality, women were not a part of their formula.

"What about us?" Tatiana would complain during the cell's political discussions. "Women deserve equal treatment in a just society. Besides, in Nicaragua we head three out of every four households."

"One struggle at a time, compañera," a cell member would answer. "Once we liberate the country, we can work on liberating the poor, and then women." The men in the cell would all agree, with the exception of Edmundo, whom Tatiana had convinced to join her cause. But the other men ignored Edmundo, and they never forgave him for including women in their cell.

"A woman's role within the movement should be to provide men with sexual companionship. That's it," a cell member said during a political discussion.

"Yes," another agreed. "But even that's problematic. It'll eventually create conflicts among us."

Tatiana kept her bitterness over such comments to herself.

Wanting to prove that a woman could do anything a man could, Tatiana asked for more responsibility within el Frente. She pestered the leadership in León so much, becoming as irritating as a pebble in a shoe, that an order finally came directly from Carlos Fonseca Amador that she be placed in charge of a safehouse, where members whose identity was known to la Guardia could hide. Although Tatiana was at first thrilled, seeing the assignment as a chance to prove a woman's worth, she became disillusioned when she discovered that she was also expected to clean, cook, wash, and mend the compañeros' clothes.

After several months of being in charge of the safehouse, Tatiana grew bored. She again began asking for a bigger role within the movement. She wanted either to join los guerrilleros in the mountains or to work alongside her male camaradas in urban operations.

"Please, Tatiana. Please stop asking for these assignments," Edmundo would beg her. "They're risky. Now that we're lovers, I don't want you exposed to any danger." Tatiana felt trapped even more. All because of her sex.

It was around this time that she first noticed the surveillance. Two men were meeting every day, in the small restaurant across the street, apparently to chat. Something about them, something she couldn't quite put into words, made Tatiana wary. But no one else was alarmed.

"We're not going to abandon a perfectly good safehouse based only on a woman's intuition," said the cell leader.

Undaunted, Tatiana continued watching the men. She became obsessed with them, certain that they worked for Somoza's National Security. On the third day of her countersurveillance, one of them dropped a newspaper, and when he bent to get it, through her binoculars she spotted the service revolver he kept attached to the inside of his waist, above his right hip. That evening, Tatiana led a well-planned evacuation of the safehouse and, shortly before dawn, she returned by herself to retrieve two pistols and a portable typewriter they had been forced to leave behind.

"Why did you do that?!" Edmundo yelled at her. "Don't you know you could've been caught?" But Tatiana's handling of the situation earned the respect of León's Sandinista directorate.

"She's earned the right to participate in something larger," Carlos Fonseca Amador declared when he heard about Tatiana's bravery.

Along with three men from her cell, including Edmundo, she began training for their biggest operation to date: robbing the local branch of el Banco Nacional. They spent weeks planning the assault, observing the guards, studying the layout, keeping a record of the comings and goings of customers to learn the busiest days and hours. At last, Tatiana and her compañeros were ready, believing they had foreseen every possible scenario, every possible outcome. But sometimes things go wrong for no reason. Of the four Sandinistas involved in the robbery, two escaped with the money. Edmundo fought valiantly, but died the instant he was shot; and Tatiana was captured as she tried to escape into Subtiava.

In a prison cell of la Oficina de Seguridad Nacional, Tatiana suffered tortures that tested the limits of her endurance. For once, she was happy she didn't know much about el Frente's operations. If she had, she would have told her captors everything just to put an end to the pain. The black hood they always kept over her head disoriented her. She lost track of time. Her cell was air-conditioned, and the temperature was kept close to freezing. Perhaps all this wouldn't have been that awful, if she also hadn't been stripped of all her clothing.

At first embarrassed by her nudity, within days Tatiana lost her shame, and soon she stopped paying attention to her jailers' lewd comments. During the first few weeks (or was it months?) she was beaten, left tied to a wall for hours, and given frequent electric shocks with wires that were connected to a nearby socket.

Tatiana survived the beatings and the shocks—with valor, as her torturers later said—but what finally broke her, what finally shattered her defiant spirit, was the night (or was it day?) that seventeen men visited her cell and, one at a time, raped her. Although she was kept hooded during the entire ordeal, she swore that she recognized the voice of el Hombre himself, el Dictador, among the perpetrators.

After that day (or was it night?), Tatiana withdrew to a place far within herself where everything was white, like a blank sheet of paper. "Once I'm released," she'd mumble into the hood, "I'll rewrite my entire life." And Tatiana began to do this even before her captors set her free. Mentally, she rehearsed, over and over, every step she would take to become the most feared member of el Frente. Tatiana also thought about how, from the moment of her release, she would not accept anything other than equal treatment from her compañeros. More important, she decided that never again would a man touch her.

Tatiana's torturers, convinced that she had been crushed, convinced that she would never again pose a threat, released la guerrillera amid a public relations campaign that lauded the dictator's magnanimity: *Anastasio Somoza Debayle: A Compassionate Leader* read the headline of *Novedades,* his personal newspaper.

Tatiana's torturers never suspected that she had such an extraordinary reserve of strength. After only a few months in Costa Rica, where she recovered in the house of an uncle, she returned to Nicaragua determined to fight Somoza and la Guardia Nacional until the end. The only aftereffects of the torture were that she avoided rooms with air-conditioning and that she couldn't stand the smell of men.

"Stay away from me!" Tatiana— code name Sandra—would growl if a new recruit came on to her. Holding her revolver against his temple, she'd say, "You better pray that your smell doesn't make me gag. Because, then, the only thing that will cure me is a bullet through your brain." Soon, no Sandinista in his right mind made an advance toward her.

"See that woman over there?" veterans would tell new recruits while they pointed out the fierce guerrillera. "If you want to come out of this alive, you'll be wise to stay away from her. We'd rather one of Somoza's bullets kill you than one of hers." Tatiana, meanwhile, developed quite a following among young female recruits, which in time she would learn to use for her pleasure.

On the battlefield, Tatiana became respected for remaining calm, rational, and collected, even in the most critical situations. Compañeros asked to be in her squad because they knew that under her leadership, with her cold, calculating mind, the odds for their survival would increase. And they were right. Tatiana knew just when and where to engage the enemy, and not once did she make the wrong decision. For years, just like Sandino five decades earlier, she and her men moved swiftly through the jungles of northeastern Nicaragua, proving impossible to trap, and frustrating la Guardia Nacional in its quest to eliminate communists from the face of the earth. Her men respected her, but they always kept themselves at a safe distance.

During the final offensive, Tatiana's squad fought in several of the uprising's bloodiest battles. It wasn't until the last week of la Insurrección that she lost a crew member, and that was through his own carelessness. El compañero, a victim of his craving for sweets, stopped in the middle of the street to buy cajeta de coco during the siege of León, making a perfect target for a Guardia sharpshooter. Tatiana had grown fond of every guerrillero on her team, and that loss hurt her almost as much as when she lost Edmundo. But the last days of the dictatorship were not a time to shed tears. The suffering, the years of fighting against a brutal, ruthless enemy, were coming to an end. Soon, Tatiana knew, el Frente would hold the destiny of the nation in its hands.

After the Sandinista victory, Tatiana was placed in charge of a prisoner of war camp. She distinguished herself for converting once sadistic men, who had been notorious torturers during the dictatorship, into meek, docile creatures. After their release they wouldn't step on a cucaracha. Soviet and Cuban advisers observed Tatiana's techniques, and they praised her talent for rehabilitating difficult cases.

"There's little we can teach Tatiana," one Soviet intelligence officer said. "She's a consummate professional who has a knack for this sort of thing. Plus, she enjoys her work immensely."

Because of Tatiana's unique skills, el Ministerio del Interior assigned her to la Oficina de Seguridad Nacional, where she was placed in charge of monitoring the conservative wing of the Catholic Church. She found the work demanding but satisfying. And today, as the Lada pulled into the compound of El Chipote, Tatiana wanted to concentrate on her biggest challenge to date: the pope's March visit. But first, she had to neutralize Bernardo Martínez.

Tatiana didn't return the guard's salute as she rushed into the building. Her mind was fixed on one thought: how to destroy the visionary's spirit before the end of the day. As Jorge Pineda had reminded her, time had run out. She stepped into her office and turned on the fans—a plywood board covered the hole where an air conditioner once had been. Tatiana sat at her desk, opened the top drawer, and pulled out the file labeled "Cuapa." Flipping open the folder, she began to review the case.

The first step Tatiana ordered was an investigation into Bernardo Martínez's past. The agents found nothing of interest. *His life had been unremarkable until the time of the apparition,* they wrote in their report. *When we discovered that the subject had never been married, nor known to have ever had a romantic affair with a woman—other than a close, but apparently chaste, relationship with a certain Blanca Arias—we immediately suspected that he was a homosexual. Our investigation along these lines uncovered nothing concrete.*

Tatiana then sent two agents to Cuapa on a pilgrimage: a man and a woman posing as a married, devoutly Catholic couple. Upon their return to the capital, they confirmed that Bernardo was condemning la Revolución. The woman had asked, during one of his daily talks at the apparition site, what la Virgen had to say about the Sandinistas. According to their written report, Bernardo answered:

La Virgencita doesn't approve of the Sandinistas because they are atheists, and atheists never deliver on any of their promises. She wants us all to pray the rosary so we can stop the spread of communism throughout the world, but especially to stop it here, in Nicaragua. La Virgencita also said that the road to peace in this continent goes through our country, that we must protect democracy. The agents' report also stated that Bernardo used counterrevolutionary code phrases, such as *the great danger, the obstacle to peace,* and *the approaching darkness.*

Tatiana had then tried to bribe Bernardo. One of her Soviet

mentors had taught her that most men have their price because, as Marx wrote: *The forces of colonialism and imperialism have, throughout the centuries, indoctrinated the masses in the selfish notions of capitalism.* Three agents visited the seer at his home.

"Don Bernardo, the government is prepared to offer you a finca: ten manzanas of clean and fertile pastures," the head agent proposed. "You probably already know the place. It's called El Triunfo. A monseñor from Granada left it to the Church in his will. We confiscated the land after an audit showed that the fees to transfer the ownership had not been paid. You'll also be given ten heads of cattle. All you need to do, don Bernardo, for El Triunfo to become yours, is to say that la Virgen supports la Revolución, that Christianity and Sandinismo are the same thing."

"I'm sorry, but I can't do that. I can't betray Nuestra Señora. Her message is sacred."

The agents moved to the opposite side of the seer's living room, where they conferred in private. When they returned, the same man spoke, saying, "How about this, then, Bernardo? All you have to say is that la Virgen has nothing against la Revolución."

"I would also betray her by saying that," the visionary said, refusing the bribe.

After the agents left, an informer reported that Bernardo grew suspicious. He moved into Cuapa to live with a friend in her elegant seven-pillar home on la Calle de los Laureles. Sure now that Bernardo couldn't be convinced to modify la Virgen's message, Tatiana ordered a smear campaign. The Sandinista press—television, radio, and newspapers—gave detailed accounts of the visionary's emotional instability. These reports also suggested that the seer's use of marijuana had aggravated his already fragile mental state. Plus, Bernardo de Cuapa was far from being a saint.

Several women in el pueblo, in fact, claimed that he was the father of their children. This proved, the stories reported, that the apparition was nothing more than Bernardo's ploy to earn money to support his numerous offspring as well as his drug habit.

The attacks against the visionary in the media were relentless. But surprisingly, if anything, his credibility increased. Believers in la Virgen's apparition in Cuapa, that is to say the vast majority of Nicaraguan Catholics, rallied in support. Instead of rejecting Bernardo de Cuapa, the faithful turned him into a symbol of resistance. In response to his growing popularity, at Tatiana's suggestion, the comandantes issued a decree forbidding the press from reporting on the apparitions until these had been officially approved by the Vatican.

With that law, Bernardo's story was no longer discussed in public. That didn't stop the pilgrimages. On the contrary, since news of the apparition became scarce, the number of pilgrims visiting Cuapa increased, eager now to hear la Virgen's message directly from her messenger.

Tatiana was then inspired by another assignment she was coordinating in which the archbishop's press secretary, a priest, was being set up so that reporters would "discover" his affair with a married woman. In Bernardo's case, Tatiana decided to try something similar, offering herself as the bait.

"After all," Tatiana had said to one of her agents, "how difficult can it be to seduce a jincho from Chontales?"

She appeared in Cuapa one day posing as a devotee of la Virgen. Using her code name, Sandra, she visited the apparition site as one of many who had come to listen to Bernardo talk about Nuestra Señora's appearance. During Sandra's second visit to the site, as the seer described what la Virgen looked like, she pretended to faint. Bernardo stayed at her side until she recovered. Sandra then began to work on gaining his trust.

"Don Bernardo," she said that afternoon, "I have a problem and I need your Virgencita's help. The government has invited me to work for the foreign ministry. They want me to give tours for important visitors from Eastern Europe. At first it seemed like a wonderful opportunity, don Bernardo. But now I suspect that what they really want is for me to offer myself to these gentlemen. The classes I'm taking are teaching me how to put on makeup, how to dress, how to walk provocatively. Do you understand what I'm saying? I live with my mother, and we're very poor. We can use the money, but I'm not sure I want to do this. That's why I need Nuestra Señora's guidance. And yours as well, if you'd be so kind."

Bernardo spent the next few mornings with Sandra, going for walks by the river, resting under a genízaro, and there counseling her. Within a few days she seemed more at ease, less tormented: laughing at his jokes, catching fish with him; they even splashed water at each other, just like children.

Things were ready for the next phase of her plan, Sandra thought: to set up the visionary for the incriminating photographs that would later appear in the papers—without her face being revealed, of course. By the end of the first week, as they sat under the genízaro, enjoying the flowing river, she said, "Bernardo, I want to see you tonight."

"Well, we're having a prayer meeting this evening. Why don't you join us?"

"No, Bernardo. I want to see *you*."

"¿Por qué? Is there a problem?"

"No, Bernardo, I want to *be* with you . . . *alone. Tonight.*"

Sandra was now sure that Bernardo understood, and she was

sure that he *was* interested. He promised to meet her in front of the church at eight o'clock. What she didn't anticipate was, as he later stated under questioning, that he would call Padre Domingo to seek his advice.

"I don't know, Bernardito," the parish priest said. "The whole thing seems suspicious to me. I mean, what would a young, intelligent, attractive woman, as you describe her, want with a fifty-two-year-old tailor? If I were you, I'd avoid seeing her altogether."

That night, Sandra waited in the park until eleven o'clock. Although she hated to admit it, Bernardo's rejection angered her. Sandra returned to the inn, dismissed the photographer, packed her things, got in the jeep, and shortly before midnight drove back to Managua, all alone on the dark, desolate highway.

By now, Tatiana faced a growing problem: the crowds in Cuapa were getting larger, and el Ministerio del Interior wanted results. More assertive measures were necessary. But Tatiana preferred to keep the operation simple, not like the one involving the spokesman for the archdiocese, over which she lost control and, in the end, the evidence against the priest seemed fabricated. Tatiana wanted the operation in Cuapa to go unnoticed. She sent three agents to bring Bernardo to Managua as quietly as possible. They returned empty-handed. Their plan, a good one really, or so Tatiana thought, had been to offer Bernardo a ride to the apparition site as he began the five-kilometer walk for his daily presentation. Once inside the car, they would chloroform the visionary and whisk the sleeping man straight to El Chipote.

"What actually happened was eerie, compañera," the lead agent said. "Bernardo accepted our offer, but when he climbed into the car the engine died on us. The other two agents worked on it for a while, and Bernardo, in a hurry now to get to the site, stepped out of the vehicle. As soon as he did, compañera, the engine started. But when he got back in, it stopped. Bernardo stepped out again, and the engine started. He climbed back in, and it stopped. Finally, he caught a ride in another passing car." Scratching his head, the agent concluded, "If I didn't know any better, compañera, I would say that la Virgen was protecting him."

In the end, Tatiana had no choice but to become more forceful. She ordered another three agents to kidnap Bernardo and bring him to Managua, using whatever means necessary. Two nights later, the men quietly broke into the house with the seven mahogany pillars on la Calle de los Laureles, intending to gag and tie the visionary, and then carry him out. But that plan failed as well.

"Compañera, he's a lot stronger than he seems. Even though we surprised him, and there were three of us, we couldn't subdue him. He hit me on the head with a heavy wooden crucifix, and I almost passed out. Then his cries for help woke the entire neighborhood. We had to run out of there. If los cuapeños had caught us, I suspect we would have been lynched. You know how savage chontaleños can be."

Tatiana now thought that the entire affair with Bernardo de Cuapa had gotten out of hand. How difficult could it be to bring a madman who talks to la Virgen María under control? This time, she and her agents couldn't afford to fail. By now, everyone in Cuapa knew that the Sandinistas wanted to get their hands on Bernardo. The whole town was on the watch, protecting him. She and her men needed to think of something subtle. Tatiana called a meeting of every agent who had ever been involved with the case.

"This is getting ridiculous, compañeros. We need to find out what would persuade Bernardo to come to Managua of his own free will. Any ideas?"

The agents remained silent, pondering the question Tatiana had posed. Finally, one spoke, "Well, more than anything, he wants to become a priest. I think a written invitation from the archbishop's office stating that he's been accepted into the seminary would bring him to Managua immediately."

Even Tatiana, who was difficult to impress, was stunned by the simple genius of this plan. At once, they drafted this letter:

Estimado Bernardo:

Greetings in the name of Nuestro Señor Jesucristo. It is with great pleasure that I inform you that the Council of Bishops has accepted you as a student in the seminary. As a favored son of Nuestra Señora, we are sure you will succeed in your efforts to become a priest.

Due to the difficult situation that the Church is currently facing, and because it has come to our attention that the government has been targeting you specifically, we ask that you come at once with Padre Francisco Madrigal, the bearer of this message, to Managua.

For your own safety, please tell no one where you are going. We will inform your friends and relatives in Cuapa regarding your whereabouts at a more appropriate time.

Su hermano en Cristo,

Monseñor Julio Buitrago
Assistant to the Archbishop

The agent, alias Padre Francisco Madrigal, delivered the letter. In his written report, he described Bernardo's response as simple and to the point: *La Virgencita told me this day would come.* While the agent waited in the vehicle, Bernardo went into the seven-caoba-pillar house, packed a few belongings, and left without telling anyone. According to the report, *The visionary never showed signs of suspecting anything. On the ride to Managua his demeanor was peaceful and beatific. He didn't even seem alarmed when, instead of driving to the seminary, the car pulled into El Chipote.* Without uttering a word, Bernardo stepped into his cell—the same one that had held Tatiana years before. It wasn't until the guards began stripping the visionary of his clothes that he protested.

"Por favor," Bernardo pleaded, his hands open, palms facing up, in supplication, "let me keep my dignity."

The guards tied him up and left him naked. The temperature of the cell was kept so low that the motor of the air conditioner strained from overwork. At intervals that were impossible for Bernardo to predict, the agents roused him from his sleep by dipping a live electrical wire into the thin layer of water that covered the floor. But no matter how much they tortured the seer, no matter how terrifying the threats, no matter what they promised, Bernardo de Cuapa refused to recant.

"I can't betray la Virgencita," he would mumble, exhausted, but firm in his resolve.

Following Tatiana's meeting with Jorge Pineda, her jefe in el Ministerio del Interior, after ten days of trying to break the prisoner without success, she had only one afternoon left in which to accomplish the task. She closed the folder and placed the *Cuapa* file back in the top drawer of her desk. It was now time for Tatiana to speak to Bernardo personally. She ordered the guards to untie him from the wall. After they had done this, Tatiana entered his cell for the first time since the seer had been imprisoned.

Bernardo de Cuapa sat on the floor, legs stretched out before him, with his back against the wall. He kept his head down, too tired to raise it. Tatiana waited for him to look at her, but when he didn't, she spoke.

"Hola, Bernardo."

The seer had not heard a woman's voice since the nightmare had begun. Bernardo looked up, squinting as he struggled to recognize the person standing before him. At last, he said, "Sandra, are they keeping you here too?"

"Bernardo, they've asked me to try to convince you to sign a document where you state that you've made up the entire story about your Virgencita. If you do this simple thing, you can go home and live out the rest of your life in peace. Wouldn't you like that?"

"Yes, Sandra. I would. But I can't. I can't betray her."

"But Bernardo, you can leave this place right now if you just say that you invented everything. They're even promising to give you la finca they offered you earlier. Think about it, Bernardo. That's very generous. You can return home a wealthy man, and no one would ever blame you for changing your mind."

"I know, Sandra, I know. But I also know what I saw and what I heard. The apparition of Nuestra Señora was real. I can't lie about that."

"You know, Bernardo," Tatiana said, squatting next to the prisoner and speaking softly, "I've been reading about your saint. Do you really want to send young men to die in a doomed religious crusade, just like San Bernardo did in Europe? Are you aware what happened to his crusade? It ended in disaster. Few returned home of those who went in the name of your God to liberate the Promised Land. Your namesake's righteousness cost thousands of lives. Is that how you, Bernardo de Cuapa, wish to be remembered? Do you want to be responsible for all the deaths that will surely result from a war in Nicaragua?"

Bernardo shook his head.

"Well, then, you can change all that and help us avoid the pain of seeing mothers weeping next to the coffins of their children. All you have to do is recant, Bernardo. If you really want to end your suffering, just say that you made the whole foolish thing up."

At last, after ten days without showing signs of breaking, Bernardo looked at Sandra, and began to cry. His sobs became so wrenching that even Tatiana, experienced at crushing men's spirits, was moved. When Bernardo de Cuapa tried to speak, out of his mouth came an incoherent, tormented howl. Finally, he bawled, "I can't, Sandra. Even though it might save my life, and the lives of others, I can't betray la Virgencita."

"In that case, there's nothing more I can do for you, Bernardo. I'm very sorry." She leaned toward the visionary, and kissed him on the cheek.

Tatiana left the room. Four agents had watched the exchange through the one-way mirror. They now awaited Tatiana's instructions. The interrogation confirmed what she had begun to suspect: that nothing could get Bernardo de Cuapa to recant. One option was to make him disappear. But that would give the Church a martyr. She certainly didn't want that on her hands. All Tatiana could hope for was to hurt the visionary deeply, to cause him such agonizing pain that it would be a while before he appeared in public again.

Without saying a word, Tatiana looked each agent bluntly in the eyes. They understood perfectly that their boss's orders were not to be countermanded. After Tatiana was certain she had their unconditional allegiance, she looked through the glass at Bernardo, who was still crying. Without the slightest tremor in her voice, she said, "Let him just walk out of here once it's dark outside. But before you do that, rape the bastard."

TERTIA VISIO

(The Third Apparition)

July 8–September 6, 1980

Bernardo

ON JULY 8, I returned to the site. About forty persons joined me, eager to see la Virgencita for themselves. We arrived shortly before noon. We sang a few hymns, and then prayed the rosary. We stayed there until the day began turning to dusk. But just like last month, she didn't appear. I had prayed all month long that la Virgencita would come today. That made my disappointment even bigger because I had really believed that my prayers were being heard. And this time, people weren't as kind. Some said I had made them waste an entire day. There were a few who even suggested that I was making up the story of Nuestra Señora's apparition.

That night, feeling terribly alone, I prayed the rosary. I was so sad that I did so distractedly. Remembering that el Señor doesn't like prayers said like that, I began to say a second rosary. When I finally finished, I was terribly exhausted. I fell asleep almost instantly. Soon, I began to dream.

In my dream, I was at the apparition site, kneeling before the morisco tree where Nuestra Señora had appeared. I began to pray a rosary for Nicaragua and for the rest of the world, just as she had instructed. When I finished, I remembered that Padre Domingo had asked me to pray for all the priests, nuns, bishops, cardinals, and the pope, for they are in special need of la Virgencita's blessing. Thinking about them, I started to pray a second rosary.

After I finished, I remembered that my friend Chepita had asked me to pray for her brother, Fernando, who was in the Juigalpa jail. Three weeks ago, in a cantina, after a few drinks, he had gotten into an argument. The discussion became bitter, and his rival ran to the police station, falsely accusing Fernando of making statements against la Revolución. He had been locked up ever since. Chepita was worried because the guards wouldn't allow her to visit her brother for more than a few minutes at a time. And when she did see him, they weren't given any privacy; someone always stood nearby, listening to everything they said. Still in my dream, I remained on my knees and began to pray a third rosary, this time for Fernando.

But I didn't finish. Having prayed the rosary four times— twice awake and twice in my dream—I was worn out. I was also worried because in the dream I had to hurry home to feed the pigs. In a rush to leave, I decided just to pray three Hail Marys for Fernando. I lifted my arms, raised my eyes toward the heavens, and began.

Once I finished, I glanced at the pile of rocks in front of the morisco tree. I was startled to see a young man standing there. Immediately I knew he was an angel. His body was bathed in light, making him look almost transparent. He hadn't shaved for about three days, which I found interesting. The stubble looked good on him, though. He was tall, wore a simple white tunic, and, like Nuestra Señora, his feet were bare.

He was friendly and open, and had a calmness that comforted me. But I didn't feel as free to talk to him as I do with Nuestra Señora. I didn't know what to say. Happily, el Angel spoke first.

Bernardo, your prayer has been heard. He said nothing more. Confused, and still on my knees, I scratched my head, asking myself just which one of my prayers he was talking about. El Angel, reading my thoughts, said, *Go tell the prisoner's sister not to worry. On Monday, he will be released. But tell her to go visit him on Sunday. For once, the guards will allow her to speak to him in privacy. She must warn him not to sign a document in which he admits to stealing money. The prison commander will tempt him this way, saying that if he signs he can go home, but he must refuse. Tell the sister to return to the jail on Monday with one thousand córdobas: that's what it will cost to get him released. After she pays, he will be set free.*

"Thank you," I said.

Seeing that I had a chance to present a few of the hundreds of petitions I'd been receiving, I began with those from my relatives. I chose my cousin Liduvina's because she had come all the way from Zelaya just to speak to me.

"Señor Angel, my cousin has two problems: the first one is about her teaching job. She's afraid she's going to lose it. She believes that the Sandinistas are going to ask her to renounce her faith in Jesús. My cousin knows that to betray Nuestro Señor would be terrible, but she doesn't want to lose her job either. She doesn't know what to do."

Tell your cousin not to be afraid, el Angel replied. *Tell her to remain firm and to not resign. The school's director will try to intimidate her, but she should not abandon her job, no matter what. As a teacher who believes in el Señor, she will do much good for humanity.*

"Thank you, Señor Angel. I'll tell her that. Her second problem is about her father and brother: they become violent when they drink."

Tell your cousin that she should instruct everyone in her family to be patient. They should not scold her father when he is drunk. Then, Bernardo, I want you to tell him to stop drinking gradually; he should not try to quit all at once. Little by little, el Señor will remove his desire for alcohol. El Angel then looked at me sadly. He paused, saying nothing for the longest moment. At last, he sighed and then continued speaking.

Liduvina's brother faces a bigger problem. Tell him that he will be robbed and during the robbery he will be shot in the foot. This is only a warning, though. Later, the criminals will return. The second time they will kill him.

I was horrified when I heard this. "Can I change my cousin's fate if I pray several rosaries a day for him?"

No, Bernardo. This is how he's destined to die. But if he follows your advice he will live a little longer. Before I had a chance to recover from this alarming prophecy, el Angel began to repeat, word for word, everything Nuestra Señora had asked of us. He reminded us to pray the rosary every day, in family; to pray it during the quietest part of the day, when there are no distractions; to love one another and to fulfill our obligations to each other; to forgive one another and to work for peace; to avoid the path of violence; to change our ways so that we can avoid Armageddon. And he reminded me to share her message with the world.

The instant el Angel finished, he vanished. I woke up and immediately prayed the rosary. Afterward, I thought about the dream. As with last month's, I could remember everything, every single detail.

The next day I told Chepita about the dream, but I asked her to keep it a secret. I didn't want people to know that I was now talking to angels in my sleep. Already many were saying that I was crazy, ready to be shipped off to el Kilómetro Cinco, the psychiatric hospital in Managua.

"How can that be, Bernardo? I doubt they're going to release Fernando," she replied after I finished telling her what el Angel had said.

"Chepita," I answered, "have faith in el Señor. Do everything el Angel has asked, and it will turn out well." She promised that she would. And then we prayed the rosary together.

Chepita visited her brother on Sunday, just as el Angel had asked. And as he had prophesied, the guards allowed her to be alone with him for as long as she needed. "They'll give you a document to sign. Don't do it, Fernandito," she said. He promised to do as she asked.

When Chepita returned to Cuapa, she went to see don Iván, a moneylender who never forgives anyone who's late in paying. He's also known for not handing out a single centavo without collateral. He loaned Chepita the thousand córdobas. When she handed him her mother's wedding ring, don Iván said, "You don't need to do that, Chepita. I trust you."

"Don Iván, why didn't you take the ring?" I asked him a few days later.

"It was the strangest thing, Bernardo, but a voice in my head told me just to give Chepita the money without accepting anything from her. I just had to obey."

I told don Iván that la Virgencita would bless his trust.

Monday morning, Chepita returned to the jail. "Niña Chepita, I've concluded the investigation into Fernando's case. He's guilty of subversive activities, but if you pay a fine of one thousand five hundred córdobas, I'll release him into your custody."

"Señor, I'm just a poor schoolteacher. I can't afford to pay that much," Chepita answered.

The official thought about it for a moment, and then he said, "I understand. I'll reduce the fine to one thousand, then."

Chepita paid the amount. A few minutes later, she was crying in Fernando's arms, thanking la Virgencita.

On the bus ride back to Cuapa, Fernando asked, "Chepita, how did you know what would happen? El jefe woke me up before dawn. He said that if I signed a document saying that I had stolen money from the Vargas family, he would let me go. If I refused, he said, I would stay in prison for a long time. I said no, because of my promise to you. But, honestly, I was scared to death because I believed I would never go free."

After Chepita returned to Cuapa, she asked for my permission to tell everyone about my dream, and about how everything I predicted had come true. I said yes. She must have been very convincing because many who doubted me dropped by the house later to apologize. Yes, that story ended happily, just as el Angel had foretold.

My cousin Liduvina's concern about her job ended happily as well. The director of her school, a teacher sent here from Cuba, tried to get her to sign a document in which she renounced her faith in Jesús. But when he saw that my cousin wasn't going to do that, even when he threatened to fire her, he gave up. Since then, he has never bothered Liduvina again.

The story also ended well for mi tío, Liduvina's father. He agreed to give up drinking, gradually, just as el Angel had suggested. Faster than any of us could have hoped for, he has given up guaro altogether. We hope that it's forever.

Sadly, el Angel's predictions about Liduvina's brother have also come true. The day after Fernando was released from prison, I went to visit my cousin. He lived far away: a two-hour bus ride east on la carretera to Rama, then another two hours on a terrible dirt road to La Batea; from there I walked to La Ardilla, where I rented a horse, and then I rode across el Río Mico until I came to a village called La Tigra. From there it was still another hour to my cousin's finca. He liked living deep in the mountains with his wife and two children. As soon as we were alone, I told him about my dream: about him first being shot in the foot and later killed. But his heart was already as hard as la Piedra de Cuapa. My warnings didn't move him.

"Primo," I said, "you should come back to Cuapa. You need to avoid the approaching danger, and you should stop drinking as well, but do it gradually." Immediately after I finished saying this, my cousin went inside the house and returned with a bottle of guaro and two plastic cups.

"Primo," he said, "if all along you've been hinting for me to invite you for a drink, you should have just said so." That made me angry. But I didn't say a word. After talking for a little while more, I left for Cuapa. On the trip back home I felt sad and helpless. All I could do was pray a rosary for him.

Less than a week later, I heard that two men had robbed my cousin and that he had been shot . . . in the foot. I made the long trip back to his farm to see for myself what had happened.

"Two masked men came and demanded that I give them all my money. Instead of handing it over, I ran inside the house and closed the door behind me. From the other side the men pushed, trying to force it open, but I managed to keep it shut. Then one of them put the barrel of the gun in the gap under the door and shot me." As my cousin said this, he lifted his left leg and showed me the wrapped foot. A doctor from La Batea had removed the bullet from his heel. "In spite of the pain, primo, I was still able to hold the door closed. Los bandidos left, but they were pissed, encachimbados. They went away shouting that they'd be back. They ended up taking some cheeses and two mules I had just bought."

"Primo," I said, "don't you see that el Angel's predictions are coming true? Sell the farm and come back to Cuapa. I'm sure you'll find work there. It's not worth losing your life over this finca."

"Everything you've told me, primo, about el Angel and all that, are just coincidences. I plan on living a long life. Nothing you say, no matter who told you to say it, is going to scare me into giving up mi finquita and going to work for someone else. How about a drink?"

I left feeling very sad, knowing that unless my cousin had a sudden change of heart, it would be the last time I'd see him. On my way back to Cuapa, I prayed several Rosaries for him.

On September 6, as I was heading to church to pray the rosary before el Santísimo, I saw don Fulgor, the telegraph operator, running toward me and waving something in his hand. When he reached me, he was out of breath.

"Bernardo, tengo malas noticias," don Fulgor said, once he could speak. He handed me a telegram. I opened it and read that my cousin had been shot and killed.

I'm happy that la Virgencita hasn't given me the gift of prophecy. Whenever I knew what would happen, it was because it had been part of a vision. Those little glimpses into the future seemed almost like an accident. And although I was aware beforehand of my cousin's destino, it didn't make the pain any less. If anything, it made it worse. Knowing what would happen and not being able to do anything about it made his death seem more tragic.

Don Fulgor stared at me anxiously. At last, he said, "I'm sorry, Bernardo."

"Don Fulgor, it was foretold that my cousin would die this way. It was so foretold." I folded the telegram and returned it to him. Then I went on to church. That afternoon, the rosary I prayed was for my cousin's soul.

chapter nine

THEOTOKOS
(The God-Bearer)

November 1988

Germán Sotelo

ONLY TWO months ago I was waiting anxiously, my shirt soaked in sweat, inside the dingy, muggy halls of General Augusto César Sandino International Airport. I expected that day to be the most important of my life. When the flight from Panamá landed, my heart was beating so fast you would've thought I was about to embark on my first sexual adventure. But just like that experience, the whole thing turned out to be a big disappointment.

If you think about it, it's easy to imagine my excitement. After all, Jaime Jaramillo Solís, the Great Ecuadorian Writer and one of Latin America's most renowned novelists, was spending a month in Nicaragua to conduct research for an article he was writing about life under the Sandinistas. And the Nicaraguan Ministry of

Culture had chosen me, Germán Sotelo, Nicaraguan poet, novelist, dramatist, and, most important, literary theorist, to be his aide. Just imagine that.

Jaime Jaramillo Solís is but merely one of dozens of Great Writers who have visited our country in recent years. The Great Argentinean Writer who died not too long ago, the one who wrote that brilliant novel in which you hop from chapter to chapter, was a frequent visitor and a big supporter of la Revolución. The Great Colombian Writer, the one who won el Premio Nobel, often drops by to let the Sandinistas know that he's behind them. The distinguished-looking Great Mexican Writer, who writes in Spanish but speaks perfect English, has also been here. The Great English Catholic writer, the one who has written several novels about Latin America, has been here a couple of times. Even a Great Pakistani-Indian-British Writer came by for a quick visit. (It was ruined a bit when at a reception in his honor, a curandera read his palm and solemnly declared that a dark cloud of persecution hovered over him.) Thus, as you can see, writers from all over the world are coming to take a closer look at our little social laboratory. And now, we can add the name of Jaime Jaramillo Solís to this prestigious list. And I was more excited than anyone else in this country because I would be at his side the entire time.

I admit that it's true that the Great Ecuadorian Writer has been ostracized by his peers. That's because they write from the left, while he writes from the right. Early in his career, Jaime Jaramillo Solís defended revolutions everywhere. He was a close friend of Fidel's, but he and the bearded one had a falling out. Ever since, Jaramillo Solís has been an outcast. But that didn't bother me at all. In that respect, we were kindred spirits. Or so I thought.

Why was I, then, with so many other Nicaraguan writers in

better standing with el Ministerio de Cultura, chosen to be the Great Ecuadorian Writer's aide? The only way to answer this question is to tell you a little bit about myself.

I was born in Ocotal, Nueva Segovia, in the beautiful pine-studded mountains of northern Nicaragua. From an early age, I stood out for being exceptionally bright, especially gifted in writing. When I graduated from la escuela secundaria, my parents, making a big sacrifice, sent me to the Jesuit university in Managua to study law. Although I graduated with honors, I was unhappy because I knew I was missing my true calling: to critique, and produce, literature. During my years as a law student, I spent every spare minute writing poetry and reading books on literary theory. I was even able to blend both obsessions flawlessly in my first poetic collection: *Memorias del deseo.*

In this work, I attempted to fuse, in verse form, the notions of the Russian formalists with those of Ferdinand de Saussure. I wrote an erotic epic poem that sought to demonstrate that nar-remes, mythemes, functions, roles, modalities, and types of events are perpetually intertwined in lucid temporal sequences according to the rules of syntax. I failed in that aim. What I accomplished, instead, was a dissection of the theories of Gérard Genette when I created a body of work where the analepses and prolepses constantly disrupt the chronology of the sexual experience. In other words, the lines between scene and summary were erased; thus the reader is constantly challenged to discern whether what he has read was a mimesis or a diegesis. Needless to say, my work was fantastic! ¡Genial!

Nevertheless, the book didn't sell very well. To be honest, it didn't sell at all, so to speak. My parents bought the hundred copies that were printed and set them ablaze in a bonfire. They said that the contents of my erotic poem embarrassed them. It's just as well that no copies survived. My poetic masterpiece was too far ahead of its time. I don't believe readers will ever be ready to understand what I was trying to achieve.

Not all was lost, however. At a conference on Central American Literature, held in Guatemala City during the early seventies, a professor from the University of North Dakota recognized my genius after I argued with him for three hours about how the existence of God can be proven through semiotics. Mine was a perspective that, inexplicably, theologians and philosophers have missed. Dazzled by the genius of my oral dissertation, he offered me a teaching assistantship. I accepted, of course. How could I not? It was a dream coming true. Poets and literary critics are as plentiful in Nicaragua as coconuts, and much less appreciated. A doctoral degree from los Estados Unidos in this majestic field would assure that I stand out in the crowd. ¡Bendito sea el logos!

I breezed through my studies. During my years as a graduate student, I read every book I could get my hands on, especially those on literary theory—my passion, my never-ending fountain of inspiration.

By the time I received my doctorate, I had started to enjoy life in los Estados Unidos. I decided that I wanted to stay there, so I tried to find a teaching job. But I had a slight problem: I had never made the effort to learn English. Why did I need English if my field was Spanish? Since I didn't get a job offer, I returned home. But that was fine. I could then devote my energies to la Revolución, which had just gotten under way.

From the moment I showed up, I was suspect. A Nicaraguan with a Ph.D. in Spanish from los Estados Unidos? CIA. No doubt about it. To this day my fellow writers are absolutely sure that I'm here to spy on them. To be honest, this belief makes perfect sense to me. After all, the vast majority of my colleagues are rabid Sandinistas. They were writing articles against Somoza at a time when doing so could be deadly. I, on the other hand, was safely tucked away in North Dakota . . . freezing my ass off, but far from danger. After el Triunfo, many of my fellow writers, because of their militancy in el Frente, received juicy government posts. I got nothing. But I don't care. No, I don't care at all. I mean, la Revolución is just a temporal matter. Literary theory, on the other hand, can lead us to eternal truths. And no one in this country understands or experiments with literary theory as brilliantly as myself.

Yet I have to admit that I'm hurt when my colleagues say behind my back that I'm as mad as Don Quixote de la Mancha. That just isn't so. For one, I believe that the knight-errant wasn't insane. He consciously went about living his life as a work of art, as a work of fiction. His awareness of himself as a character pulled the other characters into his invention, the way the Pacific Ocean, with its treacherous tides, draws careless swimmers, tossing them around as if they were nothing more than ants. The knight-errant understood, perfectly, that each of us has a role in this one-act play of God's creation that we call life. Literary theory, when taken seriously, helps us understand the role our Maker has assigned us. We can live and die creatively as we struggle against the fierce tides of existence. So once we realize that we are part of a fictional work, we can then find grace, and that leads us to redemption. I guess that the next time I'm compared to Don Quixote, perhaps I should say thank you.

As you can see, it doesn't bother me one bit to be an outcast. I prefer the isolation, in fact. It allows me to be original, unique. Plus, I don't feel obligated to write works that praise our socialist experiment. Instead, I can focus on absorbing every conceivable literary theory in preparation for my next masterpiece.

I think you now understand why I was chosen to be Jaime Jaramillo Solís's aide. I'm already out of favor with the cultural elite of la Revolución, so it doesn't matter if I'm seen with a right-wing author who's notorious for his scathing attacks on Marx, Lenin, Fidel, socialism, and communism. I, Germán Sotelo, was the Ministry of Culture's natural choice.

For the Great Ecuadorian Writer's visit, I rented a spacious, comfortable, air-conditioned house in Bolonia—a once wealthy neighborhood of Managua whose former inhabitants now hang out on Miami's Calle Ocho, ordering Cuban sandwiches. The house has a great office, with a picture window that faces a lush garden with a fountain at the center. When I first saw that room, I envisioned Jaime Jaramillo Solís inspired, typing away at a feverish pace. By putting him in such a placid setting, I hoped that he would feel relaxed enough to share his boundless knowledge of literature with me. He, too, has a doctorate: from la Sorbonne. His doctoral thesis is a dazzling look into Rubén Darío's rejection of the discourse of the common man. Therefore, based on his obvious appreciation of our national poet, I had every reason to believe that the Great Ecuadorian Writer would treasure his time in Nicaragua.

The problem was that as soon as I greeted Jaime Jaramillo Solís at the airport, I found him to be arrogant. His haughtiness revealed that he was utterly sold on his self-importance. Dressed in a Gucci suit, he looked me up and down, snickering at my guayabera, which was somewhat frayed from so many washings. Didn't he know what the U.S. economic embargo had done to our choices in clothing? But what do you expect? The Great Ecuadorian Writer couldn't concern himself with such mundane things. After all, the man *is* a genius.

As I drove him home, I didn't waste any time mining his wisdom. I asked him several questions about his first novel: *El martirio de los gatos.* "Did you attempt to prove what Shakespeare argued in *Henry V,* which is, according to Yuri Lotman, that with regard to the topic of nationhood, a nation becomes conscious of itself when it creates a model of itself? Or did you intend to prove that national identity is merely an accidental discursive formation? Or, as a third-world artist, were you consciously building an imaginative vision of a gestatory political structure? And, as you suggest in the novel's final chapter, is Frantz Fanon correct when he theorizes that international consciousness grows within the heart of national consciousness?"

Jaime Jaramillo Solís turned in the passenger's seat to face me squarely. For a moment, I felt like an insignificant insect that a greater creature contemptuously examines to determine whether or not to let it live. After a long, awkward pause, he replied, "I just wrote a damn book about a boy in a military academy who likes to torture cats. At that time, all I hoped for was a little money and, if I was lucky, a little fame. That's it. So, please, don't ask any more obnoxious questions during the rest of my stay here."

At first I attributed his moroseness to jet lag. But after a couple of days went by and his mood didn't improve, I realized that he was nothing more than un gran pendejo. Yes, a real asshole. But, like myself, he's a literary genius.

Still, in spite of my sweeping knowledge of literary theory and literature, in spite of being the only writer in this country with a goddamned Ph.D. from los Estados Unidos, Jaime Jaramillo Solís barely tolerated my presence. He constantly sent me on meaningless errands. For instance, I thought that he had taken a tremendous liking to fritangas, especially the first ones I introduced him

to: those with fried ripe plantains and roasted strips of meat that
had been marinated in the juice of sour oranges, all topped with a
cabbage, tomato, and vinegar salad. I thought the Great
Ecuadorian Writer really loved them because every night he asked
me to go buy an order.

"Germancito," he would say, "I want another fritanga. But it
has to come from the same place you bought it the first time." Well,
that fritanga stand is on the other side of Managua, close to el
Mercado del Mayoreo. It takes almost two hours to go there and
bring the food back. But if a fritanga would help inspire Jaime
Jaramillo Solís, I was willing to drive all the way to the Costa Rican
border. Still, I have to admit that my feelings were terribly hurt
when I discovered that, all along, he had been throwing the food
away. One morning I found the untouched fritanga at the bottom of
the kitchen trash can. If he wanted me out of the house, he should
have just said so.

The Great Ecuadorian Writer seemed to hate not only me
but also everything in Nicaragua. I know for certain that he
despised Managua. "I used to think that Tokyo was the most difficult city to get around in, but now I vote for this dump. And it
doesn't help, Germancito, that your capital looks like an abandoned movie set of a city bombed to ruins during an air raid." Yes,
he hated the food; he hated the heat; he hated the muckiness; he
hated the potholes; he hated the diesel fumes of the buses; he hated
everything.

It was easy, therefore, for Jaime Jaramillo Solís to find plenty
of rubbish to write about life under the Sandinistas. From the
beginning I had a feeling that he had only come looking for dirt
and, if anything, in Nicaragua there's always plenty of dirt to be
found, no matter what the regime. The material to inspire Jaime

Jaramillo Solís's attack on the Sandinistas was everywhere: in the cries of mothers whose sons had been drafted; in the outrage of merchants who were furious at the government's price-fixing; in the indignation of journalists whose articles were censored every day; in the quiet resignation of the campesino who, frustrated at being told what he should plant, dropped el machete and picked up a rifle instead. The shortcomings of the entire country were laid out before the Great Ecuadorian Writer like a detailed outline. All he needed to do was to sit down and type.

I did find it puzzling that Jaime Jaramillo Solís didn't want to interview any writers. "They've all gone too far to the left. Their artistic integrity was compromised the moment they became apologists for la Revolución," he pronounced emphatically.

I felt like asking, "Well, what about me? Why don't you interview me?" But I kept my mouth shut. If he had taken the time for a formal literary dialogue—a conversation that should have been recorded for posterity—I would've gladly expounded on the novel I'm thinking about writing. When I finish it, this work will epitomize the perfect marriage between the creative process and literary theory. In my novel, I will incorporate Roman Ingarden's notions about how we experience literature as a unique event in our consciousness. Applying Husserlian principles, of course. My twist? Thieves steal the *Lebenswelt* of my characters at the Siete-Sur bus stop in Managua. In order for them to recover their lost horizon of expectations, they have to compare notes with each other based on the few memories the thieves have left behind. ¡Genial!

El Bastardo de Ecuador, however, didn't interview me. What's worse, throughout his visit, I felt that I wasn't much help at all. I served only as his chofer, and as his cachimber boy: driving him around and running stupid, meaningless errands. He didn't need someone as talented as me for that. The most interesting thing I did the entire month was to tape-record the interviews he conducted. Before long, I even began to find that chore rather boring. Still, I did get to hang around while he spoke to some very influential people.

When the Great Ecuadorian Writer interviewed the cardinal, for instance, he learned about the supposed apparition of la Virgen, in Cuapa. For some reason, this story really caught his attention. And I can understand why. After all, the entire phenomenon is a glowing example of Victor Shklovsky's concept of defamiliarization. La Virgen's message, and her appearance, has disrupted our nation's ordinary language and habitual modes of perception. She has rendered unfamiliar what were once common points of reference. Thus, it has become impossible for Nicaraguans to use conventional codes of representation with regard to the gap between religion and politics. In other words, the apparition has deadened our powers of discernment. In the process of deciding whether the event represents a truth, or not, we have become unfamiliar to ourselves. La Virgen's appearance has even disrupted the dreams being forged by our emerging socialist system, thereby impeding political development and change. Still, although I find the entire thing somewhat intriguing, I would never waste my time writing about it.

When Jaime Jaramillo Solís told His Eminence that he wanted to interview the visionary, the cardinal's assistant, a stern-looking monseñor, urged the Great Ecuadorian Writer to be cautious. "Five years ago, the Sandinistas put Bernardo through a terrible ordeal. What they did to him is unspeakable. He was found wandering the streets, completely naked. Bernardo was so traumatized, so uncommunicative, that we couldn't think of sending him back to Cuapa. We had no other option but to hide him in the seminary. For his own protection, of course. Por favor, don't ask him what the Sandinistas did to him. Bernardo, at last, seems to have come to terms with that dreadful incident, as well as with the reality of his situation. The time is coming when he'll be able to return home and quietly live out the rest of his days."

The following morning we drove to the seminary, just off la Carretera Sur, to interview Bernardo Martínez. Padre Jerónimo Peña, the director, a priest so gentle he reminded me of San Francisco de Asís, greeted us in the lobby. On our way to meet the seer, he led us through the seminary's beautiful gardens. The splendor of the setting encourages spiritual reflection. I could sit here all day and happily muse on literary theory. The grounds reminded me of the pastoral novels of Spain's golden age: bucolic, serene, and full of wise, poetic beings. Dozens of young men strolled about, speaking to each other in hushed voices. Others sat quietly, under trees, apparently meditating. And many others sat by themselves, reading books. The trees shaded the corridors, and with the seminary being up in the hills outside the capital, along the highway that leads to El Crucero, the coolness was refreshing. The Great Ecuadorian Writer commented on how pleasant it was to escape Managua's suffocating heat.

"Padre," he went on, "the Catholic Church in Nicaragua can't complain about a lack of young men interested in the priesthood. You have more students in this seminary alone than all the seminaries of Ecuador put together have. La Revolución has been good to you. God's business is booming."

I expected Padre Jerónimo to take the comment in good spirits, like a compliment, or at least as a joke. Instead, the priest's face grew somber, and he stopped walking. He looked intently at

Jaime Jaramillo Solís. I could tell the director was trying to see if the
Writer was trustworthy. At last, Padre Jerónimo spoke.

"Please don't reveal what I'm about to tell you. If you do, the
lives of these young men will be in danger." The director removed
his glasses, thoughtfully biting on the end of an arm, before continuing, "Dr. Jaramillo, we are not experiencing a surge in young
men who have heard el Señor's calling. The reality is this: the
majority have expressed an interest in the priesthood only because
once they're admitted into the seminary, they become exempt
from military service. Thus, as you can see, we've not been too dis-
criminating in whom we admit these days. All we ask of those
who come here is that they partake in the sacraments."

"They're here, then, to avoid the military draft?" the Great
Ecuadorian Writer said softly, almost to himself. He looked around,
assessing the revelation.

"Yes. Sadly, this is the case with most of our seminarians.
There are," the priest added with a smile, "a few who have truly
heard the calling."

"Of course. And don't worry, Padre, I will not print a word of
this without getting your permission first."

Padre Jerónimo nodded in thanks, and we continued walking
along a wide, open corridor that led into a second garden, more
beautiful than the first, bursting with the colors of roses and
bougainvilleas. In the center stood a large concrete statue of la
Virgen. Before it, seated on a bench, was an older gentleman, distinguished looking and with graying hair. A group of young men
surrounded him. They sat at his feet, on the grass, laughing at
something he had just said.

"There's Bernardo," said Padre Jerónimo. "He's quite a storyteller. Like the saint he's named after, he's able to draw a crowd

with the skill of his tongue. He's full of delightful anecdotes. You know, he has helped us keep these young men in good spirits. Since they can't leave the seminary, his tales are highly sought after. It's difficult for many of these boys to be in here. They're locked up, unable to go out. They don't know when, if ever, they'll be able to return to the world outside. Bernardo's stories entertain them. We've been blessed that la Virgen has sent him to us."

When the seminarians saw the director coming, they rose to their feet—all of them, including Bernardo. I was surprised by how tall the seer was. He didn't look one bit like the crazed, stooped-over, toothless campesino the press had been describing.

As was often the case wherever I escorted the Great Ecuadorian Writer, several in the group were speechless when they realized who was there visiting. Jaime Jaramillo Solís greeted each seminarian with a handshake. It was obvious that many of them had read his work. Starstruck, they kept their mouths wide open, unable to respond to the Writer's greetings. Really, the only person who seemed unaffected by the Literary Giant was Bernardo.

"Jóvenes," Padre Jerónimo said to the seminarians, "our illustrious guest is here to visit with Bernardo. Please allow them some privacy."

Reluctantly, the young men left, glancing back over their shoulders as they exited the courtyard. After expressing his hopes that the Great Ecuadorian Writer would enjoy the remainder of his time in Nicaragua, Padre Jerónimo also said farewell. Once alone with Bernardo, Jaime Jaramillo Solís asked if he could conduct the interview right there, on the same bench where the visionary had been talking to the seminarians. El cuapeño merely nodded and gestured for us to sit. I brought the tape recorder out of my briefcase, checked inside to make sure it had a new cassette, and turned it on.

The Writer and the visionary chatted for two hours. Jaramillo Solís jotted down a few notes on his pad and followed no program of questioning, at least from what I could see. He relied entirely on inspiration. I recorded every word of their conversation. Once we finished, as we drove back to the house, I asked the Great Ecuadorian Writer what he thought about the interview.

"Well, the fellow didn't really have much to say, did he?"

If the visionary didn't have much to say, I asked myself, why did he spend two hours talking to him? I then asked the novelist/essayist/playwright, "Do you believe that la Virgen appeared to this man?"

For once, after nearly a month in Nicaragua, the Great Ecuadorian Writer looked at me as if I had asked a question worthy of his consideration. He thought about his answer for quite a while before responding, "Personally, I don't believe in these types of manifestations of the divine. However, Germancito, as Shakespeare wrote: 'There are more things in heaven and earth, Horatio, than are dreamt of in your philosophy.'" In this instance, I couldn't agree more.

As a gift for *La Prensa,* in what the Great Ecuadorian Writer said was a protest against censorship, he wrote a brief article about Bernardo and la Virgen. I must confess that I found the essay rather disappointing, far below Jaime Jaramillo Solís's usually high standards. But in all fairness, he didn't put much effort into the piece, composing it that afternoon in less than thirty minutes. The Great Ecuadorian Writer, in few words, describes the apparition, putting anti-Sandinista words into la Virgen's mouth; he mentions, without going into detail, that the Sandinistas harassed Bernardo; and he concludes that the way in which Nicaraguans align themselves with regard to la Virgen de Cuapa reflects what side of the political chasm they're on. Thus, in Jaramillo Solís's view, Bernardo's story represents a test of whether a person supports or rejects the Sandinistas. La Virgen, then, sits on the axis of the nation's conflict.

The Great Ecuadorian Writer spent only a few more days in Nicaragua before flying back to Spain, which, for the moment, he calls home. Before leaving, he revealed to me that he was considering running for president in his country's next elections. "God save Ecuador if he should win," I said to myself.

I was relieved when, at last, I dropped him off at the airport. When the time came to say farewell, all he did was to reach out, place a hand on my shoulder, and shake his head. What was *that* supposed to mean? I really don't think I'm as insufferable as he made me out to be.

"Vaya con Dios, pendejo," I mumbled to myself as I watched his jet take off.

The day before, as Jaime Jaramillo Solís was packing his suitcase, I said, "Don't forget your tapes."

"You can keep those, Germancito," he answered. "I have what I need in my notebooks, and up here," he added, tapping a finger against his temple. Great, I thought, I spend several weeks lugging around a tape recorder, and for what? Nothing. I was left with a shoebox full of cassettes to store. Oh, well, I thought, I can record music over them, as I found most of the interviews too boring to save.

About a month later, just as I began to recover from the Great Ecuadorian Writer's visit, nostalgia, with its delightfully manipulative ways, made me miss him. Misty eyed, I opened the box of tapes and listened to several interviews. Hearing his pedantic phrasing and his deep, melodic voice once again almost made me cry. I could feel his presence in the room. The interview that immediately gripped me was the one Jaime Jaramillo Solís conducted with Bernardo Martínez. In retrospect, there was something very literary about their two-hour exchange, something both the Great Ecuadorian Writer and I had initially missed. To better study their discussion, I asked a student at the university to transcribe the whole thing, word for word.

When I studied the document, I was astonished to discover that the interview highlighted Michel Foucault's theory whereby he posits that the disciplinary techniques used in modern prisons are also present in every institution in contemporary society. In other words, *they*, those who govern us, control even the minutest details of our lives. Thus, the microphysics of power reaches past the stated limits of law and repression to render the individual a subject in, as well as subject to, the corrective mechanisms of the state. Power, in this manner, regulates not only speech but also the most intimate recesses of a speaker's self. Therefore, both the rulers and the ruled are forever trapped in a vast web of discreet local conflicts. ¡Genial!

As proof, I submit this small sample of their conversation:

TRANSCRIPT

Interview of Bernardo Martínez by Jaime Jaramillo Solís!!!
Taking place sometime in October 1988
Seminario Menor, Managua
Transcribed by (and it was an honor) Sonia Bendaña
Third-Year Student
November 1988

JAIME JARAMILLO SOLÍS!: Bernardo, why don't you begin by telling me a little about your educational background.

BERNARDO MARTÍNEZ: Well, I studied through the fourth grade in the Colegio Centro América. That was many years ago, when the school was in Granada. It's in Managua now. I completed the fifth and sixth grades in a public school, in Juigalpa. That's in Chontales. I then completed the first three years of secundaria in Cuapa. I actually helped bring the high school to Cuapa. Next month, I'll finish the last year of secundaria. Si Dios quiere, I'll finally have my bachillerato.

JJS: Are you finishing secundaria here in the seminary?

BM: No. Sor Milagros from el Colegio de Nuestra Señora de la Victoria allowed me to study in that school. It's nearby, in El Crucero. For two years I've been going there every day to help with the repair of the buildings, and to help with some new construction as well.

JJS: So you'll be a high school graduate at last. How old are you?

BM: Fifty-seven.

JJS: That's amazing. Most people in your position would have given up long ago. What's your secret?

BM: Mi abuelita always said that I'm very stubborn. I've always wanted to go to school. I've always wanted to be more than just a campesino. But going to school has been very difficult for me. First of all, mi abuelita didn't have the money to pay for it. And then, I'm not the brightest of students.

JJS: How long have you been here, in the seminary?

BM: I'm going on six years now.

JJS: Do you ever go out?

BM: Seldom. It's not safe for me out there. I feel safe working with las monjitas, because their Colegio is nearby. But theirs is one of only a few places I've visited in more than five years.

JJS: In essence, then, you're a prisoner here.

BM: I guess you can say that.

JJS: Why don't you study here, in the seminary? I understand that you'd like to become a priest.

BM: More than anything in the world.

JJS: So, after you graduate, why don't you continue studying here?

BM: Well, it's not that simple. The archdiocese would have to allow the seminary to accept me as a student.

JJS: Are you saying that the archdiocese has not supported your wish to become a priest?

[*Silence.*]

What's their reasoning, Bernardo? What's their objection?

BM: I've been told that I don't have enough education.

JJS: What do you need? A degree from escuela secundaria?

BM: Yes.

JJS: What's the problem, then?

[*Silence.*]

Bernardo, if you have the proper degree, and the vocation to become a priest, why aren't they accepting you?

BM: Well, a gringo priest and a bishop have both told me that I'm not bright enough. Then there's the problem with la Virgencita.

JJS: I don't understand.

BM: There are those who think I'm crazy because I've seen and spoken to Nuestra Señora. A priest needs to be stable. My visions make them question . . .

JJS: Your sanity?

BM: I guess so.

JJS: Well, Bernardo, for what it's worth, I believe that if anyone belongs here, studying to become a priest, it's you. Who better to become an apostle of the faith than someone who has experienced the divine? In many societies the visionaries are the priests.

They are the ones equipped to communicate with the gods. You've experienced that, thus you are closer to your god. Sometimes, when a person is especially blessed, others feel threatened. Is that what's going on in your case?

BM: I don't know. That question is too difficult for me.

JJS: All right, Bernardo, let's move on to another subject, shall we? How has the apparition changed your life?

BM: La Virgencita's appearance has brought me the greatest joy imaginable . . . but also the greatest pain. I've changed a lot since she first came. I'm now someone completely different. I was a forty-eight-year-old tailor living a simple life in Cuapa when she appeared to me. I had also been the town's sacristán for nearly thirty years. Volunteer work, no pay. When I look back on all that now, I had everything I ever needed, really. I took care of my animals, tended my garden, and made clothes. And then, all of a sudden, I'm caught in the middle of a storm. But now I'm at peace, here in the seminary. To be honest, I also feel trapped, unable to move forward. You know, I only want to serve Nuestro Señor and Nuestra Señora. I'm doing the best that I can here, but I feel it's not enough. In one of her appearances she told me that I would not be happy in this lifetime; she said that I would suffer greatly. Well, her prophecy has come true.

JJS: Have the Sandinistas been responsible, to any extent, for your suffering?

BM: Yes, they have. Definitely.

JJS: What have they done to you?

BM: Well, they spied on me while I was in Cuapa. They sent men to try to bribe me. They even offered to let me have El Triunfo—that's a finca near el Cerro Tumbé—if I said that la Virgencita wore rojo y negro, the Sandinista colors. They also sent a woman named Sandra to seduce me. And once they tried to kidnap me. After that, I came here to hide. I've been here ever since.

JJS: But the Sandinistas arrested you, didn't they?

[*Silence.*]

Rumors are that they held you for a couple of weeks and tortured you; that they tried to get you to deny the story of the apparition, to say that you had made the whole thing up. Am I right?

[*Silence.*]

Bernardo, you need to let everyone know the truth about what happened to you. People need to see the Sandinistas for what they really are. I can make your suffering known to the entire world and, in the process, make the story of the apparition known. But you need to help me, Bernardo. What did the Sandinistas do to you?

[*Silence.*]

Well, Bernardo, I have no other choice but to respect your decision to remain silent. Still, I think you're making a mistake. It doesn't matter now, though. I have just one more question. Since the apparition, what has been the saddest thing for you?

BM [*long pause*]: That la Virgen de Cuapa and her message have been forgotten. That, for me, is the saddest thing.

JJS: I'm sorry. I must have missed something here, Bernardo. I don't understand. Everyone in Nicaragua knows about la Virgen's apparition. As far as I can tell, no one has forgotten her. What do you mean?

BM: I mean exactly what I said, that the message of Cuapa has been forgotten. No one talks about la Virgen de Cuapa anymore. The priests and the bishops have fallen silent. There are no more pilgrimages to the apparition site. Very few people visit now. No one is spreading her message anymore. Nuestra Señora de Cuapa has been forgotten. That's the saddest thing for me. It's also the most painful.

JJS: But, Bernardo, didn't la Virgen say that you're her messenger?

BM: Yes.

JJS: Then, and excuse me for saying so, it seems to me that until you're dead, the things you're complaining about are your own fault. It's up to *you* to make sure that neither she nor her messenger are forgotten. As long as you remain silent, locked in here, you'll be failing her. You have to act, my friend. You need to get out there and preach because if you don't, no one else will. And might I add that, at fifty-seven, you don't have much time left.

[*Silence, and after a long pause, the tape recorder is turned off.*]

As I stated earlier, this conversation clearly illustrates the different discourses used by those who rule and those who are ruled. Based on this transcript, I'm inspired to write a play about language and power. But in my work, there will only be questions. The powerless will be rendered silent. Fantastic! ¡Genial!

tercera parte
PAZ

chapter ten

KEKARITOMENE
(Thou That Art Highly Favored)

November 1993

Paulina Thompson

BY THE TIME Bernardo Martínez's plane touched down on the runway, Paulina Thompson and her husband Jake had been waiting in the Los Angeles International Airport for over an hour. The visionary's impending arrival had made Paulina so nervous that as they left their house to meet his flight, she first forgot her sweater, then her purse, and finally the thick coat Bernardo had requested to help him ward off the winter cold. Throughout his wife's crisis, Jake waited patiently in the driveway, sitting behind the steering wheel and enjoying the smooth idle of his BMW. Each time Paulina ran out of the house, only to discover that she had forgotten something else, he urged her to remain calm, assuring her that Bernardo's visit would go well.

Two months earlier, Paulina had read in the church bulletin

that a convention of seers of the Blessed Virgin Mary was going to be held in Los Angeles. The parish's secretary gave her the organizer's telephone number, and Paulina called to ask if Bernardo Martínez, from Nicaragua, would be there.

"Yes. His attendance has been confirmed," replied the woman at the other end. Paulina heard the rustling of paper as the list was being put away. After a brief pause, the woman asked, "Ma'am, do you speak Spanish?"

"Yes, I do," Paulina replied.

"Please don't feel obliged, ma'am, but we need to ask a favor. Mr. Martínez is arriving a few days before the convention begins, and he plans to stay a couple of days afterward. Rather than paying for a hotel, he's asked us to help him find a Spanish-speaking family he can stay with. Could you possibly help us out?"

Paulina was thrilled. The request rewarded her unyielding devotion to the Blessed Mother, and she also welcomed the chance to renew her ties to Nicaragua. She had left her country of birth nearly thirty years earlier—long before the mass exodus of the 1980s—and hadn't returned since.

Paulina Thompson—maiden name, Paulina Vigil—was from Diriamba: one of three daughters and four sons of a devoutly Catholic couple. Although the family lived comfortably, in a spacious house a block west of the clock tower, they weren't rich. From kindergarten through graduation from high school, Paulina attended el Colegio Inmaculada Concepción. There, the nuns instructed her dutifully in the veneration of la Virgen. And at home Paulina prayed every night with her grandmother Inés before the image of María Auxiliadora.

Her fervent devotion to Nuestra Señora was evident so early that at age ten she was accepted into las Hijas de María. Also, for two years in a row, Paulina honored la Virgen by winning Carazo's high school essay contest, sponsored by the local Catholic schools and dedicated to la patria. The first time she triumphed with the composition "Nicaragua de María," and the following year with "María de Nicaragua."

When Paulina graduated from high school, she chose to become a secretary. (Teaching, the other option open to women, didn't interest her.) Dr. Buenaventura Canales, a kind and generous patrón and owner of el Beneficio de Café El Milagro, gave her a job. While working at El Milagro, Paulina stumbled after she met and fell madly in love with Ramón Arévalo, Dr. Canales's nephew. Paulina found the athletic young man—a star on the Caciques de Diriangén Fútbol Club—unbearably handsome: with blond hair, blue eyes, and a soft, captivating, boyish face.

She often wondered why someone like Ramón would be interested in her. Yes, she was pretty. Paulina combed her short wavy hair back to reveal large honey-colored eyes, a small, perfectly contoured nose, and full, glistening lips. And her figure, bordering on voluptuous but still thin, drew los piropos of the men who sat every afternoon in el parque. (Their comments did upset her whenever they trespassed the boundaries of chivalry.) Even so, Paulina continued asking herself out loud: "If Ramón Arévalo could have any girl in Carazo, why is he interested in me?"

But Ramón Arévalo *was* interested in her. And their courtship perfectly matched her childhood dreams. A year after they met, he asked Paulina to be his novia, and she answered yes. Then, most formally, dressed in a dark suit, a tie, and holding a dozen yellow roses in his hand, he visited her house to ask for her parents' permission. They consented, but not without setting some ground rules first: Ramón could visit Paulina from six to nine o'clock every evening, but he was expected to eat dinner at his own house, there would always be someone else in the same room with them, and whenever they went out a chaperone would go along.

What Paulina's family failed to see (or did they close their eyes to it?) was that their daughter and her novio spent plenty of time alone at El Milagro. It was there, amid the coolness of the coffee bushes, that she fell from grace, giving herself completely to the man she adored. And in spite of Paulina's belief that their ardor gravely offended Nuestra Señora, for several weeks she continued loving Ramón with fiery abandon.

Their passion came to an abrupt halt the day don Buenaventura discovered his secretary and his nephew showering together in El Milagro's plantation house. A man with a strict moral code, Dr. Canales had no choice but to inform Paulina's parents.

"You've disgraced us!" her father exclaimed in a hiss that evening. "Now, to restore the family's good name, you'll have to marry that sinvergüenza!"

Marrying that scoundrel would certainly solve Paulina's predicament. She'd become an honorable woman, and at the same time she'd earn la Virgen's forgiveness. Her dreams over the past few months would become reality. Ramón and she: husband and wife, father and mother, devout Catholics.

Ramón's parents agreed that the respectable thing to do was for their son to marry Paulina. The young man thought differently. He vanished. Some said into Costa Rica; others said Honduras.

"Now you've been soiled forever, Paulina," her mother lamented. "An honest man will never have you for his wife."

"We have no choice but to send you away," her father sentenced, "before our private shame becomes public knowledge. We're sending you to live with your tía Antonieta," his sister who, many years before, had settled in Los Angeles and married a sensible, hardworking gringo named Fred.

Feeling rejected and tainted, Paulina locked herself away, waiting as all the arrangements for her departure were being made. She envisioned being alone for the rest of her life, without a husband and without the children she had always yearned for. Guilt racked Paulina's soul and although the priest granted her absolution, she could not forgive herself for lowering her guard and delivering her maidenhood to Ramón Arévalo, whom she had once thought of as her destino.

What most disturbed her was the shame. Paulina couldn't step out of the house thinking that her face had become eternally marked by the lust that had consumed her in the Edenic breezes of the plantation. Like Eve, Paulina had been tempted, and she drowned in the embarrassment of knowing that she had loved the taste of the apple. Because of her sin, which she was certain everyone in Diriamba knew about, she was being expelled from Paradise, and as she stepped into the automobile that would take her to the airport, her eyes were cast on the ground in ignominy. After Paulina boarded her flight, still bitter over being forced into exile and blinded by tears, she swore never to return to Nicaragua.

As her tía Antonieta and Fred drove Paulina to her new home, her aunt said, "The first thing you have to do is learn English." She had pronounced these words sternly, Paulina thought, to prove that she was serious. "We've enrolled you in an adult school. If you learn the language quickly, you'll do fine here."

As Fred steered north on the Pasadena Freeway, the immensity of Los Angeles intimidated Paulina. The streets and houses dashed by in a single, blurry motion, like scrolling images on a movie screen that never seemed to end. It would suit her well, she thought, to hide out in this vastness, an outcast because of the mess she had made of her life.

The English classes were a welcome relief. They helped to take Paulina's mind off of Ramón Arévalo. The school atmosphere inspired her. Paulina's classmates had come from all over the world and, although the course had already been under way for three weeks, they accepted her into their fellowship. A bond, a spirit of family arose out of their struggle to "become Americans"—an expression their teacher often used in class. To become something she was not wouldn't be easy, Paulina thought. But she was determined to try, hoping that maybe by reinventing herself, she would find release from her shame.

When Paulina first arrived in the United States, the nation was in mourning. Their young, handsome, Catholic president had recently been assassinated, and the fear of an uncertain future cast a gloom over her adoptive homeland.

Yet Paulina found Americans resilient, a people for whom it seemed that adversity was nothing more than another hurdle in the track of life. She believed that a saying she had learned in class best explained their outlook: "If life hands you lemons, make lemonade."

Paulina liked that attitude, and soon began to love life in the United States. She enjoyed the country's intricate rhythms, its tireless beat. And she was learning English so rapidly that after only a couple of months she was holding long conversations with Fred, who marveled at how effortlessly she absorbed the language. "Jeez, you're like a sponge," he would say.

Within a few weeks, Paulina's new life had fallen into a comfortable routine. In the mornings she attended classes. She'd then go home for lunch. Afterward, she'd walk five blocks to Exposition

Park, sit always at the same picnic table, and do her homework. When done, she'd feed bread crumbs to the pigeons and the squirrels. Then she'd head back home to make dinner for her hosts, who always returned exhausted from their jobs. All in all, Paulina thought, life was good. Still, her fall from grace continued to haunt her, an undesirable specter.

One afternoon, as Paulina was studying, a man sat down across from her at the picnic table. At first she refused to look up, not because her tía Antonieta had warned her about talking to strangers, but because she resented the intrusion. But she couldn't resist glancing up from her homework when he placed a large, bright red apple on the picnic table, right before her eyes. Paulina found the gesture so appealing that she ignored her tía's warnings.

"Hi, my name is Jake Thompson. I see you every day, sitting here alone, working on whatever it is you're working on. I just had to meet you," he said, rather shyly she thought, as he held out his hand. As Paulina shook it, she examined the intruder. He would have never stood out in a crowd. He seemed so . . . average: thin, with brown eyes, an elongated face, and dark brown hair. The only thing exceptional about him was his height: over six feet.

"Are you from Los Angeles?" Paulina asked.

"Well, I'm originally from Iowa. But I've been living in California for twelve years now," he answered. He then smiled playfully. "And, no, I don't eat a lot of corn."

Paulina was puzzled. It was clear that she had missed yet another joke. But as Jake sat there grinning, she peered into his eyes and saw deep into his soul. Without really understanding how, although years later she attributed the certainty to la Virgen's intercession, Paulina instantly knew that before her was one of the kindest men on the planet, just the opposite of Ramón Arévalo in every way. She was sure Jake would never abandon her; this made her feel that maybe there was hope, that perhaps she did have a chance for another relationship.

"And where are you from?" Jake asked.

"I used to be Nicaraguan, but I'm an American now," she replied. Although Paulina meant it as a joke, her answer was also serious.

"I pass you every afternoon when I walk in the park," he said.

"And why do you walk at this hour?" she asked. "Don't you have a job?"

"Well, I walk here to get away from the university."

"Are you a student?" Paulina asked, the prospect exciting her.

"No." Jake looked hesitant. For a moment, she thought he wanted to hide something. At last, he admitted, "I teach there."

"What do you teach?" She hoped Jake would answer literature, philosophy, art, music, or something romantic along those lines.

"Medicine."

Jake was not that much older than Paulina, but since adolescence he had devoted himself entirely to his dream of becoming a physician. As a student, and later as an intern, his genius for research astounded his professors. After Jake finished specializing in neurophysiology, he was urged to teach while continuing his research.

That afternoon, Paulina and Jake spent a couple of hours talking, and before saying good-bye, he asked, "Will you be here tomorrow?"

"Well, Jake," Paulina answered, holding up his gift, "you know what Americans say: 'An apple a day keeps the doctor away.'"

When Paulina returned home and told her tía Antonieta and Fred about the meeting, she asked, "What exactly does 'Don't bet on it' mean?"

At the wedding, several months later, Fred kept on leaning over to his wife and whispering, "I can't believe Paulina landed herself a doctor after only a year here." He finally stopped repeating himself when Antonieta's pinches began to turn his arm blue.

Jake was the man Paulina had always hoped for. When she sensed that he was serious about her, she, with great trepidation and remorse, confessed her impure past. Paulina expected Jake to rise from the bench and walk away without looking back, vanishing into the pine trees. But she knew that she would have never been able to live with herself had she concealed her mortal sin. Besides, she was afraid that Jake, knowledgeable about the female anatomy, would return her to her tía Antonieta's house when, on their wedding night, he discovered that she wasn't a virgin.

"What kind of man would want to marry a desecrated woman?" Paulina would often ask herself, overcome with guilt, as she stood before the mirror.

After her confession, Jake, with an amused smile, asked, "Are there any children I'll have to adopt?"

Jake loved being married to a Nicaraguan, always calling Paulina "my hot-blooded little Mexican." The first couple of times he said this, she went into a detailed explanation about the difference between a Mexican and a Nicaraguan. When she saw Jake's grin, she knew that, once again, she had missed the joke.

The only problems that Jake, a man of science, had with his Latin American wife revolved around Paulina's preposterous superstitions. For instance, after his afternoon run, she would get angry when he showered, saying he was sure to catch pneumonia if he got wet after 5:00 P.M.; or after ironing, she would refuse to open the refrigerator because it would give her arthritis; or they couldn't have fish for dinner because eating seafood during the evening was bad; or whenever she was pregnant, before going out of the house, she needed to know if there would be an eclipse because she didn't want her child to be born with a horrendous birthmark; or whenever she wanted to make a baby's hiccups go away, she would put a piece of thread in her mouth, moisten it, and then stick it on the infant's forehead; or whenever a family member had a cold, they could not touch a pair of scissors because the illness would prolong itself another three days; or when she once broke a mirror, she threw handfuls of salt on the shards to ward off bad luck; or when she had her period, people couldn't stand downwind because air carrying the vestiges of her menstruation would make them sick; or she'd always be on guard because someone, intentionally or unintentionally, could give one of her children mal de ojo just by looking at the child while thinking wicked thoughts. Jake did find some of her beliefs endearing. For instance, whenever they walked together down a street he had to be on the outside of the sidewalk, nearer to the street, to show the world that he was a gentleman.

One of Paulina's superstitions, above all others, puzzled Jake: whenever they attended a wake or a funeral, as soon as they returned home, they had to get out of their clothes and jump into the shower to fend off the specter of death. "I have to shower even if it's after five o'clock?" Jake would ask, frustrated because his wife failed to see the paradox. Plus, Paulina would not allow him to wear those clothes again until they had been washed or sent to the cleaners. And then, when a colleague of Jake's brought her infant to a funeral and she asked him if he would like to hold the child, Paulina came charging out of nowhere to forbid her husband from doing so.

"Only a parent can hold a child in the presence of death. Otherwise, the baby's life will be shortened. I know what I'm talking about, Jake," she said resolutely.

In spite of these odd beliefs, Paulina made Jake happy.

"God blessed us with four wonderful children, your job at the university, and this house," she'd often say as she stood before the large picture window in their living room. Their home rested high on a cliff on the Palos Verdes Peninsula, overlooking the Pacific Ocean. Yes, life couldn't have gone better for Paulina, and for this she thanked her devotion to the Virgin Mary.

Jake, on the other hand, wasn't religious. "My parents are Presbyterians," he explained to Paulina early in their relationship. "But attending church was never an important part of our family's life." Before their wedding, then, at Paulina's request, Jake converted to Catholicism and later, as the kids were growing up, he showed a genuine interest in their religious education.

At the beginning of their marriage, Paulina noticed that the statues of the Virgin Mary she placed in every room of their house confused him, as did all the candles she lit before her. "You know, Paulina, someday you're going to burn the place down," he warned. But after a couple of years, Paulina discovered that he was el duende who sometimes lit or replaced the candles that went out.

Paulina's devotion to the Blessed Mother became such a natural part of their lives that Jake was hardly surprised when she asked that the family go to France for their vacation because "I've always wanted to visit the shrine at Lourdes." The following year they went to Portugal to visit Fatima. After that they traveled to Ireland to visit Knock. And the next year they drove to Mexico to visit the shrine of la Virgen de Guadalupe.

Afterward, Jake would tell her that the pilgrimages always left him feeling as if his load in life had gotten a bit lighter.

Throughout their entire marriage—nearly thirty years— Paulina had not once expressed an interest in visiting her homeland.

Still she had, very quietly, kept her patria close to her heart. From Palos Verdes, she had suffered with her compatriotas through the earthquake, through the bloody uprising that overthrew Somoza, and through the violent decade of the Contra War. And now that doña Violeta was in power, she prayed fervently that her people would, at last, find peace.

Paulina's family now all lived in the United States. Her own parents were in Miami, and she visited them often. One of Paulina's sisters, who lived in San Francisco, had kept her informed of the lives of relatives and friends. Through her, she learned that there was no point in returning to Nicaragua, that almost everyone she had known and loved had chosen exile or had died. Simply put, there was no one there left to visit.

But one story nearly compelled her to pack her bags and embark on a pilgrimage to Nicaragua. Years back, around 1983, if Paulina remembered correctly, her sister told her that the Blessed Virgin Mary had appeared to a campesino in a small Chontales town called Cuapa. The instant Paulina heard about the apparition, she knew it was true. She couldn't explain why, but she was certain, beyond any doubt, that Nuestra Señora had visited her country. Paulina begged her sister, who was very involved in San Francisco's Nicaraguan community, to send her more information. Not long afterward, in the mail, Paulina received a booklet: *Relación sobre los sagrados eventos de Cuapa.* She read the seer's account of what happened over and over, until she had memorized every detail. Throughout the following years, she repressed a yearning, to her a seemingly irrational desire, to hop on a plane to Managua, rent a car at the airport, drive to Cuapa, visit the apparition site, drive back to the airport, and hop on the next plane back to Los Angeles. But the lingering shame over her conduct with Ramón Arévalo prevented her from doing so.

That is why, when Paulina was asked if she would be willing to host Bernardo Martínez during his stay for the Convention of the Seers of the Blessed Virgin Mary, without hesitating a second, she answered yes!

As the passengers on the flight from Houston filed down the ramp, Paulina scanned their faces trying to recognize the visionary. She had pictured Bernardo de Cuapa as a short, stooped, aged campesino, his face withered from a lifetime of work in the sun, wearing a sombrero on his head, caites laced with thin leather straps onto his feet, and a pair of white cotton pants held up by a coarse rope tied around the waist. Nervously clutching Jake's hand, Paulina's anxiety grew as the exiting passengers trickled to just a few; and then she nearly panicked when the airline employee closed the door to the gate. She looked around to see if she had missed the seer. A couple of families had remained behind, loudly celebrating their reunion.

Then Paulina saw him. At first she wasn't sure. The man who stood there, looking lost and worried, didn't fit the image she had formed in her mind. He was tall and distinguished looking, not at all like a campesino. If anything, he reminded her a little of the British actor James Mason, in the latter part of his career, only with a darker complexion. Paulina approached the man.

"¿Bernardo Martínez?"

"Sí," he replied, an expression of relief blossoming on his face.

"Hola, I'm Paulina Thompson, and this is my husband, Jake. You'll be staying with us during your stay in Los Angeles."

"¡Gracias a la Virgencita! I thought no one had come to pick me up," he said.

As they walked through the terminal, Bernardo studied the signs in the building. He listened distractedly to Paulina's nervous chatter about airplanes and flying, and replied to her questions about his flight politely, but in brief sentences.

Once they were inside the car, Paulina saw Bernardo caress the rear leather seat, running his hand up and down the back. By the look on his face, that simple act soothed him greatly. "Is this your first time in the United States?" she asked.

"No, it's my fourth."

"Was it difficult for you to get a visa?"

Bernardo smiled, his gaze wistful as he retrieved the pleasant memory. "The United States Embassy gave me an open visa. I'm told that they rarely do this. It never expires." The seer smiled again, and then continued. "A couple of years ago, a Marian group from Pittsburgh invited me to give a talk about the apparition. I saw it as a chance to raise some money for the Church of Nuestra Señora de la Victoria, in El Crucero—that's where I've been assigned for the last few years. I accepted the invitation because it was something I thought la Virgencita wanted me to do. I took my application to the embassy and they told me to return a few days later for an interview. When I came back, they asked me to sit in the waiting area. I sat down next to a lady who talked a lot. She kept going on about how unfair the gringo system was for giving visas.

"'They want to humiliate us,' she said. 'Very few are granted, you know.'

"While she complained, she was also praying for a visa because she wanted to visit her daughter in Nueva Orleans. Well, all her talk made me nervous. I surely didn't want to be humiliated. I began to pray to la Virgencita that my request for a visa be denied so I would never have to suffer through the experience again. We waited for a couple of hours. Then two people from the embassy came out to talk to us.

"A woman, very businesslike, said to the lady, 'We're giving you a visa for thirty days. But you have to be back in Nicaragua before it expires or you'll never receive another one. ¿Comprende?' The lady was so delighted, she jumped up and down, as if she had won a big prize in a contest.

"The other person, a man, had come to talk to me. He was very friendly and he smiled all the time he spoke. He introduced himself as Victor something or other. He smelled of cigars and his voice reminded me of the sound of sandpaper. 'I want to thank you for everything you've done for your patria,' he said as he shook my hand. I still don't know what he meant by that. He then said, 'We're giving you an open visa. You can travel to los Estados Unidos any time you want, and you can stay there for as long as you like.' I was shocked. Obviously, la Virgencita wanted me to have this visa.

"As the lady and I were leaving, she turned to me and said, 'Why did you get a visa like that?'

"'No tengo idea,' I answered.

"Well, that upset her. 'See what I mean about the gringos?' she said. 'They gave you a better visa just to humiliate *me.*'" Paulina enjoyed the way Bernardo smiled when he finished telling the story.

"So he can come and go any time he wants?" Jake asked Paulina after she finished translating. She nodded in reply.

"How are things in Nicaragua?" she then asked Bernardo.

"Tense. Not as bad as they were a couple of years ago, but there's still a lot of hatred left over from the war." Bernardo's expression grew somber, and he continued, "Just two weeks ago, someone destroyed the statue of la Virgen that was at the apparition site. The caretaker found her in pieces shortly after dawn. We don't know who did it. That same night someone broke into the church building and threw the consecrated hosts all over the place. People today have so little respect for what is sacred. The police investigating the case have accused the caretaker. But I know it wasn't him. He's a believer."

"Who does Bernardo think it was then?" asked Jake after Paulina's translation.

"Who else could it be but Sandinistas?" Bernardo replied sadly. "La Virgencita has become so politicized. I'm still accused of having made up the entire story as part of a plot against la Revolución. I just want us to live en paz, like she asked us to."

"Do people in Nicaragua know about the attack? It's important that everyone be made aware of this sacrilege," Paulina said, outraged and pointing a finger at Bernardo. He flinched, as if she were accusing him of the act. "Perdón, Bernardo."

The seer then smiled, and replied, "The incident has been reported on television, on the radio, and in the papers. Most people become angry, as you just did."

"Maybe something good will come out of it, then," said Jake. "Maybe it will help bring Catholics together."

Bernardo listened as Paulina translated and then replied, "It's true. There are more visitors at the site now. And interest in the apparition has grown the past couple of years. I'm afraid I had stopped spreading her message. I thought that my work as her messenger was done. I settled on being safe, on hiding in el seminario. But then I realized that I couldn't do that and expect people's devotion to Nuestra Señora to grow. The last few years I've been working harder than ever to let everyone know what she's asking of us."

"So there's more interest in la Virgen de Cuapa now?" Paulina asked.

"Yes, but without the madness of the early days. The devotion of the people is more mature now. And the interest in her appearance in Cuapa should continue increasing. Two books are being written about la Virgen: one by a priest who has been gathering information for twelve years, and another by a couple who lives here, somewhere in los Estados Unidos. That should help spread her message even more."

"Well, what about you? You said you were in the seminary. Are you studying to become a priest?" Jake asked.

"Eight months ago I finished my last course in theology."

"But you haven't been ordained?" Jake asked.

"No. I'm still a deacon."

"When will you be ordained, then?" Paulina asked.

"Whenever the bishop decides that I'm ready," Bernardo replied, smiling. "I have to be patient and obedient. He, with Nuestra Señora's help, will know when the time is right."

After Jake pulled the car into the garage, Bernardo said, "I'm going to the other side of the road for a moment. I think I see something." The seer walked across the street, toward the edge of the cliff. Both Paulina and Jake followed him. The colors of the setting sun ran deep red and bright orange, mixing against a background of different hues of blue.

"The sunsets from up here are beautiful," Paulina commented.

"Yes," Bernardo agreed, "I can see that. But I'm not really looking at the sunset. I'm looking at that cloud," he said, pointing toward the northwestern sky.

Paulina and Jake both looked in that direction. There, against a powder-blue backdrop, a cloud glowed strangely, seeming to cast a light of its own.

"You're right, Bernardo," Jake said. "There's something odd about that cloud. I'll get my camera." When Jake returned he took several photographs, until the film ran out.

"Ay, that cloud is beautiful," Paulina sighed. The three stood there until the sun finally set and the cloud was engulfed by darkness.

As soon as Bernardo stepped into the house, he was drawn to the statue of la Inmaculada Concepción that Paulina kept in the hallway leading to the bedrooms. He walked up to her, touched her feet, and made the sign of the cross. He then said a brief, silent prayer.

Afterward, Paulina showed Bernardo to the guest room. "Dinner will be ready in about thirty minutes," she said. When Bernardo came to the table, he held a package that had been carefully wrapped in white tissue paper. After they finished eating, he rose from his seat.

"I know that you're a believer. So, I want you to have this," he said, handing Paulina the package.

As she unwrapped the present, Paulina's expression was of delight. But before she had finished removing the tissue paper, it had changed to concern.

"Is something wrong?" Bernardo asked.

"Her hand broke off," Paulina answered, pouting. She searched through the tissue paper until, at last, she found the small missing piece.

"Yes, that's been a problem," Bernardo explained. "I insisted that the statue look exactly as Nuestra Señora did when She appeared to me. The artist warned me that since She would be cast only in plaster, without wires inside, her hand would be weak, and that it would break off easily. Unfortunately, I didn't listen. But the hand's easy to glue back on."

"Oh, Bernardo, don't worry about it. It doesn't really matter. She's beautiful!" Paulina placed la Virgen de Cuapa on the dining room table. The nine-inch image looked exactly as Paulina had imagined her, based on the seer's description in la *Relación de los eventos sagrados de Cuapa*. Nuestra Señora had a beautiful mestiza face; a shawl covered her long brown hair and it was wrapped around her neck, dangling over her left shoulder and ending just below her knee; golden threads hung from the end of the shawl; a ribbon, light blue and gold, was tied around her waist; she wore a modest white dress, and at the bottom Paulina saw the toes of her bare feet sticking out; and Nuestra Señora stood on a white round cloud that also served as the statue's base. La Virgen's left hand rested on her thigh, over the shawl. Her right hand, the missing one, would have extended out, waist high, with her palm open and facing up. The only thing that differed from how Paulina had imagined her was that the shawl in the statue was light blue, whereas in Bernardo's transcribed account it had been beige. "You know what, Bernardo," Paulina said, "I won't glue her hand back on." For an instant, Bernardo looked perplexed. Seeing this, Paulina quickly added, "I'll put the hand away somewhere safe, and I'll glue it back when I make my pilgrimage to Cuapa. Having her like that, without a hand, will remind me to fulfill this promesa."

Over the next few days, Paulina took Bernardo out on several tours of Los Angeles. This included a day at Disneyland, which he loved, at first. But as they were riding the boat on "It's a Small World," the seer began to cry.

"Bernardo, what's wrong?" Paulina asked, alarmed.

"Nothing, really. It's just that it makes me sad to think about all the children in Nicaragua who will never have a chance to see this."

"I worry about Bernardo, Jake," Paulina said to her husband that evening. "He's so innocent, just like a child."

The Convention of Seers of the Blessed Virgin Mary began on Bernardo's fourth day in Los Angeles. Paulina loved hearing the favored ones tell about their visions. She sat in the front row during Bernardo's presentation, and when he finished she was proud of him. Paulina thought he had an engaging, folksy way of telling his story. But she didn't like the work of the interpreter that the convention organizers assigned to him. Paulina was sure she would have done a better job. The woman didn't know the English names for many of the trees, animals, and fruits the Nicaraguan seer mentioned during his talk.

Paulina's list of future pilgrimages grew during the convention. She heard the stories of visionaries from Spain, Rwanda, Syria, Argentina, Italy, Vietnam, Egypt, Iraq, Venezuela, and many other countries. She was only disappointed that none of the seers from Medjugorje, Bosnia, had attended. In spite of this, Paulina found the experience magnificent.

The day the event ended, when Jake returned home from work, he walked into the house excitedly. As soon as he saw Paulina and Bernardo, he reached into his briefcase and brought out a packet with the photographs he had taken the evening the seer had arrived.

"Tell me what you see," Jake said, handing the pictures to Bernardo.

The visionary looked at them, and when he was halfway through the stack, he broke into a grin. Without saying a word, he handed the pictures to Paulina. Within a few moments, she exclaimed, "¡Dios mío!" She rose from her seat, rushed to the bed-room, and returned with the statue of la Virgen de Cuapa. "Look," she said, "the cloud's a perfect outline of her!" And in the last pho-tograph Jake had taken that evening, Paulina swore that la Virgen was missing a hand.

On Bernardo's last day in Los Angeles, he asked his compa-triota if she would drive him to the home of "la reina de los Nicaragüenses en Los Angeles." Doña Esmeralda Saavedra, "the queen of Nicaraguans living in Los Angeles," came to California in the late 1950s. She quickly deciphered the city and soon was helping her compatriotas to settle and find work. In return, all she wanted was their adoration. Doña Esmeralda's house, located in the heart of the Pico District, became the gathering place for the exiled. She lived in a part of Los Angeles where Paulina and Jake never ventured. As the wife of a physician who lived in the affluent Palos Verdes neighborhood, Paulina had lost touch with her fellow Nicaraguans—whose numbers in Los Angeles had swollen to nearly one hundred thousand during the 1980s. Not once during her marriage to Jake had she sought out her compa-triotas, with the exception of her tía Antonieta, who was happily retired and living with Fred in Palm Springs. Plus, she still believed that she bore the mark of her fall from grace—one her fellow Nicaraguans would instantly detect.

Once Paulina parked the BMW near the inner-city address Bernardo had scrawled on a piece of paper, she became nervous. She grew even more anxious when she saw that most of the cars parked on that street sported decals of Nicaragua's blue-and-white flag. Every Nicaraguan in Los Angeles, it seemed, had come to see the seer.

As they approached doña Esmeralda's house, she fought the urge to hold Bernardo's hand. People were crammed in the living room, talking so loudly that their voices could be easily heard half a block away. Over the years, Paulina had forgotten just how noisy her compatriotas could be. When she and Bernardo entered the building, the din died down, and everyone parted to let Nuestra Señora's messenger enter. Paulina saw that in a room to the side, doña Esmeralda had created a large shrine to la Virgen de Cuapa. On the opposite end of the living room, a short, stocky woman sat in a prominent spot, reigning over the gathering from her high-backed, hand-carved mahogany chair. A small crowd surrounded doña Esmeralda as they humbly addressed her with their petitions. As soon as the queen spotted Bernardo, she motioned for everyone to be silent. At once, the house became eerily quiet.

"¡Ideay, Bernardo!" doña Esmeralda said loudly enough for everyone to hear. "I'm angry at you. Why didn't you stay here with me, in my house?"

Instantly, the word *ideay* took Paulina back to her youth. She hadn't heard the expression for years—an expression that she was certain only Nicaraguans used. By now Paulina was so Americanized that she spoke a standard, listless form of textbook Spanish. She hadn't used *ideay* for so long she had forgotten that such a word existed. Early in her marriage, she tried to explain its meaning to Jake, who often heard Paulina use it in conversation with her tía Antonieta. But in answering her husband's question, Paulina discovered that *ideay* defied translation. It could mean anything, and to figure it out one had to know the context: "What happened?!" "Well?!" "And what do you think happened next?!" "What's your problem?!" "Can you believe it?!" "What's up?!" "What's holding you up?!" "What happened to our agreement?!" "Who do you think you are?!" "What the heck?!" And the list went on and on.

"How do you folks keep it straight?" Jake asked, wondering

how his wife's compatriotas could ever understand each other with such words. Jake looked up *ideay* in several Spanish language dictionaries, but didn't find it. He then asked a Spanish professor at his university. She just shrugged her shoulders and said, "It must just be a peculiarly Nicaraguan idiom."

"Perdón, doña Esmeralda," Bernardo said, "but I had to stay with my cousin Paulina. You know how it is with family." He looked at Paulina, his eyes pleading for her support.

"A cousin in Los Angeles?" doña Esmeralda asked. The woman's skepticism made Paulina uncomfortable.

"Yes," Paulina nevertheless intervened. "We had lost touch over the years. But that won't happen again. Right, Bernardo?"

The seer smiled and nodded.

"Well, I'm glad you agreed to come tonight, Bernardo. But remember, my feelings are still hurt. Next time you're in Los Angeles you're staying with me." Doña Esmeralda then turned to face everyone in the room. "Now that Bernardo is here, we'll take la Virgen de Cuapa on a procession around the block. When we return, we'll pray the rosary and, afterward, there'll be food and refreshments." Doña Esmeralda then clapped her hands. Four men immediately stepped into the shrine. They carefully lifted the three-foot-tall statue of la Virgen de Cuapa, carrying her on a wooden platform with extended handles. The statue was identical to the one Paulina had, except for its size—and its perfectly good hand. Paulina was surprised when she experienced a twinge of jealousy.

Every person in the house accompanied la Virgen de Cuapa on her voyage. Residents of the neighborhood came out to greet her, waving handkerchiefs and making the sign of the cross as she passed before their homes. When the procession reached busy Pico Street, on the northern end of the block, the cars driving by honked their horns to hail la Virgen. The faithful sang hymns the entire route. Although Paulina recognized the melodies, she had long forgotten the words. But the joy she felt at being again among Nicaraguans caught her off guard. Paulina remembered what she most treasured about her compatriotas: their spontaneity and passion for life. And their devotion inspired her to repeat her pledge to la Virgen de Cuapa that she would make the pilgrimage to the Chontales site where she had appeared. More important, Paulina was thrilled that no one had detected her shame.

Once the procession returned to doña Esmeralda's house, everyone crammed back inside. As soon as la reina settled her subjects down, Bernardo led them in praying the rosary. Once finished, doña Esmeralda ordered that nacatamales be served. From Paulina's first bite, the taste of el nacatamal brought back long-forgotten memories with a force that startled her. For an instant, she imagined herself back in Nicaragua.

As Paulina sat there, savoring her past, many people began to gather around Bernardo to present their petitions. He assured each supplicant that he would relay all concerns to la Virgen. Many of those who came up to the visionary didn't ask anything of him; they were happy just to touch him, believing that by doing so they were receiving Nuestra Señora's blessing.

After an hour of this, doña Esmeralda rose from her seat. She clapped and motioned for the people surrounding the seer to leave him alone. She then led Bernardo to a corner of the living room and spoke to him privately.

Throughout, Paulina was by herself. But she didn't mind being alone because she was entertained, eavesdropping on the conversations around her. She enjoyed listening to the words, expressions, accents, lilts, and raucous laughter of her compatriotas.

When doña Esmeralda finished speaking with Bernardo, she returned to her place, all the time holding his hand. Standing before her queenly mahogany chair, she raised her free hand. Soon, the gathering grew silent.

"Bernardo has asked us to help him in the important work he's doing at the Church of Nuestra Señora de la Victoria, in El Crucero. Today, with your help, I pledge to raise enough money to send him two used pickups."

The people cheered, clapped, and whistled. Paulina overheard one woman say, "¡Tan buena que es doña Esmeralda!" Bernardo stood next to la reina, holding her hand, smiling and nodding.

On the drive back to Palos Verdes, Paulina leaned toward the seer, and said, "Bernardo, what doña Esmeralda is doing is marvelous. Those vehicles will certainly help in your work with the poor."

Bernardo looked at Paulina with great curiosity, and for a moment it made her tense. Then a sad, faint smile appeared on his lips. "Ay, hija. I can tell that you've been away from Nicaraguans for a long time. In every community there's a doña Esmeralda. They make big promises before an adoring public. But afterward . . . nothing. Her admirers will never know the truth. As far as they're concerned, the trucks are already in El Crucero. I'm sorry to say this, Paulina, but that's the way of our compatriotas."

Paulina didn't say another word. Instead, she watched as Bernardo played with the radio dial until he found a Spanish-speaking station. At that precise moment, a Catholic priest was asking his listeners to join him in praying the rosary. And Paulina and Bernardo did so, finding solace in the repetitiousness of the prayers.

NULLA VISIO

(No Apparition)

August 8–12, 1980

Bernardo

THE NEXT month went by slowly. I thought August 8 would never come. In my excitement I didn't sleep the night before. Two months earlier she had come to me in a dream. And last month she sent el Angel, also in a dream. I hoped that this time Nuestra Señora would come herself; better yet, I hoped that she would come while I was awake. A lot of people laughed when I told them that she had come to me in a dream. I didn't mind them laughing at me, but I don't want them laughing at *her.*

On the day la Virgencita said she would be here, I was a bit worried because of the weather. It had been raining for twenty-four hours, and the skies showed no signs of letting up. Even so, in spite of the downpour, a group of fifteen women were waiting for me at the church, ready to go to the site. We left town shortly after lunch and headed down the old road to Juigalpa. At times it rained so hard that we couldn't see the path. Thinking we were walking straight, we'd end up slipping on the muddy embankments. But that didn't bother us. For some reason, unknown to me at the time, it was a cheerful trip—until we reached the river.

What we saw at the crossing frightened us. Usually a harmless stream, el Río de Cuapa was now flooded. It raged out of control with the waters coming down from the eastern mountains. I walked up and down the bank, trying to find some place where we could cross safely. But it looked impossible, especially for doña Justiniana, doña Ena, and doña Corina, three of Cuapa's oldest women. They had come along, they said, because they hoped to meet Nuestra Señora in person before joining her in heaven.

Wanting to keep my date with la Virgencita, I decided to ford the river by myself. I couldn't let her down. When I announced that I was going to cross, everyone protested loudly.

"¡Bernardo, ¿estás loco?! You'll drown for sure!" said doña Socorro. She was probably right. During the last rainy season, just a couple of kilometers upstream, don Arnoldo had tried to cross the flooded river on the back of his mule. Their bodies were found three days later, not far from where we stood, close to where I like to fish.

Convinced that to try to cross el río would be foolish, I turned to the women, and said, "Nuestra Señora can hear our prayers wherever we are. Let's just stay here, pray the rosary, and then return to Cuapa." We prayed, and before leaving we sang a couple of hymns.

Amazingly, in spite of our clothes being soaked like laundry left in remojo overnight and in spite of not being able to make it to the apparition site, we were all in a joyful mood. Nothing about that day bothered us. No one got angry, no one got cold, and, surprisingly, even though we all were soaking wet and got back home after five o'clock, no one got sick.

By the next morning the rain had stopped, and by midday the river was passable. I went to the site with Blanquita and doña Tula, both of whom had been with me the day before. We went there just in case la Virgencita had changed her plans because of the weather. We waited for three hours, but she didn't come.

"Bernardo, I don't think she wants to see you anymore," said doña Tula.

Her remark worried me. But there was nothing I could do, really. Before returning home, we prayed the rosary. Although I was disappointed, I wasn't sad. I don't know why, but I was sure that I would soon know the reason for her absence.

A few days later, on August 12, Padre Domingo came to Cuapa to celebrate mass. The past few months he had been very understanding, never questioning anything I had said. Still, I knew he wasn't a believer.

On this day, from the moment Padre Domingo arrived, he seemed different, preoccupied. He celebrated mass somewhat distractedly, without his usual passion. That's when I began to worry about him.

Afterward, as we ate lunch, the priest said, "Bernardo, I have a favor to ask."

"If I can do it, Padre, I will," I answered.

"I want you to go with me to the apparition site. But be quiet the entire way, please. Don't say a word until I ask you to. And do not, under any circumstances, point out the pasture or the spot where she appeared. Can you do that?"

"Yes," I replied, although puzzled.

The only thing Padre Domingo knew for sure was that el potrero was somewhere along the old road to Juigalpa, but he had never been there. Not once. I didn't know what he was up to, but whatever it was, I was happy to help. He's a good man.

As we walked there, Padre Domingo kept looking around,

as if trying to recognize something. But true to my word, I kept my mouth shut. Shortly after crossing the river, as we approached the site, he stopped, placed both hands on his hips, glanced around, and nodded. He then walked straight to the entrance to mi potrero. I followed him, in silence. At the gate, he stopped.

"Bernardo, will you please pray three Hail Marys with me?" he asked. I did so happily.

The prayers seemed to give Padre Domingo strength. From the gate, he walked directly to the spot where she had first appeared. When he got there, he brought out his handkerchief and wiped the sweat from his brow. He glanced around one more time. Then he stared at me without saying a word, but I could clearly see the look of amazement on his face.

"This is where she appeared. Am I right, Bernardo?" he said, pointing to the bed of rocks before the morisco tree.

"Yes," I answered, shocked. "How did you know, Padre?"

"I was here. The night of August 8, I was here . . . standing on this very spot . . . in a dream."

I became so excited that I grabbed him by the shoulders. Forgetting the respect one should have for a priest of the Church, I shook him. "Did she appear to you, Padre Domingo? Did Nuestra Señora appear to you in that dream? Did she talk to you?"

Padre Domingo looked at me blankly; his expression said nothing. "That information, Bernardo, I'll reserve for myself, and for the Church investigation that will now certainly follow. All I can tell you is that four nights ago, I was here."

"Padre," I said, excited, "now I know why she didn't appear to me. She wanted *you* to believe. She wanted to make you a believer." The priest didn't answer. He just stood there; ready to return to

Cuapa. But first I asked him the question that had been worrying me most. "Padre, will Nuestra Señora return? I'm afraid that she won't appear again."

Placing both hands on my shoulders and looking me straight in the eyes, he replied, "Pray, hijo. Pray and she will come." Padre Domingo was sincere; I could see that. He then smiled and said, "Bernardo, please pray another three Hail Marys with me before we leave."

My heart rejoiced as we prayed, for I now knew, without a doubt, that Padre Domingo was a believer.

chapter eleven

AEIPARTHENOS
(Ever Virgin)

August 20, 1995

Sor Milagros Tijerino

"IN THE name of the Father and of the Son and of the Holy Spirit. Blessed be la Santísima Virgen María for making this day, this miracle, possible. Amén." I said this brief prayer with tears in my eyes at the conclusion of Bernardo Martínez's first mass as a Catholic priest.

I've been part of his odyssey from the beginning. Actually, I've been part of his journey even before it began. At a prayer meeting, in Managua, about a month before Nuestra Señora's first apparition in Cuapa, doña Clorinda, a woman who receives messages directly from el Espíritu Santo, announced that la Santísima Virgen María would soon visit Nicaragua. That sent all of us who had gathered in her house that evening into a loud celebration. Those were very difficult times back then, and a visit from her would certainly help make things better. Unfortunately, doña Clorinda's vision didn't include exactly *where* or *when* Nuestra Señora would appear. So I began a vigil: reading the papers every day, monitoring the news over the radio, and watching as many television news broadcasts as I could. Sooner or later I was bound to hear something about her arrival. Everyone knows that in this country, a secret is impossible to keep.

But I had to wait quite a while before the blessed news surfaced. Almost a year had passed since doña Clorinda's prophetic announcement when, at last, my informant in the archdiocese told me, in confidence, that His Grace had ordered an investigation into claims that la Virgen had appeared in Cuapa.

Cuapa? Of all places, why did she choose Chontales? That was my first reaction. Then I remembered that I'm not worthy of questioning la Santísima Virgen María.

I didn't waste any time. The next day I took a bus there to conduct my own investigation. In truth, I just wanted to help spread the happy news. I also wanted to pledge eternal loyalty to Our Blessed Mother on the very site she had consecrated.

Upon first meeting Bernardo Martínez, I reached out, took his hand, and kissed his open palm. "Thou that art so highly favored," I said, bowing before him. The Chosen One just stared at me. He looked like a frightened deer, ready to bolt off and hide in the bushes. Fortunately, on that day Padre Domingo was also in Cuapa. With his help—he's one of the nicest priests anywhere—I quickly gained Bernardo's trust. I offered to help Nuestra Señora's messenger in any way I could. Since that day I've been at Bernardo's service, in honor of la Virgen María.

During one of my first visits to Cuapa, a newspaper reporter was there. Word of Nuestra Señora's appearance had leaked out to the press. The young woman investigating the story interviewed me. I was delighted and honored to talk about la Santísima Virgen.

But the reporter completely distorted my comments in her article and she made Bernardo look ridiculous. That was terribly sad. All along I had thought that the young woman was honest and sincere. She seemed genuinely touched by Nuestra Señora's visit. After that incident I did my best to protect Bernardo from the Sandinista press, especially after those communist devils organized that awful campaign to discredit him.

That lovely American priest that headed the Church's investigation also questioned me. He was such a nice man. I never understood why los cuapeños disliked him so much. Toward the end of his stay they became downright rude, avoiding him wherever he went. I found their behavior very disrespectful. This is a man of God we're talking about.

A couple of years later, I spent two months in the seminary, not stepping out once, while I nursed Bernardo back to health after those piricuacos, those rabid Marxist dogs, tortured him. The poor man. I couldn't believe what they had done to her messenger. Although he never told anyone what happened, I heard him talking in his sleep. Yes, I heard him talking. Atheistic perverts. But to the Chosen One's glory, he was made a martyr.

A few years after that, I helped Bernardo graduate from escuela secundaria. I gave him permission to attend el Colegio de Nuestra Señora de la Victoria, in El Crucero, of which I'm the director. All he had to do in return was help us with repairs and new construction.

Through my friendship with Bernardo I have been blessed. I've witnessed many of Nuestra Señora's miracles: I've seen promesantes travel long distances to fulfill their pledges to la Santísima Virgen; I've seen men, women, and children cured of cancer, cured of deformity, cured of mental illness; I've seen relationships healed;

and I've seen many desperate lives find meaning through her intervention. I've heard their wondrous stories.

I am one of la Virgen de Cuapa's most loyal devotees. I've preached her message across the continents. I'm never without her. Literally. While traveling on business for my order, she has accompanied me to the United States, Europe, and the Orient. Wherever I go, I take along a statue, two feet tall, of la Virgen de Cuapa. She has been to Universal Studios in Florida, the Eiffel Tower, and the Great Wall of China. People stare at me because they think I'm very attached to my large doll, but I don't mind. On the contrary, I welcome their questions. Nuestra Señora's statue helps me preach her message, one that's for all of mankind.

What makes these occasions so special for me, Bernardo's ordination and his first mass, is that in spite of all the obstacles he didn't stray from his quest to join the holiest of all communities: the brotherhood of Roman Catholic priests. The Chosen One's path wasn't an easy one. By no means. Often he became impatient. At other times, despair almost made him abandon his dream. And, sadly, many times I saw doubt in his eyes. I saw him waver from the certainty that Nuestra Señora would fulfill her promise to him. But I urged him not to surrender. I wouldn't let him give up. I kept on pushing him, knowing that la Santísima Virgen María would keep her word.

It's true that Bernardo is not the most intelligent of men. It's also true that after the Sandinistas lost the elections most bishops wanted him to go back into the shadows, to return to Cuapa. They believed that he had already accomplished his mission by helping the faithful resist the communist warlords. And it's especially true that many of the cardinal's advisers believed that Bernardo just didn't have the proper background to become one of God's chosen men. But Bernardo *was* chosen . . . by the Blessed Mother of Jesús herself. If that honor didn't entitle him to become a priest, then what would?

Besides, Bernardo spent years locked up in the seminary. He completed all the coursework. The theology courses were especially difficult for him. He's someone who understands Nuestro Señor emotionally, not intellectually. While it's true that he barely passed his classes, in the end he *did* pass them. I thought it was sheer meanness to have kept him waiting for so long. The world needs priests like Bernardo: men devoted body and soul to the Church. He has the vocation, he has heard the calling, he has heard her voice, and he has responded. He has the spirit of an apostle, and the soul of a martyr, and he's devoted to God and to his fellow man.

I thought, then, that the way the Church handled Bernardo's desire to become a priest was unfair. Here's a man who has suffered more than anyone in Nicaragua in el Nombre de Cristo. He has been a model of obedience as well, doing everything his superiors have ever asked of him. And still, after years of committed service, Bernardo was repeatedly denied entry into the holiest of professions. It's true that there was that small scandal about him trying to make money by selling Agua Milagrosa de la Virgen de Cuapa when it was really tap water from the church in El Crucero. And then there's the time he dressed up in his deacon's garb and paraded through the streets of Cuapa with the statue of la Inmaculada Concepción, campaigning against the Sandinista candidate for mayor (whom he called Satanic). But he only did these things because he's a trusting soul. Sometimes people who don't have his best interests in mind, like that unpleasant woman who owns La Purísima, influence him too easily. But Bernardo is the closest thing I know to an adult with childlike innocence. That's a sign of saintliness, isn't it?

In the end, my own patience had reached its limit. Frustrated that her Chosen One wasn't yet ordained, I paid a visit to Bernardo's benefactor, the bishop of León. Surely there was something His Grace could do to help her messenger at last join the priesthood.

Thanks to my prayers to Our Blessed Mother, the bishop received me as soon as I arrived. We have known each other ever since he was a young seminarian and I was a novitiate. He greeted me with a warm embrace.

"Sor Milagros," he said, "is it my imagination or are you getting taller?" He's one of the few persons whom I allow to joke about my height. At four feet eleven inches, I tend to be sensitive about it. But the good bishop means no harm. I know that. "And I see that you're taking great care of Nuestra Señora de Cuapa," he said, referring to my statue. I thanked him for his kind words.

As soon as we were seated in his office, I didn't waste any time presenting my case. "Your Grace, Bernardo has earned the right to be ordained. Besides, he's now sixty-three. How many more good years do you think he still has before him? There's no time to spare." I punctuated my statement by pounding my fist on the bishop's desk.

My friend listened patiently, his elbows on the armrest of his chair while he kept the tips of his fingers together at the height of the large, handsome crucifix that dangles on a thick gold chain around his neck. When I finished, the bishop smiled, somewhat sadly, I thought, and, in confidence, he revealed a story to me.

"You know, Sor Milagros," he began, "I had hoped that when I ordained Bernardo as a deacon everyone would be happy. I thought it could simply be left at that. Certainly the cardinal's advisers could not object to it, since Bernardo had not entered the priesthood. And I fully expected Bernardo and his followers to be happy, since he could, in essence, perform the same tasks as a priest—with some important exceptions, as you know. Well, I was right about the cardinal and his men but wrong about Bernardo's supporters. You people are a persistent bunch. Still, Sor Milagros, I can honestly say that I was satisfied with my choice. As far as I was concerned, Bernardo could remain a deacon forever. After all, if deaconry was good enough for San Francisco de Asís, then it's good enough for him. But, Sor Milagros, something happened recently that has made me change my mind."

In all the time I've known the bishop, he has been a fair, just man. I do, however, find him a little too rational, almost to the point of absurdity. He's overly logical. His Grace calculates every ecclesiastical decision down to its minutest consequence. My friend doesn't appear to have a spiritual bone in his body. The glories of rapture must be an experience entirely alien to him. Of course, I'm exaggerating.

But let me try to explain it this way: I'm a big fan of the old *Star Trek*. I love watching the reruns on television. El Capitán Kirk is so handsome (although I would never admit that in public). But the point I want to make is that the bishop reminds me of el Señor Spock. Only a commanding force, a commanding reason, a commanding display of logic can change his mind.

"What I will tell you next, Sor Milagros, is a secret. Please don't let it leave this room."

"You have my word, Your Grace." And I kept my promise. Someone else told, and the story spread like wildfire. That's why I feel free to tell it now.

The bishop nodded and continued. "A few weeks ago, I was conducting my review of candidates for ordination. Every year, I make two piles out of the folders I've examined: one for the files of candidates whose ordination I support and another for the files of those I do not. I had been at this for hours, saving the three most difficult cases for last. First, I reviewed Bernardo's. I knew that if I approved his ordination, my decision would, in all likelihood, start a conflict between the cardinal's men and myself. And, Sor Milagros, to be honest, I don't have the time or the energy to go to war with that group. It's much easier for me to deal with Bernardo's disappointment—and the disappointment of his supporters, of course. With that in mind, I put his folder on the pile against ordination.

"The last two cases were more delicate. I had both of their files open, side by side, and I thought to ask Nuestro Señor to help guide me in making the right decision. As I sat at my desk in prayer, out of the corner of my eye I saw a faint ember of light glowing in the left-hand corner of the room. Then it grew in intensity. Suddenly, there was an exploding radiance that swept across my office, blinding me for a few seconds. While lost in the darkness, I heard the papers on my desk shuffling, as if a gust of wind were blowing them around. But, Sor Milagros, all the doors and windows were closed, I assure you. I prefer air-conditioning, as you know.

"When I could see again, I expected to find the papers scattered all over my office. But my desk looked exactly the same as it did before the flash of light . . . with one exception: on top of the two cases I had been trying to decide, was Bernardo's folder. How it went from the rejection pile to sit perfectly before me, I'll never know. But what I understand even less is that Bernardo's file was open to the form where I had marked my decision. Now, Sor Milagros, I'm positive that I checked the box denying his ordination. I know that for sure, as sure as I know that I'm sitting here, at this very moment, enjoying your company. But to my astonishment, the form was now blank, my mark completely erased. Now, this is the part where you need to brace yourself, Hermana: the approval box glowed brightly, as if guiding my pen. I instantly knew that this was Nuestra Señora's doing. Even thinking about it now makes the hairs on my arms stand up. At that moment, Sor Milagros, I knew that she was taking the decision out of my hands."

The bishop then stared at me, I think to watch my reaction. All I could do was make the sign of the cross. After a long pause, His Grace smiled and announced, "Bernardo's ordination will take place here, in la Catedral, on August 19. You're the first person to learn about it, outside of Bernardo. I'm sure he'll invite you, his biggest supporter, to the ceremony."

I was both shocked and elated. For once in my life I had nothing to say. I thanked the bishop, bade him farewell, and then paid a quick visit to la Catedral to thank el Sagrado Corazón de Jesús. Before returning to Managua, I called Bernardo to congratulate him.

"You are coming, aren't you, Sor Milagros?" he asked.

"Of course, Bernardo," I replied. "This is what we've been waiting for all these years."

Yesterday, August 19, the day we had long prayed for finally arrived: Bernardo's ordination as a priest in the Holy Roman Catholic Church. I barely slept the night before. Almost fourteen years of pleading for this miracle, and at last it was here.

Before entering la Catedral—such a magnificent building—I stood out front, looking up at the four giants that stand on the roof: two pairs of them, facing each other. They support, on their tired shoulders, the massive beams of the portals. Unjustly, ever since I can recall, the giants to the left have also had to bear the weight of a huge cast-iron bell that hangs from the center of their beam. Since I was a small child, these creatures have fascinated me: Christian Atlases who hold the fate of the Nicaraguan Catholic Church on their shoulders. After these contemplations, I greeted the two ferocious stone lions that guard the steps leading up to la Catedral. That has also been a custom of mine since childhood.

When I entered the building I dipped my fingers in the font of holy water and made the sign of the cross. Inside, la Catedral looked beautiful. Pink roses adorned the columns nearest to the altar. The Lord's table was covered with a white satin cloth, the words AVE MARIA embroidered on it. More pink roses decorated each corner. To the left, high on a pedestal, was a statue of la Inmaculada Concepción. It wasn't the image that glowed on that fateful night before Bernardo's incredulous eyes, but she was strikingly similar. Who brought her, and from where, I don't know.

Since I was a guest of honor, I was escorted to the front row. I sat down and carefully placed my statue of la Virgen de Cuapa next to me. Because of my height, I insisted on an aisle seat so I could see who had attended. Nothing could stop me from taking in every detail of the miracle of Bernardo's ordination.

La Catedral was full of devotees of la Virgen de Cuapa. The faithful were here from all over the country. I even saw a group of people who had come all the way from los Estados Unidos—a banner they brought with them said so. Knowing that she had touched so many lives, far beyond our borders, filled me with joy. I could feel her loving spirit among us.

The ordination ceremony is one of my favorites in the Catholic Church. It's always a moving experience to welcome a new member into the holiest community of men. I envy them. Sometimes I wish I had been born a man so that I could have joined the priesthood. But these thoughts are only momentary lapses. I'm happy serving Nuestro Señor as a nun.

On this evening, the one of Bernardo's ordination, I did feel my usual twinge of envy. But I was truly delighted for her messenger. This was Bernardo's evening, and we were gathered to witness him become, at long last, a priest in Christ's Church.

I was beginning to pray, thanking Nuestro Señor por el milagro, when the organ player struck low, solemn chords on the keys of his noble instrument. Everyone rose to their feet, straining their necks to watch the entrance of the celebrants. I, of course, seated on the aisle, had no problem.

Fifty seminarians led the procession, followed by the deacons. After their entry, there was a break in the procession. Then Bernardo, walking alone, his gaze lost in the heavens, entered la Catedral. After another pause, the priests entered. At last, my friend, the bishop, entered the temple. He looked magnificent in his holy regalia, ready to preside over the blessed event.

Once the procession had concluded, His Grace welcomed all of us who had supported Bernardo throughout the years. To my embarrassment, he mentioned me in particular, which he really shouldn't have, as there are many others who also helped Bernardo on this difficult journey. When the bishop finished speaking, he took his seat while Padre Jerónimo Peña, director of the seminary (and one of the gentlest priests I know) presented the candidate to His Grace and to the congregation.

"Those who approve of Bernardo Martinez's ordination, please applaud to show your support," he said. Well, of course, everyone clapped and cheered and wept.

When at last we quieted down, the bishop stepped up to the microphone and said, "I cannot begin this ceremony without saying a few words about the message Nuestra Señora entrusted to Bernardo, in Cuapa, fifteen years ago. Her words are an invitation for us to love and forgive one another. She calls upon us to fulfill our obligations to our families and to society. She asks us to pray and to contemplate the mysteries of the holy rosary, every day. She also invites us to ask el Señor for the strength to face adversity, the strength to attain true repentance, and the strength to live a Christian life. For this message, we thank Bernardo, who today, with you as witnesses, will be ordained a priest in the Catholic Church."

His Grace then turned to her Chosen One and asked, "Bernardo, are you firm in your decision to fulfill God's ministry faithfully?"

"Sí, lo estoy," Bernardo answered. The candidate then kneeled before the bishop, who swore him to obedience.

My eyes became misty when, immediately afterward, Bernardo, showing the discomfort of his aged bones, lowered himself to the ground to lie prostrate—his face and mouth pressed against la Catedral's grimy floor—in a gesture that demonstrated his unworthiness for the priesthood. For the longest time he lay there, arms spread out like Cristo on the cross, unmoving, while the rest of us sang the Litany of the Saints, calling upon Jesús and the entire Comunidad de los Santos to intercede before the Almighty on Bernardo's behalf.

I also shed tears during the Imposition of Hands. His Grace and all the priests, in this ancient practice that goes back to the Apostles, laid their hands on Bernardo, praying in silence for him.

Afterward, His Grace presented Bernardo with the gifts to help him fulfill his priestly obligations: his stole, his chasuble, his chalice, and his paten. The bishop, with his sacred authority and divine voice, said, "Bernardo, accept from the holy people of God the gifts you are to offer to him. Know what you are doing, and imitate the mystery you celebrate; model your life on the mystery of the Lord's Cross."

His Grace then anointed Bernardo's hands with sacrum chrisma, God's holy oil. This prepared Bernardo for his divine duties, cleansing his hands so they could hold the blessed vessels, the instruments of priests. After the purification of Bernardo's hands, he would be able to offer communion to those in grace, to anoint the sick, and to bless the poor.

The bishop then said, "El Padre anointed Nuestro Señor Jesucristo through the power of el Espíritu Santo. May Jesús preserve you to sanctify the Christian people and to offer sacrifice to God."

His Grace and the priests then came forward. Each of them walked to Bernardo and gave him the kiss of peace. When they had concluded offering the candidate this sign of brotherhood, Bernardo Martínez, the Messenger of la Virgen de Cuapa, was, at last, a priest. Her Chosen One then walked up to the altar to join his hermanos en Cristo. At that point, my tears were flowing like the waters of the Jordan.

Before closing the ceremony, His Grace shared a few thoughts on Nuestra Señora's Chosen One. "Bernardo's ordination is, I believe, a miracle. He came from humble origins and didn't learn to read until he was nearly twenty years old. But since childhood, he has served el Señor and his people quietly and faithfully. He became a leader in his Church in el pueblito de Cuapa. And when this humble servant standing before us today was forty-eight, Nuestra Señora rewarded his faith with a vision—a vision that changed his life forever. She entrusted him with a message intended for all of humanity, not just for those of us living in this long-suffering nation. But her apparition also marked the beginning of Bernardo's Calvario. Admirably, in spite of the ridicule, in spite of the humiliation, in spite of the anguish, and in spite of the torture, he has remained true to Nuestra Señora, and to her Son, not once doubting her promise that he would one day become a priest.

"At the age of fifty-eight, when most of us are thinking about relaxing and enjoying the remainder of our lives, he graduated from la escuela secundaria. After that, although faced with many obstacles, he successfully completed his coursework in the seminary. And today, after a long and at times sorrowful journey of fifteen years, with all of you gathered here as witnesses, Bernardo Martínez has been ordained a priest of the Holy Roman Catholic Church.

"Tomorrow, on the feast day of San Bernardo de Clairvaux, which will also be Bernardo's sixty-fourth birthday, he reaches the summit of his quest when he celebrates his first mass in his beloved Cuapa. I hope everyone here today will attend."

Our applause reverberated throughout the cavernous building. I'm sure that our three great poets—Rubén Darío, Alfonso Cortés, and Salomón de la Selva—whose remains are in eternal repose on these hallowed grounds, were also rejoicing. The bishop waited patiently for the ovation to end.

He was about to continue when a woman in the congregation, unable to contain her emotions, shouted, "¿Quién es la más guapa?"

All of us, in single voice that made the thick walls of la Catedral shudder, replied, "¡La Virgen de Cuapa!"

His Grace looked annoyed. He's very formal, you know. He likes religious ceremonies to be solemn, respectful. But, really, after all these years of waiting, we couldn't restrain ourselves any longer. I believe that the Holy Spirit had moved the woman to call out the question. After all, la Santísima Virgen María was the real reason we were there that day; the real reason this vast Catedral was packed full.

My friend then overcame his irritation and, smiling, said, "Damas y caballeros, por favor, welcome Padre Bernardo Martínez into the priesthood."

We rose to our feet. The sound of our clapping swirled around and around, bouncing off every niche, column, and ceiling arch. This time, His Grace appeared to enjoy our display of affection for Bernardo. After several minutes, when the applause finally died down, Padre Bernardo Martínez stepped up to the microphone.

"I want to thank our bishop who, from the beginning, has been very supportive of me. It's through the goodness of his heart that I stand before you today, at last a priest. I want to thank my teachers in the seminary, and my classmates, who gave much of their time and of their energies to help me succeed. I thank the people who have prayed to Jesucristo on my behalf. My ordination is a product of these prayers. I thank everyone here this evening for your help. I especially want to thank Sor Milagros Tijerino, who has been at my side through it all and has not once abandoned me. Thank you, mi hermana en Cristo. Once again, my deepest thanks to each of you. Finally, I wish to thank Nuestra Señora, la Santísima Virgen María, who made this day possible. Here now, standing before you, is your priest. I am yours."

Lord help me, I couldn't stop crying. Tears of joy rolled down my cheeks, and my chest heaved in convulsions. I looked around and saw that all present had tears in their eyes as well. Even His Grace, who is so stern, so stoic, was dabbing the corners of his eyes with his handkerchief.

After the ordination ceremony, His Grace hosted a lovely reception. Long lines of devotees of la Virgen de Cuapa waited their turn to touch, embrace, and be blessed by her Chosen One. I stayed in the background with my statue, rejoicing in the glory of this miracle. After all, I can talk to Bernardo almost anytime I wish.

I was enjoying my third Rojita—the strawberry soda that always helps me keep my emotions under control—when my good friend, the bishop, came to sit next to me.

"Your Grace," I said, "that was a beautiful ceremony. I was moved to tears several times."

"I know, Sor Milagros," he replied. "I was watching you closely." His Grace smiled, placed an arm around my shoulders, and gave me a big squeeze. "I have one question for you," he said, leaning back and looking pleased with himself. "Are you happy now?"

I didn't have to think about the answer. "Yes, Your Grace. Yes, I am. Very happy. This is a miracle I've long prayed for. I'm elated, knowing that she has heard my prayers. And you, my friend, were la Virgen's gracious agent."

"Sor Milagros, I just obeyed her wishes. Nothing more." He smiled, reached out, and squeezed me again. His Grace then rose, bowed before my statue of la Virgen de Cuapa, and hurried to the food table. Yes, I'm happy, I thought. Bendito sea Nuestro Señor.

After the reception I slept in el Convento, in León. Two nuns from my Colegio also stayed there. We woke up well before dawn for the long trip to Cuapa, but we didn't mind. We were thrilled to attend Padre Bernardo's first mass. Along the way, we stopped at San Benito, the town at the juncture that leads to Chontales, to buy a copy of *La Prensa*. There, before my eyes, spread out like a miracle, was the day's headline: *Bernardo de Cuapa Ordained a Priest*. I read the article out loud to mis hermanas en Cristo, and we were thankful for the privilege of being part of Bernardo's spiritual journey.

Getting to Cuapa was difficult as usual. There are so many potholes on the highway that it seemed we would never make it. But Sor Beatrice is an excellent driver. She got us there safely, and with an hour to spare. We arrived just as a procession was getting under way. Los cuapeños were taking la Inmaculada Concepción, the very same statue that had illuminated for Padre Bernardo long ago, on a journey of thanks, carrying her up and down every street in el pueblito.

Her Chosen One led the procession; dressed in his new chasuble, ready to perform his first celebration of la Eucaristía upon their return. We sang hymns to Nuestra Señora along the entire route. The procession was back at the church exactly on time for mass to begin.

Three priests awaited us at the entrance, ready to concelebrate with Padre Bernardo. Once again, I had privileged seating in the front row, along with my statue of la Virgen de Cuapa.

The church was brightly decorated with streamers, banners, and flowers. I was happy to see a huge crowd in attendance. The building couldn't hold everyone, and people were spilling out into the park. Fortunately, Padre Francisco, the new parish priest, thought ahead to place loudspeakers outside so those who couldn't fit inside could still follow the mass.

Padre Bernardo officiated rather nervously. But that's understandable. At times, it was also obvious that he had learned to read late in life, stumbling over the more difficult words when he read el

Evangelio. At moments the Gospel sounded like a scratched record, caught in a groove, until Padre Bernardo got unstuck and could move forward.

For fifteen years I had been anxiously waiting to hear Padre Bernardo's first sermon as a priest of the Holy Roman Catholic Church. I expected that, once ordained, la Santísima Virgen María would illuminate him every time he stepped into the pulpit. I had believed that every Sunday, moved by el Espíritu Santo, he would give a homily that would lead everyone to repent of their sinful ways and lead saintly lives. But to be honest, I found the messenger's sermon rather ordinary. If anything, Padre Bernardo kept straying from the topic, making it difficult for me to follow his thoughts.

His choice of subject was certainly appropriate: the need for Catholics to be responsible parents. As an example, he shared how his abuelita, with the right combination of kindness and firmness, raised him to become the man and the priest standing before us today. From early on, that understanding woman taught him the importance of venerating la Santísima Virgen María.

As best as I can remember, the clearest part of Padre Bernardo's sermon went something like this: "Teach your children to pray the rosary as soon as they are able to understand." He then made an interesting confession. "When Nuestra Señora told me that she wanted everyone to reflect upon the appropriate passages of the Bible while they prayed the rosary, I had no idea what she meant. Although mi abuelita, doña Eloísa, taught me to pray when I was barely learning to walk, she never said anything about los Misterios. And that's because she didn't know about them herself; or no one had taught her. I was nearly fifty years old before I realized that, all along, I had been praying the rosary incorrectly. In doing so, I was leading the people of Cuapa astray." Padre Bernardo looked sad.

For a moment I thought he was going to ask for our forgiveness.

"But that doesn't matter," he continued. "Nuestra Señora knows what's in our hearts, and she accepts our prayers as long as they're sincere. So, parents, teach your children to pray. But don't make the same mistake mi abuelita made; teach them correctly.

"Also," he went on, "teach them to respect the people God has chosen to carry out his work: priests and nuns. Mi abuelita, after every mass, would make me kiss the floor the priest had stood upon because Jesús, in the person of one of his representatives on Earth, had been there to celebrate la Eucaristía. I know no one does this anymore, so just ask your children to pray for us. ¡Bendito sea el Señor!"

During the consecration—the transformation of the bread and wine into the body and blood of Cristo—I saw tears streaking down Padre Bernardo's cheeks. They left glistening little rows where they washed away the dust that had gathered on his face during the procession. Later, while he was giving communion, I noticed his hands shaking, even though as a deacon serving in the Church of Nuestra Señora de la Victoria he had given communion thousands of times before. I guess being among his people made him nervous. But los cuapeños responded with love, making this one of the most moving masses I've ever attended—and I've been to nearly a million of them, let me assure you.

At the conclusion of mass, after Padre Bernardo finished giving us the Blessing of el Señor, two of the priests concelebrating with him asked for permission to say a few words. The first one, Padre Miguel, announced, "I've been researching la Virgen's apparition in Cuapa for fourteen years. At last, Nuestra Señora has been kind enough to reward my efforts. My book about the blessed event will be ready to present to the pope during his upcoming visit to Nicaragua." We broke into a joyous ovation. Now His Holiness will know how blessed Nicaragua has been. And we will be blessed to have the pope among us once again. I'm happy he's returning because during his first visit the Sandinista turbas heckled him mercilessly during the mass he celebrated in Managua.

Then Padre Francisco, Cuapa's new parish priest, told everyone of a recent miracle. As he spoke, his voice cracked, and there were tears in his eyes. "The miracle I'm about to share with you has affected me personally. My niece, who is sixteen years old, was dying of cancer. After we asked la Virgen de Cuapa for her intercession, Nuestra Señora smiled upon her. At my niece's most recent visit to the clinic, the doctors pronounced her cured." At that news we began to clap and to cry.

At the reception afterward, once again the lines were long. Los cuapeños were eager to greet Padre Bernardo and receive his blessing. I stood at the rear of the room, leaning against the wall while embracing my statue, deeply moved to see the way his people put their arms around him. Many of them wept with joy. I, on the other hand, celebrated quietly his entrance into the holiest community of men.

I was almost moved to tears when doña Blanca's turn came. She and Padre Bernardo held each other tightly, both of them crying. She's a dear friend of his from childhood. What happened to her boy during the war is very sad; it broke everyone's heart here in Cuapa. I know that the tragedy also devastated my friend. "Elías was like a son to me," Padre Bernardo had once shared with me.

By the time I had finished drinking my fifth Rojita, my lips now red, the line to greet my friend had dwindled to only a few. I walked over there to wait my turn. Before long, I stood before him, ready to receive my first blessing from *Padre* Bernardo.

He broke into a wide grin when he saw me. Without saying a word, he opened his arms wide and held me in a strong embrace. I was very surprised when he began to sob uncontrollably. I clung to him tightly. I had been there all along for him; I was not about to abandon him now.

After a few minutes, Padre Bernardo was calm enough to speak. He released me from his embrace and, instead, held me firmly by the shoulders. With tears flowing freely down his face, he said, "Sor Milagros, la Virgencita had promised that this day would come. But I do confess that sometimes it seemed that only a miracle would fulfill her promise. Sor Milagros, I am ashamed. Throughout all these years, many times I have doubted her word. I've been weak in my faith. Do you think she will ever forgive me?"

chapter twelve

HUMILITAS

(Humility)

January 15, 2000

Nicolás Salazar

TODAY I'M preparing arroz a la valenciana for Bernardo, even though he prefers pollo frito for lunch. He especially likes the fried chicken from that famous Guatemalan chain (the name of which escapes me at the moment) because they have machines that suck out all the fat. But today I simply can't afford it; doña Nora didn't leave me much money. Still, I think that he'll like my rice dish: it's nutritious, and there's plenty of it. Besides, what's more important, much more important than the food, are our weekly conversations. Every Monday he stops by the house to eat; and afterward he takes a short nap before his long five-hour trip back to Tonalá.

I've known Bernardo for nineteen years now. We met not too long after Nuestra Señora's apparition. Doña Nora owns La Purísima, the largest religious supply store in the country, and she saw a good business opportunity in her visit to Nicaragua. Relics, portraits, cards, and statues are big sellers here, you know. Don't get me wrong, doña Nora's not only interested in profits; she's also sincerely devoted to la Virgen. At the time Nuestra Señora appeared to Bernardo, however, the store was barely surviving. But then, all businesses were suffering during the 1980s, with the Sandinistas in power. Ours was no exception. During their reign, the whole damn country went to pot.

I've always hated communism. Marxism's bad for people who like to make money. Besides, los comunistas are arrogant creatures. They can never admit to being wrong. Back in the 1950s, that senator from los Estados Unidos, Joseph McCarthy, was right about them. Like he said, since you can't trust those cucarachas it would be better to wipe them off the face of the earth. It's a shame how los Americanos turned their backs on such a wise man. But the gringos paid for it later: Cuba, Vietnam, the hippies, Woodstock, rock music. Los comunistas were responsible for all that mess. Back in the sixties, los Rolling Stones were really Soviet agents indoctrinating América's youth in the ways of Leninism. I'd bet everything I own on it.

And I have a question for all those who believe that human rights come before order, like that weakling Jimmy Carter: What good did la Revolución do for Nicaragua? I'll tell you what communism did for our country: it left us ten years behind the rest of the world and with seventy thousand dead. That's what those Sandinistas, those sinvergüenzas did. They're scoundrels. For ten years the most productive thing they did was parade around in olive green uniforms imitating their hero, Fidel.

And I'll never forgive those hijueputas for what they did to Bernardo. Sons of bitches. Months went by before doña Nora and I discovered that he was hiding in the seminary. We had given up hope of ever finding him, believing los comunistas had made him disappear. And then Bernardo stayed locked up in there for years. During the latter part of the 1980s I barely got to see him.

I wish that I could say that Nicaragua has gotten better since we got rid of the Sandinistas. But it really hasn't. Those godless freaks have been replaced by the Miami Boys, los Ricos Bolos: wealthy, hard-drinking, cocaine-snorting Nicaraguans who left for Florida during the 1980s and returned once it was safe, waving their dollars in our faces. By the time we had defeated los comunistas we were so broke that we'd sell our own mothers for next to nothing. But let me ask these questions: Where were the Miami Boys when the rest of us were standing in long lines? Where were they when we were resisting the Sandinistas as best as we could? We stayed behind trying to save the place, and they're the ones who returned to reap the glory.

One can see los Ricos Bolos ride around the country in their late-model sports-utility vehicles. They hide behind tinted windows while the rest of us are still struggling to get by. And with their gringo money, the Miami Boys have bought their way into plush positions of power where they're robbing the country blind—and with immunity to boot. These people have no scruples. They don't seem to care about who's going hungry. In fact, they look at the rest of us with contempt. All they care about are their offshore bank accounts, their mansions, their beach houses, their yachts, and their SUVs. Money laundering—that's their business. They're not that much better than the Sandinistas.

All this confirms what I've been telling everyone for ages: the world is coming to an end, just like Nostradamus predicted. I've read every book written about the Great Seer and I'm convinced that if we listen to him we'll be ready for what's ahead. For centuries, Nostra-damus has been warning us of our demise. Look at his track record: the Great Visionary predicted the rise of Napoleón, Franco, and Hitler, as well as the bombing of Hiroshima. He even predicted the date of his own exhumation. So how can you even dream about ques-tioning him when he says that the Third World War started in 1999?

Everyone says I'm crazy because the date has already passed and nothing has happened. Remember this, sometimes the really big wars start quietly. Look at the Second World War, for instance. Who took notice as the Nazis began invading other countries? And we've yet to see Nostradamus's true sign of the coming of Armageddon: a shattering explosion above the skies of a giant city where towers of death plunge to the ground. When we see this we'll know our end is near. My friends say that I'm a pessimist, but why should we even try to make the world a better place if we're doomed?

"No. I'm a realist," I reply.

I've suggested to Bernardo that he ask la Virgen what's in store for us. And while he's at it he should ask her for details like where and when. Between Bernardo and Nostradamus, we would know everything. That way we'll have enough time to cleanse our souls and prepare for the end. Nuestra Señora wants the entire human race to die noble, Christian deaths. Why do you think that she is appearing everywhere these days? Bernardo just shakes his head and smiles when I say this. But doña Nora yells at me, telling me to shut up. She says that I'm always talking nonsense, that I'm always saying nothing but disparates. But at our final hour I will be vindicated. Everyone's last words will be: "Don Nicolás was right after all."

Thanks to Bernardo I'm ready for the hour of my death. It would suit me fine if the end of the world came right now, at this very instant. But I hope I die before Judgment Day arrives. I don't want to be around to see the suffering that's in store for sinners.

Once a week, when Bernardo drops by, he listens to my confession. It's funny, although at the time of his ordination we had been friends for almost fifteen years he knew almost nothing about me. But once he had the authority to absolve my sins, I told him my entire life story. The day we sat down in the backyard under the guachipilín tree, it had been forty years since my last confession. I had fallen into a dark abyss, far from the light of Nuestro Señor Jesucristo. But Bernardo and la Virgen de Cuapa brought me back from the shadows. I'm at peace with my Creator now. Like I said, I'm ready to die.

The first time I confessed my sins to Bernardo I cried throughout. My soul had become a black, foul, hideous thing. For forty years I had been carrying around the burden of my evil deeds. I admitted to everything wicked I had ever done, from the beginning. I told Bernardo how my mother—who now rests in heaven alongside the saints—used to force me to pray the rosary every day. And I confessed how much I hated that. I also confessed that, when I was twelve, I used to sell the mirrors that my friend Erasmo would steal from his mother's store in Granada's marketplace. Afterward, with the money I had made, we'd go to el Parque Colón to get something to eat, and then we'd go to the movies where we'd masturbate and smoke cigarettes in the balcony. One may say that those are the small sins of little boys, but if you don't do something to straighten children out early, they'll go on to become big sinners. Bernardo agrees with that.

I also told Bernardo how my mother, desperate over my recklessness, had to borrow money from the family she cooked for so that my brother and I could attend el Colegio Salesiano. She put us in their boarding school to keep us from roaming the streets. At the time I resented being sent away. Immensely. And I confessed that once I was locked up behind the school walls, I developed the attitude of a rebellious prisoner, always plotting against the guards: tall, somber priests dressed in black cassocks. But that experience, my forced imprisonment in the hallowed halls of Catholicism, ended up saving me. Los padres Salesianos turned me into a disciplined person.

As I told Bernardo, the severity of their punishments taught me obedience, making me submissive to the teachings of the Church. Like I said, if you don't straighten kids out early, they'll be condemned to everlasting damnation. When my mother put me in el Colegio Salesiano, she really ended up saving me from hell.

Amazingly, Bernardo and I crossed paths there without knowing it. He told me that he had worked in el Colegio for a month as a janitor. As it turns out, we were in that sanctuary at the same time. I was in the fourth year of secundaria back then. Sometimes, as they say, the world is as small as a handkerchief.

Eventually, the priests beat the rebelliousness out of me. I surrendered to their righteousness. I even became a decent student, as well as a devout Catholic. I stood out as an athlete too, playing baseball and soccer. El Colegio Salesiano won a national championship in each sport thanks to me. During my confession, I acknowledged that my saintly mother had done the right thing by locking me up in that school, and Bernardo fully agreed.

When I was in my last year of escuela secundaria, I met Teresa de Jesús Medina. Even though I had been quite a troublemaker, I was still pretty inexperienced when it came to girls. Because of that, when I finally managed to snare my first novia . . . well . . . everything happened too fast. Before I knew it we were engaged and then—zap—married. Her mother and an Italian nun at the school Teresa attended rushed us into tying the knot. I now realize that we were far too young. But no one's to blame. That's the way things were back then. In that respect, kids are better off today.

Sadly, my marriage to Teresa was doomed from the start. The things we wanted in life were too different. I hadn't even decided if I was going to attend my Colegio's graduation ceremony, and Teresa was already pushing for me to go to medical school. It didn't matter to her that I hated being around sick people; she just wanted to be married to a doctor. I, on the other hand, have always been happy with a steady job and a steady paycheck. Teresa would become angry at what she called my "lack of ambition" and yell, "I would've been much better off marrying a tailor!" Bernardo smiled during this part of my confession. Not many people know this, but he had been a tailor before la Virgen's apparition.

Yes, our differences were far too many and too big to overcome. For instance, Teresa was stuck on appearances: dresses, jewelry, makeup, things like that. I was perfectly happy with clean clothes and a watch that worked. She liked to go out: dancing, movies, concerts, plays, trips to the beach. I just wanted to stay home, lie in my hammock, and read detective novels, which I still love doing. She liked nice things: furniture, china, a stereo, a television. I was thrilled to have a reliable car; I couldn't care less about the make or what it looked like. She took risks. I was cautious, never changing anything in my life unless absolutely necessary. She wanted fidelity. And I, being more highly sexed than your average macho stud, needed other women. Teresa always said that was the biggest problem in our marriage.

During my confession, I admitted that my affairs hurt Teresa. But I did try to be discreet. And Bernardo believed me. If my wife hadn't been insanely jealous, if she hadn't sent people to spy on me, she never would have found out about the other women. Things would still be fine. We'd probably still be together because, like I said, I hate change. I really do. I always made it a point to leave my lovers whenever I thought that the situation started to become too involved, that they might want me to leave my family and change my life. Even though it would break my heart, I'd say good-bye to these lovely ladies to become a model husband to Teresa and an excellent father to my three kids . . . that is, until the next woman came along. Still, for as long as it was humanly possible I'd do the right thing and devote myself to my marriage.

But a real man has urges that will make him sick if he represses them. That's been proven scientifically in a study conducted in the former Soviet Union. (Comunistas may be terrible rulers, but they're excellent scientists.) Nursing homes in the Ukraine, for instance, are full of old, useless men who repressed their sexual urges when they could still get it up. When I informed Bernardo of this during confession, he nodded.

In spite of the distractions other women created in my routine, I was always able to slide easily back into my regular, everyday life. None of them could get me to break free from the small iron cage my existence had become—until I met doña Nora. For nearly twenty years—the time Teresa and I had been married—I worked for Telcor, Somoza's communications monopoly. Contrary to what one may think, the Somozas ruling over us didn't bother me at all. Their benevolent dictatorships were always good to me. What people don't seem to understand, then and today, was that as long as you kept your nose out of politics you were fine. Like I said, what was important to me was a steady job with a steady paycheck. Since I had both of those things, I was perfectly happy.

One day, then, as a total surprise, the top man at Telcor introduced doña Nora as the new customer service manager. Everyone
in the office immediately hated her. She's an abrasive, manipulative, conniving woman with the body of the cork, the kind that
comes in a jug of wine—with large breasts, though. The only
reason she got the job was because her brother was a minister in
Somoza's cabinet. At first I disliked her—more than any of my
coworkers, I'd say. For that reason, as I told Bernardo during confession, no one was more surprised than I when, two months after
she was hired, I found myself with my face buried deep in her
bosom, the two of us going at it frantically on top of her desk.
Even though we kept our affair as discreet as possible, the others
in the office started to suspect that something was up. Still, things
would've gone just fine if the accountant hadn't leaked the news
that I had received the biggest pay raise in the office that year.
Some pendejo called the head of Telcor, who came down from his
air-conditioned penthouse office and caught us red-handed
during one of our private "strategic-planning meetings."

We both got fired. In my case, twenty years of faithful service
meant nothing to those bastardos. I was out of a job, and what
worried me more was that I didn't know how I was going to tell
Teresa. But as I was packing my things, doña Nora asked me to
come work for her in a religious supply store she was opening.
Well, I really had no choice. Plus, all the time we had spent
working closely together had made me grow fond of the cantankerous old broad. Her stern, coarse, domineering ways reminded
me of my virtuous mother: Que en paz descanse la santa. Yes, may
that saint of a woman rest in peace.

Doña Nora offered me more money than I was making at

Telcor, so I simply told Teresa that I had found a better job. But my wife knew me better than to believe that I would make such a big change without thinking it over for at least a couple of years. From the beginning, she suspected another woman was involved. That made the transition difficult for me. I had to work overtime setting up smoke screens so Teresa would think that my relationship with doña Nora was strictly a matter of business. I tried. Honest I did.

What made things easier was that La Purísima really took off. Within less than a year, we had become the most successful wholesaler and retailer of religious items in all of Nicaragua. Of course, during the time of the Somozas, every business succeeded. All you needed to do was to set up a shop and—boom—you were rich! I miss those days, especially the way the Somozas kept los comunistas in check. Anyway, the extra money I brought home seemed to appease Teresa. She began to ignore me, almost as if she had resigned herself to my infidelities. She didn't seem to care what I did or with whom as long as I brought in the money. Instead, she became entirely devoted to our three children. A few months after I had started working for doña Nora, I felt more like a guest in my own home than a husband and father. And that was just fine with me. I could come and go as I pleased, my affairs now my own business.

During my confession, I explained to Bernardo that for six years La Purísima flourished. (Doña Nora's useless son drained a lot of the profits, but my first confession in forty years wasn't the appropriate time to complain about that.) Then the world started to go to hell. Nostradamus's predictions started to come true when the war to overthrow Somoza began. Los comunistas terroristas sucked the lifeblood right out of this country. Incredibly, los Estados Unidos turned its back on Somoza just like it did with the noble Senator

McCarthy. After our beloved leader left, our economy fell into ruins. No one had any money, so no one was buying anything. La Purísima started to go downhill.

The only good thing that came out of la Revolución was that it helped me resolve my personal situation. I got rid of Teresa once and for all. I sent her and the kids to live in los Estados Unidos. I said that I'd join them as soon as I could. Of course, I never had any intentions of going. Our marriage had already come to an end. Since Teresa wouldn't accept it at the time, I thought it was better that she find out on her own, far away from me. Besides, she hated living under the Sandinistas. Really, then, as I saw it, I did her and the kids a big favor. (Bernardo nodded again after I said this.)

During my confession, I insisted that all along I had remained faithful to the Catholic Church. Even though twenty years have passed since I sent Teresa away, we haven't gotten divorced. But once she and the kids were gone, I moved in with doña Nora. Our relationship was quite lustful at the beginning and, because of that, I was living in mortal sin. But before long, we settled into a quiet coexistence, like two old dogs no longer interested in playing frisky games. (Don't think for a second that this means that I've lost my manliness. I still desire other women— very much so.)

When I finally reached the end of my confession, Bernardo absolved me of my sins. He took me gently down the road to repentance and redemption. Because of Bernardo I'm at ease with the tough choices I've had to make in my life. That's why I believe he's a saint, just like my mother.

How was it, then, that I became close to Bernardo? During the first year of la Revolución, La Purísima barely survived. How can you expect to sell anything when people are having trouble feeding themselves? But gracias a Nuestro Señor Jesucristo, Nicaragua's a devoutly Catholic country. We know that the soul comes before the body. In spite of being poor, then, the faithful kept on buying statues, portraits, rosaries, candles, crosses, and missals. They weren't purchasing in the same quantities as before, of course, but we were keeping ahead of our creditors—barely. Still, we were thankful for the business we had. Although doña Nora and I were poor, just like everyone else under the communist yoke, we were happy, living alone at last and in peace.

But it was hard to keep La Purísima afloat. We devoted ourselves to the store's survival, although some days barely a customer walked in through our doors. That's why as soon as doña Nora heard about la Virgen's apparition in Cuapa, she smelled the scent of profit. She has quite a nose for that.

Doña Nora rushed to Chontales to find Bernardo, and when she did she offered to help him spread Nuestra Señora's message. At first he was suspicious of her, and for good reason: los comunistas had been trying to intimidate him; they wanted him to shut his mouth about the apparition. But before long Bernardo saw that doña Nora hated the Sandinistas just as much as anyone else. After that, whenever he visited Managua, which was whenever la Virgen had a message for the archbishop, he would stay at our house.

During one of his first trips to the capital, doña Nora took him to a sculptor. The poor man ended up making at least twenty-five models of la Virgen de Cuapa before an image finally met Bernardo's approval. The statue they finally settled on was absolutely beautiful, perfect—with the exception of her right hand, which tends to break off easily. But doña Nora insisted that Nuestra Señora be made with her hand out, palm open and facing up, just like Bernardo had seen her during the first apparition.

"People will pay more if something's authentic," she said to me. We began to sell her statues at La Purísima, and for several years la Virgin de Cuapa was the store's best-selling item. Sadly, with the passage of time and the Sandinista threat gone, people are forgetting about her. We have about a thousand statues in the back, gathering dust.

Still, as I said before, during the early 1980s, doña Nora, Bernardo, and I were happy. But Dios does not want us to be happy for long. Just ask Nostradamus. Suffering reminds us of the pain we will endure in hell if we are not faithful to the Church's teachings. That's why Nuestro Señor sent Agustín back to live with his mother.

Doña Nora's son is useless. For years he lied to his mother, telling her that he was attending college in los Estados Unidos. Every month she'd send him a big check dreaming of the day he'd return to Nicaragua as an engineer. Whenever I'd mention my doubts about Agustín actually going to classes, doña Nora would shout, "Mind your own business, imbécil! You sent your children away, so what the hell do you know about raising a child!" I can never criticize Agustín because in spite of everything she still has a blind spot to his failings. In her eyes, he's perfect.

Actually, this guy is just like his father—whom doña Nora divorced shortly after Agustín was born—a loser and a drunk (although he's from a prominent family: the *Dávilas*). Worse yet, instead of attending college, Agustín hung out with junkies in the alleys of Miami. He knows drugs like American soldiers know condoms, just ask any former contrarevolucionario who trained with them along the Honduran border (may Dios forgive them).

Fortunately, I wasn't the only one who was onto Agustín. During a trip to the United States, doña Nora's brother stopped by to visit his nephew, and he came back alarmed. "You've got to stop sending Agustín money and bring him back immediately, Nora! That boy's in bad shape!" he said. She didn't listen, of course. Her angelito could do no wrong. Besides, that was during Somoza's reign, when money was plentiful.

A few months after the Sandinistas took over, however, doña Nora could no longer afford to support Agustín's "studies." She sent her son a letter that said, succinctly, *I'm out of money. Come home.* Included in the envelope was a plane ticket. My life has been a living hell ever since. I'm sure there's a prediction about Agustín in one of Nostradamus's quatrains. The problem is that I haven't been able to find it yet.

Agustín's a miserable human being. I'd prefer to hang out with Sandinistas, any day. When he's drunk or stoned, he's belligerent. And when he's sober, which is rare, he's even more belligerent. He'll commit any act, no matter how repulsive, to get his daily fix. Which drugs he uses, I don't know. But what I do know is that Agustín disappears into Managua's worst neighborhoods, with whatever money he can get his hands on, and he doesn't return until he has spent every last centavo. He will then demand money from his mother, and if she doesn't give it to him, he becomes violent, smashing things against the wall. He once beat doña Nora—when I wasn't around, of course. Another time Agustín tried to start something with me, but even though I'm old, he knows that I can still put up a fight, so he keeps his distance. That doesn't stop him from threatening to break my brittle bones, though.

That's why I'll never understand what Rocío saw in el Demonio, which is what her mother nicknamed Agustín (and it's an appropriate one because he *is* a demon). Rocío was absolutely gorgeous. I would have cherished a fling with her. She was also intelligent: an educated woman, with a college degree. I always ask myself, why did she fall in love with such a pitiful human being? Just one of life's mysteries, I guess. Nuestro Señor sabe lo que hace. Still, if he had a plan, if he knows what he is doing, why did he let the best thing that ever happened to Agustín end in tragedy?

Two days before Rocío accidentally killed herself (although doña Nora says that a suicide is still a suicide) she came by to visit me. I had seen her growing sadder each passing day. Rocío was suffering because el Demonio had poisoned the once close relationship she had with her mother.

"Don Nicolás," she said pleadingly, "if anything should ever happen to me, I want you to promise that you'll take good care of Lourdes."

"Don't be silly," I answered, "what's going to happen to you?"

"I just need you to make this promise, don Nicolás!" she said. The urgency in her voice startled me. As Rocío reached out to hold my hand, the tears in her eyes stunned me. If only I could have foreseen what was about to happen. If only I had started studying Nostradamus back then, perhaps I could've prevented the catastrophe.

"Of course, my dear," I said. "I promise to take care of your little girl." It was easy for me to make that pledge because Rocío was beautiful, and I could never say no to a beautiful lady. So when doña Nora brought Lourdes to live with us, I began to look after the infant as if she were my own flesh and blood. I got to be the doting grandfather I never had the chance to be with my own grandchildren.

Lourdes became the center of my existence, and at the time I needed something to fill that void. Since el Demonio had returned from los Estados Unidos, doña Nora and I had grown apart. Before Lourdes came to live with us, my life had become a boring, empty routine—even for someone like myself who loves routines.

I'd spend the entire day minding La Purísima, and immediately after I closed up shop, I'd have a light dinner, get into my pajamas, and watch television until I fell asleep. Doña Nora and I barely spoke to each other after Agustín, her angelito, came back into the picture. I firmly believe that el Señor sent the baby to lift the oppressive loneliness that had covered my soul like mold spreads on the bathroom walls during the rainy season. I would do anything for my little girl, and that was easy because Lourdes was bright, funny, and loving: the reincarnation of her mother.

Lourdes grew up to be more beautiful than her mother had been. Her slender body and long legs caused traffic accidents. As a teenager she started to wear tight white pants, which highlighted her perfectly rounded hips. (I tried to forbid her from wearing those, but doña Nora told me to let the girl wear whatever she wanted.) Wherever Lourdes went, she drove men crazy. More important, she turned out to be much wiser than Rocío. Lourdes was kind to everyone, but she was also sensible. She knew exactly how to handle her father. Her poise around el Demonio amazed me. I could never be as patient as she was with that walking disaster. But Lourdes would tell me, "He's my father, don Nicolás, for better or for worse, and it's my duty as his daughter to give him whatever happiness I can in this lifetime."

That's why I believe it's good that Agustín would disappear for days at a time in search of his fixes. Lourdes, then, wouldn't have to deal with his foul, violent moods as often. Still, I know that she suffered because of el Demonio, just as her mother had before her. But I also believe that I was able to give Lourdes some stability by being the one man she could always rely on.

My relationship with her had a nice tension, too. Lourdes used to call me her viejito lindo as she rubbed my shoulders. And although I'm old, she flirted with me as if I were a young stallion. She used to tell me that she wouldn't have a novio until I could deal with it. Wasn't that wonderful? Lourdes's love helped keep me alive.

"¡Me valen verga las predicciones de Nostradamus!" I used to say back then. Yes, I didn't give a shit about the Great Seer's predictions about gloom and doom. Life with Lourdes was good.

Bernardo's weekly visits lifted our spirits as well. When Lourdes was a child, she'd sit on his lap and recite Darío's poetry. Now *that* was real poetry, not like the crap so-called poets write today. Their verses don't even rhyme. Lourdes made Bernardo and me cry; her splendid recitations breathed such life into Darío's poems.

Later, when Lourdes was old enough, I let her choose Monday's lunch menu: we'd have pollo frito a lot because she loved the Guatemalan fat-free fried chicken, just like Bernardo. And whenever doña Nora fired another maid—as she did yesterday—Lourdes would help me by setting the table. Our gatherings at the dining room with Bernardo were, by far, the highlight of our week.

It's ironic, but after Bernardo was ordained and assigned as parish priest of Tonalá—a hot, dusty pueblito way up north, close to the Honduran border—we actually got to see more of him than when he lived nearby in El Crucero. That's because when he comes to Managua every week to raise funds for his parishes, he needs a place to rest. It's a long trip back to Tonalá.

Still, it's a shame that Bernardo was sent so far away from here, and even more shameful that he's not in Cuapa. He always dreamed of being the parish priest of his pueblo. But los mafiosos surrounding His Eminence don't approve of Bernardo. They criticize his humble origins and his poor schooling, and they're embarrassed by his encounters with la Virgen. That's why they were dead set against his ordination. It was fine for them to use Bernardo when it served their purposes, especially when the Church was at war with the Sandinistas. But once that threat was over, they hoped that he would simply fade away, that he would return quietly to his tailoring in Chontales.

Nuestra Señora, though, had bigger plans for Bernardo. She promised that he'd become a priest, and she kept that promise. And although the bishop of León assigned him to the farthest reaches of his diocese, Bernardo's still able to perform miracles. Nothing he does ever surprises me. I know that he has been anointed by Dios to do his will. In just a few years Bernardo has built more chapels, schools, nursing homes, and day-care centers than any other priest in the country. He's done his work so well that his bishop has now given him the task of rebuilding the church in El Sauce. This building, once majestic and full of history, now lies in ashes since it burned down a couple of years ago. No other priest wanted that responsibility. But let me assure you, Bernardo will get the job done.

The government owes Bernardo a medal as well. Just a few months ago, he did something heroic, and no one acknowledged it: not the papers, not the radio, not the television, not anyone. The country woke up one morning to discover that a certain congressman was not who he claimed to be. He wasn't even alive. He was dead. Legally, that is. Turns out that during the war this man vanished. His fellow contrarevolucionarios declared that he had been killed: blown to so many bits that they didn't even bother recovering what was left of him. Years later, with a new identity, he surfaced as a candidate for Congress. Of course, back then none of us really knew who he was. And guess what? He won! Is this a great country or what?

His web of lies began to unravel when a woman, a campesina, appeared before the cameras claiming to be his wife and demanding that he support the four daughters they had together. The congressman denied everything. In front of the microphones and cameras he pretended to be livid.

"I've never seen that woman in my life!" he shouted. "The whole thing is a Sandinista plot to discredit me!"

Under his new identity, he married the daughter of an influential politician, and he has four daughters with her. And when reporters dug a bit deeper, they discovered a third wife, with whom he has four daughters as well. This guy puts me to shame. Throughout all this, he still had the nerve to continue denying everything.

The hoax was finally up when a reporter found the congressman's father. Guess where the old man lives? In Cuapa, of all places. He's a poor campesino and a devotee of la Virgen de Cuapa, so he can't lie.

"Yes," the startled man said before the press, his voice trembling, "that's my son. I was told he had been killed in the war. I'm happy he's still alive. But why hasn't he tried to contact me?" Well, knowing that the gig was up, the congressman locked himself in la Asamblea, the Nicaraguan Hall of Congress. And he took a hostage . . . himself.

Holding a gun to his head, he threatened to blow his brains out if anyone got near him. For hours he paralyzed our government, which, really, when you think about it, is not all that hard to do. Employees in la Asamblea were thrilled because they got the day off. In the meantime, the "dead" congressman refused to surrender or to talk to the police. At long last, he stated that there was only one person he'd negotiate with: Bernardo de Cuapa.

It was a Monday, after lunch, and we had all just gone down for a nap. Before we knew what was going on, police cars, their sirens blaring, surrounded our house and whisked Bernardo away to la Asamblea.

"Do you think he'll be all right, abuelito Nicolás?" Lourdes asked with tears in her eyes.

"Let's pray so," I replied.

To avoid reporters, the police snuck Bernardo into the building through an underground entrance. Within minutes, the congressman surrendered. And life in our paisito, our quirky little country, returned to normal. I'm not kidding. The man is still serving in congress—with his fake identity, his three wives, his twelve daughters, and the rest. But did Bernardo get any credit for saving the day? Absolutely not.

That doesn't really matter, though. What has been recognized is Bernardo's gift for bringing people to prayer. His bishop recently commented during a radio interview that Bernardo's parishioners are the most pious in his diocese. El pueblo of Tonalá spends more time praying the rosary than any other community in the country. That's why I believe that Bernardo should be canonized while he's still alive; he deserves to be made a saint before the world comes to an end. This pope had better hurry up, too. Neither he nor Bernardo is getting any younger. Whenever I'm around my friend, I can feel his holiness, his proximity to the divine. I have no doubt that someday he'll be declared un santo: San Bernardo de Cuapa. I have no doubt about this. Nostradamus probably already foretold his sainthood; it's just a matter of me finding the right quatrain. And Nuestro Señor has blessed me, infinitely so, by allowing me to be close to Bernardo in this lifetime.

Although Lourdes and I seldom got to see Bernardo celebrate mass, every week we prayed the rosary with him. Lourdes was devoted to la Virgen de Cuapa, and to Bernardo as well. She liked to make him laugh. Whenever he visited, Lourdes would greet him by saying, "¿Cómo está hoy, San Bernardo?" Hilarious. She was, as I said, the light of my life. Bernardo was very fond of her, too.

You can understand, then, why her tragedy has devastated us. I say it's another omen of the advent of the Apocalypse, another sign of the approaching storm that will bring to an end mankind's circle of suffering, which we have been condemned to because of our sins.

I begged doña Nora not to take Lourdes that day, almost two months ago. I begged her to let Lourdes stay home. My little girl didn't want to go either; she didn't want to leave me at home by myself. Every Saturday, we'd watch Sábado Gigante together. It has been a tradition of ours for the last ten years. We thought that don Francisco was a riot, a comic genius. But doña Nora assured me that they'd be back in time for the beginning of the show. She also thought it would be good for Lourdes to get a little sun in Pochomil, where a friend owns una casa playera, right on the beach.

"It all happened so fast," doña Nora said afterward, barely able to speak through her sobs. "Before we knew it, don Nicolás, a current had dragged Lourdes far into the ocean. You know how dreadful the tides in the Pacific can be. We saw Lourdes waving frantically, signaling for help. All I could do was cry for help. Soon she went under, tired of fighting those monstrous waves. Some fishermen working nearby got to where she had vanished as fast as they could. One of them dove in, found her, and brought her back to the surface. Then they rowed as fast as they could to shore. We managed to get Lourdes breathing again and rushed her to the hospital. But the doctors say there's nothing more anyone can do but wait. But they doubt that she'll regain consciousness. We've lost her, don Nicolás."

I wish my life had ended at that moment. For seventeen years I had kept my promise to Rocío, and in the end I failed her. Lourdes is in worse shape than doña Flor de María, her other abuelita, who since Rocío's death, many years ago now, has been catatonic. The last two months have been horrible for me. It's been the most painful time of my life. Lourdes just lies in her bed all day, her eyes closed. My little girl can't move, talk, see, or hear. I can't stand seeing her like that. Every time I've tried to enter her bedroom it feels like my lungs are going to stop working. And when I come out, I'm bawling; I'm begging el Señor to take me as well. Señor mío, I say, this cross is far too heavy for me to bear.

The most I can do to help Lourdes is to sit in my recliner, which I've placed right outside her door, and pray. I must be up to twenty Rosaries a day now. Sometimes when I'm praying, I get the same eerie feeling I used to get when Lourdes was a baby. Back then, out of the corner of my eye, I'd catch a glimpse of her mother, entering the room where the infant was sleeping. Of course, I used to tell myself that it was just my imagination. After all, Rocío's death had occurred just a few weeks before, and we were all feeling fragile.

But it's happening all over again. A few times now, while praying, I've seen Rocío going into Lourdes's room. The strange thing is that I've seen doña Flor de María go in there as well. But that can't be because she's still alive, sort of. I blame these visions on my state of mind, which is pitiful. I want the whole thing to be a nightmare. I desperately want to wake up and find that Lourdes is all right. But this is not a dream; I know that.

"Bernardo," I implore every time he visits, "please ask la Virgen to heal Lourdes. Please ask her for that miracle."

Bernardo looks at me sadly, his eyes full of compassion. At

last, he'll say, "I pray for Lourdes every day, Nicolás. La Virgencita knows what's best for her. All we can do is to have faith and trust her judgment. She knows what Nuestro Señor has in mind for your little girl."

It calms me when he says this. I know that not every tragedy can be fixed through a miracle. How many times has doña Nora asked Bernardo to intervene with la Virgen on Agustín's behalf? All of our prayers haven't helped el Demonio overcome his uselessness and his addictions. They've become even worse since Lourdes's tragedy. No one has seen him for over a month. It's his worst binge ever.

Today, after Bernardo and I finished eating lunch—he enjoyed el arroz a la valenciana, by the way—he asked me to join him in Lourdes's room to pray the rosary. At first I refused. I haven't been able to step in there for the past week. But Bernardo was insistent, so much so that I couldn't say no.

When I went inside and saw her lying there looking so helpless, my heart skipped and my lungs felt like they were about to collapse. I started to tremble. Bernardo reached out and held my hand.

"Be strong, Nicolás. Be brave for Lourdes, please."

I nodded, biting my lip to avoid breaking into sobs. We placed chairs next to Lourdes's bed, getting as close to her as we could. And we began to pray. As we were reflecting on the fourth glorious mystery, the Assumption of Nuestra Señora into heaven, I felt them enter and move slowly across the room: invisible lives that are, in spite of everything, very real. This time I knew for sure that Rocío and Flor de María were present and praying alongside us. But I said nothing. Bernardo was immersed in prayer, lost somewhere deep in his chant, oblivious to their presence. I was not afraid to have them with us, not in the least. On the contrary, I found their spirits comforting, and I prayed with more fervor than ever.

When we finished the rosary, I waited in silence for a few minutes, allowing time for meditation. Bernardo and I sat there, saying nothing, simply staring at Lourdes. When I sensed that he was about to rise from his chair, I leaned forward and whispered, "Bernardo. . . ."

He put a finger across his lips, telling me to remain quiet. After a few moments, he lowered it, smiled at me, and said, "Yes, Nicolás. . . . I know."

QUARTA VISIO

(The Fourth Apparition)

September 8, 1980

Bernardo

ON SEPTEMBER 8, I returned to the apparition site. All month long I had prayed for la Virgencita to return, just like Padre Domingo had said I should. About sixty people joined me on this day: men, women, and children. This included a large group that had come all the way from Juigalpa. I couldn't help being a little suspicious of the juigalpeños since there were a few Protestants among them. As we all know, they don't believe in Nuestra Señora.

"Maybe they came to ridicule you, Bernardo," doña Tula said. At first I thought that perhaps she was right. But then, the more I reflected on it, the more I realized that they had come because Nuestra Señora wanted them to, and who am I to question her motives?

When we arrived at the site, those of us who were Catholics kneeled before el morisco, and we began to pray the rosary. As we prayed, I became a little distracted, feeling sorry for the small tree. The devout had been tearing off leaves and branches and carving away at the bark. It looked like el morisco would become the first victim of the people's devotion to la Virgencita. I put those distracting thoughts out of my mind and concentrated once again on praying. And I thanked el Señor for helping me do this. As la Virgen said, he doesn't like us to pray in a hasty, distracted manner.

As soon as we had finished the rosary, I saw the familiar flash of light. "Nuestra Señora is coming!" I shouted. I heard a murmur spread through the crowd. I could feel many of the people there becoming afraid. I, on the other hand, began to feel giddy, even blissful, for I knew that I was about to see her again.

Then came the second flash of light; and there, standing before me, on a cloud, was la Virgencita. But this time, she *was* a "Little Virgin"—a child of about eight. She was so precious! She wore a simple beige tunic. The only thing adorning her clothes was a pink ribbon tied around her waist. Her head was uncovered. For the first time I could see her hair: shimmering brown, light in color, and falling about nine inches below her shoulders. Her eyes, as always, were the color of honey. A lovely, soft blue light radiated from la Niña Virgen. Although she was appearing as a child, I had no doubt that she was also Nuestra Señora.

I glanced back at the people with me. "Can you see her?" I asked. "She's here!" They looked at me sadly, shaking their heads.

I turned back to look at her and immediately forgot everything else. I just stared at her in rapture. She then began to speak to me in the sweet, pure voice of a child. I listened closely to her message, the one I had learned by heart months ago. She repeated everything once again, reminding us to pray the rosary every day, in family; pray it during the quietest part of the day, when there are no distractions; love one another; fulfill your obligations to each other; forgive one another and work for peace; avoid the path of violence; and change our ways so that we can avoid Armageddon. And she concluded by reminding me to share this message with the world.

Once she had finished, as pleasantly as I could, I said, "Please, Señora, let everyone see you! Let them see and hear you so that they may believe. These people have come here today, some from far away, because they want to meet you. Please, Señora." La Niña Virgen only stared at me, saying nothing. Once again, I tried to convince her. "Please, Señora, do this favor for me."

For a moment, I thought she was considering my petition. After a while, she replied, *No, Bernardo. It is enough for you to give them my message. For the ones who believe, this will suffice. The incredulous will never believe, even if they should see or hear me.*

To be honest, her reply disappointed me. I wanted the others to see her as well. The burden of being the only one who could see her was becoming a heavy cross for me to bear. I wanted others to help me with the job of being her messenger. But I reminded myself that even though she *was* a child, she was still Nuestra Señora. I knew that I needed to show respect, that I didn't have the right to keep insisting that she let others see her. Being chosen to spread her message was my honor and responsibility alone. I had to learn to accept that. I decided, then, to stop trying to talk her into showing herself. Instead, I went on to a question many cuapeños wanted me to ask.

"Señora, we're ready to build a temple on this site to honor you. Would you like that?"

No. El Señor does not want buildings. He wants you, his living temples. Restore those sacred temples for el Señor. With that, he will be gratified. For him it is more important that you love and forgive one another. For him it is more important that you work for peace, and not merely ask for it.

La Niña Virgen then smiled at me, and the cloud began to rise.

Instead of on October eighth, I will return on the thirteenth.

La Virgencita and the cloud continued rising, slowly climbing until they cleared the ailing morisco, and then, little by little, she faded away.

chapter thirteen

HYPAPANTE
(The Meeting)

May 8, 2000

Padre Ginés Hidalgo and the Pilgrims

GINÉS HIDALGO firmly believed that el Señor had always intended for him to be Cuapa's parish priest. He had been chosen since the dawn of Creation. There was no other explanation for how he, a native of Toledo, could have ended up in rural Nicaragua, in a remote pueblito, cherishing the assignment. The Spaniard had grown to love this land. But what mattered most to the priest was that he believed he was making a difference in the lives of the villagers. Of course, Cuapa, like any small community anywhere in the world, had its share of envies, jealousies, intrigues, and gossip, but Padre Ginés believed that any halfway competent priest would be able to rise above the pettiness. He was indeed sincere when he told his family back in Spain that Cuapa was home.

Padre Ginés enjoyed being the custodian of the spiritual lives of these simple folk. But what the Spaniard liked best was his role as guardian of the legacy of la Virgen de Cuapa—even though that title rightfully belonged to his good friend, Bernardo Martínez. But it was Padre Ginés, and not Bernardo, who was there every day to greet the pilgrims who visited the apparition site; it was he who answered their endless questions about Nuestra Señora's apparition; it was he who joined them in prayer for their petitions; and it was he who first heard the reports of her miracles. Yes, the Spaniard thanked Nuestro Señor every day for allowing him the honor of being in his service as Cuapa's parish priest.

And today, the twentieth anniversary of her first apparition, the honor was especially meaningful. In fact, Padre Ginés was finding the distinction a bit overwhelming. As the hour of the commemorative mass approached, he lit a Belmont cigarette and began pacing nervously up and down the length of the sanctuary's concrete platform. The simple, open-air structure—with a red, half-moon zinc canopy to provide shade for the important guests—was erected precisely for this occasion. For a moment, as the Spaniard looked over the construction of his design, his chest swelled with pride.

A few weeks before, the cardinal had asked Padre Ginés to say the opening words for the ceremony. The priest happily accepted, believing it a privilege, but he never anticipated a crowd of this size: at least seventy thousand pilgrims had gathered on the Chontales hillsides. If the Spaniard had known this many people were coming, he would've started working on his speech as soon as His Eminence had asked. But now, what made the priest's head ache in panic was that with less than an hour to go before the beginning of mass, he had no clue what he was going to say.

The previous night, Padre Ginés thought that he would have time to reflect upon his opening words during the early hours of the morning, shortly after dawn. He had planned to arrive early at the site and sit under the mango tree to jot down a few notes before supervising the final preparations, but by the time the sun had begun to peek over la Sierra de Amerrisque, things were quite hectic. A good twenty thousand devotees of la Virgen de Cuapa had already taken the best spots, and it seemed that every single one of them wanted a few moments alone with the Spaniard. How could the parish priest of Cuapa tell a wealthy Miami exile, who might surprise him with a generous donation, to get lost so that he could think about his speech?

No, there were far too many distractions for Padre Ginés to dwell on inspirational thoughts. He was, nevertheless, getting lots of practice at the microphone, trying to maintain order.

"To all vendors: Do not set up your booths on this side of the river. Please sell your merchandise on the other side. This side is hallowed ground. It's not a marketplace. Gracias."

"To all bus drivers: Please park on the open fields on the other side of the river. We have made them available for that purpose. Please do not park your vehicles along the side of the road. Gracias."

And that's the way things had gone ever since dawn.

As Padre Ginés oversaw the installation of fluorescent lights in the sanctuary, the reparation of the wooden confessionals along the hillside, and the cleaning of the latrines, he hoped that he hadn't used up his most stirring words on those announcements. For the opening of the celebration, he wanted to say something that would immediately seize the hearts of the faithful. But at this moment he had too many responsibilities; it was impossible for him to think about his speech. Worse yet, the morning had gone by like a flash of lightning: in another half an hour the eleven o'clock service would begin . . . that is, if the cardinal and his bishops showed up on time.

Padre Ginés looked worriedly over the hillsides while he lit another Belmont. The toasted browns of the dry season made everything look barren. And the heat of the day made it feel like a desert, too. The sun was now almost directly overhead, tilted just slightly to the east, but still beating down relentlessly on the crowd. As the priest scanned the sea of hats and umbrellas, he wondered how many would faint before the mass was over. But things could have been much worse. Fortunately, a light rain—a sprinkle, really—had fallen on the dry fields that morning.

"Madre Santísima," Padre Ginés had prayed the night before, "please deliver us from dust." And la Virgen de Cuapa, as she had done so many times before, listened to the Spaniard's plea.

Two days earlier, when the vendors started appearing, a benevolent chaos descended on el pueblito. These merchants earned a living traveling from feria to feria, selling whatever they could. For the last day and a half, along the old road to Juigalpa, on the northern side of the river, pilgrims could buy pizzas, parrots, hats, fritangas, umbrellas, ice cream, raspados, carved wooden animals, güirilas and cuajada, rosquillas, fried chicken, apples from the state of Washington, enchiladas (Chontales style: rice and meat turnovers, deep-fried, and not to be confused with the Mexican dish), polvorones, atol, arroz con leche, and cosas de horno. There were also Rojita stands everywhere: "The Official Soft Drink of la Virgen de Cuapa," as Padre Ginés jokingly referred to the strawberry soda. His parish, of course, received a percentage from the sales. The vendors sold religious items as well: rosaries, scapularies, prayer books, bottles of holy water, and images of saints and of la Inmaculada Concepción. Padre Ginés, however, strictly prohibited anyone from selling statues of la Virgen de Cuapa.

"I will not allow her to be commercialized," he would repeat whenever someone proposed a way of making money off of her apparition.

The pilgrims also began arriving two days ago, and with them came the noise. Padre Ginés didn't mind the competition between the choirs, the chichero bands, and the announcements blaring at full volume through the loudspeakers. But what he wouldn't tolerate were the hundreds of men with their radios tuned to the playoffs of the national béisbol league. Around ten o'clock that morning, the Spaniard had walked through the crowd asking the fans to turn those chunches, those contraptions, off. But the priest knew that his efforts were for nothing; he was sure that as soon as he was out of range the games would be on again—every doble-play and jonrón echoing through the hills. Still, the priest thought, it's important to try to teach people to respect this site, this living temple.

As Padre Ginés continued pacing across the sanctuary platform, smoking another Belmont and praying to el Espíritu Santo—asking that the opening words descend upon him—he looked out upon the crowd and recognized several familiar faces. There was Sor Milagros: a monja so short that the statue of la Virgen of Cuapa she always carried around was almost as tall as her. To the right, walking across the eastern hillside and towering over everyone, was Padre Damián. Although the American priest's biretta was black, the Spaniard could see that it was soaked with sweat. Another gringo, a tall, thin man smoking a cigar, accompanied Padre Damián. They seemed to be looking for someone. "Rounding up the usual suspects, I guess. Dios me perdone," mumbled Padre Ginés, while making the sign of the cross, "but I've never liked that man."

The Spaniard waved enthusiastically when he saw Heriberto,

the parish priest from the Church of La Merced in Granada, and Padre Ginés's best friend among the Nicaraguan clergy. He hoped that Heriberto would not be in a rush afterward; he wanted to spend some time chatting with him, catching up on the latest ecclesiastical gossip.

Padre Ginés then waved happily to Blanca Arias, Cuapa's most generous parishioner. As usual, she was dressed in mourning. Poor thing, the priest thought, doña Blanca will never be able to put her son's death behind her. The entire pueblo as well seemed obsessed with the tragedy: Elías's death was like an iron umbilical cord, too tough to cut, that kept cuapeños tied to the sorrows of war.

But Bernardo was nowhere to be seen. He had arrived in Cuapa late yesterday afternoon to celebrate the mass for last night's vigilia. As usual, he gave a rambling, stream-of-consciousness sermon that had people yawning. After forty minutes of this, many cuapeños just got up and left. Padre Ginés had advised Bernardo many times that he needed to prepare his talks beforehand and to keep them brief. But it seemed that his friend couldn't help himself. In spite of this, Bernardo's presence gave the event greater meaning. What would this anniversary be without the seer? After all, today's crowd was a tribute not only to Nuestra Señora but also to her messenger.

Is that doña Teresa I see over there? I saw don Nicolás earlier, carting something around. I thought they had gotten divorced ages ago and that she had moved to los Estados Unidos. I'd say hello to them, but they probably wouldn't remember me. I was a good friend of their son, and as a teenager I used to drop by their house once in a while just to hang out. Anyway, it's good to see that they're still together.

Poor Ginés, stuck in this part of the world that God almost forgot. It takes la Santísima Virgen herself to get people to come out here of their own free will. If it weren't for her, Cuapa wouldn't even be on the map. In fact, el pueblo doesn't appear on most maps. Why Ginés doesn't hustle to bring more people here—religious tourists maybe?—is beyond me. I would die from sheer boredom if I had been assigned to these backwoods. Gracias a Dios for my assignment in La Merced. I *love* Granada.

My uncle, Monseñor Orlando García Sánchez, que en paz descanse, almost went out of his mind when he was the parish priest of Cuapa, ages ago. Yes, may he rest in peace. Although he spoke fondly of his days in Chontales, he also said that those fifteen lonely years of exile in cattle country were enough to last him a lifetime.

The monseñor would often tell me that that's why he would never allow anyone to remove him as parish priest of La Merced. What's more, his last request was that I make sure that he be buried in the church. That proved a difficult promise to keep. The bishop of Granada was adamantly against the idea. I had to take a firm stand against His Grace until he changed his mind. In the end, the bishop gave his blessing, but my lack of submission to his authority angered him. He even threatened me, saying that he was going to assign me somewhere in Chontales. ¡Por el amor de Dios, no! But time has sorted everything out. Gracias a Nuestro Señor, His Grace seems to have forgotten the entire incident.

My cantankerous old uncle, el monseñor, lived just long enough to hear about la Virgen's visit to Cuapa. I gave him the news eighteen years ago, during the last days of his life. He motioned for me to sit at his bedside, and with great difficulty he asked, "Heriberto, did someone named Bernardo Martínez have anything to do with the apparition?"

"Sí, tío. He's the man who saw her," I answered, amazed that he would know.

My uncle smiled, closed his eyes, and never said another word.

Why on earth did I have to make this promise to la Virgen? Of all the things I could have pledged for a miracle, I had to think up this one. Oh well, I have no choice now but to keep up my end of the bargain. No other choice. But let me tell you, dragging this huge cage with five hundred doves inside isn't easy for an old man. Even though I'm wheeling them around on a cart, it's tiring, especially when I walk uphill. The worst part is the way people point and stare at me. I feel like a clown. But it's worth it. For what la Virgen has given back to me, every single embarrassing moment is worth it.

And, really, now that I'm here in the middle of this crowd, dragging around a cage full of pigeons isn't all that bad. I'm learning that young women are attracted to birds. If I had known this when I was younger, I would have dragged around a cage full of doves all the time. Take these two hot Miami Mamas, for instance. They've been asking me all kinds of questions about my little pets. I guess there's not much animal action up there in Florida. Well, if they want to, they can take me back to los Estados Unidos with them because *I'm an animal!*

Who am I kidding? I know everyone sees me as un viejo verde. And I guess I deserve to be called a dirty old man. But it hurts, especially when in my mind I still see myself as a young, macho stud. I especially feel like a stallion today, surrounded by beautiful, broad-shouldered young girls wearing blouses held up only by spaghetti straps.

Now hold on a second! Over there's a mature woman I can sink my bridges into. Although she looks stern, all dressed up in mourning, she's still sexy. She has very shapely legs for someone her age. Doña Nora pointed her out to me earlier. Turns out that she's one of the wealthiest persons in Chontales. Good-looking and with money! I like that! But doña Nora also told me that she has never recovered from her son's death, that the tragedy left her devastated. I came very close to knowing how she feels. Perhaps now that doña Nora and I are strictly business partners I can offer this woman some *consolation*.

Doña Nora doesn't need me anymore. The center of her life is now Agustín. He absorbs her attention like a rosquilla soaks up café con leche. Look at him, over there, kneeling at the fence before the statue of la Virgen. El Demonio is pretending to pray. He's such a hypocrite. I bet the second he walks back into the house he'll start his reign of terror all over again, making us miserable with his threats, his beatings, and his demands for money.

Even on their worst days my three kids are better than el Demonio at his best. I know they're here today with Teresa, but I'll never be able to find them in this crowd. My daughters promised me that they'd come to Cuapa for this anniversary. So they're here . . . somewhere. Teresa and my son keep their distance from me, and I understand that. Perfectly. I gave up being a husband and father quite a few years ago. But my girls still talk to me. On this visit from los Estados Unidos they've stopped by the house several times to see me—when doña Nora or Agustín aren't around, of course. They're returning to Houston in a few days. The girls tell me that they love it there. As anyone can see, I *did* do the right thing by sending them away. So why is my son still angry at me? Oh, well, at least my daughters understand.

The one thing that really bothers those two is my relationship with Lourdes. They're very jealous of her. But Lourdes is my miracle, mi milagro. I've tried to make them understand that. I was praying so hard to la Virgen de Cuapa that, at last, she heard me. My little girl woke up one day and climbed out of bed as if she had just finished a siesta. I nearly wet my pants when Lourdes stepped out of her room to kiss me. That was the happiest day of my life. Even Bernardo says that her coming out of that coma is one of his favorite miracles.

That's why I'm dragging around all these pigeons. One day, while Lourdes was still in that near-death sleep, closed off to the world, in a desperate, prayerful moment, I heard a voice in my head say, *Promise Nuestra Señora that if she heals Lourdes you'll take five hundred doves to the next anniversary of her appearance, and that you'll release them during Communion.*

Well, I promised her that, and she took me up on it. I couldn't be happier. I don't give a damn anymore what Nostradamus has to say. I have my little girl back and life looks grand. Except that el Demonio is still around.

Nicolás hasn't changed one bit. Although twenty years have passed since I last saw him, he's still a hopeless skirt chaser. But now, at his age, it seems pathetic. Just look at him over there flirting with those young women. He should be ashamed of himself. He's old enough to be their grandfather. The man has no sense of decency.

I feel sorry for Nicolás, though. He hasn't aged well. He looks much older than seventy-four. If I didn't know better, I'd say he's ninety. But my daughters tell me that he's in a difficult situation. Nora's son is always threatening to beat him up, and I hear they got into a fistfight just a couple of weeks ago. But as we say in the States, "He made his bed, so now he has to sit on it."

My girls told me about the miracle of Nicolás's "little girl." I'm happy for him. And for her as well. Although I don't think her family should let her wear those pants in public—they're far too tight. And why would anyone wear white in Chontales with all this dirt around?

Now look at Nicolás. He's flirting with the widow. I must admit she's very striking. I always said that Nicolás had good taste in women. Except for Nora, that is. She reminds me of a tree stump . . . with large breasts. But as we Americans say, "Give to each what is their own."

At first it was hard for me to get used to life in the United States. I was a middle-aged woman, alone, with three children—although they were almost adults by then. Learning English was difficult. I used to make mistakes all the time, and people would laugh at me. But I applied myself, and now I'm fully bilingual. My children say that I speak English like a chump. And Houston is home now. I know that the kids never want to come back to Nicaragua to live. They have good careers, solid jobs, and their own families to think of. I'm proud of them. We have wonderful lives in los Estados Unidos.

So I'm surprised to discover, after twenty years away, how much I miss my country. I'm also surprised by how much I've forgotten about this place—especially how noisy Nicaraguans are. Over there by the pavilion, for example, some women are singing, but the prerecorded music blaring through the loudspeakers is drowning them out. It's just as well because they're awful. Only a tambourine accompanies them, and whoever's playing it is way off the beaten path. And if all that noise were not enough, two chichero bands—one on each side of the sanctuary—are dueling with each other. The trombones, trumpets, tubas, saxophones, clarinets, and drums are each doing their own thing. I don't know why, but my son loves chichero music. He says it's "funky, like Dixieland," whatever that means. But all I hear are musicians playing loud and out of tune. The racket everyone's making is so wild that I can't even hear myself meditate.

Although I'm thrilled to be here, at the site where la Virgen appeared, I'm more excited about seeing Bernardo again. I still remember the silly schoolgirl crush I once had on him. Sadly, after that relationship, I went on to make the biggest mistake of my life: I married Nicolás. But our children are not a mistake. They've turned out to be wonderful people.

Take my son, for instance. He has been very loyal to me, taking my side all these years by refusing to talk to his father. I'm not saying that what he's doing is right. On the contrary, I always counsel my boy to fire up the peace cigar with his dad. But he won't. He's stubborn. Just like Nicolás, I guess.

Today, my boy sat by my side all morning. But I told him to go out there and mingle, so he went to talk to a couple of gringos who teach at an "ultra-orthodox Catholic American university" here in Nicaragua. I don't know what that means, but it sounds scary. When my son told me this, I pretended to be impressed. After my boy said that he was going to bring the professors by later to introduce them, he begged me not to mention my favorite piece of American college trivia:

"Do you know that William Walker, the Yanqui who invaded my country in the middle of the nineteenth century, declared himself president, made English the official language, and instituted slavery, had three degrees from a university in Tennessee?"

I promised my son that I wouldn't mention these very interesting facts.

Getting back to Bernardo, I remember being head above shoulders in love with him. But no matter how hard I tried to get him to be mi novio and get him to give me my first kiss, he ignored me. I'm ashamed to admit that for many years afterward I went through life believing that he was gay. Little did I know that all along he was destined to become a saint.

Just who does this old man think he is? He looks ridiculous carting all those birds around.

"Señora," he says to me, "would you like to hold my pigeon?" Yes, it's true that he has a dove in his hand, but everyone in Nicaragua knows what *paloma* also means. Viejo verde. Can't that dirty old man tell by the way I'm dressed that I'm in mourning?

To be honest, he must have been somewhat handsome in his days. I can still tell. I especially like his voice. But by the looks of him, he's been through hell. It's true that I'm lonely. But not *that* lonely.

I am alone, though. Both of my parents died in the early eighties, and it was perhaps for the best because my father, don Isidoro, absolutely hated the Sandinistas—even though his grandson was one of them. Worst still, if living in a communist country didn't do it, Elías's death would have killed him for sure. Yes, it's a good thing that by then don Isidoro had already passed away.

Bernardo, the one person I trust completely in this world, left

Cuapa a couple of years after la Revolución, and he hasn't returned to live here since. I know that something horrible happened to him in Managua; and whatever it was changed him, making him distant, aloof. For the longest time I could barely talk to Bernardo—a conversation with him felt like talking to someone at the other end of a long tunnel. For years, he hid in the seminary, and sometimes when I'd go visit he'd refuse to see me. But he's finally his old self again. Well, almost. Gracias a Dios.

Bernardo seldom visits Cuapa now that his bishop has assigned him way out there in Tonalá. But when he does, he always stays at my house, and it's so good to have him there. He spent last night in my home—exhausted after the long sermon he gave during the mass. Whenever Bernardo's visiting, which is not often enough, I feel much less alone.

I survived Róger's death by trying to become everything Elías could ever want in a mother and more. But the pain of losing my husband all came back in one swift earth-shattering blow on August 1, 1985. Early that morning, just as the sun was rising, the sound of gunfire made us all hide under our beds. The battle didn't really last long. The contrarevolucionarios easily overran the poorly trained Sandinista militia stationed in the garrison. What we didn't know at the time was that the attack was merely the bait in a trap. The contrarevolucionarios were counting on the Sandinistas sending reinforcements from Juigalpa. I was told that Elías tried to talk his jefe out of sending troops down the faster route.

"It would be better to take the old road to Cuapa, compañero, the one that runs along the apparition site," he advised. "The main road is dangerous. There's at least one spot where they could easily ambush us: a pass between two small hills about two kilometers before you get to Cuapa. If they catch us there, we'll be defenseless, like pigs going to don Casimiro's to be slaughtered."

El jefe refused to listen to my son's warnings. "La Revolución needs to be defended, compañero! And we need to act decisively. We can't waste time sending troops along the back roads," he said. He then ordered a convoy of raw recruits, teenage boys from this area, to their deaths. My son, in charge of the operation, died alongside them. And at their funerals, I was able to cry alongside their mothers.

Doña Tula almost got caught in the middle of the attack. She was returning from the village of Llano Grande, where she had gone to catch up on the latest gossip. She said that Elías probably didn't know what hit him. In the blink of an eye, in a mother's heartbeat, at the very pass he had warned his jefe about, a rocket grenade struck the cab of the lead truck, which exploded instantly, with Elías inside. Perhaps my son didn't know what hit him, but it sure hit me, right where it hurts the most.

The irony is that when the contrarevolucionarios came back to boast about what they had done—right before they went out into the woods to execute the Sandinista officials stationed in Cuapa—the people were aghast to learn that the fellow commanding their forces was el Muerto. Elías had spared this man's life years before.

"Strange are the paths of pity," Bernardo said back then.

The war was so cruel, pitting brother against brother while the two superpowers that were really at the heart of the conflict hovered above us, pulling our strings like macabre puppeteers. When the killing finally ended, I did not want revenge. All I wanted to know was what had happened to el Muerto. At long last, someone found out that he's working in a Miami supermarket, bagging groceries and cleaning up the storeroom. Dios sabe lo que hace. But I do wish that God had made his purpose clear to me.

Still, there's something of Elías still alive and nearby, a chele, a being of light, like an ángel: Magdalena and Gerardo's eldest son. Shortly after Somoza's fall, Elías told me all about his affair with Magdalena. He did this because from the moment he first set eyes on the boy, he was convinced that the child was his. The boy has now grown into a fine, handsome young man of twenty. He's attending college in Juigalpa and will one day have a degree in agricultural science. I've paid for his education, and I'm paying for his younger brothers and sisters to go to school as well. He calls me Mamá Blanquita and stops by at least once a week to have lunch with me.

When I look into his green eyes, I see Róger, and I see my son. That's why, in mi testamento, I'm leaving him everything.

Why does that woman keep on staring? She's beginning to scare me. There's something not quite right about her, but I can't put my finger on it. For instance, what's up with her hair? That mess on top of her head looks like a wig. And those oversized sunglasses are only there to hide her face; I know it. Even though I can't see her eyes, I can *feel* her staring at me. I wish she would stop doing that—it gives me the creeps.

This reminds me of the time I ran into the ghost of Colonel Arrechavala in the streets of León. Seeing his spirit on the back of a stallion late one night scared the crap out of me. At the time I was in León visiting a few friends who attend la universidad there. It's true that we had smoked a little dope that evening. I even tripped and fell in the middle of the street, getting my white pants all covered in mud. But I do know what I saw.

I'm here in Cuapa today to help mi abuelito Nicolás fulfill his pledge to la Virgen. He offered that if she released me from my coma he would bring five hundred doves (which I think is so sweet!) to the next anniversary of her apparition. But I'm also here because mi mamá and mi abuelita asked me to come.

I know that sounds strange, but I'm telling the truth. When I was laying in bed, shut out from this world, both my mother and mi abuelita Flor de María dropped by every day to visit. They'd sit at my bedside and tell me their stories. At last, I was able to bring the missing pieces of my life together and weave my own story into a beautiful quilt. I especially loved getting to know my mother. We're so much alike. Now I know why mi abuelito Nicolás keeps on saying that I am her reincarnation.

Although I had the impression that we were conversing through mosquito netting, their figures indistinct through the gauzy material, I have no doubt that their visits were real. I treasured our conversations. I didn't want to leave that world; I was happy there. I was filling a hollow, an empty space that had me longing for completeness.

One afternoon, toward the end of one of their visits, they began to say adiós for good. I was so sad that I began to cry. But mi mamá, reaching out to hold my hand, said, "It's time for you to go back, Lourdes. There's no reason to be unhappy. From now on you'll have the both of us in your heart. Forever."

"Lourdes, mi amor," mi abuelita Flor de María then said, "I need you to do a favor for me. Go visit my brother Pedro. Thank him and Susana for taking care of me all these years. Let them know that I appreciate everything they've done. Also, tell them to get things ready for my departure. I know that you've never visited them before, but they are the only relatives you have left on your mother's and my side. After I'm gone, please drop by to see them as often as you can. I'm sure that with time you'll come to love one another."

As we said our farewells, I hugged both mi abuelita and mi mamá. We promised to meet again in a brighter world. But, to be honest, I now hope that's not anytime soon.

Three days after I awoke, I went to visit mis tíos, just like mi abuelita Flor de María had asked. They were delighted to see me. And then I saw her, or at least the shell she had become. When I gave them her message, mis tíos both cried, and they believed me without question. That same day, they began the preparations for mi abuelita's death, which happened two days later. Ever since then, I visit mi tío Pedro and mi tía Susana several times a week.

I had never been to see them before because mi abuela Nora said that they blamed me for my mother's death and that they wanted nothing to do with me. But, thanks to mi abuelita Flor de María, I've been able to recover that part of myself—a part I thought I had lost forever. She hung on to life all those years just so I could return to the family. And once I had, she was free to go. I'll always love her for that.

That girl in the tight white pants is making my heart swoon. When I first got here I was trying to make eye contact with a cute little chela, the blond gringa over there, sitting on the pavilion and holding a parrot. But then this old fart came and sat next to her. He put his arm around the blond and began kissing her on the neck. I think they're a couple. Who's to account for taste these days? But now I've found this tasty morsel. I'll see if I can get to know her before the day is done.

Dios me perdone. Conversion, though, is a process, and I swear that I'm doing the best I can to become a good Christian again. But there's still a big sinner living inside of me, and that sinner is especially tempted by luscious young women wearing tight white pants (which, incidentally, I find absurd in this place since, before long, her pants will be filthy). The biggest sins in my life, however, are not of the flesh but of cruelty. They are the sins of a warrior. Of these, I promise, I have fully repented and mended my ways.

At one time Catholicism was my greatest enemy, the cause of all of my country's problems, or so I thought. Christianity, I believed, had taught the people to accept every injustice in return for some nebulous reward el Señor would give them in the afterlife. But now, many years later, I've accepted Jesús as mi salvador personal and I've learned to respect Christians. And I must admit, the devoutness I see here today, in Cuapa, is impressive.

The lines of people standing on the hillsides, awaiting confession under the blazing sun, are longer than the lines people made during the 1980s to get their food rations. There must be at least fifty priests out there working their ears off. The faithful are crammed several rows deep along the fence that protects the statue of la Virgen. Those in front have their faces pressed against the bars. They look stunned by their own devotion, staring wide eyed at Nuestra Señora. Others are crying without shame.

A young man wearing a cap, advertising the tennis shoes with the swoosh, is removing bark from the tree nearest to the statue. With a pocketknife he is cutting perfect little squares and carefully placing them in the outstretched hands of the believers. His labor has left the base of the tree blanched. I overheard the local parish priest—a gruff, chain-smoking Spaniard—say that every two years he has to plant a new, almost fully grown tree. The morisco upon which she appeared, which was still alive the last time I was here, didn't survive the relic seekers.

Two men are crouching beside the tree-carving youth. They're removing bucketfuls of dirt from the atrium, and people are grabbing the dark, rich soil by the handful and putting the clumps into plastic bags. Yes, when I look around, it's the face of devotion that I see in Cuapa. How foolish of me to ever think that I was capable of destroying my people's faith.

Although I walked away from politics many years ago, I still have to wear disguises whenever I leave my house. People still remember me. On occasion, one of my "cases" will recognize me, walk right up, and spit in my face. Other times, they'll run away in terror. I can't even go to Metrocentro without wearing something to hide my identity. Can you believe that? Even in a damn shopping mall I'm not safe. That's why I'm wearing this uncomfortably hot wig and these ridiculously large sunglasses. But I guess I can count myself lucky. At least there were no Nuremberg trials after we fell from grace. For sure, I would have hung from the gallows.

What people have forgotten is that we were in the middle of a shitty war back then—una guerra de mierda. We were the last sneeze of the cold war. And you had to be ruthless if you were going to survive in state security. During the 1980s there was no room for compassion, no room for mercy. The spy games I had to play against CIA agents were particularly nasty. Whatever I needed to do to gather information considered vital to the survival of la Revolución, I did. And gladly. To hesitate during the war made a warrior weak, and in this arena the weak didn't survive. I can take you to their secret graves. But don't you ever believe that you could tell the good guys from the bad guys on the scorecard;

each team would go to any length to obtain whatever it thought was necessary. All's fair . . . , as they say.

But no. Those of us who ended up on the losing side will never be forgiven. It's the winners who become heroes. Take, for instance, those two gringos walking among the crowd, looking for something or someone: Victor and his faithful companion, Padre Damián. Back in the eighties I knew everything about them. Do you think they played the game by honorable rules? I know that priest helped send a few Marxists in several countries to meet Nuestro Señor. Part of my job was to put a stop to whatever those two were up to. Which makes me wonder, what the hell are they doing here? Hasn't anyone told them that the war's over? Oh, well, it doesn't matter to me anymore. I'm out of that scene for good. At this moment, that sweet young thing in the tight white pants is far more important than anything else in the world, and I prefer it that way.

I just want to forget the past. And I pray that some day everything I did during the war will also be forgotten. I'm here today to ask for la Virgen's forgiveness. If Nuestra Señora forgives me, I can then ask Bernardo to forgive me for what I ordered my men to do to him. And if I receive his forgiveness, then, just maybe, I can begin to forgive myself.

What a nice man, that American priest. And he's so tall! He even towers over Jake! With such broad shoulders, it's a shame that he's so flabby. Although his black cassock hides most of the bulges, I can still see rolls of fat underneath. Why does he wear that outfit in this heat? Priests are allowed to dress more comfortably these days. Just look at the rest of them here today, dressed casually. And why does he wear a biretta? It's soaked in sweat. I haven't seen a priest wear one of those things on his head for ages. In those clothes the poor man is bound to faint before the day is over. The sun is relentless, unforgiving.

To be honest, if I hadn't talked to him first and found him so charming, his appearance would have frightened me. Still, even though his looks are intimidating, that's no reason for the people of Cuapa to be disrespectful. After all, he *is* a priest. Jake and I arrived in Cuapa yesterday, in time for la vigilia, and we noticed that whenever the American priest passed before a group of cuapeños, they'd chuckle, point to him, and say "¡Mirá, vos, regresó Darth Vader!" I wanted to give them a piece of my mind, but Jake said it's better for me to stay out of it. Since my husband is usually right about things like this, I followed his advice.

Although almost forty years have passed since I left my country—swearing never to return—the people are exactly the same as I remember them: messy and irreverent. They throw trash anywhere they please. Nicaraguans are talking now about tourism being the future of the country. Do they really expect to see bus-loads of foreigners interested in seeing an entire nation treated as a landfill? It's such a shame too, because Nicaragua *is* beautiful. But you never know, maybe the first busloads of tourists will tell Nicaraguans to clean up their act or else they'll stop coming. And maybe mis compatriotas will listen.

And then there's the noise. I had forgotten how loud Nicaraguans can be. The loudspeakers are blasting out announcements and religious music, the bands of chicheros are competing to see who can play the loudest, the women are singing off-key, and hundreds of radios are tuned to the béisbol games. It's all too much. At times I have to put my hands over my ears. I'm sure that tonight I'm going to have a migraine. But at least Jake's here and he can prescribe something.

"I really haven't missed much," I lean over to tell my husband. "Very little has changed in all these years." But Jake's not really listening; his mind is off somewhere, wandering. He's enthralled with the view. We were smart to arrive here early enough to get a shady spot under this mango tree, halfway up the hill to the east of the sanctuary. Gazing at the sights myself, I have to admit that the mountain ranges of Chontales are majestic. Even though it's toward the end of the dry season, the countryside still looks green to me. At the same time, the mountains are rugged, not unlike some I've seen in Arizona. That austere peak rising to the north is certainly mesmerizing. To the south, la Piedra de Cuapa is kind of interesting, but I still can't see why the locals are so proud of that thing. Now that I think about it, that monolith reminds me of a pimple.

While Jake devotes himself to studying the countryside, I look at the people. Here, today, gathered on this site, is a nice portrait of Nicaragua. People from every walk of life are here. The literate and the illiterate, the wealthy and the poor, the whites, the indios, and the mestizos. I only wish a few costeños had shown up, but they're Moravians—the veneration of la Virgen María is not on their religious agenda. Well, at least most of Nicaragua is here.

Take, for instance, that wealthy family sitting over there on a blanket. By their brand-name clothes, their coolers packed with food, the bottled water, and the canned soft drinks, you can tell they lived in Miami during the Sandinista years. "They think they're here on a picnic," I tell Jake.

The campesinos are just as easy to spot. The men are wearing white shirts, khaki pants, cowboy hats, and boots—with the spurs still on. The women are wearing simple dresses—the colors faded—which they don't mind getting dirty as they sit carelessly on the ground.

The urban poor, on the other hand, look like walking advertisements. Their clothing is living proof that free enterprise has returned to Nicaragua, with a vengeance. Many wear used garments, donations from the United States that were shipped here after Huracán Mitch. For instance, I can hardly believe that grandmother sitting over there wearing a T-shirt that's obviously promoting some rock group: ANTHRAX—THE BOVINE DEATH TOUR. That little old man walking toward us, who looks like he's the town drunk, has a T-shirt on that asks DON'T I MAKE YOU HORNY? Definitely not.

The young men from the cities can be spotted because they all seem to be wearing caps of their favorite sports teams. Looks like the San Francisco Giants are pretty popular this year. And quite a few young men are wearing basketball tank tops, which I think is smart on a hot day like today. They have the names Jordan, O'Neal, and Bryant sprawled across their backs. And someone important must be here today because a lot of men are wearing caps that say "Bodyguard."

Curious, I turn to a woman sitting next to me and ask, pointing to a cap, "Señora, who's here today? Why are there so many bodyguards?"

The woman smiles, leans forward, and whispers in my ear, so that Jake won't overhear, "Señora, 'Bodyguard' son condones."

Condoms? They're wearing caps advertising condoms? At a celebration for la Virgen? With ¡Sí a la Vida! banners all over the place? Well, I'm right. Little has changed. Nicaraguans are as irreverent as ever.

Although not much is different from when I used to live here,
I now realize that I stayed away from my country for far too long.
More than six years have gone by since I promised Bernardo that I
would make a pilgrimage to Cuapa, but fear of facing my past kept
me away. But as the twentieth anniversary of the apparition of
Nuestra Señora approached, I knew I couldn't put off my pledge to
la Virgen de Cuapa any longer. She has given me so many blessings.

I'm glad we came. All these years I had been afraid to see
Ramón Arévalo again. Turns out that he died a long time ago—
from alcoholism, they say. Poor thing, he didn't turn out to be
worth the grief after all. I thought that everyone in Diriamba
would remember that out of lust I had surrendered my virginity to
him, but it was quite the opposite—no one remembered that
Ramón and I had been an item. Relieved, and with a clean slate, I
began to enjoy visiting relatives and friends whom I believed had
left the country. Reliving my youth has been fun. I realize that no
matter how hard I had tried to distance myself from Nicaragua,
how much I tried to reinvent myself, trying to become an
"American," I missed my homeland. I'm happy now that I had the
courage to return. And Jake, the best thing that has ever happened
to me, has promised that from now on we'll come back to visit once
a year. He actually likes it here.

The only item left on my list of things to do is to see Bernardo.
I brought along the statue of Nuestra Señora that he gave me when
he visited Los Angeles. And I also brought along a tube of Krazy
Glue to fix her broken hand—just like I promised I would six years
ago. I want Bernardo to be the one to do it, and now that he's a
priest I'll ask him to bless my beloved image of la Virgen de Cuapa.

As I turn to look toward the sanctuary, an old man pulling a
cart catches my eye. On top, there's a cage. "Are those pigeons he has

crammed in there?" I ask Jake. "There must be at least a couple hundred of them." The old-timer's chatting away with a widow, trying to hand her a bird he's holding. When she finally takes the pigeon, he reaches into the cage to get another one, and the top accidentally flies open.

"Look, honey," I say to Jake, pointing at the birds as they take flight, happy to have regained their freedom.

"Oh, my . . . ," said Jake, at last looking toward the cage on wheels. "By the way that fellow is jumping around, I don't think he meant for that to happen."

Suddenly, there's absolute silence. The lull is a blessed relief to my aching ears. A hush has fallen over the gathering as everyone stops whatever they are doing to look up at the doves, now circling directly above our heads. Someone has turned off the deafening music that was playing over the loudspeakers. The soundman probably thinks the release of the doves signals the beginning of the ceremony. Those listening to the béisbol games turn off their radios. The choir of women abruptly cut the out-of-tune singing. Even the chicheros stop playing their cheesy music to stare up at the freed birds. And I, happy to have left my gilded cage on the Palos Verdes Peninsula to return home for this visit, reach out to hold Jake's hand.

Padre Ginés Hidalgo anxiously paced across the sanctuary platform, smoking another Belmont. The tension running through his neck became a dull, aching knot when el sacristán announced that the luxury bus bringing the cardinal and his bishops had arrived. The Spaniard still had no idea what he was going to say. His mind was like a blank sheet of paper with time running out during a final exam. To make matters worse, the whole day had been rapidly descending into chaos. How could anyone expect him to think of the opening words *and* control a crowd of seventy thousand? Impossible. But he continued to think frantically, hoping that at the last moment something inspirational would come to him. Perhaps a speech modeled on the Sermon of the Mount. Blessed are those who come to Cuapa, for they will eat tortillas and cuajada. No, he mustn't get silly. Time was quickly running out.

A news producer from Univision, accompanied by a reporter and a cameraman, added to Padre Ginés's fretfulness. She had come all the way from the United States for the occasion. What puzzled the priest was that an experienced newsperson, one who works for Univision no less, would also seem nervous.

"Padre, I was one of the first reporters to write about the apparition. I botched the story back then, and I promised her that someday I would get it right," she said, although because of his own pressing concerns, the priest was not interested in her explanation. "And, years ago, la Virgen performed a miracle for me; she made sure that my mother's breast cancer didn't recur. I owe her this story. Could you arrange an interview with Padre Bernardo for us?"

The Spaniard wanted to reply, "Get in line, Señora." Instead, he reached out, patted her gently on the arm, and said, "I'll see what I can do."

Padre Ginés turned his back on the woman and continued his pacing. He prayed desperately for el Señor to allow the opening words to pour down on him, suddenly and hard, like rain during a tropical storm. But all the priest heard in response to his plea was the noise and the chaos. Just as he was about to give up hope, everything became silent. The Spaniard quickly turned toward the crowd—every face was raised heavenward.

"What is it? Is the sun playing tricks again?" he asked el

sacristán, who was standing next to him. And then he saw a flock of doves ascending slowly, in widening circles, before they began to fly northwest, in the direction of Managua.

"Gracias a Dios everyone has quieted down," he said to himself. And then the crowd turned its attention toward el potrero gate. The people rose to their feet, like a huge ocean wave, as the cardinal and his bishops marched in, dressed in their stoles and chasubles, ready to perform mass. The pointed peaks of the miters they wore on their heads made their advance toward the sanctuary visible to every single person in the huge gathering.

Caught by surprise, Padre Ginés threw his cigarette away and rushed to put on his vestments to concelebrate in the day's Eucharist. By the time the procession had reached the sanctuary, Padre Ginés was dressed, but not ready—the words he frantically needed were still out of his grasp. As the cardinal and his bishops ascended the platform they spread out along its length, where the altar had been placed on that day so all the concelebrants could face the multitudes gathered on the hillsides. Once the clergymen were in their places, Padre Ginés saw Bernardo, standing to the right of the cardinal.

Nineteen years ago, the visionary had received a message from la Virgen. Bernardo had dictated her words to the Spaniard, who had copied them down and given the sheet of paper to the notary of the archdiocese, who in turn had placed it in a sealed envelope. On the cover, the notary had written: *To be opened by the archbishop on the twentieth anniversary of my first appearance*. Today, after waiting patiently all these years, Padre Ginés observed with eagerness as the current notary stepped forward and handed the message to the cardinal. His Eminence broke the wax seal, opened the envelope, brought out the sheet of paper, unfolded it, and began to read. Although the Spaniard had written down the message long ago, he perfectly remembered every single one of her words: *On May 8, 2000, the archbishop (who will by then be a cardinal) and his bishops will all come together for the first time to venerate me on this site.* After the cardinal had finished, he turned to Bernardo, nodded, and smiled. He then passed the message on to the bishops. Padre Ginés watched their reactions closely. He was pleased by the looks of amazement on their faces when each of them finished reading. Each man glanced at the cardinal. His Eminence responded by nodding, to which the bishops would bow, their miters accentuating the gesture.

When each one had read the message, the note was returned to the cardinal. He placed the paper carefully back inside the envelope and gave it to the notary, who placed it inside his cassock and left. The cardinal then looked toward Padre Ginés and nodded. The moment of truth had arrived.

"May el Espíritu Santo illuminate me," Padre Ginés mumbled to himself as he made the sign of the cross while stepping up to the microphone. He tapped it twice with his right index finger and was rewarded with two dull thumps. He looked at the crowd covering the hillsides. People were packed so densely together that not a single square yard of grass could be seen. Padre Ginés then took a deep breath and, placing all his faith in Nuestra Señora, began to speak.

"Buenos días, devotos de la Virgen de Cuapa. We have gathered this morning to celebrate the twentieth anniversary of her first appearance at this very site. On that day, she made this, the ground upon which we stand today, hallowed. Years later, after her visits to this holy pasture had reached their end, her messenger, Bernardo Martínez, distressed over our capacity for violence, came to believe that we had forgotten that Nuestra Señora had been here, that she had come to visit us here, in Nicaragua. Bernardo de Cuapa thought that we had forgotten the message of peace and of hope that she had brought to us twenty years ago."

Padre Ginés paused for a moment. He gazed at the crowd. He saw that they were hanging on his every word, listening in total silence. Raising his voice slightly, the priest then asked, "Did you ever forget that she was here?"

"¡NO!" the crowd responded in a single voice. Many shook their heads. Others lifted a hand with an extended index finger, waving it from side to side in denial.

"Have you *ever* forgotten that she was here?"

"¡NO!" The crowd's reply sounded like rolling thunder, spreading in ripples through the valleys.

"Will you ever forget that she was here?"

"¡NUNCA!"

Padre Ginés paused again, allowing the reverberation of the reply to seep into the hills of Chontales. The crowd remained silent. So silent that, for a moment, the Spaniard could hear the birds singing. After a slight pause, he continued.

"Make it so, then. Que así sea. Never forget that Nuestra Señora has honored Nicaragua with her presence. And never forget her message. You Nicaraguans can be a forgetful bunch. It's true that I'm not really one of you. From my lisp, you can probably tell that I'm from Spain. But I have lived among you for twenty-two years, and I have eaten as much gallo pinto, as much rice mixed with beans, as any of you. This, therefore, gives me the right to be firm when I say,

"Never forget her message.

"She came to this very spot, and with Bernardo as her messenger, she said, 'Don't ask for peace, work for it.' Nuestra Madre,

Our Mother, María, came to you at the dawning of terrible war between brothers, and she pleaded with you: 'Don't ask for peace, work for it.'

"Never forget."

The hillsides became a glittering movement of handkerchiefs as Padre Ginés watched people dabbing at their tears. He had done his job, and he was grateful that el Espíritu Santo had descended upon him after all. He said a brief, silent prayer of thanks. It was now time, he thought, to bring his role in today's ceremony to a close.

"*¿Quién es la más guapa?*" he shouted into the microphone, his right index finger pointed toward the heavens.

"*¡La Virgen de Cuapa!*" seventy thousand pilgrims shouted back.

The priest waited, not moving a muscle, until the echo had died down, and then, in a soft voice, but one that every single person on the hillsides could hear, he said, "Ni quien diga lo contrario."

He looked toward the cardinal, who smiled in approval. Padre Ginés, then, with a slight bow of his head and a slow sweeping wave of his arm, motioned for His Eminence to step up to the microphone. The crowd broke into a loud and sustained ovation.

Yes, Padre Ginés thought once he stood in place among the bishops and priests, la Virgen de Cuapa is the most beautiful Virgin of all.

Don't let anyone tell you otherwise.

Amén.

chapter fourteen

KOIMESIS

(To Sleep Eternal)

November 22, 2000

Diego Miranda

AT EL KIOSKO of el Parque Central of Juigalpa, Diego Miranda ordered a glass of tiste and then sat under the shade of el guanacaste tree. The next bus to Cuapa didn't leave for another hour. The rather unexpected trip had caused havoc in his busy writing schedule. But Diego couldn't put it off till later. Bernardo Martínez's death, which had happened on October 30, had left too many questions unanswered.

The seer's remains were buried in el pueblo's old church on November 1: All Saints' Day.

"Does Bernardo's burial on that day have a special significance?" Diego had asked himself. Of course, similar questions had been plaguing him for months: Was Bernardo a saint? Were his visions real? Did he make up the story of the apparitions hoping that it would help him fulfill his lifelong dream of becoming a priest? Did he have the slightest idea of the remarkable chain of events his vision would trigger?

Diego didn't have the answers. But what he *did* know was that Bernardo's tale was so full of twists of fate, so replete with small marvels, that even if the former college professor spent a lifetime trying to deconstruct their significance, the task would prove impossible. To solve every riddle, Diego would have needed a miracle. And why waste one on such minor concerns?

Several years ago—four? five?—Diego Miranda could have used a miracle for himself. He certainly had needed one to save him from the bloodcurdling midlife crisis that made him walk away from his wife and children. He certainly had needed a miracle to prevent him from giving up a distinguished position as an associate professor of comparative literature—with tenure—in a well-respected university in the United States. He definitely needed one to forestall his falling into a dark pit of depression, where he would remain for three—four?—years. And at the time, he could have especially used a miracle to stop him from packing up his belongings and moving to Nicaragua. That, his friends all agreed, was sheer lunacy.

Throughout his life, Diego Miranda had been a Latino golden boy. From kindergarten through high school, his teachers in San Gabriel, California, had called him a "model student," a young man of "unlimited potential." His parents, both Nicaraguan, had immigrated to the United States in the early 1950s and raised him to blend, as seamlessly as possible, into their new homeland. They wanted their son to become an "American"—as things were back then, before people started placing a hyphen between heritages. (Paradoxically, Diego's parents sent him on long vacations to their homeland to visit relatives and to stay in touch with his Nicaraguan side.)

Diego earned a scholarship to attend a prestigious Bay Area university, where he earned respectable grades. Shortly after graduation, he married his college sweetheart: a beautiful Southern Californian blue-eyed Americana with whom he had two children. Theirs was the picture of an idyllic family.

Passionate about literature, after a couple of well paid but miserable years as an insurance executive, Diego returned to graduate school and continued studying, earning many honors, until he completed his doctorate.

Through his hard work, Diego had become a model for other sons and daughters of immigrants who, like him, were trying to find their place in the United States. "Look at Dr. Miranda," people would often say, "Latinos *can* succeed if they put their minds to it." And Diego accepted that platitude as a compliment. He considered himself, in all modesty, a living example that persistence and dedication had its rewards, regardless of one's origins. Indeed, Diego Miranda had it all: a beautiful wife, two wonderful kids, a prestigious job, two highly rated Japanese automobiles, a beautiful home, and a summer cottage by the lake. What more could a Nicaraguan-American want?

Life was good.

But in reality, when one closely inspected the nuts and bolts, up until Diego's spectacular midlife crisis his existence had been a rather drab and uneventful affair. He had spent most of his years with his nose between book covers, his creativity bogged down by the boring nuisances of committee work and grading stacks of student papers. And at home he'd spent considerable time with a pen in hand, writing out the checks to pay the mortgages.

Throughout Diego's climb up the ladder, he hadn't noticed

rigor mortis setting in. His slide into crisis had started discreetly, he realized years later, with an uneasy feeling that life was passing him by too fast. In a way that had quietly crept up on him, like a ghostly shadow, his life at home and his work at the university had become a mix of thoughtless and dull routines. What once had been a soothing tempo, a distinct rhythm that inspired him, like the steady slapping of conga drums, had gradually turned into a monotonous rattle of empty, worthless chores.

To the outside observer, Diego was living the American dream. But in fervently pursuing that mirage, the son of immigrants let his responsibilities get the best of him. He became a workaholic: striving for perfection. As a college professor, Diego published numerous articles and books, he competed for national grants and won, he received various teaching awards, and, as the ultimate recognition of his worth, he was given tenure. Still, in spite of these victories, a hollow feeling haunted him. His successes, no matter how impressive, had become meaningless.

By nature an overachiever, Diego had always, since childhood, tended to be dissatisfied. Whatever he accomplished, whatever sterling reputation he had built for himself, whatever he owned, had never been enough. The bar of his expectations, already set too high, was pushed even higher in his pursuit of the American dream. His mother had often pointed this out.

"Hijito, why are you killing yourself? Relájate. Enjoy life a little. Take a vacation." His wife agreed.

But Diego Miranda, an All-American-Latino boy, continued playing the game with ardor. He became the consummate consumer, working endless hours to accumulate the properties, the gadgets, and the toys. And he became stuck with the bills that went along with his aptitude for purchasing. By the time Diego reached middle age, his life was cluttered beyond hope. One morning, he woke up believing that everything had gone wrong. Way too wrong. He felt as if he were trying to get onto a Los Angeles freeway—through the exit ramp.

It was about then that the dream started, the one that recurred night after night for months. It began with Diego enjoying a hike through a splendid forest. The air was charged with the scent of pine needles. The moss and ferns added a serene, vibrant green to the scenery. His dog ran happily ahead of him. Suddenly, a rabbit would appear, and the dog would chase after it down an unknown path. Diego followed behind as fast as he could, running and calling the dog's name. When he'd finally give up, he'd discover that he was completely lost. As he stood there worrying about how he was going to find his way back home, he'd hear a woman's voice, lovely and soothing.

"Diego, do not be afraid. I am here for you."

He turned to see a beautiful and slightly terrifying being. Her stunning violet eyes probed his soul.

An angel?

"Who are you?" he'd ask.

"Diego, I've come only to deliver this message: First, you will suffer through many changes, painful changes. But this path will someday lead you to her. When you get there, the story will be waiting."

"What story?"

"The one that is waiting for you," she'd answer before walking into a bright light that had started to seep through the trees. After she'd disappear, night engulfed the forest. In the darkness, Diego would hear cries that frightened him—the cries of lost souls, of other middle-aged men who had failed to find their way out of the forest and were condemned to roam it for eternity, their destinies unfulfilled.

Diego would wake up in a cold sweat. The dream returned night after night. Stress, angst, and confusion started to lay siege upon him. Without realizing it, Diego became detached. At work, he'd stare vacantly as students and colleagues spoke to him. He'd answer their questions in short, terse sentences. Alarmed over Dr. Miranda's mental state, they'd walk away, sadly shaking their heads. At home, Diego would sit for hours in front of the television, remote control in hand, watching nothing but reruns of sitcoms from his childhood.

"Honey, please go see a psychiatrist," his wife suggested. Of course, being a stalwart Latino male, he refused.

Then Diego's body started to break down as well. A vain person, he had kept his jet-black hair (people asked themselves if he dyed it, which he did) perfectly combed and his thick beard immaculately trimmed. Plus, Diego had kept himself in excellent shape: his compact, wiry body was nothing but lean muscle mass from running seven miles a day and doing one hundred sit-ups afterward. In spite of this, the blitz with which the midlife crisis hit him caused its ravages. First came the maddening headaches, and then the perpetual feeling of being bloated, full of gas. Thereafter came the hot flashes and the cold sweats, alternating with implacable force. But Diego didn't become truly alarmed until his heart would suddenly start galloping as if it had entered a race. Several nights he woke up panic-stricken, his chest tight. He imagined his arteries compressed, conspiring to stop his blood from flowing.

He needed to escape.

Two questions began to haunt his every waking hour:

Can a man change his life?

Can a man walk away from his responsibilities and achievements and forget it all?

Diego was afraid that he was caught in a death trap. He had also started to believe that he was living the wrong life, someone else's and not his own. He wanted to hop off the treadmill and run far away from everything he had become. The associate professor of comparative literature watched helplessly as his present scuttled by, headed so resolutely toward the future that he could no longer remember his past.

Ridden by these anxieties, Diego called his best friend, Cuevitas, a Cuban-American who had been his college roommate during the undergraduate years. They were so much alike that from the moment they met they were certain that, in another life, they had been twins. Cuevitas now owned a successful insurance agency and lived a comfortable life in Coral Gables, Florida. Diego, sobbing over the phone, told his friend everything.

"Sí, hombre, of course you can change your life," Cuevitas said firmly. "Don't despair. Take it easy, Dieguito. It's funny, but I'm going through the exact same thing right now, Hermano. Gemelos always, remember. We're twins, Brother. Besides, it's natural to go through something like this at our age. Sooner or later it happens to all men. It's the fork in the road where we have to choose the path that means the most to us. But, Dieguito, all you really need to do is to simplify your life and reconnect with a happier time in your past. I'm going back to explore my Cuban roots. That's going to heal me, I'm sure of it. You should try to reconnect with your Nicaraguan roots, Diego. And listen, a santera performed a cleansing on me just a few days ago. Now I feel great. I suggest you do something along the same line."

A week later, Diego received a telephone call from Cuevitas's ex-wife informing him that his twin had driven to the southernmost key in Florida, stepped out of his car, and jumped into the ocean, clothes and all, and that no one had seen him since. Cuevitas had gone under.

Afraid that he would do something similar, afraid that he was on a raceway destined for a head-on midlife collision from which he would not come out alive, Diego, in a metaphor he thought up as a tribute to his friend, parked his car, stepped out of the vehicle, and walked away.

Yes, Diego could have used a miracle to stop his life from going into a tailspin. His existence had become a horrifying, spiraling descent into hell. But the miracle he needed never came. Diego Miranda, Ph.D., associate professor of Comparative Literature, had died. The shell of the person he had once been packed what little he needed and left for Nicaragua on a quest for meaning, on a search for the woman (angel?) who had beckoned him in his dreams.

Strangely, in spite of the torment the dreams had caused, to his waking mind, what she said made a kind of sense. Although Diego's existence had been cast into the abyss of doubt, there was one thing he was absolutely sure of: he wanted to write. He *needed* to write. Writing, Diego was certain, would lift him out of the wretchedness he had sunken into. Beyond all questions, writing would save his soul—word by word he would claw his way out of the dark pit of despair. But what would he write about?

When Diego decided to change his life, without really understanding why, he knew that he needed to return to the country of his parents' birth—a country in which he had spent some of the happiest moments in his life—to find the story the dream woman had promised. He was positive of this. Although he couldn't say why, Nicaragua felt like a sacred draw. Diego was being called the way a Muslim is called to Mecca. For the time being, writing scholarly works was out of the question. Dr. Diego Miranda had already died once. The resurrected Diego Miranda, a modern-day Lazarus, would now make his bid for a grain of immortality: he would write a novel.

Once in Nicaragua, Diego lived on the tightest budget he had known since his days as an undergraduate. In the beginning, he had absolute faith that the mysterious "she" mentioned in his dreams would meet him here, and Diego was sure that, sooner or later, the story would find him. But as the pages torn from the Cerveza Toña calendar began accumulating in a worrisome stack in his desk drawer, self-doubt started to chip away at his certainty. After nearly a year of just milling about, without having found the story, Diego was ready to give up, pack up his things, and head back, in humiliation and defeat, to the States.

And then, just as he was about to relinquish his dream, the miracle he desperately needed happened: the novelist, through an acquaintance—Germán Sotelo, a kooky college professor obsessed with literary theory—met Padre Bernardo Martínez.

The seer shared his story with Diego. The writer couldn't believe his luck. A saga right out of the realm of magical realism had fallen into his lap. Before long, the voices of his characters started to buzz, like an insistent swarm of bees, inside of Diego's head. And the more Diego the novelist heard, the more obsessed he became with retelling the priest's tale. It was then that Diego realized that the only way to accurately convey the remarkable paths of Padre Bernardo Martínez's experience, and keep it believable, was in the form of a novel—his novel.

Who did Diego need to thank for this gift? Padre Bernardo? La Virgen de Cuapa? The dream woman? All he really knew was that in a flash, like the one immediately preceding one of la Virgen's apparitions, the story was there, floating on a cloud.

Diego and Padre Bernardo began to meet frequently, the novelist taking volumes of notes during their informal chats. Diego also read every account he could get his hands on about la Virgen's apparitions in Chontales. He made a quick trip to San Francisco de Cuapa (el pueblo's real name, but everyone knows the town as just plain "Cuapa"), and although his time there had been somewhat brief, coinciding with the commemoration of the twentieth anniversary of her first apparition, he felt he had sized up the setting well enough to write convincingly about it.

At last, the day after the ceremonies, Diego was ready to sit down in front of his laptop.

"I want to write your story," he had said to Padre Bernardo. Diego had been surprised that not once did the seer ask him what he intended to do with the information. "But I must warn you, I intend to write it as a novel."

"As long as you remain true to her message, you have my permission—and my blessing," the seer answered.

"Padre Bernardo," Diego pressed on gently, but hoping to make himself clear, "you do understand that what I'm writing is fiction? I'm not a historian. My account of your story will stray from the truth—many, many times. A novelist makes up things; a novelist *lies*. We invent the things we don't know, or reinvent the things we find dull." Diego suspected that because Padre Bernardo had learned to read so late in his life, distinctions between fiction and nonfiction weren't always perfectly clear.

Padre Bernardo just smiled and answered, "What I think really doesn't matter. She told me some time ago that she had chosen you to write this book."

To this day, whenever Diego recalls the visionary's reply, a piercing chill runs down his spine and he finds himself fighting back the tears.

Within a week of that conversation, Diego began to write his version of Padre Bernardo Martínez's life. Every day, as part of his writing ritual, Diego lit a candle before his nine-inch tall statue of la Virgen de Cuapa and said a brief prayer asking for her blessing. Gradually, as the numbers of pages in his first draft grew, he started to believe that he had indeed been chosen, just as Bernardo, to help spread her message. But this did not make Diego fearful; rather, the more Diego delved into the visionary's story, the more his life was invaded by a blessed sense of peace. And as the novel progressed, the writer moved from darkness to light, from sin to grace, from hopelessness to redemption. He became so absorbed in the project that he barely noticed the months quickly passing by. Then, without warning, the novelist received a telephone call telling him that the seer had passed away.

After Diego hung up, he remained in the same seat for an hour, stunned by the news. Just a few weeks ago, they had spent a morning together, Diego checking a few facts. The seer had seemed in good health. The only problem the novelist had ever detected with Padre Bernardo was a chronic back problem that forced him to walk slightly slanted to the right.

Diego had just assumed that Padre Bernardo would live to see the novel completed. While it was true that the visionary's death gave the story its ending—for months the novelist had been wondering where to bring the narrative to an end—by no means did this literary convenience make him happy. Padre Bernardo had been a good, decent man. Diego genuinely believed that the world needed more Bernardos—people who sacrifice themselves as they try to create a utopia, however unrealistic their visions may seem to others.

"What's a life lived without passion?" Diego had often asked his students.

After he recovered from the shock of the seer's death, an unexplainable curiosity, one that bordered on morbidity, overcame Diego. He wanted to know every single detail about Padre Bernardo's last moments. Aware that Padre Ginés Hidalgo, the parish priest of Cuapa, had been at the visionary's bedside during his death, the novelist decided to interview him.

He had met the Spaniard once before, briefly, before the mass in celebration of the twentieth anniversary of la Virgen's first apparition in Cuapa. That day, when Diego spoke to Padre Ginés, the priest seemed agitated and distracted, so the novelist merely introduced himself, deciding at that moment not to trouble the Spaniard with his writing project. Still, with only that fragile connection, he gathered up his courage and phoned the parish priest of Cuapa to request an interview. Diego was surprised when, in a still thick Castilian accent, Padre Ginés offered to reserve an entire day, November 22, to answer his questions.

Diego arrived in Cuapa a few days early to conduct some last-minute research—for the sake of cultural and geographical accuracy. His friends had cautioned him against taking his car. They argued that the rainy season had probably made the already dreadful roads to Chontales even worse. If Diego took his vehicle, they said, by the time he returned it would need new shock absorbers.

"Better to take the bus, Diego," they all suggested.

"Easy for them to say," the novelist muttered to himself during the miserable bus ride from Managua to Juigalpa.

Three and a half hours after leaving the capital, Diego was sipping tiste in el Parque Central of Juigalpa. His joints were sore after the trip on an overcrowded yellow bus that failed to dodge the majority of the enormous potholes and, according to the lettering on its side, had put forth its best years of service transporting school children in Wilkes County, North Carolina. Once Diego had arrived in the capital of Chontales, he was thankful for his friends' advice. His vehicle would have been demolished.

The twenty-two-kilometer voyage from Juigalpa to Cuapa was also bumpy, traveling along a wide, poorly graded dirt road. The bus traveled so slowly that it took almost an hour to cover the relatively short distance separating the city from the town. At first, Diego, sitting next to a window, amused himself by gazing out upon the hilly countryside. The fields were the vibrant tropical green that marks the end of the rainy season. At times, between hills, to the right, la Piedra de Cuapa would rear its tip to greet him. Soon, perhaps lulled by el duende of the monolith, and in spite of the rough ride, Diego fell asleep.

A jarring movement, sharper than the rest, woke him. He looked out of his window and stared sadly as the bus passed the stern monument for the more than forty young Sandinista recruits—mostly teenagers—who had been killed in a Contra ambush. Indeed, Diego realized, the steep slopes on both sides of the highway and the massive boulders gunmen could hide behind made this stretch a perfect death trap.

"What had the war been for?" the novelist sighed to himself, lamenting the suffering of the 1980s. He then made the sign of the cross and said a brief, silent prayer for Elías Bacon.

Yet the knowledge that Cuapa was right around the bend quickly lifted Diego's spirits. As soon as the bus pulled out of the curve, he saw her standing there, greeting all visitors: a concrete whitewashed statue of la Virgen de Cuapa, her right hand open and with the palm facing up. A rustic sign pointed pilgrims toward the apparition site: two kilometers south along the old road to Juigalpa. Before reaching the statue, to the right of the turnoff, stood the home where Bernardo had lived until the Sandinistas' mistrust of his visions made it dangerous for him to continue living alone.

Another kilometer east, the bus reached the top of a hill: the entrance to Cuapa. From that vantage point, the novelist could see most of el pueblito sprawled out across the valley. The community looked so small that Diego still found it hard to believe that ten thousand called Cuapa home.

As the bus rolled into the heart of el pueblo, Diego looked to the right, down la Calle de los Laureles. There was Blanca Arias's elegant seven-caoba-pillar house—the mahogany columns, holding up a red tile overhang, once again impressed the novelist.

Diego grabbed his bags as the bus approached the next corner, his final stop—five and a half hours after leaving Managua. He stepped off the bus and walked the short block south to doña Queta's new hotel.

"I'd like a room for six nights," he said to the owner's niece, a young, exuberantly pregnant woman. She looked at him with open curiosity. The novelist could read the question on her mind: *Why do you want to stay in Cuapa this long?* But out of politeness, she kept it to herself.

The hotel had been recently constructed. The walls of Diego's tiny room still smelled of wet concrete, but it was clean and had a private bathroom. Compared to the inn where the writer had stayed during his previous visit, this was five-star lodging. Diego took a cold shower, thankful that there was water. The biting iciness felt marvelous as it ran down his back. He then lay down· to read for a few minutes, to unwind a little before lunch. But Diego was so exhausted that once again he fell asleep.

By the time he woke up it was midafternoon. Although there still were several days to go before the writer's interview with Padre Ginés, he decided to visit la Casa Cural to alert the Spaniard of his arrival. Diego walked across town, through el Parque Central, climbed the fifteen steps to the new church, and went around the building to the house in back. The parish secretary sat behind a desk, shuffling documents while sucking on a bonbón. The lollipop had tinted her lips a light shade of purple.

"Buenas tardes, ¿se encuentra el Padre Ginés?" Diego asked.

"No. He's out hunting with an Englishman who's visiting Cuapa."

"What are they hunting?" the novelist asked, more in the spirit of friendly conversation than out of curiosity.

"Fish," she answered succinctly.

"Oh, so you mean they're fishing," he corrected.

The secretary glanced up from her papers, looking at Diego as if he had just insulted her. "No," she answered, rather impatiently. "Padre Ginés went to el Río Murra to *hunt*. He shoots fish with an AK-47."

Only in Nicaragua, Diego thought. One had to admire a priest who fished with such a weapon. "He must be a fine fisher of men as well. Although I certainly hope he uses a gentler weapon for that," Diego said to the secretary.

She stared at him. Not the faintest trace of a smile appeared on her lips.

Seeing that he wouldn't be able to greet Padre Ginés, Diego opted to visit an old friend. "If you don't mind, Señorita, I'd like to see where Bernardo is buried."

The secretary grabbed a large key ring from her desk drawer, rose from her chair, and motioned for the novelist to follow. They walked out of la Casa Cural, past the new church, down the fifteen steps, and across el parque to the old church. She unlocked the building, turned on the light, and said, "Let me know when you're finished."

"Sí, y gracias," Diego answered.

The novelist strolled toward the front. In the middle of the floor, flush on the surface, not far from the altar, was a huge marble slab that had not been there during his previous visit. It marked the seer's grave.

PADRE BERNARDO MARTÍNEZ

20 DE AGOSTO 1931–30 DE OCTUBRE 2000

Inscribed on the tomb were the words: MARÍA, VOS SOS MI MADRE, MADRE DE TODOS NOSOTROS, PECADORES.

Diego visited with Padre Bernardo for a while. He told him that he was in Cuapa researching the final chapter of the book. Then he asked for Padre Bernardo's and la Virgen's blessing on the project. Before leaving, Diego walked to the empty wooden niche that stood against the building's northern wall. He reverently ran his hand along its length. It was the same niche that held the statue of la Inmaculada Concepción the night she illuminated for Bernardo, over twenty years ago. It was still in the exact same spot. The image had been moved to the new church and was kept locked, behind a glass door, to protect her from vandals and relic seekers.

Diego said farewell to Padre Bernardo and returned to la Casa Cural to let the secretary know that he was done. Afterward, he walked to the park and sat on a bench, under the shade of a guayacán tree, to rest. Before long, an old man came by selling wooden animals he had carved by hand: bulls, pigs, parrots, and giraffes.

"¿Cómo se llama, Señor?" Diego asked the vendor.

"Juan Espinoza, para servirle."

The novelist scratched his head, he knew he had heard the name before, but just couldn't recall where. Don Juan's creatures were so primitive and outlandish that Diego thought cuapeños were very kind when they later described him as an artist. But, although ugly, the carvings did have plenty of personality.

While don Juan chatted with Diego, people began to gather around them, curious to learn something about the stranger.

"Why are you here? There isn't a rodeo coming up, nor is it the usual time for pilgrims," a woman selling rosquillas asked.

"I want to learn more about la Virgen de Cuapa and about Bernardo," Diego responded.

He didn't dare mention that he was writing a novel about la Virgen's apparition in their pueblo. Why should he even try? How would he explain historical fiction to people who were barely literate? How would he tell them that they had been recreated as characters and placed in imaginary situations that, although not entirely true, would try to recapture the essence of their lives? How would he explain something that he had trouble understanding himself?

"¿Sos un creyente? Are you a believer?" don Juan, the woodcarver, asked. The old man took a step toward the novelist, staring intently at him. The entire group became silent. Every man, woman, and child awaited Diego's reply. Although he knew that there was only one correct answer, he became nervous.

"Of course I believe!" he answered emphatically. But Diego wasn't really sure if he was telling the truth.

The gathering applauded. Within moments, the meeting became a celebration of Nuestra Señora's visit. Los cuapeños sang all the hymns to la Virgen de Cuapa they knew, including one don Juan himself had written. The elders shared their stories with Diego. They also told him every miracle they had heard about. The list soon grew too long for the novelist to remember. Within thirty minutes, his mind was saturated. Using the excuse that he hadn't had lunch yet—which was true—Diego bade the group farewell and told them that he was going to eat at doña Queta's restaurant.

"Try la sopa de huevos de toro," don Juan said, winking. "Doña Queta's bull testicle soup is excellent. Powerful stuff as well. Be careful, it'll keep your bed sheet raised high, like a flag in the night." The woodcarver walked off, chuckling to himself.

As Diego turned to leave, an ancient woman with wild white hair and inquisitive eyes, who had been among the group listening keenly to what everyone had to say, grabbed the writer by his shirtsleeve and took him aside.

"If you want to hear more stories about la Virgen, or about Bernardo, or about anyone else in this town, I know them all. I know everything about everyone," she whispered, as if they were involved in a conspiracy.

"Muchas gracias, Señora. I'll be here for several days. Perhaps I can look you up later," the novelist whispered back.

"Well, all you have to do is ask for me. My name is doña Tula. Everyone here knows me."

Diego thanked her and left. At doña Queta's he ordered la sopa de huevos de toro. "Don Juan Espinoza recommended the soup, and he was right. It's excellent," he said to doña Queta's niece, who smiled timidly as she took the empty bowl away.

During the remainder of Diego's stay in el pueblito, he spent several hours each day at the apparition site. He'd sit on the bench closest to the statue of la Virgen de Cuapa, under the shade of the sanctuary's canopy. He'd be as still as possible, gazing at the image for hours: her delicate face, her hands both open, her palms up, and her head covered with a light blue shroud. La Virgen wore a simple beige dress. A cape, adorned with gold-colored embroidery along the edges, covered her shoulders. By any account, she was beautiful. Diego could easily see how Bernardo had fallen so completely in love with such a magnificent being.

When Bernardo's story had first mesmerized Diego, he had come to expect la Virgen de Cuapa to be the dream woman who had visited him so often. But when he finally saw a statue of la Virgen, he was surprised and disappointed that the women were not one and the same. And since his arrival in Nicaragua the dream had never recurred. The question, then, lingered—who was this woman, the one who had led him here? The answer, Diego would never know.

During the novelist's first visit to the site he met the Englishman—a bright young man with a doctorate in philosophy from Pembroke College of Oxford who was traveling through Central America. The philosopher, a Catholic, had heard the story of the apparition, liked it, and was considering writing an essay about la Virgen de Cuapa.

"The whole thing is inspiring, isn't it?" he asked Diego.

"Yes, it is," the novelist answered, not sharing how much time, pain, and effort he had already invested on a similar quest.

The Englishman was staying at doña Queta's as well, so the two began to dine together at the hotel restaurant. Afterward, they'd linger at the table for a while, drinking Victorias and comparing notes on academic life between the continents. The complexities and rituals of Oxford left Diego perplexed.

Later on those evenings, Diego and the Englishman would leave the restaurant and sit on plastic chairs on the hotel's narrow deck. There, they'd continue talking, smoking Cuban cigars, and admiring the majestic genízaro tree in the park across the street. Its branches, extending about sixty feet from the trunk in a generous green canopy, made the tree look like a colossal weeping willow.

Young boys from the neighborhood, excited about having a foreigner in Cuapa, would join them. They asked the Englishman endless questions. Since, at first, the boys didn't have any idea where his homeland was, the philosopher led them, like the Pied Piper, to the monument under el genízaro: a globe of the world with a statue of la Inmaculada Concepción standing on top, arms open and spreading her message throughout the planet. The Englishman climbed atop the base and pointed out England on a disproportionately drawn map of the world: the island looked a lot like Cuba and was located a stone's throw off the shores of Portugal. When the philosopher left, a couple of days later, on his way to Honduras, Diego missed him and his Cuban cigars.

Over the next couple of days Diego continued visiting the apparition site. The hours he spent there in quiet contemplation were a balsam to his soul. The deep wounds of his midlife crisis seemed to be closing. Diego Miranda no longer felt guilty, confused, and like a fool. He had quietly resigned himself to the damage he had caused, and he prayed fervently to la Virgen de Cuapa that she help his family find peace as well.

The last few days the novelist spent in Cuapa he'd wake up at dawn, get dressed, and walk to Bernardo's former potrero (which years ago the seer had donated to the Catholic Church). He'd take something to eat and drink and would return to el pueblo shortly before sunset. He began to fantasize about moving to Cuapa and setting up a writer's colony—a creative spiritual haven for others who, like him, needed to write their way out of despair. He found the serenity of this part of Chontales inspiring. Time moved slowly here, and everything in Diego's life, after only a few days, almost made sense once again.

On November 22, Diego showed up punctually at la Casa Cural for his appointment with Padre Ginés Hidalgo. He brought along two presents for the priest: a bottle of red Chilean wine and a Cuban cigar. The Spaniard—a man of about fifty-five, medium height, with a slightly protruding stomach, a handsome face, plenty of boyish charm, and a ready smile—was waiting. In spite of Padre Ginés's youthful good looks, Diego could tell that the parish priest had seen a lot of life—the deep creases along his forehead bore the evidence.

"I left the entire day open for you," the priest said in greeting.

"Gracias, Padre Ginés," Diego answered as he returned the surprisingly vigorous handshake.

"Where are you staying?"

"At doña Queta's."

"You should try her sopa de huevos de toro. It's excellent. The secret to her bull testicle soup is the way in which Néstor Urbina, the butcher, castrates the animals. He's learned how to do it so delicately that those poor creatures aren't even aware that they've lost anything. The huevos Néstor cuts are always tender." As Padre

Ginés finished saying this, he formed the tips of the fingers of his right hand into a cluster, brought it to his lips, kissed it with a loud smack, and released the bunch, leaving his palm open, facing up.

"Thank you for the advice, Padre. I may just do that," the novelist replied, somewhat embarrassed. He was ashamed to confess that he already had succumbed to a temptation that, in that instant, seemed excessively sensual.

The two men sat down in the living room, which also doubled as the office for la Casa Cural. In a room to the right, there was a pharmacy where the parish sold medicine to the poor for whatever they could afford to pay. To the left there was a bookcase filled with novels in Spanish, Portuguese, and English. In a corner of the living room, behind Padre Ginés, a television set was blaring, but the loudness didn't seem to bother the priest. His secretary, absorbed in the plot of a soap opera, paid no attention to the two men. After Diego opened his notebook to the list of questions he'd prepared, he looked up. Behind Padre Ginés, on the screen, a man and a woman kissed passionately.

The Spaniard lit a Belmont, inhaled, and, with the smoke still deep in his lungs, said, "Let's get to work. What's your first question?"

"I appreciate that, Padre. Well, to start things off, how long did you know Bernardo?"

"For twenty years. I met him shortly after Nuestra Señora appeared. In fact, I was the first person the archbishop appointed to investigate the case."

"I thought that was Padre Damián. The gringo priest."

"No. His Eminence first asked me to look into her apparitions. I'm not sure what happened after that, but after only a couple of weeks I was pulled from the investigation. Padre Damián just came in and took over." Padre Ginés leaned forward conspiratorially, and whispered, "Between you and me, I never cared much for that man."

"I understand," Diego agreed diplomatically. "So you've known Bernardo since this all began?"

"Yes. And years later, when he was hiding in the seminary, I became his confessor. You can say, then, that I knew him just as well as anyone, if not better. Most of what he told me, however, I'll take to the grave," Padre Ginés added firmly.

"Of course, Padre. I would never want you to reveal anything he said to you during confession. Let me, then, ask you a personal question. How do you like being assigned here, in Cuapa? I mean, you're an educated man," the novelist said, pointing to the bookcase, "and yet here you are, living among mostly illiterate campesinos."

Padre Ginés chuckled as he crushed his cigarette in the ashtray that was on the coffee table. He leaned back and, speaking loudly for his secretary's benefit, who was dusting the pharmacy during a commercial break in her soap opera, said, "Did you hear that, Matilde? The writer says I'm an educated man. You see, I'm not the only one who thinks so." He smiled at Diego and continued, "You know something? I love it here! Seriously. I admit that at first I was a little distraught over the idea of coming to Cuapa when my bishop mentioned it to me. But from the moment I drove back into this town, after many years away, I knew that I had come home. Being the parish priest of this pueblito is her precious gift to me. I'm honored and happy to be here, serving her, and serving los cuapeños, of course." Padre Ginés smiled, pulled another Belmont out of the pack, and lit it.

"Padre Ginés, why do so few people know that la Virgen continued appearing to Bernardo?"

"Because she told Bernardo that the messages given at the site were for the entire world. After those apparitions, the rest of her messages were only for Bernardo or for the bishops. She never stopped appearing to him, as you know. Shortly after my investigation began, I'd see Bernardo strolling along the old road to Juigalpa, talking to himself. I asked him once if he was all right. 'Yes, of course,' he answered. 'La Señora and I are just taking a little stroll and chatting.' They did that frequently, it seems."

"Padre, there's something about her message I never fully understood, and Bernardo didn't help me clear it up. Why did she always repeat her message verbatim? Virtually every single word is the same each time, without variation."

"May Bernardo forgive me for saying this," Padre Ginés said, leaning forward to crush the cigarette in the ashtray, "but he was far from being the brightest man on the planet. He was clever, no doubt about it. He was good at solving common, everyday problems. But the only way Bernardo could be sure about accurately spreading her message was by memorizing it word for word. What's not told in the published accounts is that the first time she appeared, he asked her to repeat everything over and over again until he knew it like he knew the Lord's Prayer.

"'Señora, soy muy bruto,' he said to her. 'I'm as dumb as a stick. Please repeat your message once again so I can get it right. Otherwise, I'll forget what you said and make a mess out of everything.' That's why the message is always exactly the same."

"Well, then, Padre, if la Virgen wanted Nicaraguans to love one another, why was she so partisan? Why did she oppose the Sandinistas so strongly?"

"Ah, but you see, she *didn't* oppose the Sandinistas. Most people assume that was the case, but they're wrong. She came to Cuapa out of love for *all* Nicaraguans. Never once did she even mention the Sandinistas, by name or otherwise, in her messages."

"But, Padre Ginés, Bernardo said, in public no less, that she mistrusted the Sandinistas."

"Listen. Whenever you relay someone else's message you will, at some point or another, get it mixed up. El Señor knows we clerics have done our own share of it with Jesucristo's message. Everyone has been guilty of that sin because we impose our own interpretations and anxieties upon the speaker's intentions. That's what happened in Bernardo's case. It's as simple as that."

"Padre, tell me this, then, did the Sandinistas really torture Bernardo? I've heard several people express their doubts about that."

"I can't share that information with you, I'm afraid. What he told me regarding that was in absolute confidence."

"I understand, Padre Ginés. Let me move on to another subject, then. Why do you think she chose to appear in Nicaragua?"

"That's easy to answer," the priest said, waving about the hand in which he held the Belmont he had just lit. "She was here to guide Nicaraguans through their darkest hour. She knew that a civil war was approaching, that the blood of brothers would soon be flowing like rivers. Interestingly, the bishops, through Bernardo, asked her the same question. Her reply surprised them: *Because the future of peace in this continent runs through Nicaragua and no one seems to realize it.*"

"And why did she choose Cuapa?"

"That's a mystery. Why Cuapa? Why Bernardo? We'll never know. What I believe is that she chose Bernardo because he had the simple mind and the pure heart of a child. But that's only my guess. Why exactly she chose a poorly educated tailor from Cuapa, we'll never know."

Padre Ginés paused and stared at Diego. For a moment the novelist became nervous, thinking that the priest would want to know when was the last time he had been to confession. "Let me ask *you* a question," the Spaniard finally said, breaking the silence. "Have you been to the apparition site?"

"Yes, I've spent many hours there this week."

"Good. Good. Tell me, then, what did you feel while you were there?"

Diego did not hesitate an instant in replying. "Peace, Padre. I found peace, both within and outside of myself. It's something I've been trying to find for years. I'd dare say that my time there is helping to heal some serious wounds to my soul."

"¡Excelente! That's usually the answer I get when I ask that question. All I can tell you is that for some reason, tied to Bernardo, she chose to bless his pasture. She told him that she didn't want us to build any shrines there. Nuestra Señora also insisted that she didn't want her apparition in Cuapa to become commercialized, as has happened at other sites. Have you seen anyone here selling relics, or peddling anything else having to do with her visit? Of course not. Why? Because she expressly asked that this not be done. She told Bernardo, *I want this to be a place of quiet, of reflection, of rest, and of healing. I want this to be a place where families can feel free to bring their lunch and enjoy a nice day in my company. I want this to be a quiet place where weary souls can come and find renewal.* But you ask me *why* she chose Cuapa? That, Señor, we'll never know."

"Have there been any recent miracles, Padre Ginés? Has anything out of the ordinary happened since Bernardo's death?"

"We try to downplay the miracles. That's intentional. We don't want her apparition here to become a carnival. Instead, we want to encourage genuine devotion to Nuestro Señor Jesucristo and his teachings. Do you understand what I'm saying? The people of Cuapa respect and appreciate that. They've learned to take the miracles in stride."

Diego glanced down at his notebook; only a couple of questions remained on his list. "Padre Ginés, Bernardo's death was sudden, wasn't it? I saw him just a few months ago and he seemed fine."

"Yes, it was sudden. But at the same time not unexpected," the priest sighed. He crushed the cigarette he had been smoking in the ashtray. He immediately took the last Belmont out of the pack and lit it.

"What do you mean by 'not unexpected'?"

"Bernardo had predicted his death," Padre Ginés answered calmly as he exhaled a thick, light blue cloud of smoke.

"He predicted his own death?" Diego asked, leaning forward. He was eager to capture every word of the Spaniard's reply.

"Yes. A few months ago Bernardo called me. 'Padre Ginés,' he said, 'Nuestra Señora spoke to me last night. She told me that my work on earth was complete, that I had done everything she asked me to do. She said that I should get ready to go, that I should put my things in order.'

"'You're being ridiculous, Bernardo,' I answered. 'You're not talking about going on a picnic or a trip to el mercado. You're talking about dying!'

"'Yes, I know,' he answered.

"And you know what? Bernardo sounded *happy. Ecstatic!* Like a child who's just been told that the family's going out to eat ice cream. Several months went by, and, to be honest, I had put the entire conversation out of my mind. I thought it was nothing more than one of Bernardo's mystical misinterpretations. Then, about five weeks ago, I received a call from Managua letting me know that Bernardo had undergone an operation."

"What was wrong with him?" Diego asked, closing his notebook.

"Supposedly a simple prostate problem. But when the doctors opened him up, they found his insides riddled with cancer. They sewed him back up and told him to go home, that there was nothing more they could do for him. What the doctors couldn't believe was that Bernardo was absolutely free of pain. With cancer of that type and at that stage, the pain should have been unbearable."

"What happened then?" the novelist asked.

"Bernardo's last wish was to die in Cuapa. As soon as Blanca Arias could, she brought him here and took him straight to her house. The instant I was told he was back, I rushed to see him. I found him in bed, resting comfortably. Throughout his last days he was lucid, except for the moments of rapture."

"Rapture?"

"Yes, rapture," answered Padre Ginés, who, for the first time since the beginning of the interview, seemed stirred by the discussion. "Nuestra Señora would drop by to visit him several times a day. Bernardo would lay there, his right hand extended, grasping nothing but air."

"'What are you doing?' I'd ask.

"'La Señora is here with me. We're holding hands right now.' And Bernardo would stare longingly, like a lover at his beloved, at some vacant spot on the wall, at someone the rest of us in the room couldn't see."

Padre Ginés's eyes filled with tears as he recalled that moment. Diego thought about waiting until the priest recovered, but the novelist, sensing that the culmination of his own quest was close at hand, couldn't wait any longer, "Please, Padre, continue."

"Although Bernardo was very weak, he still found the strength to pray the rosary, over and over. On his third day back in Cuapa, doña Blanca called and asked me to hurry to Bernardo's bedside. Within minutes, I was at her house.

"When I stepped into Bernardo's room, he looked at me and smiled. He then said, 'Padre Ginés, would you be so kind as to give me the last rites?' His request surprised me. He didn't look like a man on the verge of dying.

"'Why now, Bernardo?' I asked.

"With a beatific smile that made me wish I had taken along my camera, he replied, 'Because la Señora has said that it's time for me to join her.'"

Padre Ginés's voice cracked. Diego waited in silence. He felt his throat closing in on him as well. As he glanced toward the pharmacy, he saw that the parish secretary was enthralled with the conversation. The soap opera was no longer blaring. Without Diego realizing when, she had turned the television set off.

After the Spaniard regained his composure, he continued. "I cried throughout his confession. Afterward, as I anointed him, my tears fell, mixing with the holy oils. By the time I gave Bernardo communion, they were streaming down my face. I don't remember crying like that since I was a child.

"Throughout the ritual, Bernardo smiled blissfully at someone standing at his side, someone none of us could see. When I finished administering los Sacramentos, he looked at me and said, 'Gracias, querido amigo, y adiós.' He then turned to each person in the room, saying 'Adiós' as well.

"Bernardo looked once again toward where la Virgen stood,

smiled at her, and then, very serenely, said, 'Señora, en tus manos encomiendo mi espíritu.' After entrusting his soul into her care, Bernardo closed his eyes and, very peacefully, went to sleep."

Padre Ginés used his shirtsleeve to wipe away the tears. Although he found it difficult to continue, he insisted on going on, his voice at times croaking. "At that moment, the most extraordinary thing happened. And I will never forget this, no matter how long I live. Everyone in that room felt Bernardo's soul rise from the bed and hover in the air. Then we all quivered when we felt his being merge with la Virgen's. Suddenly, their spirits, now joined together, swished right through us like a gust of wind, letting us experience every bit of Bernardo's joy and leaving us with a blessed sense of peace. And immediately after that, everything in the room, every single person, every particle of air, every molecule within the walls of that small universe, absolutely everything, became saturated with the most incredible, the most passionate fragrance of red roses."

ULTIMA VISIO
(The Last Apparition)
October 13, 1980

Bernardo

THE DAY at last arrived when la Virgencita promised to return. That month had gone by painfully slow, so when October 13 finally came, I was more than ready. And I wasn't alone. About seventy persons met me in the church at midmorning, eager to go to the apparition site. The gathering felt like una fiesta. While at the church, we prayed the rosary, we sang, and at noon we had a nice lunch—a roasted pig that Blanquita had ordered her cooks to prepare for all of us. As soon as we finished eating, we left. The pilgrimage was colorful. On our way to el potrero, people picked the wildflowers growing along the old road to Juigalpa. The group, excited about meeting Nuestra Señora, sang hymns the entire way.

When we arrived at the site, the first thing we did was to place the flowers on the bed of rocks where she always appears. We then kneeled before the morisco tree and began to pray. It was our second rosary of the day.

There were dark rain clouds directly overhead, and they showed no sign of leaving. But that didn't disturb us because we were too excited about la Virgencita's visit.

433

As we reflected upon the third joyful mystery, the Birth of Nuestro Señor Jesuscristo, I began to feel the giddiness that always takes hold of me right before she appears. Since I didn't want to interrupt anyone's prayers, I remained silent and tried my best to concentrate on praying.

Once we finished, we began to sing a hymn. Suddenly, from the heavens, breaking through the clouds, a circle of light descended upon us. The brightness enclosed the entire group, like a glowing halo. I looked around and saw that every person was looking up, toward the sky. Every single face was gloriously illuminated. Many of those who had come along were pointing upward, commenting on the rainbow of colors swirling above.

"¡Miren allá!" doña Tula exclaimed, pointing west toward the sun—a bright, crimson-red ball—as it hovered above the hills. At that moment, we realized that we couldn't explain where the light shining directly above our heads was coming from.

A drizzle began to fall, but it didn't bother any of us. The day was so hot that we found the mist refreshing. Several in the group touched their clothes. Amazed, they shouted for us to do the same. When we did, we were surprised to see that we were not getting wet. I then glanced around and saw that the ring of light continued surrounding us.

I looked toward the heavens again. That's when I saw the first flash. Everyone gasped, and I was happy that they had seen the burst of light as well. An instant later, the second flash followed. I lowered my eyes toward el morisco and there, standing on a cloud that rested on the bed of wildflowers, was la Virgen, beautiful as ever. She looked exactly the same as the first time she had appeared to me.

Marcelita, doña Aracely's four-year-old daughter, began running toward Nuestra Señora, arms open, ready to embrace her. Doña Aracely sprang quickly from the crowd, grabbed the child, and brought her back.

"What are you doing?" the mother scolded.

"Mami, la bella Señora is calling me. Let me go, please. I want to be with her."

A murmur rose from the group when they heard the child's words. Doña Aracely responded by clutching Marcelita even tighter in her arms. She later told me that she was afraid that her daughter would join the invisible being and be taken away—forever.

"La niña's right!" I shouted. "Nuestra Señora is here! Look at her!" I cried, pointing toward the flowers. No one said anything. No one other than the little girl could see her. Frustrated, I began to implore la Virgen.

"Please, Señora, let them see you. They're all here because they want to see you. They're good people. They won't betray you. I promise you that."

Bernardo, not everyone can see me.

"Look!" I exclaimed in spite of her words, turning back to face the crowd. "Don't you see her? She's right there, standing on that cloud right above the wildflowers!"

"*I* can see her!" Marcelita answered. A few people started sobbing, but I didn't look back to see who they were because my gaze now belonged only to la Virgen. Later that day, about five persons, including Blanquita, confessed that Nuestra Señora had made herself visible to them.

"Please, Señora, let everyone see you," I begged once again. This time, in reply, she just shook her head.

"Look toward the flowers," I shouted to the group. "She's there! Look!" I wanted everyone to see her, to see that I was not crazy. I was so desperate that I pleaded with her yet again.

"Señora, please let them see you so they can believe. Many people don't believe that you've come to visit us. They say that I'm crazy, completamente loco. They say that it's really the devil who is appearing to me. Others say that you are dead, that you have rotted and turned into dust, like any mere mortal. Please let them see you, Señora! ¡Por favor!"

She didn't answer. Instead, la Virgen placed her hands on her chest and slightly lowered her face. Her expression became one of deep sorrow. She grew pale and her shawl, once beige, began to turn gray. Then she began to cry. That broke my heart.

I started to cry as well. My chest began to heave out of control. I soon began to wail because, somehow, I could feel every bit of her grief.

"Señora," I sobbed, "please forgive me for what I said! It's my fault you are crying. You are angry with me. Please forgive me! Don't be angry with me, Señora. ¡Perdón, por favor!"

I am not angry, Bernardo. I never become angry.

"But I see you crying. Why are you crying?"

I am sad to see how people's hearts have hardened. But you, and those who believe in my Son, have to pray for a change so they may once again experience pure innocence and pure love in their hearts.

I couldn't answer her. I was crying so hard that I could barely breathe. My chest felt like a sponge being squeezed by a giant hand. All I could do was let out loud, broken howls.

I felt guilty for having insisted that she allow everyone to see her. I could feel her tears dripping onto my soul, and they burned my heart.

While I sobbed uncontrollably, She began to repeat her message.

I want everyone to pray the rosary, every day, not only during the month of May. I want everyone to pray it with their family. Teach your children to pray the rosary as soon as they are old enough to understand. Pray the rosary at the same time of the day, once the chores of the home have been completed. El Señor does not like prayers that are said in a hasty, distracted, or mechanical manner. Make sure that when you pray the rosary you take time to reflect upon the appropriate passages of the Bible. Renew the first Saturdays. You received many favors from el Señor when you last did this. And above all, I want everyone to live la Palabra de Dios.

As I continued sobbing, she went on.

Love one another. Fulfill your duties and obligations to each other. Forgive one another. Work for peace. Do not ask el Señor for peace. You need to work to make peace among yourselves; otherwise it will never happen. Do not choose the path of violence. Never choose the path of violence. Since the earthquake, your country has suffered much, and now dark, menacing clouds cover it again. Your suffering and the suffering of all of humanity shall continue if people don't mend their ways.

Pray, mi hijo. Pray the rosary for the entire planet. Tell believers and nonbelievers alike that grave dangers threaten the world. I am begging el Señor to delay his judgment. If you don't mend your ways your dependence on violence as a way to settle differences will bring forth Armageddon.

When la Virgencita had finished repeating her message, I remembered that many cuapeños had asked me to present their petitions to her. By then I had stopped crying, so once again I could speak.

"Señora, people have many favors they want to ask of you." But now, as I knelt before her, I couldn't remember a single request from the long list I had memorized for today's apparition.

After a few moments, I gave up trying to remember and said, "Señora, I have forgotten them all, but I'm sure you know what each person wants. All you need to do is tell me whether or not their prayers will be answered. I'll then personally deliver your message to each of them."

She looked at me, her eyes sad, and replied in a soft, low voice, *Bernardo, they are asking me for things that are not important. They should be asking for greater faith and patience to help them bear their crosses. I cannot take away the suffering that is part of living in this world. Those are the crosses we all bear. I, for one, witnessed my Son's Crucifixion, and I later held his tortured body in my arms. Instead, everyone needs to listen to and act upon this message: love one another, resolve your differences by talking to each other. Do not take the path of violence. Never take the path of violence. Ask for faith, and you shall be rewarded with patience.*

"Comprendo, Señora," I answered. She smiled and stared at me for a long time.

Finally, she said, *Bernardo, you will not see me at this site again.*

Fear instantly gripped me. I couldn't bear the thought of never seeing la Virgen again. I became so terrified that I began to scream, "Don't leave us, Señora! Don't leave us! Madre mía, don't leave us! Don't leave us, Madre mía!"

Do not worry, Bernardo. Tell everyone not to worry. I am here, with every one of you, though you may not see me. I am mother to all of you, and a mother never forgets her children. Whenever you need me, invoke me with these words: "María, you are my Mother, Mother of all of us, sinners. María, vos sos mi madre, madre de todos nosotros, pecadores. María, you are my Mother, Mother of all of us, sinners."

When she had finished repeating the invocation, she gazed tenderly upon me and smiled. The cloud then started rising, la

Virgen going higher than I had ever seen her go before. When Nuestra Señora reached the lowest rain clouds, she continued to ascend, and then, slowly, she disappeared within.

Although I knew that she would always be with me, I couldn't help but feel as if my soul had been ripped out. I couldn't bear the pain and the sorrow. I couldn't imagine living the rest of my life without seeing her again. My misery was so devastating, my heart so broken, that I threw myself on the ground that day, not caring what anyone thought. I didn't even care that the dirt and the gravel were grinding into my face, cutting me and leaving scars that you can still see today. Believing that I would never see her again, all I could do was bawl. All I could do was to let out a single loud wail, like when I was a child and mi abuelita Eloísa had just finished punishing me.

In the name of Nuestro Señor Jesucristo, and in the presence of Padre Damián, the priest our beloved archbishop has appointed to record this miracle, I, Bernardo Martínez, swear that everything I have said about la Virgen's apparition in Cuapa is absolutely true.

POSDATA

ON MAY 8, 1980, the Virgin Mary appeared to Bernardo Martínez—
a poorly educated, forty-eight-year-old tailor—in a cow pasture on
the outskirts of the town of Cuapa, in Nicaragua. This "true" incident took place less than ten months after the Sandinistas overthrew
the half-century-old Somoza dynasty and two years before the full
onset of the Contra War, the bloodiest military conflict in that
nation's history.

My interest in Bernardo's story arose when I returned to
Nicaragua—after nearly a twenty-year absence—and met the seer, in
March of 1999. By that time the country had been at peace for a
decade. Upon hearing Bernardo's life story, I immediately knew
that the best way to capture its many dramatic and magical dimen-
sions was through fiction. As Joseph Campbell posits in *The Hero
with a Thousand Faces,* to try to render miraculous events in a
straightforward manner, narrating them as the truth, will always
lead a writer into bathos. In other words, in striving to accurately
describe the sublime nature of Bernardo's experience, I would have

inevitably overreached and toppled into the absurd. His tale, and the tales of his compatriots, deserve better.

Two books on la Virgen's appearance in Cuapa were extremely helpful in providing me with facts, as well as inspiration: Padre Jorge Rodríguez's *Cuapa: Historia y Mensaje,* and Stephen and Mariam Weglian's *Let Heaven and Earth Unite.* Also, Stephen Kinzer's classic account of life in Nicaragua during the 1980s, *The Blood of Brothers: Life and War in Nicaragua,* was especially helpful in my attempt to capture the spirit and tension of those turbulent years. Moreover, Kinzer perfectly understood the impact Bernardo's vision had on Nicaraguan politics. It is no coincidence that the war correspondent for the *New York Times* tells the story of la Virgen's apparition in Cuapa to begin the chapter that deals with the grave conflict between the Catholic Church and the Sandinista government.

What you find in these pages, then, is Bernardo Martínez as I have recreated him, and as seen through the eyes of the other characters—every one of them, beyond argument, fictional. Nevertheless, most of the events related within, even the miracles, have their basis in occurrences that have taken place, or are believed to have taken place.

A few incidents, in particular Bernardo's imprisonment and torture, are highly contested with regard to their veracity. Various accounts published in newspapers and books critical of the Sandinista era assure us that this tragic mistake did indeed occur. But when I asked Padre Bernardo if this episode really did happen, although he admitted that Sandinista securities forces had detained him, he denied being tortured. Several individuals close to him, however, insist that Bernardo Martínez, preferring to forget the sad episode, would have never acknowledged being raped while in prison.

Regardless, one of my objectives was to immerse the reader in the lives of Nicaraguans during the latter part of the twentieth century. To accomplish this, I took liberties with regard to dates, characterization of historical figures, places, and events. My hope is that this novel will give readers some insight into what it has meant to be a Nicaraguan during such tumultuous times.

Bernardo de Cuapa died on October 30, 2000. His remains are buried in the town's old church, just a few steps away from where the image of la Virgen first illuminated for him. The Nicaraguan Catholic Church has declared his former cow pasture, the place of the apparitions, a holy site.

El Pueblo de San Francisco de Cuapa is most welcoming to all pilgrims and visitors.

ACKNOWLEDGMENTS

INFINITAS GRACIAS to those who helped and encouraged me during the writing of this book:

Nina Forsythe (and Rob, Hannah, and Asa, too)
Rhonda Patzia (and Michael)
Benjamin Murphy
Brian Sullivan

Joaquín Sirias, my father (q.e.p.d.)
Padre Gregorio Raya
Aracellis Vargas
Robert Mullin
Julia Borek
Bill Mulcahey

Sue Betz and the good people at Northwestern University Press
(for their faith)

Julia Alvarez (who rekindled the flame)

Virgil Suárez (who helped me, by example, with the most
    difficult chapter of this book)

Elaine Markson (who believed)

Magee (with all my love)

Padre Bernardo Martínez (q.e.p.d.)

La Virgen de Cuapa

ABOUT THE AUTHOR

Silvio Sirias was born in Los Angeles and grew up there and in Nicaragua. He is the author of *Julia Alvarez: A Critical Companion,* the editor of Salomón de la Selva's *Tropical Town and Other Poems,* and the coeditor of *Conversations with Rudolfo Anaya.* He lives in the Republic of Panama, where he is working on his second novel.